OUR MAN IN LONG BRANCH

"No," said Horny,
for whom things were going much too fast.
"I mean, can't you let me know what this is all about
first? I guess it's some kind of CIA thing, but—"

"Oh, Horny, you're tiresome. Look.
The CIA was disbanded years ago, after the scandals.
Didn't you know that? There's no such thing any
more. What we have here is just a Team.
With a job to do."

"Then what kind of job—"

The man stood up,
and suddenly looked a lot taller. He said in a flat
voice, "You have two choices, Hake. Take the oath.
Or go to jail for evasion of service.
That's only a five-year sentence, but they'll be hard
years, Hake, they'll be very hard years.
And then we'll think of something else."

"Pohl's latest novel is an unqualified success.
Entertainment with an all-too-believable setting."
—*Library Journal*

"A thoughtful, funny book. Four stars."
—*The West Coast Review of Books*

THE
COOL WAR

Frederik Pohl

A Del Rey Book

BALLANTINE BOOKS • NEW YORK

A Del Rey Book
Published by Ballantine Books

Copyright © 1979, 1980 by Frederik Pohl

Portions of this novel have appeared in somewhat different
format in *Isaac Asimov's Science Fiction Magazine*.

All rights reserved under International and Pan-American
Copyright Conventions. Published in the United States by Ballantine Books, a division of Random House, Inc., New York,
and simultaneously in Canada by Random House of Canada,
Limited, Toronto, Canada.

Library of Congress Catalog Card Number: 80-23589

ISBN 0-345-30137-4

Manufactured in the United States of America

First Edition: April 1981

Paperback Format:
First Edition: March 1982

Cover art by Murray Tinkelman

1

THE day they came for the Reverend H. Hornswell Hake was his thirty-ninth birthday, and his secretary, Jessie Tunman, had baked him a cake. Because she liked him, she had only put two candles on it. Because she was Jessie, she dumped it in front of him with a scowl. "That's very kind of you, Jessie," he said, eyeing the coconut frosting he couldn't stand.

"Yeah. Better eat it fast, because your nine o'clock people are getting out of that kiddie-car of theirs right now. Aren't you going to blow out the candles?" She watched him do it. "Well, happy birthday, Horny. I know you'd rather have chocolate, but it gives you blackheads."

She did not wait for an answer, but closed the door behind her.

Naturally she had caught him stripped down to his shorts, doing his barbells in front of the mirror. Now that he had stopped exercising he was freezing; he quickly put the weights away, pulled on his pants, drew lined boots over his sweatsocks and began to button his shirt, covering the great network of scars that curved under his left nipple. By the time his first counseling people showed up he was sitting behind his desk, looking once more like a Unitarian minister instead of a jock.

Another marriage down the tube if he didn't save it. It was a responsibility he had accepted long ago, when he took the vows at the seminary. But time didn't make his job easier. He greeted the young people, offered them birthday cake and got ready to hear their complaints and accusations one more time.

Hake took all his ministerial duties seriously. Counseling he took more seriously than most. And of all the kinds of problem-solving and support his congregation asked of him, the kinds involving marriage were the hardest and the most demanding. They came to him for marriage counseling, bright-faced, with a youthful, sophisticated veneer covering their tender, terrified insides; and they came to him again later on, most of them did, with the frayed look of anger and indigestion that went with divorce counseling. He gave them all the best he had.

"I really love you, Alys!" Ted Brant yelled furiously.

Hake gazed politely at Alys. She was not responding. She was staring tight-lipped into the corner of the room. Hake repressed a sigh and kept his silence. That was half of counseling: keeping your mouth shut, waiting for the about-to-be-married or the considering-divorce to come out with what was on their minds, really. His feet were cold. He reached down inconspicuously and rearranged the afghan he had wrapped around them.

A knock on the door broke up the tableau, and Jessie Tunman peered around it. "Sorry," she said urgently, "but this seemed important." She left a note on the glove table and closed the door again, smiling at the young people to show that she was not really interrupting.

Horny shook his feet out of the afghan and padded over to look at the note:

A man from the Internal Revenue wants to talk to you right away.

"Oh, God," he said. His conscience was as clear as most, which is to say not all that clear. Not that he expected to have any real problem. But he was used to having non-problems that turned out to be interminable annoyances. One of the good things about being a clergyman was that so much of what people spent money on was, for you, deductible: the house larger than a single man really needed, justified because so many rooms were used for church purposes, like counseling and wine-and-cheese parties; the occasional travel that he liked so much almost always to attend seminars, church conventions and professional courses. But the bad thing about that good thing was that, when you had so much deductible, you had to spend a lot of time proving it.

Ted Brant was looking at him now, with the expression of a man conscious of a grievance. "I *thought* this session was about the *ruin* of our *marriage*."

"It is, Ted, it is. I'm sorry for the interruption. Still," he said, "actually it comes at a good time. I want you to try talking to each other privately about some of the things we've discussed. So I'm going to leave the room for ten minutes. If you don't know what to say, well, Alys, you might go on with what you think about sharing the cooking: that was a good point you made, about your feelings about a dirty kitchen. Don't ever apologize for feelings." He pointed to the wine decanter and the coffee maker. "Help yourselves. And have another piece of cake,"

In the anteroom Jessie was cranking the mimeograph machine, counting turns: *Shhhlick, shhhlick, shhhlick.* She paused to say, "He's waiting for you in his car, Horny."

"In his *car?*"

"He's kind of a funny guy, Horny. I don't like him. And, listen, the heat's gone off again. I went down and switched over to methane, but there's no pressure."

"The coal man said he'd come today."

"He never comes till late afternoon. We'll be icicles by then. I'm going to have to use the electric heater."

Hake groaned. The power rationing made life difficult when winter hung on to the end of March, as it was this year. The electric company had installed a sealed fuse on the main. It was not supposed to blow out short of thirty amps, but the fuses were not all that accurate. If one did blow out, they had to wait for a repairman to come from the company, shortly to be followed by a cop with a summons for power-piggery. Hake said, "If you have to, you have to. But turn off some lights. And go in and turn off the heater in the study. There's enough animal heat in there anyway."

She said virtuously, "I hate to disturb the young folks."

"Sure you do." What she said was the truth. She preferred to listen at the door. He put a sweater on and went out to the porch. The winds were coming straight off the Atlantic, and either surf-spray or a drizzle was blowing in on him.

The rectory was a house a hundred and fifty years old, from the great days of Long Branch when presidents came up to take the summer ocean air (and died there, a couple of them). It was past those days now. The scrollwork on the wooden porch was soft with rot, and the Building Fund never seemed to keep up with replacing the storm windows and the tiles that flew off the roof every time the wind blew. At times it had been a summer home for a wealthy Philadelphia family, a whorehouse, a speakeasy, a dying place for old people, a headquarters for the local Ku Klux Klan, eight or ten different kinds of rooming house—and vacant. Lately, mostly vacant. The church bought it at one of those times because it was cheap.

Hake rested his hand on the rail for the chair-lift, no longer used since his rebirth two years before, and clutched his scarf, looking for his visitor. Among the rubble of street excavation that seemed to be the chronic state of the roadway it was not easy to see all the cars— But then he saw it. No mistake. In a block sparsely lined with three-wheelers and mini-Volkses, it was the only Buick. And four-door at that. And gasoline driven. *And it had the motor running.*

Horny Hake had a temper, learned in the free and outspoken kibbutz where he had spent his childhood, where if you didn't yell when you were sore no one knew you were around. He jumped down the steps, flung open the wastefully heavy door, leaned in it and blazed, "Power pig! Turn off that God-damned motor!"

The man at the wheel threw away a cigarette and turned a startled face to him. "Ah, Reverend Hake?"

"Damn right I'm Reverend Hake, whoever the hell you are, and what's this crap about my tax return?" He was shivering, partly from the wind and partly from fury. "And *turn off that motor.*"

"Ah, yes, sir. Of course." The man switched off the ignition and began to roll up the window with one hand, trying to stretch to the open door on Horny's side with the other. "Please come in, sir. I'm surely sorry about keeping the motor running, but this weather—"

Hake irritably slid in and shut the door. "All right. What about my taxes?"

The young man struggled to get a wallet out of his hip pocket and extracted a card. "My ID, sir." It read:

T. Donal Corry
Administrative Assistant
Senator Nicholson Bainbridge Watson

"I thought you were from Internal Revenue," said Hake suspiciously, turning the card over in his hand. It was handsomely engraved and apparently made from virgin linen stock: another kind of piggery!

"No, sir. That statement is, ah, inoperative at this point in time."

"Meaning you lied?"

"Meaning, sir, that this is a matter of national security. I did not wish to risk exposing a sensitive matter to your associate, Ms. Tunman, or your counselees."

Horny twisted around in the padded leather seat and stared at Corry. He began mildly enough, but his voice was rising as he finished: "You mean you came up here, stinking up the air in your big-assed Buick, got me out of a counseling session, shook up my secretary whom I can't pay enough to afford to antagonize, scared me half to death that I was being audited on my tax return, and all you wanted was to tell me some Senator wanted to come up and see me?"

Corry winced. "Yes, sir. I mean, that's about the size of it, Reverend Hake, except that the, ah, Senator is not really involved either. That too is inoperative. And he isn't coming here anyway. You're going there."

"I can't just take off and—"

"Yes, you can, Reverend," the man said firmly. "I've got your travel papers here. Eight fifteen to Newark, Metro-

liner to Washington, get off in Maryland, as indicated—
you'll be at your destination at a quarter of one and briefing
will be completed by two at the latest. Good-by, Reverend
Hake." And before Horny knew it, he was outside the car
again, and that pestilential eight-cylinder motor had started
up, and the car roared into an illegal U-turn and away.

"Are we in trouble, Horny?" Jessie Tunman asked
anxiously.

"I don't think so. I mean, I guess it's only routine," he
said, roused from abstraction.

"Well, that's good, because we've got enough trouble
already. I was just listening to the radio. There's a riot in
Asbury Park, and the garbage men just went on strike, so
there's going to be methane rationing if they don't get it
settled by tomorrow."

"Oh, lord."

"And I still can't get any heat in here, and you'd better
get back inside because I heard them yelling at each other
a minute ago."

Hake shook his head mournfully; he had almost forgotten
about the marital problems of his parishioners. But they
were far more rewarding than his own, and less perplexing.
He perked up as he went back through the door. "Well,"
he said. "What have you decided?"

Ted Brant looked around the room and said, "I guess I'll
be the one to tell you. Alys definitely wants a divorce."

That was a body blow; Horny had hoped he'd got them
reconciled. His voice was angry as he said, "I'm sorry to
hear that, Alys. Are you sure? I don't hold marriage as
an inviolable sacrament, of course, but my observation is
that people who divorce almost always repeat the same
sort of marriage with new partners. No better, no worse."

"I'm sure that's what I want, Horny," said Alys. The
reddening of the eyes and the streaks of her makeup
showed she had been weeping, but she was composed now.

"Is it Ted?"

"Oh, no."

"Walter?"

"No. It isn't Sue-Ellen, either. They're all just as fine as they can be. But not for me. They'll be happier with somebody else, Horny."

Walter Sturgis gazed at her with eyes leaking slow tears. He was breathing heavily. "Oh, Horny," he moaned. "I never thought it would end like this. I remember the day I first met Alys. Ted introduced us. They were recently married, just the two of them. I'd always liked Ted, but I just never thought of a plural marriage with him until I met Alys, so pretty, so *different*. And then when Sue-Ellen came along, we all fitted together. We proposed the day after we met."

"Actually it was about two weeks after we met, dear," said Sue-Ellen with some difficulty. She had been crying too.

"No, honey, that was after you and I met; I mean after the two of us met Ted and Alys. Horny," he said despondently, "if Alys won't change her mind I don't know what I'll do. I'll never find another girl like her. And I'm sure I speak for Ted and Sue-Ellen too."

Long after they had gone Horny sat in the gathering darkness, wondering where he had failed. But had it been his failure? Wasn't there something in the essential grinding, grim grittiness of the world that was destroying social fabrics of more kinds than marriage? The strikes and the muggings, the unemployment and the inflation, the jolting disappearance of fresh fruits from the stores in summer and of Christmas trees in December, the puzzling and permanently infuriating dislocations that had become the central fact of everyone's life—wasn't that where the cause was, and not in his failure?

But the failure felt like his own. And that was almost a pleasing thought. At least it was a useful one. He had been a minister long enough to recognize that any insight into guilt was a possible starting place for a sermon theme. He picked up the microphone, thumbed the switch and started to dictate before he realized the red operation light hadn't gone on.

At the same moment Jessie Tunman opened the door without knocking. "Horny! Did you turn on your heater?"

He looked guiltily down, and there it was. Not glowing. But warm and clicking to itself from thermal strain.

"I guess I must have."

"Well, you did it that time. We've blown the input fuse."

"I'm sorry, Jessie. Well, the coal man will be here pretty soon—"

"But then the blower won't work, because there's no power for it, will it? You'll be lucky if the pipes don't freeze, Horny, and as for me, I'm getting a cold. I've got to go home."

"But the church newsletter—"

"I'll run it off tomorrow, Horny."

"My sermon! I haven't even started dictating it!"

"You can dictate it tomorrow, Horny. I'll type it up."

"I can't, I have to go— I have to do something else tomorrow."

She looked at him curiously. "Well," she said, puffing her gray cheeks, "when you get up there Sunday morning maybe you can do a couple of card tricks. I have to go now, or I'll be sick, and then I won't be in tomorrow either."

He watched her zip up her quilted jacket and transfer her spiral silver safe brooch from blouse to coat. As she was leaving there was someone at the door, and for a moment Horny's hopes ran high—the man from the electric company? Maybe the coal man, maybe both of them together? But it was only the policeman with the summons for power-piggery. "That's your fifth offense, Reverend," he smirked, blowing into his reddened hands. "Maybe I should just leave a couple of blank ones for you to fill out, save me a trip next time?"

Horny stared at him, a big, beefy man with a gay knot on the shoulder of his uniform jacket, leather bracelet at his wrist, American flag in between. He was not the kind of person Horny Hake looked to argue with. A hundred rejoinders rose to his lips, but what came out was, "Thank you, Sergeant. Sure is lousy weather, isn't it?"

II

HE barely made it to the bus station on the boardwalk by 8:15, but then the bus was late. By the time it limped along he had had ten unprotected minutes in the unending bitter wind. The first section of the tandem was full already. He found a seat in the second bus, but that meant sitting next to the charcoal generator, which was old and leaky and backed smoke into the bus every time the driver throttled down. He might have slept, but for the matter of his sermon for the next morning. No sense putting it off. He took the lid off his battered portable typewriter, balanced it on his knee and began to type: *Finding Something to Love in Everyone.*

Well, that was a start. When you came right down to it, there was something lovable in every human being. Jessie Tunman? She was a hard worker. The world would fall apart without Jessie Tunmans. The coal man? Out day after day in every kind of weather, keeping everyone's home warm. Sergeant Moncozzi— He drew a blank on Sergeant Moncozzi, disrupted his chain of thought, sat with his mind skittering in a hundred directions for a minute and then crossed out what he had written and typed in a new title: *If You Can't Love, Then Tolerate.*

"Excuse me," said the lady next to him, "are you a writer?"

He looked up at her. She had got on in Matawan, a tall, skinny woman with an old-fashioned wedding ring belligerently displayed on her finger, hair an unlikely yellow, face made up so heavily it had to be concealing wrinkles. "Not exactly," he said.

"I didn't think so," she said. "If you were a real writer you'd be writing instead of just staring at the paper like that."

He nodded and went back to looking out the window. The tandem bus was creaking up the long slope of the Edison Bridge, the motor groaning and faltering to make forty kilometers an hour. It was all right on the straightaway, but on anything more than a three percent grade it could not even reach the legal limit of eighty. Down below the river was choked with breaking-up ice laced together with a tangle of northern water hyacinth. A tug was doggedly trying to clear a path for a string of coal barges running upstream.

"When I was a girl," the woman said, leaning across him to peer out the window, "this was all oil tanks." She rubbed a clear spot on the window and scowled at the housing developments. "Dozens of tanks. Big ones. And all full. And refineries, with the flames coming out of the top of them where they were burning the waste gas. Waste gas, young man! They didn't even try to save it. Oh, I tell you, we had some good times in 1970." *If You Can't Love, Then Tolerate.*

Exercising his tolerance to the full, Horny said, "I guess there have to be places for the people to live."

"People? Who's talking about people? I mean, where's the oil now, young man? The Communists have it all, what the Jews left us. Wasn't for them, we'd have good times again."

"Well, madam—"

"You know I'm right, don't you? And all this crime and pollution!" She sank back into her seat, neck craned to stare at him triumphantly.

"Crime? I'm not sure I see how crime comes into it."

"Plain as the nose on your face! All these young people

with nothing to do! If they had their cars they could ride around with a six-pack and a couple of girls, and who could be happier? Oh, I remember those times, until the Jews spoiled it for all of us."

Horny Hake fought back his temper. She was, of course, referring to the Israeli reprisals against the Arab League, the commando and air attacks that had blasted open every major oilfield in the Near East, causing the Abu Dabu firestorm and a thousand lesser, but immense, blazes. "I don't agree, madam! Israel was fighting for its life."

"And ruining mine! Talk about pollution. Do you know they increased the particulate matter in the air by *seven point two percent*? And it was just to be mean."

"It was to save their lives, madam! It wasn't the Arab armies that put Israel in danger. They proved that six times. It was the Arab oil, and the Arab money!"

She looked at him with dawning comprehension, then sniffed. "You Jewish?" she asked. "I thought so!"

Hake swallowed the answer and turned back to the window, steaming. After a moment he put the lid back on the typewriter, slid it under the seat, closed his eyes, folded his hands and began practicing his isometric exercises to relax.

The trouble with the question was that it had a complicated answer, and he didn't like her well enough to give it. Hake didn't think of himself as Jewish—well, he wasn't; but it was more complex than that. He didn't think of himself as a minister, either, or at least not the kind of person he had always thought of as a minister, back when he was a kid. Considering how his life had changed in the past two years, he wasn't altogether sure who he was. Except that he was himself. Physically he might be somebody new, but inside he was old Horny Hake, whose choices were limited, not too lucky with women, not too financially successful. Maybe not even too smart, at least compared to the bright new kids out of the seminaries. But the center of his own personal universe, all the same.

The first memory Horny Hake had of his early life was being carried, hastily and not very carefully, through the wheat fields of his parents' kibbutz. The sprinklers were going, and the sour smell of the grain was heavy in the sodden, sultry air. He was maybe three years old at the time, and it was way past his bedtime.

He woke up with a yell. Something had scared him. It was going right on scaring him: crunching, roaring blasts of sound, people shouting and screaming. He didn't know what it was. Little Horny knew what rocket fire sounded like well enough, because he had heard the kibbutz militia practicing in the fallow fields every week. This was different. He could not identify these terrifying eruptions with the orderly slow fire of the drill. Neither had he heard people shriek in agony and fear when rockets exploded. He began to cry. "Sssh, *bilmouachira,*" said whoever was carrying him, gruff, scared, a man's voice. Not his father's. When he realized that neither his mother nor his father was with them, that he and the unknown man were all alone, he stopped crying. It was too frightening for tears.

At three he was still young enough to be treated as a baby, too old to like it. He also disliked the physical sensations of where they were; it was unpleasantly hot, but the mist from the sprayers was clammy cold. "Put down, *magboret!*" he yelled, but the man who was carrying him didn't put him down, he clamped a dirty, calloused hand that tasted of grease and salt over Horny's mouth. Then Horny recognized the hand. It was old Ahmet, the Palestinian electrician who ran the milking machines at the kibbutz, and babysat for Horny when his parents flew into Haifa or Tel Aviv for a weekend.

By all rights Horny's life should have ended right there, because the PLO commandos had them dead to rights. What saved them was a diversion. Horny remembered it all his life, a tower of flame that seemed to reach the sky. He got it confused in his mind, as he grew up, with the Abu Dabu firestorm, when the Israelis dumped their shaped nuclear charge into the oilfields that gave the Arabs their muscle. It was impossible, of course. Probably what had actually exploded on the edge of the kibbutz was no more than the tractor gas pumps. But it kept the commandos busy enough for long enough to save his life.

Horny never saw his father again. None of the male

militia at Kibbutz Meir survived the first strike. Horny's mother lived, but she was too seriously wounded to go back to farm life. She took the baby and returned to America, lived long enough to marry a widower with five children and bear him Horny's half-sister. It was the best she could do for her son, and it wasn't bad. He grew up in that family in Fair Haven, New Jersey, well cared for and well educated.

That was in the last Arab-Israeli war, the fourth after Yom Kippur, the second after the Bay of Sharks, the one that settled things forever. Growing up after it, Horny had been alternately full of resolve to return and build up Israel again (but Israel did fine without him) and determination to help his new country as a thermodynamic engineer, able to solve the problems of wiped-out oil reserves. It didn't work out that way. It might have, if he hadn't spent so much of his childhood in a wheelchair. But after two years of MIT he began to perceive that technology didn't seem to deal with the kind of problems people came to him with: the invalid young man was a repository for all confidences, and he found he liked it. He switched schools and objectives. The next step was the seminary, and he wound up a Unitarian minister.

He had not married. Not because he was in a wheelchair; oh, no, any number of young women had made it perfectly clear that that wouldn't stop *them*. At the seminary he had paid a shrink for a dozen fifty-minute hours to find out, among other things, why that was. He was not sure he had had his money's worth. It seemed to have something to do with pride. But why that much pride? He had learned that he was full of unresolved conflicts. He hated Arabs, who had killed his father, and ultimately his mother too. But the man who hid him out in the wheat and saved his life was also an Arab, whom he loved. He had been brought up as a Jew, a non-religious Jew, to be sure, but in an atmosphere saturated with dreidels and Chanukah candles. But both his parents had been born Protestants, one side Lutheran and the other Methodist, who had happened to admire the kibbutz lifestyle and been accepted as volunteers in the exciting years when all the second-generation kibbutzim were flocking to the cities and the agro-industrial settlements were desperate for warm bodies.

So he wound up a minister in a Unitarian church in Long Branch, New Jersey, between a pizzeria and a parking lot, and all in all he liked it well enough. At least until the last cardiac operation, two years before, that had changed things around.

Now he was not really sure what he liked. What he disliked was clear enough. He disliked crime, and filth, and poverty, and meanness; and most of all he disliked bigots like the woman beside him. He maintained silence all the way to Newark, where he got out while the bus driver stood in the doorway with his shotgun until all the passengers were safely inside the terminal, just in time to catch the Metroliner to Washington.

The Metroliner was a four-bus string, with a pilot, copilot, stewardess and conductor. From the outside it looked glittering and new. Inside, not quite so new. For one thing, in his coach section three of the windows were stuck open. For another the woman from the Long Branch bus followed him aboard, evidently anxious to renew the conversation.

For the first twenty miles Hake tried to feign sleep, but it was hard going. Not only was the window behind him open, but for some reason the air-conditioning was full on and icy drafts caught him in the temple every time he leaned back and closed his eyes.

At the rest stop at the Howard Johnson's outside Philadelphia, he got out, went to the men's room, came out and stood gloomily surveying the Philadelphia Slag Bank until the pilot tapped his horn impatiently. He leaped in at the last minute, followed closely by a girl in a denim zipper-suit, who gave him a surprisingly inviting smile. The smile collapsed when he sat down in the front seat, next to a large black woman counting rosary beads. The girl hesitated, then went back to the next vacant seat, and gratefully Hake fell asleep.

He woke up quite a long time later realizing that someone was talking to him in a penetrating whisper. "—to bother you, but it's important. Would you please come back to the toilet with me?"

He sat up suddenly and looked around, feeling frowsty with sleep and somewhat irritable. His black neighbor was gone, replaced by a Puerto Rican woman holding a baby with one hand and a copy of *El Diario* in the other.

The voice came from behind him; he turned and met the eye of the girl in the zip-suit.

"Turn back!" she whispered tensely. "Don't look at me!"

Confused, he followed orders. Her whisper reached him. "I think you're being watched, and I don't want any trouble. So what I'll do is I'll go back in the toilet. Nobody pays much attention to that. The one on the left; it's got a broken seat so nobody uses it much. Will you?"

Hake started to ask what for, but swallowed it. He said instead, "Where are we?"

"About half an hour out of Washington. Come on, tiger, I won't hurt you."

"I have to get out pretty soon," Hake said. "I mean, I'm not going all the way into Washington—"

"Will you please come back and quit arguing? Look, I'm going back to the toilet now. Wait one minute. Then you just get up and stroll back and come right in. I'll leave the door unlatched. There's plenty of room, I already checked it."

"Lady," said Hake, "I don't know exactly what's happening, but please leave me alone."

"Oaf!"

"I'm sorry."

She whispered angrily, "You don't even know why I want you to come back there, do you?"

He paused, surprised. "I don't? Well, then, I guess I don't."

"So *come*. It's important." And she got up, turned around in the aisle to scowl at him, and headed toward the back. None of the other passengers were watching, having reached the terminal phase of mass transit where they were asleep or engrossed in whatever they were doing or cataleptic.

For a moment Horny Hake seriously thought of following

her, just on the chance that it would be interesting. She
really was rather a nice-looking woman, years younger than
he was but not so young as to be embarrassing. There was
very little chance that she intended to cut his throat or
infect him with a communicable disease. He didn't have a
lot to lose, he was sure; but just at that moment the bus
slowed and the driver leaned over, eyes still on the road.
"Here's your stop," he called.

Would have been interesting; should have taken a chance,
thought Hake, but that's the story of my life. As he got out
of the Metroliner, at a private driveway marked Lo-Wate
Bottling Co., Inc., he looked back and saw the girl emerging hurriedly from the toilet, staring at him with resentment
and rage.

Hake opened his sealed instructions and read them again
to make sure:

> *Debus at Lo-Wate Bottling Co. entrance. Proceed on
> foot ¼ mi. to entrance marked* Visitors. *State name
> to receptionist and follow her instructions.*

Clear enough. The building marked *Visitors—Market
Analysis—Sales & Promotion* was two-story, ivy-covered,
a veteran of the decentralization years of the '60s and '70s,
but well maintained. The receptionist was a young man who
listened as Hake gave his name, then asked, "May I see
your travel orders?" He did not trouble to read them, but
put them, backside up, under a hooded bulb that emitted a
faint bluish glow. What the receptionist saw Horny could
not see, but evidently it was satisfactory. "The gentleman
with whom you have an appointment will see you in about
ten minutes," he said. "Please be seated."

It was almost exactly ten minutes, by Hake's watch. The
receptionist had been nice enough to let him use the
waiting-room john—he hadn't dared, in the bus, although
the girl's talk had put the idea strongly in his mind. Then
the receptionist beckoned to him. "The gentleman with
whom you have an appointment will see you now. This
lady will escort you there. Please follow the following instructions. Walk ten paces behind your escort. Do not look

into any offices. Check any camera, film, microphones or recording devices here. If you have any undeveloped film or magnetic tape on your person it will be damaged."

"I don't have anything like that," said Hake.

The young man nodded, unsurprised. Thinking it over, Hake remembered the thirty-second pause in the vestibule on the way in, waiting for the automatic door to open; no doubt at the same time capacitators probed for metal on his person.

His escort was a little old lady, motherly and smiling, who tottered along at slow-march, crying in a thin, piercing voice: "Uncleared personnel coming through! Uncleared personnel coming through!" Hake didn't look into the offices because he was getting the uneasy feeling that something was going on that had high stakes involved and orders had better be followed; but he was aware of a rustling of papers being covered and charts being turned to the wall from every doorway they passed.

It did not surprise him that "Lo-Wate Bottling Co." was some sort of government installation. Even if he had not expected it, "follow the following instructions" would have been a dead giveaway.

All the walls were bare, except for what looked like ventilators but might have concealed surveillance equipment; government-issue cream-colored paint; no windows visible anywhere. Hake wondered about the outside of the building. Surely there had been windows in it? But maybe they were dummies.

The motherly woman reached her destination—a closed door that bore a frame for a nameplate, but instead of a name it had a number: *T-34*. The guide carefully checked it against a card in her hand, knocked twice and waited. When the door opened she averted her eyes and stared at the ceiling. "The gentleman with whom the gentleman had an appointment is here," she said.

Hake walked in and shook the hand of the gentleman, accepted a seat and a cigarette and waited.

The gentleman slung himself into a fat leather chair behind a steel drawerless desk, and lit a cigarette of his own. He was short, slim and hairy: not only a Waspro that

fluffed out in all directions, but a sloppy beard and side-
burns. His general appearance was not of a man who
had decided to grow long hair and facial hair, but of
someone who simply stopped doing anything about it at
some remote point in time. He wore chinos and an Army
jacket, without insignia, over a blue work shirt open at the
throat; and around his waist he had a gunbelt with a
holstered .45.

"I imagine," he said, "you're wondering what you're
doing here, Horny."

Horny let out a long breath. "You are very right about
that, Mr.—"

The man waved a hand. "My name doesn't matter. I
suppose you've already figured out that this is some kind of
cockamamie cloak-and-dagger operation. If you haven't,
you're pretty dumb. So we don't give real names to people
like you, but you can call me—" he paused to lift a corner
of one of the papers on his desk—"ah, yes. You can call
me Curmudgeon."

"Curmudgeon?"

"Don't ask me why, I don't decide these things. Now, the
first thing we have to do is recall you to active service.
Please stand up and repeat the oath."

"Hey! Hey, wait a minute. I'm thirty-nine years old and
draft-proof, and besides I'm a minister."

"Oh, yes, you certainly are. You're also a fellow who
took ROTC in college, right?"

"Now, that's ridiculous! I wasn't *really* in Rotsy. I was
in a wheelchair. It was just some kind of public relations
thing, for extra credit—"

"But you took the oath, and when you signed up you
signed for twenty years in the Reserve. And that hasn't
changed, has it? So stand up."

"No," said Horny, for whom things were going much
too fast. "I mean, can't you let me know what this is all
about first? I guess it's some kind of CIA thing, but—"

"Oh, Horny, you're tiresome. Look. The CIA was disbanded years ago, after the scandals. Didn't you know that?
There's no such thing any more. What we have here is just
a team. With a job to do."

"Then what kind of job—"

The man stood up, and suddenly looked a lot taller. He said in a flat voice, "You have two choices, Hake. Take the oath. Or go to jail for evasion of service. That's only a five-year sentence, but they'll be hard years, Hake, they'll be very hard years. And then we'll think of something else."

It took about three seconds for Horny Hake to catalogue his alternate choices and realize that he didn't have any; reluctantly and sullenly he stood up and repeated the oath.

"Now, that's much better," the man said warmly. "The first thing I have to do is give you three orders. Remember them, Horny. You can't write them down, but I'm recording the orders and your responses—which, in each case, are to be, 'I understand and will comply.' Got it? All right, first order: This project and your participation in it are top secret and are not to be discussed with anyone at any time without the specific authorization of me or whoever replaces me in the event I die or am removed. Got that?"

"I guess so—"

"No, that's not it. 'I understand and will comply.' "

"I understand and will comply," said Hake thoughtfully.

"Second order: The declassification of any material relating to this project can be only at my explicit order in writing, or that of my successor. It is without time limit. You are bound to it for the rest of your life. Okay?"

"Right," said Hake dismally.

"Wrong. 'I understand—' "

"All right. I understand and will comply."

"Third: This security classification also applies to the fact that you are recalled to active duty. You may not inform anyone of this."

"What am I supposed to tell my church?" Hake demanded. The man wagged his head. "Oh, all right: I understand and will comply. But what *am* I supposed to tell them?"

"You're very sick, Horny," Curmudgeon said sympathetically. "You have to take time off."

"But I can't just leave—"

"Certainly not. We'll supply you with a replacement. And," he went on, "there are certain advantages to this from your point of view. For payroll procedures, you will be placed on retainer by Lo-Wate as a consultant at an annual salary equal to a GS-16—which, if you don't know, is currently about $83,000 a year, counting bonuses and cost-of-living. That's, let's see—" he took a notebook out of his inside shirt pocket—"looks like better than thirty thousand more than you're making now from your church. And we'll take good care of you in other ways. The Team takes care of its people."

"But I like being a minister!" Even as he was saying the words, he felt their total irrelevance. "Why me?" he burst out.

"Ah," said the man, all sympathy, "how many people have asked that question? Men dying on a battlefield. Girls being raped. Children with leukemia. Of course," he said, "in your case it's a little easier to explain. We put through a sort for persons on active service or capable of being activated for our team. Age at least twenty but no more than forty-five, of Middle Eastern but non-Jewish and non-Moslem extraction. I guess there weren't all that many, Horny. Then we evaluated in point scores. Point scores," he said confidentially, "usually means that we don't really know who we want. We figure out a couple of things— Eastern-Mediterranean languages, knowing the customs of the area, free of obligations that would interfere with leaving for parts unknown for prolonged periods. That sort of thing. And you won, Horny, fair and square."

"You want me to go be a spy in the Middle East?"

He coughed. "Well, that's the funny part. It says here your first mission will be in France, Norway and Denmark. It's a strange thing," he said philosophically, "but every once in a while the system screws up. Well. It's nice talking to you, but you've got two other people to see before you leave. Let me have you taken to your next appointment."

The next person was a plump and rather pretty woman, who said at once, "How much history do you know?"

"Well—"

"I don't mean Romans and the Dukes of Burgundy, I

mean over the last couple of decades. For instance. Why hasn't there been a shooting war in the last twenty years?"

Well, he knew the answer to that. No one had the heart for a shooting war any more, not since the brief violent bloodbaths that had splashed up and smeared twenty small countries in a couple of decades. For one thing, they were bad for business. Oil roared with pain when the Israelis demolished the Arab fields. Steel screamed under the squeeze of price-fixing. Banking wept under currency controls.

"I would say," he began judiciously, "that it's because—"

"It's because it's too dangerous," she said. "Nobody wins a war any more—if the enemy knows a war is going on."

"I beg your pardon?"

"There are two ways to win a race, Hake. One is to beat your opponent by sheer force. The other is to trip him up. They're playing trip-him-up with us. Why do you think we're so short of energy in this country?"

"Well, because the world is running out of—"

"Because they manipulate our balance of payments, Hake. The mark is up to three dollars, did you know that? And what about crime?"

"Crime?"

"You've heard of crime, haven't you? It's not safe to walk the streets of any city in America today. Even our highways aren't safe, there are bus robbers in every state. Do you know why you can't get an avocado for love or money? Because somebody—*some*body!—deliberately brought in insect pests that wiped out the crop."

Horny said, "I think you jumped over something about crime. I didn't quite get that part."

"It's plain, Hake! Somebody's encouraging this lawlessness. Cheap Spanish and Algerian porno flicks that show muggers and highwaymen doing it to all the girls. They *look* crude. But, oh, how carefully engineered! War is not all bombs and missiles, my boy. It's hurting the other fellow any way you can. And if you can hurt him so he can't prove it's happening, why, that's one for your side. And that's what they're doing to us, Hake. Here, have a look at this tape." And she threaded a cassette into a viewer.

Horny stared at it, bemused. It started way back, back before the Big Wars entirely. The peace-loving British had pioneered in this immoral equivalent for war as far back as the nineteenth century: they found a good way to discourage resistance in subject populations by encouraging them to trip out on opium. America itself had exported cigarettes and Coca-Cola around the world. Now, according to the tape, it was becoming state policy, and William James was turning in his grave. China flooded the Soviet Union with Comecon vodka at half the market price. It was not a weapon. No one died. But twenty percent of the steelworkers in Magnitogorsk were absent with hangovers on an average working day. Tokyo flooded the Marianas with cheap, high-quality sukiyaki noodles, reminding the voters of their ancestry just before the referendum that rejoined the islands to Japan. During the London water shortage just before the completion of the Rape of Scotland waterworks, Irish nationalists went around turning on hydrants and covert sympathizers left their taps running. It worked so well that Palestinian refugees, circumcized and trained for the occasion, repeated the process in Haifa to such an extent that two hundred thousand acres of orange groves died for lack of irrigation.

By now such tactics had become well institutionalized, and wholly secret. Everybody did it. Nobody talked about it.

Horny Hake was horrified. As soon as he began to understand the thrust of what he was being shown he burst out, "But that's *animal*. Wars are supposed to be all over!"

The woman replaced the cover over her projector and sighed, "Go through that door, there's somebody who wants to study you."

The somebody turned out to be a sandy-haired young man with spectacles, who looked a little like Hake. "Jim Jackson," he said, standing up. "I'm your replacement."

"Replacement for what?" Hake demanded.

"You're going on a sabbatical," said Jackson, watching Hake's expression thoughtfully. "Right word?"

"Sabbatical? It's a minister's vacation. I thought I was supposed to be sick."

"Oh, shit," said Jackson crossly, "have they changed the plans again? Well, anyway, I'm going to take over for you while you're on active duty."

Hake looked at him jealously. "Are you a minister?"

"I'm whatever they tell me to be," Jackson shrugged. "They say 'You're an account executive' or 'You're a TV producer,' and I do it. You'd be surprised how easy it is when you're a boss. When somebody else is the boss it's harder, but I manage. Sometimes I screw up but usually nobody notices."

Hake was horrified. "A minister has a tough job! How can you possibly take over a congregation?"

"Oh, I think it'll work out," said Jackson. "They told me this assignment might be coming up so I went to a church last Sunday. Doesn't look so hard. I picked up a batch of mimeographed sermons on my way out that ought to keep me going for the first few weeks anyway. Of course," he said, "that was a Baptist church and I understand you're Congregational. Or something like that. I suppose there are doctrinal differences, but I'll manage. I already checked out some books from the library: oldies but goodies like *On Being a Woman* and stuff by Janov and Perls. What else do you do?"

"Counseling," said Hake immediately. "The sermon's nothing by comparison. All the people in the church can come to me with their problems, any time."

"And you solve them?"

"Well," said Hake, "no, I don't always *solve* them. That's a sort of structured old-fashioned kind of way to look at it. You can't *force* solutions on people. They have to generate their own solutions."

"How do you get them to do that?"

"I listen," Hake said promptly. "I let them talk, and when they come to the place where the pain is I ask them what they think they could do about it. Of course there are some failures, but mostly they perceive what they have to do."

Jackson nodded, unsurprised. "That's how I handled it when I was a judge, too," he remarked. "Get the two lawyers into chambers and ask them not to waste my time, tell me what they *really* think I should do. They'd almost always tell me. I hated to give that job up, to tell you the truth."

By the time the little old lady returned to conduct Hake out into the real world he was reconciled to the fact that this fantasy had forced itself into reality. Incredibly, he was about to become a spy in a war that he had not even known was going on. *Mad!* he thought, following the lady's leper cry down the hall, while the offices around him slammed doors and bustled with the hiding of secrets from his eyes-front gaze. *Mad!*

He waited by the side of the road for his bus to pick him up. It was wholly mad, but interesting; Hake found himself accepting it as a sort of lunacy high. At least for some time he would not have to worry about blowing his overload fuse or dealing with Jessie Tunman's temper. And the extra money would be welcome enough. Hake was not overpaid. Like most preachers, he had moonlighted at a number of occupations over the years—hustling magazine subscriptions and ghosting masters' theses in school, when he was still chair-ridden; later, when he became a jock, he was counselor at a camp for delinquent boys one summer, and the year following had even driven the little hydrogen-propelled truck that squirted detergent on the heliostats for the local solar power facility. There were important requirements for a minister's sideline job. It should be either dignified or inconspicuous. No parishioner wanted to see the shepherd of his soul checking out soup cans at the supermarket.

Being a spook might not qualify as dignified, but it was guaranteed to be inconspicuous. There was, of course, the question of right and wrong. That was hard to handle. Hake dealt with it by postponing it. He saw no way out of doing what he was told, so he would do it—trusting that anyone who charged him with evil-doing later, even his own conscience, would forgive it as a temporary aberration in a life otherwise not too bad.

And viewed as madness—i.e., as a sort of penalty-free vacation from the irritating world of objective reality—it was certainly exciting enough! Almost pleasurable, in fact. Anything might happen. He told himself, with a little thrill of excitement, that he had to expect the unexpected . . . and so he was not even surprised when, instead of the bus, a three-wheeled telephone company repair truck whined to a halt in front of him. Not even when the double doors opened to reveal four people in masks, two of whom pointed guns at him while the others jumped out, grabbed him and threw him inside.

There were no windows in the van, but Hake couldn't have seen out of them anyway. He was made to lie down on a collection of only approximately level toolboxes and cases of repair parts. He was not allowed to get up until the truck stopped and, now polite and unviolent, the men led him into a normal-looking split-level ranch home in the timeworn style of sixty years earlier. It did not astonish him that he recognized the girl in the doorway. She was tall, slim and really quite pretty, if you didn't mind some strange behavioral quirks; she was, in fact, the one who had tried to pick him up in the bus.

They moved him like a puppet, talked about him as if he weren't there. "Search him," said the girl, and one man held him while another expertly turned out his pockets. The holding wasn't necessary. Horny had no intention of resisting while the two other men still had their guns pointed in his direction. "Give me his stuff," she said.

"Bunch of junk, Lee."

"Give it to me anyway." She filled her cupped hands with the litter from his pockets. It was not very impressive. Wallet, return ticket on the Metroliner, keys with a rabbit's-foot chain, summons for power-piggery, the folded sheets that were supposed to be his sermon—

"Hey," he said. "Where's my typewriter?"

The girl looked furiously at one of the men, who ventured, "I guess we left it in the truck."

"Get it! Bring it in the kitchen. You keep an eye on him, Richy." And the man with the bigger gun pushed him face down on a lumpy couch, while the girl and the other two retired from the room. The couch smelled of generations of use, and when Hake tried to move his face away from it the man called Richy warned, "Don't try it, pal."

"I'm not trying anything." Stubbornly Hake kept his face averted. Now he could study the room, though there was not much to study. It was dark because the picture window had been covered long since with translucent, then opaque, plastic to conserve heat. Which he could have wished they had conserved better because, now that he was not moving, he was cold. In the feeble light from two candles Hake worked at trying to memorize Richy's face. A perfectly ordinary face, youngish, with a red-brown beard. He wondered if he would be able to identify it in a police lineup, and then wondered if he would live to try. Although he was past being surprised he was not past being scared, and this was beginning to scare him.

"Bring him in," called the girl.

"Right, Lee. Get up, you." Horny let himself be shoved into the kitchen. It was brighter than the other room, but smelled, if anything, even worse, as though the ghost of long-dead garbage-disposal units had left their greasy deposits to sour in the drain.

The girl was sitting on the edge of a chrome and plastic kitchen table, older than she was. "Well, Reverend H. Hornswell Hake," she said, "do you want to tell us who you really are?"

It caught him by surprise. "That's who I am," he protested.

She shook her head reproachfully. "You a minister? Cripes. Worst cover I ever saw." She poked through the litter on the table: his papers and his typewriter, opened, with the roller lifted out and inches of the ribbon unrolled—to look for microfilms, maybe? "Look at this driver's license! It's dated three days ago. Real amateurish. Anybody would have known to backdate it a year or two, so it wouldn't look so phony."

"But that's when it had to be renewed. Honest, that's me.

Horny Hake. I'm minister of the Unitarian Church in Long Branch, New Jersey. Have been for years."

Richy nudged him with the gun, into an aluminum-tube chair. "I suppose you've never heard of yo-yos," he sneered.

"Yo-yos?"

"Or hula hoops. Don't even know what they are, do you?"

"Well, sure I do. Everybody does."

"And you know about them better than other people because you're a toy designer, right? Don't crap us, Hake, or whatever your name is. What we want to know is, what kind of toys are you exporting these days?"

Hake sat and blinked up at them, silent because he could not think of any answer that he was sure he should make. Except, "I don't know what you're talking about."

Lee sighed and took over. "Just start out by admitting you're a toy designer, why don't you? In fact," she said, "that would be smart, don't you see? If you don't admit that much you'll cause curiosity, which would lead people to suspect that some security matter is involved."

"But I'm not! I'm a minister!"

"Oh, God, Hake, you're such a pain." She glanced morosely toward the bigger of the armed men, who was standing by the door with a .32 automatic hanging loosely from his hand in an ostentatious kind of way. It had a long tube attached to it that Hake supposed to be a silencer. That was also ostentatious, as well as highly unpleasant.

"Want me to try with him?" the .32-automatic man rumbled.

"Not yet. Not unless he keeps this up. Listen, Hake," she said, "I can see you're new at this game. Damn Team, they don't give you proper briefing. Let me tell you the rules, all right?"

"Would you tell me the name of the game, too?"

"Don't be a wise-ass. Here's how it's supposed to go. We've kidnapped you, so obviously we're breaking the law. You're okay as far as the law goes, but you don't want to stay kidnapped. Got it so far? That's the first level of meaning to what's happening here. Now, on the second level, let's say you're really just an ordinary toy designer—"

"I'm not!"

"Oh, shut up, will you? Let me finish. Say you're a toy designer, and you never heard of the Lo-Wate Bottling Company, alias the Team. Why do you think we kidnapped you? You might suspect we're from Mattel, or say Sears Roebuck or somebody, maybe. Just plain old industrial espionage, you know, trying to get your new designs. A little rougher than most. But still just commercial, right? Well, in that case there's a special way you should act. You should cooperate with us. Why? Because your boss wouldn't expect you to for God's sake risk your *life* just to protect a new yo-yo design, even if you were expecting to ship a hundred million of them to the Soviet Union. Got it so far? There's a limit to what you should put up with just to keep the new fall line from a competitor."

"Well, that's probably true, but—"

"No, Hake, no 'but' yet. That's if you're just a toy designer, really. But now let's go to the third level. Let's suppose you're a toy designer who is actually working for the cloak-and-dagger boys. Let's say you know these yo-yos carry a subsonic whistle that drives people crazy when their kids play with them. Not fatal. Just enough to make them tense and irritable. Let's say you've figured out that the adult hula hoops are going to cause more slipped disks and sacroiliac disorders than the Soviet economy can put up with—just for instance, right? So what do you do in that case? Why, you act just the way you would on the second level, because you wouldn't want us to know you weren't just an ordinary toy designer. What you *don't* do, on either level, is lie to us about what you do for a living, because, you see, we already know that; that's why we brought you here," she explained.

"But I'm still on the first level! I'm a minister!"

"What rot," she said scornfully. "And next you're going to tell me you went to the Team headquarters just to get a diet cola?"

"Well," he said uncomfortably, and stopped.

"You see? No answer! You can't even make up a decent lie! Very bad briefing they gave you!"

Hake had to agree that he couldn't give her an answer—

not any answer at all, not after Curmudgeon's very explicit orders. But he agreed silently. It was a pity no one had explained to him what to do in a case like this. Where were the poison capsules in the false teeth, or the secret radio that would alert Headquarters and bring a hundred agents slinking in to save him?

The girl was waiting for a response. He said desperately, "All I can tell you is the truth. The papers you have tell it the way it is. I'm a Unitarian minister. Period."

"No, Hake," she said angrily, "not period. What would a minister be doing where we picked you up?"

"Ah, well," he said guardedly, "yes, I was asked to come there."

"To talk about toys for Russia!"

"No! Nobody said a word about toys!"

"Then why were you there?"

"My God, don't you think I wish I knew? All they said was they wanted somebody with a Near East background who wouldn't be missed if anything went—" Belatedly he clamped his lips together.

His captors were looking at each other. "Near East?"

"It isn't the first time that source got it wrong."

"You think—?"

"So maybe this one isn't the toy man," said the man with the .32.

The girl nodded slowly. "So maybe we're into something entirely different."

"So maybe it's time for Phase Two," said the gunman.

"Yeah. Tell you what, Hake," she said, turning back to him. "That sort of changes things, doesn't it? I guess we've made some kind of mistake. Here, have some coffee while we figure out what to do next."

He accepted the cup morosely. The four of them withdrew to the other room and whispered together, glancing through the doorway at him from time to time. He could not hear what they were saying. It did not seem to matter. Let them conspire; there was nothing he could do about it, except to let it happen. Even the coffee was not very good, though not as bad as his precarious situation. These people did not seem like very expert kidnappers or spies or whatever they were; but how much expertise did you need to pull the trigger on a gun? He took another sip of the coffee—

As he was lifting the cup for a third sip, it belatedly occurred to him that it might not be wise to drink something just because it said "Drink Me." Poison, truth serum, knockout drops— But that was two sips too late. The cup dropped out of his hand, and his head dropped to meet the typewriter case on the table.

When he woke up the typewriter was in his lap, and none of them were anywhere in sight.

He was back on the Metroliner, heading back to Newark. Across the aisle two tiny, elderly ladies were staring at him. "He's sobering up," said one loudly.

Equally loudly the other one replied, "Disgusting! If I were his wife I wouldn't have helped him on the bus, I'd've just let him rot there. And serve him right."

THE next morning the sermon went beautifully—"So fresh and enlightening," said the president of the congregation, wringing his hand. He didn't have the heart to tell her that she had heard him give the same sermon, word for word, two years before. He didn't have the head for it, either, because the only head he had was throbbing violently. Whatever had been in the coffee had given him the finest hangover he had ever owned, and without even a night's drinking to justify it. Had to have been truth drug, he decided. They wouldn't have let him go until they were quite sure he had nothing worth telling to tell them. When you came down to it, he hadn't.

The coffee hour after the service was pure pain, but there was no way out of it. He didn't always hear what was said to him. But reflexes took over:

"You've given me a lot to think about, Horny."

"So glad you liked it."

And meanwhile his mind, between thuds of pain, was considering the world about him in a new light. The game the Team was asking him to join—was it being played all around him? That raft of water lilies that floated in every river: was that just a freak of nature, or were other nations playing that game against his own?

"Horny, the methane-burner's acting up again."

"I'm so pleased you liked it."

He thought of all the power blackouts that had hit in the past few years. Defective switches, overstressed transformers? Or somebody helping the accidents along? He recalled the dozen petty pandemics of coughs and trots, the strikes, the walkouts. The incredibly detailed rumors of corruption in high places, and perverse orgies of the powerful, that had turned half the country off to its elected officials. All of them! How many were thrown up by chance? How many were calculated strategies devised in Moscow or Beijing, or even Ottawa?

"Horny, I want to thank you for all of us. We've decided to give the marriage another chance."

"I'm glad you enjoyed—oh, Alys! Yes. What did you say?"

"I said you've made us want to try again, Horny."

"That's really fine. Yes." As she started to move off he detained her; she was one of the brightest of the parishioners, with a doctoral degree, he remembered, in history. "Alys," he said, "how would you go about researching some recent events?"

"What kind of recent events, Horny?"

"Well—I don't know exactly how to describe them." He pondered for a moment, and then offered: "It seems to me that everything has got kind of, you know, crappy over the last few years. Like the lilies that are clogging up the water intakes for all those cities in the north. Where did they come from?"

"I think they were first reported in Yugoslavia," she said helpfully. "Or was it Ireland?"

"Well, that sort of thing. If I made up a list of say thirty things that are going on that, uh, that seem to damage the quality of life, how would I go about seeing where they started, and what sort of correlations there are, and so on?"

She pursed her lips, fending off a couple of other parishioners pressing toward them. "I suppose you're researching a sermon?"

"Something like that," he lied.

"I thought so." She nodded. "Well, for openers, there's the *Readers' Guide to Periodical Literature*. And *Current Topics*. Then you might want to look at the *New York Times* microfilms, with the subject index. I'm afraid you'd have to go to New York for some of the stuff. Unless—" She looked carefully at his face. "Unless you'd like me to help you with it?"

"Would you? I'd really appreciate that."

"Why, certainly, Horny," she said, impulsively pressing his arm. "I'll come around tomorrow to talk to you about it. You've been so good to all of us, why, I couldn't deny you anything at all!" She leaned forward and kissed his cheek before she turned away.

It almost seemed that the headache was less, Hake thought gratefully. He did not think Curmudgeon would approve, but he decided to know what was going on. And with a trained researcher to help him, maybe he could find out.

On the steps of the church, a gray-haired man whose name he could not quite place stopped him and said: "Reverend Hake, may I have a word with you?"

"I'm so glad you enjoyed the sermon."

"Well, uh, yes, I did. But that wasn't what I was going to ask you. You see, I'm with International Pets and Flowers. We're expanding our operations here in New Jersey. I don't know whether you've heard of it, but we've acquired the old Fort Monmouth tract in Eatontown, and we like to have responsible local representation on our district Board of Directors in a thing like this. Could you accept a directorship?"

"Directorship? I'm sorry, Mr.—"

"Haversford, Reverend Hake. Allen T. Haversford."

"Well, I appreciate the offer, Mr. Haversford. Did you say pets and flowers? I'm afraid I don't know very much about pets and flowers. And my time—"

"No special knowledge is needed, Reverend Hake. It's a question of community welfare. We want your inputs on the way we can help carry our share of the load."

"Yes, I see that, but I'm very—"

"I know your time is at a premium, but it is quite a useful service you could do. And there's a tiny honorarium, of course. Ten thousand dollars. But the important thing is that I'm sure you could be of great help to us, and we to your church. Please say yes."

"Ten thousand dollars a *year*?"

"Oh, no. The honorarium is ten thousand dollars per meeting. There's one regular meeting each quarter—sometimes special ones, of course, when some decision is needed quickly, but they are usually quite brief. You'll do it? Thank you so much, Reverend. The other members of the Board will be very pleased."

Horny stared after Haversford, his head forgetting to ache. Forty thousand dollars a year, *plus*. And a community service too! As he turned toward the rectory he was thinking of what he could do with an extra forty thousand dollars a year; and then he caught sight of the Brant-Sturgis family. Walter Sturgis was turning the crank of the compressor of their charcoal-burner van, while the two women sat stiffly inside, red-eyed or brightly and sadistically cheerful, according to their private ways of expressing stress. Ted Brant was standing at the curb, glowering at him.

That almost brought the headache back. For the moment Hake had forgotten how jealous Ted was.

Horny had made it Rule Number One to avoid sexual entanglements within his congregation, or with other people with whom he associated in his professional capacity.

Considering that Hake's twenty-four-hour days allowed
six hours of sleep and eighteen hours in contact with some
member or another of his congregation—or some person
who was off-limits for equally valid reasons, like the wife
of another minister in the Regional Confraternity or his
fellow members of the Right to Abort Committee—that
meant he avoided sexual entanglements just about completely. It wasn't that he wanted it that way. Sometimes he
didn't even think he could stand it that way. But he knew
what happened to other ministers when they departed from
that golden rule. He was the only bachelor in Monmouth
County who never missed a meeting of the Interfaith
Singles Club—and who never failed to go home alone from
them, usually after everyone else had left because he
stacked the chairs and emptied the ashtrays to ready the
room for its next use. His vacation weeks gave him the
only romantic interludes of his life. And there weren't
many of them. Weren't nearly enough.

But the last thing he was willing to accept was any share
in the probable collapse of the precarious Brant-Sturgis
marriage. Before he went to sleep that night he had typed
out a careful list of subjects for Alys to look up for him,
and left the envelope on Jessie Tunman's desk clipped to a
scrap of paper that said only "Gv. to A.—DWS." Jessie
was not terribly smart or efficient, and she did talk a lot.
But she knew what he meant by Give to Alys—Don't
Want to See, and would abide by it.

As it happened, in the morning he almost forgot that
Alys Brant existed. He had gone to sleep with the power
still off in the rectory, and what woke him was a sudden
glare of light in his eyes and the creaking hum of his bedside electric heater going on. When he went down to the
basement to investigate, the man from the electric company
was working over the meter box. "Putting a new fuse in?"
Hake asked.

The man looked up and grinned enviously. "Hell, no,
Reverend—excuse me. I'm taking the fuse out. Didn't you
know?"

"Know what?"

"Why, you're off fusing from now on. Seems you've got

your own generator coming in, and we'll be buying from you part of the time, so you're no longer subject to rationing."

"My *what?*"

"Your new generator. It's a wind generator, go on top of your house. Should be coming in today, I guess—anyway we got a priority-rush order this morning. So you can draw up to full capacity, which is rated at six hundred amps, according to your specs plate here."

"I don't know anything about a wind-power generator!"

"Yeah, well, that's the way it goes," the man sympathized. "Your wife said she had some letter about it."

Hake repressed the urge to explain that Jessie Tunman wasn't his wife, and went to find the letter. It was on the stationery of something called The Fund for Clerical Fellowship, and it said:

Dear Reverend Hake:

We are pleased to inform you that our Board has granted your Church a beneficence for the purpose of installing generating facilities for your rectory.

Accordingly, we have ordered a Model (x)A-40 Win-Tility unit, with necessary mounts and electrical connections, and have secured the services of William S. Murfree & Co., Belmar, to effect the installation.

If there is any further way in which we can serve your Church, please advise us.

It was signed by a scribble, but Hake didn't need the name to know who it came from. He was being well taken care of, just as promised.

A thought struck him. A generator. They wanted him to have dependable power. So he spent the next half hour snooping around his office and bedroom, looking for bugs. He didn't find any.

That set him back in his thinking. It was a letdown, almost a disappointment, because if they were bugging him they were automatically providing him with a means of communication. He wanted one. That wasn't the same as saying that he had made up his mind to use it. He was still thinking about that, but he wanted the option. The thought was nagging at him that he should somehow report his kidnapping. If he had been able to find a bug he could have just said it out loud: "Hey, Curmudgeon! I got kidnapped. Somebody's broken my cover. Give me a call when you get a chance, why don't you, and we'll talk about it over lunch."

But he hadn't found a bug, and that was confusing. If the Team was not supplying him with power just so they could be sure of monitoring everything he did, then maybe his whole attitude was wrong. Maybe they were really kindly and protective, and simply providing fringe benefits for a new recruit. Maybe his negative feelings were not to be trusted.

Now that he had plenty of heat the weather had turned mild. When he took his morning run, a mile down the beach to the pier and a mile back, he was panting and pouring sweat, and as he came up over the boardwalk he saw Alys Brant's three-wheeled van sitting crookedly outside the rectory. He skulked behind the rail for five minutes until she came out and drove away, and by then he was chilled and sodden.

Still—what was the use of having privileges if you didn't use them? He stripped off the suit and flung it carelessly in the washer-dryer, hoping that it still remembered how to work, and treated himself to a long, hot shower. No doubt about it. Power-piggery could make you feel good. He hit the morning's mail joyously, disposed of it in half an hour, got his expense account up to date, wrote a marriage ceremony for two young members of his congregation ("I, Arthur, take thee, James, as long as love shall endure—"), telephoned every sick parishioner and promised to visit two of them, and even had time for twenty minutes with the barbells before his pre-lunch run. His sweatsuit was crisp and dry, but he didn't need it; he pulled on shorts and a tee-shirt marked *To Love Me Is to Love God* and started off down the beach.

And on the way back, there was Alys's van again, picking its way around the construction toward his house. "Hell," said Hake. He didn't think she had seen him, so he changed course and jogged up the wide streets to his church. On weekdays the trustees had established a nursery school to maximize use of the church facilities, and the parking lot, which doubled as a playground, was full of three-foot-high human beings and taller, tenser teachers, doing the Alley Cat to music from a battery-powered cassette recorder. "Hello, hello," called Hake, dodging past them and into the building.

As he had expected, no one had set up the chairs for that evening's MUSL–WUSL meeting. Most days that would have been an annoyance, but today it was a good way to use up twenty minutes or so while Alys made up her mind he wasn't going to be at the rectory and went away.

He pushed the chairs into a circle meditatively. Counseling didn't go as well as it used to. Or went in a different way. When he had been in the wheelchair the women who came to him told him all sorts of things—censused their orgasms, clinicked their preferences. They still did. But they sat straighter and smiled more often when they did. There was a kind of receptivity in the air that had not been there before with the women. And sometimes now the men seemed, well, fidgety. Like Ted Brant. Perhaps the ministry was a mistake. Perhaps the operation that had taken him out of the wheelchair had been a mistake, for that matter. It did seem to interfere with counseling. But he couldn't undo the operation, and how could he undo the ministry? At thirty-nine you didn't make a career change lightly—

Except that maybe he *was* making one. Clergyman to spy. It was not what he had ever intended. He had certainly not sought it. But he couldn't deny that there was something about playing cloak-and-dagger games that seemed like fun. . . .

The kids were coming back from their lunch recess, which meant the church would no longer be habitable for the next couple of hours. Hake straightened the last of the chairs and started out. On the way he paused at the suggestion box, trying to remember. Had he opened it after the service yesterday? Not that there was ever much in it. He took out his key and unlocked it; yes, there was something. A paper clip. A pledge envelope—*why* couldn't people remember they were supposed to hand them in to the ushers? A note scribbled on the corner of the service program: "Can't we have some guitar music any more?" And an envelope marked:

Rev. H. Hornswell Hake
From his friends at the Maryland phone company.
Personal.

The door to the main meeting room opened, and Hake turned, the envelope in his hands, ready to repel an unauthorized invasion of four-year-olds. But it wasn't the kids from the nursery school, it was Alys Brant. She strode toward him with a flounce of green skirts and said, "Thought I'd find you here, Horny. Here you are. Is this what you wanted?"

Hake jammed the envelope in his pocket and took from her a sheaf of photocopies of CRT prints. It took him a moment to redirect his thoughts from his friends at the Maryland phone company to the curiosity that he had hoped Alys might satisfy. The stories seemed to be about oil tankers running aground and grain silos blowing up. They were not at all what he had wanted, but his ministerial training led him to express that thought by saying, "They're just fine, Alys."

"You don't look pleased."

"Oh, no! I'm very pleased. But actually—well, I can't make much sense of these things. I was hoping for, more like books."

"Books!"

He nodded, then hesitated. "I don't know if I explained what I wanted to you very well. Doesn't it seem to you that the quality of life has got worse in the last few years? Of course, I'm older than you are—"

Silvery laugh. "You're not old, Horny, not with that bod!"

"Well, I am, Alys, but you must have noticed it too. So many things go wrong—not just tankers fouling beaches. Everything. And I thought somebody else must have noticed that and written a book about it."

"A book!"

"Or maybe a TV special?" He paused, feeling his way. It did not seem wise to say anything that Curmudgeon might construe as breaching security, so he couldn't come up and tell her that he wanted to know how long nations had been playing trip-up games with each other. "The way nothing seems to work," he said at last. "Drug abuse and juvenile delinquency. Never having enough energy, and never doing anything about it. More mosquitoes than there ever used to be. All that."

She said thoughtfully, "Well, yes, I suppose there's something. But books! You know, Horny, you're almost obsolete! Still—what you want is to browse, right? And for that we'll have to take you to a decent library." She pulled a date book out of her shoulder bag and thumbed through it. "Wednesday," she decided. "I've been thinking about going in to New York then anyway—maybe see a matinee, have a nice lunch somewhere—"

"Really, Alys, I don't want to put you to all that trouble."

"Nonsense! I'll take the car. Pick you up at the rectory around—what? Eight? It'll be fun! We'll have the whole morning to do your library thing—and then, who knows?" She pressed his hand warmly and left him standing there.

Warning bells were going off in Hake's brain. She was a very attractive woman, but under the rules a protected species. Not to mention Ted.

Belatedly he remembered the letter from his Maryland telephone friends. It said:

Dear Rev. Hake:
　　There are two questions I would like to put to you.
　　Why didn't you report what we did?
　　Why did you agree to hurt people you don't even know?
　　Please see if you can figure out the answers. Some day I will ask you for them.

There was no signature. He folded the letter up and then, reconsidering, tore it into tiny pieces, went into the men's room and flushed it down the toilet, ignoring the stares of two small boys from the nursery school. They were good questions. He didn't need to be told to think them over. They were what he had been asking himself for some time.

In the next thirty-six hours, the power-piggery summons was withdrawn because of a technical defect, and Hake woke to find that traffic had been rerouted along the ocean-front while the road before the rectory was repaired—after six years of potholes and detours! He could no longer entertain the hypothesis of coincidence. Somebody was looking out for him, and doing a good job.

The questions from his whilom kidnapper were nowhere near an answer, any more than the hundred other questions that whined around his mind like Jersey mosquitoes circling for the attack. He had no answers. He could hear them droning away nearby in every thought, while he was counseling, while he was dictating to Jessie, while he was munching a quick, and already cold, slab of pizza in his church study between another long talk with the cleaning lady about scrubbing the ladies' room and his weekly meeting with the Social Action chairman. Every once in a while the mosquitoes lunged in and stung, and then that spot itched annoyingly for a while. The rest of the time he put them out of his head.

For a wonder, Social Action finished its business in five minutes and Hake had a whole unbudgeted hour. Back correspondence? Next week's sermon? He reviewed the options and settled on parish calls. Two of his flock were in Monmouth Medical Center, one in geriatrics and one in maternity, and he was overdue for seeing both of them.

Next to counseling, Hake considered visiting the sick about the most useful thing he did, especially the old and lonely sick who had no one else to call on them. It was a whole other exercise than problem-solving, as in counseling, or in moral leadership, as in his weekly sermon. The sick and old didn't need any more leadership. They had nowhere left to go. And they had passed the point of problem-solving, since the only problem they had left was beyond anyone's solution, ever.

Rachel Neidlinger, his maternity case, was getting ready to nurse newborn Rocco and needed no comforting. Two floors higher, old Gertrude Mengel was delighted to have company. She showed it, of course, by spilling out on him her week's burden of complaints against the floor nurse and boasting about the tininess of her veins, so hard for the doctor to get a hypodermic into. Hake gave her the appropriate twenty minutes to discuss her symptoms and her hopes, most of both imaginary. As he rose to go she said, "Reverend? I've had a postcard from Sylvia."

"That's marvelous, Gertrude. How is she?"

"She *says* she's got a job making hydrogen." The scant old eyelashes fluttered to announce tears nearby. "But I think she's with those bums again."

Internally Hake groaned. Seventy-year-old Gertrude had been trying to mother her fifty-five-year-old sister ever since their parents died. It was like trying to mother a china egg in a nest, and Sylvia would not even stay in the nest. "I'm sure she'll be all right. She's not, ah, using anything again, is she?"

"Who can tell?" Gertrude said bitterly. "Look where she is! What kind of place is Al Halwani?"

Hake studied the card, a gold-domed mosque overshadowed by a hundred-meter television tower, with blue water behind them. Sylvia had done her own Hegira or Stations of the Cross all her life, tracing the passion of the counterculture from the East Village and Amsterdam through Corfu and Nepal. She had begun late and never caught up. And never would. "It's not a bad place, Gertrude," Hake was able to reassure her.

"An Arab country? For a Jewish girl?"

"She's not a girl any more, Gertrude. Anyway, there's a lot of people there who aren't Arabs. It was almost a ghost town for years, after the oil was gone, and then all sorts of people moved in."

Gertrude nodded positively. "I know what sorts of people, bums," she said.

It was no use arguing, although all the way through his bacon, lettuce and tomato sandwich in the coffee shop downstairs Hake was thinking of reassuring things that he could have said. But hadn't, because there was no point in it; she didn't want to hear. The final pay-out for being a caring minister, and giving your flock the benefit of your insights, was that more than fifty percent of the time they didn't want to receive them.

Nevertheless he had made the effort, and with that half of his mind not preoccupied with the buzzing questions he was conscious of virtue. A new question added itself to the swarm, but this one rather welcome: it was only intellectually interesting, not a worry. What had Gertrude meant about her sister getting a job making hydrogen? Hake knew vaguely where the hydrogen came from, and this Al Halwani seemed to be in the right part of the world. But he was far from sure of details. His own experience with power generation had been a long way from the theoretical level.

When the Israelis destroyed the Near East's petroleum reserve with their shaped nuclear charges, they had not burned all the oil. But what was left unpumped was highly radioactive. If the hippies in Kuwait or wherever were now generating hydrogen by burning that oil, they were releasing radioactive isotopes into the world's air. No one had said that publicly that Hake had ever heard, but Hake was now quite ready to believe that there was a lot that was never said publicly. If there was a creditable reason, that had to be it. There would be no other reason to turn down fuel that did not in any way damage the environment, when you only had to look out of your window to see how badly the environment had been damaged. And it was not as if the United States were not importing fuel already. The Mexican and Chinese wells were still pouring ten million barrels a day into American refineries, even if their prices were becoming exorbitant. Especially *because* their prices were becoming exorbitant.

Anyway, was that how the hippies were doing it? He had heard something, somewhere, about solar power. The trick was to catch the energy of the sun in mirrors or lenses, boil sea-water pure, split the H_2O into its parts, chill the hydrogen into liquid and pack it into tanks. Of course, the trick was more complicated than it seemed. To direct the sunlight to a boiler or still meant putting motors on the mirrors to follow the sun across the sky; meant keeping them clean;

meant finding a place where there was plenty of sun and plenty of water and plenty of cheap land—*and* a deep-water port or a pipeline to move the LH_2 to where it was useful. Al Halwani sounded like the right kind of place.

By the time he had turned all that over in his mind he had jogged back to the parsonage where Jessie was waiting for him with news. "A Mr. Haversford called," she announced, eyes flashing with curiosity. "He asked you to come to a special meeting of the Board of International Pets and Flowers."

"Thank you, Jessie," he said, but she followed him to his own quarters. She stood in the doorway, watching him take off his jacket and pull his sweatshirt over his head. It was one of the habits in her that he most disliked.

"I didn't know you were on the Board of IPF," she said.

"It just happened." He was excusing himself to her again, of course; what he should be saying was telling her not to come into his private rooms. But he couldn't even do that because technically she wasn't; the tips of her sensible shoes were just at the sill of the door. Inspiration struck. "Do me a favor," he said. "Call Alys Brant for me and tell her that I won't be able to make the library trip because I've got to go to this meeting."

"She'd like it better if you called her yourself," she observed.

"I know she would, but please, Jessie."

"Huh." Grudgingly she disappeared, but a moment later she was back in the doorway. "She says all right, she'll make it next Wednesday instead, same time."

Well. "All right," he said. Next Wednesday would have to take care of itself. Meanwhile he had his barbells out and began the regular series of exercises, wishing Jessie would go away and take Alys Brant with her.

Jessie didn't. She watched him bend and stretch in silence for a moment, then sighed. "You're a pretty lucky man, Horny," she observed.

"I know," he panted, turning away from her as he bent from side to side. Just having her watch him made him uncomfortable enough. When she ventured personal remarks it was worse. Personal matters seemed so out of character for a woman with all the personality traits of a retired Civil Service employee, which of course was what she was. "I'm especially lucky to have you for a secretary," he thought to say at last, but she was already gone.

Was he all that lucky? Well, sure, he thought to himself, shrugging all the pectoral muscles forward as he watched himself in the mirror. For someone who had been at death's door a couple of years earlier, whose best hope had seemed to be an uneventful and probably rather short life in a wheelchair, he had a lot of interesting things opening up.

Not that he hadn't been lucky enough before. He had survived the wars of his infancy, after all, and even in a wheelchair good things had happened. There were plenty of helping hands stretched out to a kid who was an orphan *and* a displaced person *and* handicapped: Scholarships. Grants. Medical services. Counseling. There were plenty of girls, too, who were willing to stretch out to him. The skinny tall youth in the wheelchair was appealing. More than that. Nonthreatening. "I'll ride with you in the elevator, Horny, here, let me take your books." "Horny, let me help you into the car." "Why don't you come over tonight, Horny, and we'll quiz each other for the Psych test?" Hake remained a virgin until he was twenty, at least technically he did, but not because of any lack of attractive and friendly persons willing to meet him well over halfway. What kept him a virgin, or, well, pretty much so, was something within himself. He did not want pity. And he detected it in every overture offered.

He could not remember a time when he was not sick. When he began turning blue every time he got tired, he was only four. The first open-heart operation was when he was seven, and it was a disaster; it led almost immediately to the second one, which saved his life but did not strengthen it. By the time he was in his teens the prognosis for another operation was no longer as risky, but young Hake simply did not want to go through that again. Not just the risk. The pain. Pain that anesthesia hadn't removed, hypnosis hadn't removed, even both together had made barely survivable. No. No more operations. So in his wheelchair he rolled up to receive his B.A. in psychology, and his master's in social science. At the seminary he got his doctorate after two years of being carried to some of the classes—it was an old seminary, and a poor one, and they had not been able to afford compliance with the regulations for the handicapped. But he got it. And got a ministry after it, and held it to everybody's satisfaction until, in his mid-thirties, he began turning blue again—and the third operation not only worked, it took him out of the wheelchair for good. Oh, he was lucky, all right! A whole new life when he had least expected it.

But, all the same, it was confusing.

Allen T. Haversford met him in person at the gate to old Fort Monmouth, all smiles and welcome. Haversford had a face like a toy bulldog's. It seemed small for the size of his head, and the reedy Franklin D. Roosevelt tenor voice that came out through the wattles of flesh around the mouth made him seem like a bulldog breathing helium. "So nice of you to come, Reverend Hake," he shrilled. "We've arranged a little luncheon for our trustees, but that's not for half an hour. Let me show you around."

The Fort had been mothballed decades earlier, but it was springing to life. Hake had heard rumors of building, but this was his first chance to see what was going on. Plenty was. Backhoes and bulldozers were scouring out a complicated pattern of trenches, and a pre-mix truck was lining them with concrete as fast as they were dug. "You're really making progress," he said.

"Indeed, indeed! These are going to be our fish tanks," sang Haversford jovially. "Salt-water, fresh-water. Big and small. We'll have the largest fish-fancier operation on the East Coast here. Ornamentals, tropicals, even food-fish for those who want to put in their own pools. And those will be the kennels, and over there the breeding pens. This is almost a closed-ecology system, Reverend Hake. We'll bring in livestock on the hoof; then we'll have our own abattoir, you can't see it because we haven't started construction yet, and we'll dress food for almost all the pets. Nothing will go to waste, I assure you. Meat and cereal mix for the dogs. Tilapia for the cats—we'll raise most of them ourselves.

Entrails dried and pulverized for the fish." He winked.
"We'll even use the, ah, sewage, Reverend. Yes, dung has
plenty of nutritive value! Some gets dried and processed
and fed to the stock. Some—and that includes sewage from
visitors and the staff—gets settled and filtered and we grow
algae on it; algae feed shrimp, shrimp feed fish. And the
effluent goes into our hydroponics system."

"It really sounds efficient, Mr. Haversford."

"Indeed, indeed! And so it is. Over here—" He led Hake
to a sturdy plastic bubble. "Our first greenhouse. Step inside this chamber, yes, thank you, and let me close the outer
door, here we are. We don't want to waste heat, after all."

It was uncomfortably warm in the bubble. Hake loosened
his collar as he looked around. Rows of elevated trays of
seedlings, some of them already a foot tall and in leaf, some
even in blossom. He did not recognize any of the flowers;
surely those could not be morning glories, nor those sunflowers. Haversford was proudly nipping the end off a
cigar as he watched Hake looking around. "No power-
piggery here," he boasted. "All this is solar energy! Not a
calorie of fossil fuel burned, except a little bit for the
lighting. And even that we hope to generate ourselves in
time, if we can get priorities for a photovoltaic installation
on the road surfaces."

"You're doing a fine job," said Hake, watching the man
light up. Curiously, some of the nearer flowers seemed to
turn toward his lighter.

"No, no, no! Not 'you,' Reverend Hake, please! 'We!'
You are very much a part of this, you know. Now, this
section will be orchids, plus a few tropical ornamentals that
like the damp and heat. And some experimental varieties—
we will do quite a lot of hybridizing and development
here."

"I suppose you'll feed the ones that don't work out to
rabbits or something, and then feed those to the animals?"

"What? Rabbits? Why, what an excellent idea, Reverend
Hake! I'll get our technical people to look into that right
away. You see, I knew you'd be a great asset! And now, I
think, it's about time for us to join the others for our
luncheon meeting. . . ."

The "others" were seven persons, two department heads from IPF and the other five directors like Hake himself. He did not catch most of the names, and he had not seen most of the others before. One he recognized. The black man with the nearly bald head was a member of the Board of Chosen Freeholders. But who was the other, younger black with the cutoffs and worry beads? Or the very young girl with long, blonde hair? And how many of them were on the board because the Team was paying them off?

Haversford took his place at the head of the long table—linen cloth, linen napkins, crystal and silver at the place settings. On each plate there was a cup of fresh fruit—"From our own South Carolina orchards," Haversford pointed out—but what was under the cup was what interested Hake. It was an envelope with his name on it, and it contained a check. When he peeked inside the amount sent an electric shock through him. They hadn't been kidding.

The lunch was cold meats and salads, and when it was over and the coffee was served Haversford rapped his water tumbler with his spoon. "I want to thank you all for coming today on such short notice," he said. "There are only two items before this special meeting. The first is to welcome our new trustee, Reverend Hake, which I perceive you have all been doing already. The second is to take action on the proposal of our Public Relations Committee in regard to the marmosets. Ms. de la Padua?"

The dark, athletic-looking woman at his left rose and went to a sideboard. She pulled the cloth away from a tall cage, reached in and lifted out a tiny woolly monkey. "As most of you remember," said Haversford, "at our last meeting we talked of plans to increase our exports of some of our pet lines, including the marmosets, by selecting a group of young people to go abroad and present gift specimens to other children in several countries. Subject to your concurrence—" mysteriously, he twinkled toward Hake—"subject to *all* of your concurrence, a program has been prepared. The group of children will be students from local junior high and high schools, chosen on recommendation of their teachers. They will spend three weeks abroad, traveling in France, Germany and Denmark, during which time they will give away twenty-two pairs of marmosets to schools and youth groups in nine cities. Ms. de la Padua has a detailed itinerary plus the budget for the trip and will be glad to answer any questions. And in charge of the group—and I do hope you will accept?—will be our own Reverend Hake."

"*What?*"

Haversford nodded, beaming. "Yes, indeed, indeed, Reverend," he shrilled. "Of course, there is a suitable stipend included in the budget. I know it's quite an imposition—"

"But—but I can't, Mr. Haversford. I mean, I have obligations to my church—"

"Certainly you do. We all appreciate that. But if you'll take the word of an old curmudgeon, I think you'll find that the church can spare you for just this short time. May we vote, please?"

The 'ayes' had it, unanimously, all but Hake, who did not collect himself in time to vote. "An old curmudgeon," indeed! Did he have a choice? If it was the Lo-Wate Bottling Company's old Curmudgeon, probably not.

"I wasn't supposed to go to Germany," he said. But nobody was listening.

IV

THERE were thirty-one of the kids, and they filled the whole Yellow-Left section of the aircraft, two and four abreast. The Lufthansa stewardesses moved up and down the aisles, checking seat belts and making sure that air-sick bags were in every pouch, and Horny Hake and Alys

Brant, his co-leader, followed. "You're really good with children," Alys said admiringly, as he patted two or three of the unfamiliar heads at random. "I wish I could relate to them the way you do." Then she retreated to her seat at the front of the compartment, leaving Hake to wonder why a woman who didn't think she could relate to children had maneuvered herself into being his co-leader. By the time he was in his own seat and the jet was airborne he had confronted the fact that this was going to be one sticky trip.

He fell back on a resource of his childhood: counting off the hours till it was over. Nineteen days. That came to 456 hours. Including ground travel time from and to Long Branch, call it 470. He had left the rectory—he checked his watch—nearly five hours before, so now he was a little better than one one-hundredth of the way through the ordeal. In about half an hour it would be one ninetieth. By the time they reached their hotel in Frankfurt as much as a fortieth, maybe more, and by bedtime—

"Father Hake?"

He blinked and turned away from the window. "Mrs. Brant is waving to you, Father," whispered the stew, her flaxen hair brushing his cheek. "It's all right, you can get out of your seat for this."

At the head of the aisle Alys was already standing with one hand on the shoulder of a twelve-year-old, smiling sympathetically toward him. "It's Jimmy Kenkel," she said confidentially. "He reached back and punched Martin here in the nose. Probably if you ask the stew she'll get you some ice."

Martin's nose was streaming blood. The regular passengers who had been unlucky enough to be seated in Yellow-Left, dapper tall German businessmen and alert Japanese tourists, were whispering among themselves. Hake whipped out his handkerchief and held it to the boy's face, bracing himself against the thirty-degree climb of the plane and trying to catch the stew's eye. By the time he looked around Alys was gone. By the time the stewardess brought ice the bleeding had stopped, and by the time the seat belt sign was off Martin had already revenged himself by pouring the cup of melting ice over Jimmy's head.

Enough was enough. Hake turned his back on his charges and marched to the midships bar for a drink.

"Two minds with but a single thought, Horny?" asked Alys cheerfully, turning from a conversation with a slim, uniformed man wearing waxed blonde mustaches.

Hake looked at her with displeasure. "The boy is all right, if you care. God knows what they'll be doing now they can get up and move around, though."

"You see, our minds do work alike. I was just asking Heinrich here if they could keep the seat belt sign turned on in just our compartment."

"*Ja*, that would be good. But not possible." The man stuck out his hand. "Heinrich Scholl, Father," he said. "I am your purser."

"I'm not a priest, just a Unitarian minister," Hake said testily, but he accepted a whiskey and water, compliments of the purser. The children had not yet realized they were free, and the stews were moving among them, passing out Cokes and orange juice and packets of in-flight games and puzzles. Hake began to relax. He had flown tens of thousands of miles before he was ten years old, and hardly at all since. It was all new to him, from the back-tapered wing outside the window with its peculiarly feathered tip to the topless bar-stew serving their drinks. The immensity of the aircraft astonished him. He had never fully comprehended the size of the big intercontinental jets, more than a thousand people inside one great steel sausage zapping across the sea. "But I don't see why we have to have them," he said. "These jets, I mean. What a waste of energy!"

"Waste?" repeated the purser politely. "But that is not so, Mr. Hake. For the mails alone we must have them, so why not fill them up with passengers?"

"But with energy so short—" he began, thinking of heatless days in Long Branch and the tons of fossil fuel each of those huge engines on the wing was pouring out.

The purser said kindly, "It is all carefully planned, I assure you, Mr. Hake. Air transport is a vital service. We carry valuable medical supplies, diplomatic pouches, all kinds of strategically vital materials. Why, this very aircraft carried measles vaccine from Köln to New Guinea just, let me see, just last year. Or possibly the year before."

And since then? Hake asked himself. But all he said was, "Granting that, but why so many of them? I mean, does every pipsqueak little company in the world have to have its own flag line?"

"Pip? Squeak?" repeated the purser, mustache quivering.

"Oh, I don't mean Lufthansa, of course. I mean all of them. Little countries you never even heard of. I see them coming in to the traffic patterns off Long Branch, African airlines and Latin American airlines and God knows what airlines. Couldn't America, for instance, use Air France or Aeroflot or whatever, instead of flying its own planes all the time?"

Alys laughed and pushed her glass forward for a refill. "Oh, Horny! And let them do God knows what with our mail all the way across the Atlantic? You are so naive!"

The purser nodded stiffly and said, "It has been most interesting speaking with you, Mr. Hake, but now I must attend to my duties. The flight attendants must now start serving dinner."

"And maybe you should too, Horny," said Alys, looking past his shoulder. Ten of the kids were lined up for the toilets, and some of the boys were fighting again. "It's hard on you," she commiserated, "but boy-boy fights are a man's job, aren't they?"

Boy-girl fights also turned out to be a man's job, and so, Hake found out, were some of the seamier kinds of what he had always considered pure girl questions. Tiny Brenda came to him and whispered, "Reverend Hake, I'm having my personal hygiene."

He leaned closer to her, juggling the half-eaten dinner tray. "What?"

"My friend is here," she said, blushing.

"What friend are you talking about?" he demanded, and then Alys drifted by to whisper in his ear.

"The poor little thing wants a sanitary napkin," she said. "Tell her they're in the washrooms."

"They're in the washrooms, Brenda," he said.

The girl nodded. "Some of the girls call it 'my friend.' I

call it 'my personal hygiene' because that's what it says on the bag in the bathroom in school."

"So go to the washroom," said Hake, patting her cautiously on the shoulder; and then to Alys, "Why me?"

"Because you're the father-surrogate, of course. I'm only a kind of elderly girl," she said sympathetically. "Well. It's going to be a long flight. I think I'll see if I can catch some sleep."

"Me too," said Hake hopefully, surrendering his tray to a no longer smiling stew.

The hope never materialized. All through the five-hour flight Hake and the stews quelled insurrection. At least, Hake thought, toward the end of it, he was beginning to know some of them as individuals: Jimmy and Martin and Brenda; black Heidi and little blonde Tiffany; Michael, Mickey and Mike; the big, gentle, Buddha-like twelve-year-old, Sam-Wang; the three oldest girls, all from the little religious backwater of Ocean Grove. They all looked astonishingly alike, wedge-cut hairdos and disapproved lipstick and eye-shadow, but they were not related. One was named Grace, and one was named Pru, and the shortest and strongest and meanest of the three was named Demeter. Demeter was the one who swatted the youngest boys on the rear as they stretched across adult passengers to get at each other. Demeter and Grace finked to the Lufthansa stews when three of the junior-highs were smoking in the toilet. Demeter and Pru bribed the smaller ones to be quiet with the in-flight game kits. How splendid it all would have been, if only the Ocean Grovers had been doing it all to help Hake, instead of trying to soften him up for their own misdeeds: sharing drinks with the salesmen in the first-class lounge, making illicit dates with the male flight attendants. Through it all Alys slept like a baby, head on the shoulder of the Turkish Army officer in the seat next to her. But Hake didn't sleep, and neither did the stews.

Eleven hours down, four hundred and fifty-nine to go. It was going to be a long trip.

They arrived at the immense, echoing Frankfurt-am-Main airport at two A.M., local time. Worst of all possible times:

because of the time difference, the kids were not really quite ready for sleep; but they would have to be up and presenting marmosets to a *Kinderhalle* at nine that very morning. Hake kept the children whipped into line in the transit lounge while Alys, yawning prettily, sorted through the room assignments.

Somehow Hake got them all through Customs and into the main departure hall. There were no chairs, of course; but somehow he kept them from killing each other through the hour-long wait for their chartered bus; until the driver arrived, furiously complaining in German, finally managing to explain that he had been waiting outside in the parking lot for the past two hours. Somehow he got them into their rooms at the shiny big hotel, with the baggage approximately in the right rooms, or close enough. "I've put you in with Mickey and Sam-Wang," Alys said, handing him keys. "Sam snores. And Mickey's mother says he wets the bed if he isn't got up at least twice during the night, so— Anyway, I've finished your room assignments for you, Horny," she said virtuously. "Now I think I'd better tuck in myself. It's been a long day. Oh, I've had to take an extra room. It wouldn't be fair to the children to put any of them in with me, I'm so restless. I'd keep them up all night."

He watched her sway gracefully into one of the exposed teardrop elevators, then sighed, finished signing the registration cards and counting the passports and followed to his own room.

He found the bed so delightful that he allowed himself to lie with his arms crossed behind his head for a while, enjoying the prospect of sleep before letting himself experience it. Sam-Wang's snoring blended with the mutter of the air-conditioner and the distant yammer of someone's TV set across the hall. At least his virtue was spared—no, not his virtue so much as his sense of professional morality; bird-dogging around European hotels with Alys would have seemed pretty attractive if he hadn't been her marriage counselor. But if she wasn't after his body, why was she here? For that matter, why was *he* here? He had no doubt in the world that Lo-Wate Bottling Company, or whatever the spook factory chose to call itself, was behind it all.

That was clear enough. But what was it, exactly, that they were behind? If they were sending a new agent on a mission to Western Europe, shouldn't they tell him what the mission was? Were the marmosets secret intelligence couriers? Was Curmudgeon going to turn up in trenchcoat and fedora, out of some rain-shadowed doorway, to hand him The Papers? And if so, what would the papers say? It seemed a lousy way to run an intelligence agency.

No doubt it would all be revealed to him in time. He uncrossed his arms, rolled over, buried his head in the pillow, closed his eyes—

And opened them again.

He had forgotten to put Mickey on the pot.

It would have been easy enough to go on forgetting it, but a trust was a trust. Hake pushed himself out of bed, thrust his arms into his robe and coaxed the half-sleeping ten-year-old into the bathroom. With difficulty he steered him away from the bidet to the proper appliance, but then was rewarded for his efforts and got the still unawake boy back into bed . . . just as the phone rang stridently.

Hake swore and grabbed it. A voice screeched in his ear, "Where the hell are my marmosets?"

"Marmosets? Who is this?" Hake demanded in a hoarse whisper; Sam-Wang's snoring had stopped and Mickey was rocking resentfully in his bed.

"Jasper Medina. You better get down here, Hake, and start explaining where the monkeys are. I'll be at the elevators." And he hung up.

Resentfully Hake carried his discarded clothes into the bathroom and put them back on. As he combed his hair he glowered at his reflection: that healthy outdoors face now had circles under its eyes, and this trip was just beginning! He let himself out as quietly as he could and waited for the glass elevator bubble to come for him.

Waiting for him in the main lobby was a tall, lean man with bald head and white beard, chewing on a corncob pipe. "Hake? What's your excuse for this foul-up? What do you mean, you don't know what I'm talking about? There's twenty-two pair of Golden Lion marmoset fancies coming in with you, and where are they? My boys've been all over Frankfurt tonight, trying to locate them!"

"Who are you?"

"Don't you listen, sonny? I'm Medina, from the Paris office. IPF. These are my assistants—" he pointed to four men clustered around the wall telephones, two of them talking into instruments, the other two standing by. "Sven. Dieter. Carlos. Mario. We're supposed to help out with your project."

"I sure can use a little of that," said Hake feelingly, beginning to feel more friendly. "Those kids—"

"Kids? Oh, no, Hake, we've got nothing to do with the *kids*. We'll take care of the *marmosets* for you, if you'll just tell us where they are. But not the kids. Now if you'll just—wait a minute. What is it, Dieter?"

One of the men was coming toward them, beaming. "Jasper," he said—he pronounced it "Yosper"—"these monkeys, we have found them. At the *Zookontrolle*, and all quite well."

"Ah." Medina puffed on his pipe, and then smiled broadly. "Well, in that case, Hake," he said, offering his hand, "there's no need for us to waste time here, is there? Get a good night's sleep. I'll meet you for breakfast."

Get a good night's sleep. . . . By the time the glass elevator had him back at his floor he was almost asleep already, but he forced himself to put Mickey on the toilet one more time. Then he dropped his clothes on the floor and crawled into bed, clicking off the lamp beside his pillow.

But even through closed eyes he perceived that the light hadn't gone out. When he opened them he saw why. Outside the window it was broad daylight.

Nineteen days in glamorous Europe! It was a good thing he hadn't believed in that in the first place, Hake thought; at least he was spared disappointment. Cathedrals, museums, lovely river views, castles—they saw the Cologne cathedral out of the window of a bus; the Rhine was a streak of greenish-gray through tattered clouds. In Copenhagen a

whole afternoon's schedule had to be called off, because
Tivoli was closed for repairs, having been bombed silly by
some unreconciled Frisian nationalists—good deal, or might
have been, because they needed the rest; but in practice
what it meant was an extra six hours of riding herd on the
kids. In Oslo a teacher's strike closed the schools and left
Hake's charges to present their marmosets to a red-eyed
principal taking five minutes off from the all-night contract
negotiations.

After that first morning in Frankfurt, when he had gone
to Alys's room to knock her awake—and found in front of
her door the neat brown boots of a Turkish major—Hake
stopped expecting Alys to attempt to assault his virtue. She
didn't need to. There were plenty of other targets. If she
hungered and thirsted for his flesh, she concealed it well.
She spent more time with old, bald, half-blind Jasper Medina
than with Hake. Although, to be fair, she spent more time
with Hake than she did with anybody else. Especially the
kids.

Jasper—or "Yosper"—was a puzzle. Since he was from
IPF's European customer-relations department, it followed
as the night the day that he had to be a spook. But he
offered no secret plans, conveyed no instructions; when
Hake mentioned the name "Curmudgeon" in his presence
the old man gave a cracked laugh and said, "Curmudgeon?
Is that what you think I am? Let me tell you, sonny, I'm
exactly what you'll be in another forty years—only better,"
he added virtuously, "because I accept the Lord as my
Savior, and you don't!"

But he was always there, he and his four silent helpers.
The marmosets got their grapes and mealworms every four
hours; where there was sun to make it possible, got an
occasional afternoon in the open air; were brushed and
groomed and picked over for fleas. The marmosets had
plenty of supervision.

What the kids had was Horny Hake.

By the time they reached Copenhagen, Hake believed he
had encountered every ailment young human flesh was heir
to—or heiress to; *especially* heiress to: cuts and scrapes,
sulks and sneezes, faints and fevers. (126 hours down, 344

to go—better than a quarter of the way.) By Oslo it was mostly fevers and sneezes. They weren't serious, but they kept Hake up most nights to make sure they weren't. Alys slept securely through to breakfast, explaining that Hake's long experience with counseling had made him so much better at handling night alarms that there was no point, really, in her waking—"just to be in your way, Horny." And, of course, the Marmoset Duennas did not let themselves get involved. Their lives had become pretty easy, with the number of woolly monkeys dwindling at every stop. But adamantly they continued to refuse to have anything to do with the children; one species of sub-human primate was all they had contracted for.

Sven and Dieter, Mario and Carlos—why did Hake always have difficulty telling them apart? They were very different in height, weight, and coloring. It had to do with the way they wore their hair, all in a sort of Henry the Fifth soupbowl, and the clothes: always the same, pale blue jackets and dark blue slacks. But there was more than that. They seemed to think and talk the same way. Hake often had the impression there was only one person speaking, sometimes with a German accent, sometimes Spanish, but with only one mind behind them. "Yosper says we must go to bed early, six A.M. flight in the morning." "Yosper advises do not drink this water, last month PLO terrorists filled reservoir with acid." As it seemed to Hake, the mind behind them was Yosper's.

And all of that made sense, perfect sense, if they were in fact disciplined spooks on the payroll of International Pets and Flowers, alias Lo-Wate, alias the shock troops of the cool war. But were they? Hake saw no sure signs. No unexplained absences from duty. No secret meetings. Not even meaningful glances among them, or sentences begun and left incomplete. If they were spooks, when were they going to start spooking?

More than once Hake had made up his mind to confront Yosper and demand the truth. Whatever the truth might be. But he had not gone through with it, only with hints. And Yosper never responded to them. It was not that Yosper was not a talkative man. He loved to talk. He never tired of telling Hake and Alys all the ways in which the cities they raced through were inferior to their American equivalents —not counting, now and then, the occasional place where you could get a decent *smorgasbord* or a worthwhile *Jägertopf*. And he never tired of explaining to them why Unitarians shouldn't call themselves religious; Yosper was Church of God, twice born, fully saved, and sublimely sure that the time would come when he would be sitting next the Throne, while Hake and Alys and several billion others would be deeply regretting their failures in a much worse place. But he wouldn't talk about anything related to espionage.

And he wouldn't help with the kids; and of the two failures, Hake found the second hardest to live with.

By the three-quarters mark they were in Munich. The children's sneezes were reaching a crescendo, and Hake himself was feeling the strain. He was more exhausted than he had ever been since the days in the wheelchair, and unhappy with the way his insides were conducting themselves. But there was an unexpected delight. Yosper had arranged for an American school in Munich to take the children off their hands for the whole weekend, and so the grownups had the pension to themselves and forty-eight hours to enjoy it.

The enjoyment would have been more pronounced, Hake thought, if his gut had not felt as if someone had stuffed it past its load limit with chili peppers and moldy pickles. He did not quite feel like seeing the town. Still . . . three hundred and sixty hours down, and only a hundred and ten to go! And no kids till Monday morning.

The pension turned out to be the top floor of a grimy little office building, on a side street near the intersection of two big boulevards. From the outside it didn't look like much. But it was clean and to Hake, who for fifteen days had been resentfully calculating the energy costs of jet fuel, high-speed elevators and hotel saunas, it was a welcome relief from power-pigging. He did not mind that the rooms clustered around an airshaft, or that there were no porters for the luggage. He didn't even mind the fact that he had to carry Alys's bags as well as his own—"I'm really sorry,

Horny, but I just don't feel up to lugging it." He didn't mention that neither did he.

Dinner was potluck, cooked by the proprietor and served by his wife. To Hake's surprise, Alys showed up for it. Evidently she had run out of Turkish majors, SAS copilots and Norwegian desk clerks. She spent the afternoon in her room but appeared, wan but gracious, at the head of the dinner table. As she picked up her spoon she was brought up short by Yosper rapping a fork against his glass.

"Yosper always says grace," said Sven—or Dieter—with a scowl.

"Of course," said Yosper, also scowling, and then bowing his head, "Our Lord, we humble servants thank You for Your bounty and for these foods we are about to eat. Bless them to Your own good ends, and make us truly grateful for what we receive. Amen."

As the five scowls disappeared, Mario—or Carlos—said, "It is a good custom to have, is it not so? It is like Pascal's wager. If God is listening, He is pleased. If not, no harm is done."

"Don't be irreverent," said Yosper, but mildly. "Pascal was a con-man. You shouldn't obey God's commandments to save your skin. You should obey because you know God exists, and the daily miracle of life proves it to you." Alys coughed and changed the subject.

"Horny, I haven't been idle all day," she said sweetly, handing him a couple of newspapers and a magazine. "These were in my room. I've gone through them all and marked the parts that interest you."

Yosper peered at her over his uneaten soup. "How do you know what interests him?"

"Oh," she said brightly, "it's a sort of research project I've been doing for him. He has been very interested in what he calls the increasing degradation of life—you know, all the things that mess us up— Horny, is something wrong?"

"No," he said, and then, with more conviction, "Oh, no. Go ahead. I was just thinking about something." What he had been thinking about was that if Yosper reported to Curmudgeon, he would surely report that Hake was doing a little unauthorized digging. But the second thought was, why not? He hadn't been told not to be curious. And one of the things he was curious about was how Yosper would react.

Which turned out to be not at all. The man took the napkin out of his lap, dropped it on the table and waved away the plate the proprietress was bringing over from the mahogany sideboard. "You know," he said, "I don't think this is exactly what I'm in the mood for. What do you think, Dieter? Want to try the Hofbrauhaus?"

"Good idea, Yosper," said Dieter enthusiastically—or Carlos; and all the others followed suit.

Alys said wanly, "Should we come too?"

"No. You wouldn't like it."

"Are you sure?"

He cocked his head at her—with his beard and bald head, he was beginning to look like a marmoset, Hake thought. "They have some, uh, private meetings. But," he said cunningly, "the food's remarkable. Sausage you wouldn't believe. Big mugs of beer. And *Schweinefleisch*! Pork, all pink and white, with that red cabbage and potato dumplings, and all that rich, fat gravy—"

Alys dropped her spoon. "Excuse me," she said, fleeing.

Yosper grinned at Hake. "Looks like she lost her appetite."

"Yeah. I'll tell you, Yosper," Hake said. "Actually, I don't feel too fine myself. I think I'll skip dinner and turn in early. . . ."

At least he wasn't sick to his stomach. Grateful for that, he chained the door to his room and opened the papers Alys had given him: A London *Times*, a two-day-old Rome *Daily American*, the international edition of *Newsweek*. Besides reading material, he had a secret treasure of his own: two shot-sized bottles of whiskey sours, acquired on one of the many flights when he didn't have time to drink them. Rock and rye was good for a cold, he reasoned. Who was to say whiskey sours weren't too?

They went down. And, surprisingly, they stayed down. They made him feel—well, not better. But at least different.

The buzz from the whiskey flavored the misery from the cold, or whatever, enough at least to make a change.

He thumbed through the news, for conscience's sake more than interest's:

The tax on liquid hydrogen was going up fifty percent "to finance research on making America fuel-independent within the next thirty years." The mad killer who had fire-bombed twenty-two Chicago women wearing mood rings had been caught, and announced God had told him to do it. International Harvester had delivered its 10,000th Main Battle Tank, Mark XII, direct from the production line to the U.N. scrapping grounds in Detroit. The President declared that the bargaining-counter production rate was insufficient for the needs of upcoming disarmament talks, and proposed a special bond issue to finance 5,000 additional advanced warplanes to be built and scrapped within the next five years. (He also mentioned that the income tax would have to go up to pay for the bonds.) The microwave receivers in Texas had to be shut down for ten days because of excessive damage to the Van Allen belts; as a result coastal Louisiana was battling its heaviest spring blizzard and most of Oklahoma, Texas and New Mexico were without power.

A normal enough week in America. Alys had also marked European news, but Hake didn't really care enough to read it. He had seen enough griminess and grittiness in the past fifteen days to decide that the Europeans were not really any better off than the people in Long Branch, New Jersey, as far as the quality of life was concerned.

And besides, the quality of his own life was not seeming very good just then. The whiskey sours might have been a mistake.

Dizzily he got up and peered at himself in the mirror.

He really felt sick. Being sick alarmed Hake to a degree that a man who had been well all his life might hardly understand. He inspected his tongue (reasonably pink), his eyes (everything considered, not really very red), and wished he had something to take his temperature with.

Maybe all he needed was a little more sleep, and, to be

sure, a hell of a lot more exercise. He hadn't been able to pack his barbells. He studied his belly, looking for a sign of a paunch; his dorsals, for a hint of flab. None there—yet. But he had missed two weeks' jogging and a dozen judo lessons on this trip, and how long could he continue to do that without penalty? He resolved to try to trap at least one of the Ocean Grovers into at least a Ping-Pong game the next morning.

But in the morning he was in no shape to do it, even if it hadn't been Sunday and the girls off at the American school or disrupting some unfortunate church.

He bathed, shaved, dressed and unsteadily left the pension to seek a drugstore. Within three blocks he passed two of them. Both were closed, but at least they gave him the name of what he was looking for. He excused himself to an elderly gentleman sunning himself on a doorstep and asked, "*Bitte, wo bist eine Apotheke?*" He had to repeat it twice before he got an answer, and then the words that came back at him were not helpful. But the pointed finger was.

The druggist was a young woman who wore her red hair in ringlets. She spoke no English, nor Hebrew, nor any of the varieties of Arabic Hake summoned up. If the kibbutzim had not been so strict in their customs he might at least have had a little Yiddish to try on her. But all he had going for him was ingenuity. After that had failed four or five times it occurred to him to cough dramatically against the back of his hand and pantomine drinking from a bottle. "*Ja, ja!*" cried the druggist, enlightened, and reached him something off the shelf.

Blearily Hake peered at the label. Of course, it was all in German.

Antihistamin-Effekt seemed understandable enough. But what was a *Hustentherapeutikum?* The names of the ingredients were easier to read. Science is a universal language, and by adding a few letters and subtracting some he managed to figure out some of the things that were in the bottle. The difficulty with that was that Hake was no pharmacist, and exactly what maladies were *Natriumcitrat* and *Ammoniumchlorid* good for? When he came to the dosages he felt himself on more solid ground. *Erwachsene* had to mean "for adults" (if only because the column next to it was headed *Kinder*). And *1-2 Teelöffel alle 3-4 Stunden* seemed to reveal itself.

While he was hesitating, a tall woman in a floppy hat came into the store and began peering thoughtfully at a display of cosmetics. Hake rehearsed the entire rest of his German vocabulary three or four times, and then crossed over to her for help. "*Bitte, gnädige Frau,*" he began. "*Sprechen-sie* English?"

She turned to look at him.

The face under the floppy hat was one he had last seen in a Maryland kitchen. "Pay the lady, Hake," she said. "Then let's you and I go where we can talk."

If the drugstores seemed to want to close on Sundays, the bars did not. They found a sidewalk cafe, chillier than Hake would have preferred but at least remote from other people, and the woman ordered them both big brandy-snifters of raw Berlin beer with raspberry syrup at the bottom of each glass. Hake took what he estimated to be a *2-Teelöffel* swig of the *Hustentherapeutikum* and washed it down with beer. The cold was gratifying on his palate. The taste, less so. It wasn't what his body wanted, and the pressure in his gut increased. He felt as if he wanted to burp, but was afraid to risk it. He said. "You know, young lady, I could have you arrested."

"Not here you couldn't, Hake."

"Kidnapping is certainly an extraditable offense."

"Offense? Oh, but Hake, you didn't file charges, did you?"

"There's no statute of limitations on kidnapping."

"Oh, hell, Hake, lay off the lawyer talk. It doesn't become you. Let's talk about realities, like why you didn't report me to the fuzz. Have you thought about the reasons for that?"

"I know the reason for that! I, uh, I didn't know where to report you."

"Meaning," she said bitterly, "that you had committed yourself to the spooks and knew you shouldn't involve the regular police. Right? And you were afraid to tell the spooks about it because you didn't know what would happen."

He kept his mouth shut. He didn't want to admit to her that he simply hadn't known how to contact the Team until the time had passed when it seemed appropriate. He was also aware that he shouldn't be telling this woman anything at all. Or even be talking to her. Who knew if that waiter, idly kicking at a windblown scrap of newspaper, or that teenage girl in the hot-pants suit biking down the boulevard, was not reporting to someone somewhere about this meeting?

Under other circumstances he probably would have liked being with her a lot. Whether in zipper suit or flowered spring dress and floppy hat, she was a striking-looking woman. She was at least as tall as Hake, would be taller if she wore heels, and slimmer than he would have thought of as beautiful—if, on any of their meetings, it had ever mattered whether or not she was beautiful. She was perplexing in many ways. For instance, how quaint to wear an old-fashioned gold wedding ring! He hadn't seen one of those in . . . he couldn't remember when he had seen one last.

"I don't have much time, Hake," she said severely, "and I've got a lot to say. We checked you out, you know. You're a decent person. You're kind, idealistic, if you picked up a stray kitten you'd find it a home. You work ninety hours a week at a dog job for slave pay. So what did they do to you to turn you into a killer?"

"*Killer!*"

"Well, what would you call it? They're close enough to killers, Hake, and you're just getting started with them. Who knows what they'll have you doing? When you took this job, you must have known what it meant."

It was impossible for him to admit to this young, handsome, angry woman that not only didn't he know what the job meant, he hadn't yet found out exactly what it was. He said thickly, "I have my own morality, lady."

"You exactly do, yes, and yet you're doing things that I know *you* know are violating it. Why?"

He perceived with relief that the question was rhetorical and she was about to answer it for him. Carrying on this conversation was getting pretty hard. And his ears were bothering him. There seemed to be a distant roaring. He tried to concentrate on her words, in spite of the growing evidence in his stomach that he was sicker than he had thought.

She said mournfully, "Why! God, the time we've spent trying to answer that one. What changes people like you? Money? But you can't want money, or you wouldn't be, for God's sake, a *minister*. Patriotism? You weren't even born in America! Some psychosis, maybe, because you were a cripple most of your life and the girls wouldn't go near you?"

"The girls," Hake said with dignity, "were very often willing to overlook my physical problems."

"Spare me the story of your adolescent fumblings, Hake. I know that isn't it, either. Or shouldn't be. We checked you out that way, too. So what does that leave? Why would you flipflop a hundred and eighty degrees, from being an all-giver, helping anyone who comes near you any way you can, to a trouble-making, misery-spreading cloak-and-dagger fink? There's only one answer! Hake, what do you know about hypnotism?"

"*Hypnotism?*"

"You keep repeating what I say, but that's not responsive, you know. Yes, I said 'hypnotism.' In case you don't know it, you show all the diagnostic signs: trance logic, tolerance of incongruities, even analgesia. Or anyway analgesia of the soul; you'd be hurting about the kind of people you're involved with if something didn't stop you. Even hypnotic paranoia! You pick up cues that a person not in the trance state would ignore. You picked up cues from us after we kidnapped you! That's why you didn't report us, you know."

"Oh, come off it. Nobody hypnotized me."

"As to that, how would you know? If you'd been given a post-hypnotic command to forget it?"

He shook his head obstinately. "Oh, sure," she sneered. "*You'd* know, because you're you, right? But if you weren't hypnotized, how do you explain signing up with the spooks?"

I can't, he thought. But what he said out loud was, "I don't have to explain anything to you. I don't even know who you are—except your name's Lee and you're married."

She looked at him thoughtfully from under the brim of her hat. Hake couldn't see her eyes very well, and that disconcerted him. Well, everything about her disconcerted him. "I have to go to the bathroom," he said shortly. He was not feeling well at all, and sitting out at this trashy, chilly sidewalk cafe—Munich was having some sort of garbagemen's strike, and the sidewalks were loaded with old, stale refuse—was not making him feel any better. And the distant yelling was louder and closer.

When he came back, the waiter had brought refills of the *Berlinerweissens*, and Lee had removed her hat. She looked a lot younger and prettier without it, and forlorn. She would have seemed quite appealing under the right circumstances. Which were not these. Hake realized apprehensively that he had finished the whole first beer. The syrup at the bottom had cloyed his palate enough so that he wanted the astringency of the new one, but his stomach was serving notice that it was prepared to take only so much more insult.

"As to who I am, Hake," she said moodily, "I've blown my cover to you already, haven't I? So my name is Leota Pauket. I was a graduate student at—never mind where. Anyway, I'm not even a graduate student any more. My dissertation subject was disapproved, and that's what started all this."

"I hope you're going to tell me what you're talking about."

"You bet I am, Hake. Maybe more than you want to know." She took a long sip at the new beer, staring out at the littered street. "I'm a Ute."

"You don't look Indian."

"Don't wise off, Hake. I'm a Utilitarianist. I used to belong to the Jeremy Bentham Club at school. You know: 'the greatest good of the greatest number,' and all that. It was a small club, only six of us. But we were closer than brothers. I've had to deal with some pretty crummy people since I got into this, Hake. There are bad ones on the other side too, as bad as your lot, and I can't always pick my allies. But back at school they were a good bunch, all grad students, all in economics or sociology. All first-class human beings. My dissertation advisor was our faculty rep, and she was something else. She's the one who suggested the topic to me: *Covariants and correlatives: An examination into the relationship between degradation of non-monetary standard of living factors and decreasing international tensions.* She helped—"

"Hey!" Hake sat up straighter. "Can I get a copy of that?"

"My dissertation? Don't be stupid, Hake. I told you I never finished it. Still," she added, looking pleased, "I do have the preliminary draft somewhere. I suppose I could find a copy if you really wanted to read it."

"I do. Truly I do. I've been trying to dig up that sort of information myself."

"Hum." She took another sip of the beer, looking at him over the wide rim of the glass. "Maybe there's hope for you after all, Hake. Anyway. She's the one who put us on the track of your spook friends. She said it was impossible all these things could have happened at random. Something had to be behind it. The more I dug, the more sure I was that she was right. Then she got fired. She was paid on a government teaching grant. And the grant was canceled. And then the man who replaced her rejected my whole dissertation proposal. And the new faculty advisor to the JBC recommended we dissolve it. So we did—publicly. And we went underground. That," she said, counting on her fingers, "was one, two—three years ago." Hake nodded, watching her fingers. "It wasn't hard to make sure of our facts: the United States was deliberately sabotaging other nations. It wasn't even hard to find out which agency was doing it—we had help. Then the question was, what do we do about it? We thought of going public, TV, press, the whole works. But we decided against. What would we get? A ten-day sensation in the headlines, and then everybody would forget. Just printing what these people do legitimizes it; you've been in Washington, you've seen the statues to the Watergate Martyrs. So we decided to fight fire with fire—Hake? What's the matter with you?"

He was pointing at her ring. "Now I know where I saw you first! You were the old lady on the bus!"

"Well, of course I was. I told you we had to check up on you."

"But how did you know where I was going to be?"

She seemed uncomfortable. "I told you we had help."

"What kind of help?" He was finding it harder and harder to follow the conversation, or even to sit upright in his chair. The yelling was now very close, and down the broad avenue he could see an advancing parade of marchers in white robes and peaked wizard hats. He couldn't read the placards they carried, but they seemed to be chanting "*Gastarbeiter, raus! Gastarbeiter, raus!*"

"None of your business," she said loudly, over the shouting of the paraders. "Anyway, shut up about that, Hake. I'm trying to tell you—Hake! What are you doing?"

He realized he was on the ground looking up at her. "I think I'm fainting," he explained; and then he did.

What happened next was very unclear to Hake. He kept waking briefly, then passing out again. Once he was in a room he didn't recognize, with Leota and a man he didn't know, somehow Oriental, bearded, bending over him. They were talking about him:

"You're not a doctor, Subirama! He's too sick for your foolishness!"

"Ssh, ssh, Leota, it is only something to relieve the pain, a little acupuncture, it will bring down the fever—"

"I don't believe in acupuncture," Hake said, but then he realized that it was a long time later and he was in a different place, what seemed to be a military ambulance plane, with a black woman in a nurse's uniform who peered at him queerly.

"This isn't acupuncture, honey," she soothed, "just a little shot to make you feel better—"

And when he woke up again he was in a real hospital. And it had to be back home in New Jersey, because the doctor taking his pulse was Sam Cousins, whose daughter had been married in Hake's own church. His throat was painfully dehydrated. He croaked, "What—what happened, Sam?"

The doctor put his wrist down and looked pleased. "There you are, Horny. Nice to have you back. Orderly, give me a glass of water."

As Hake was greedily taking the permitted three sips, the doctor said, "You've been pretty sick, you know. Here, that's enough water just now. You can have more in a minute."

Hake followed the glass wistfully with his eyes. "Sick with what?"

"Well, that's the problem, Horny. Some new kind of virus. All the kids got it too, and so did Alys. But it doesn't bother young children much. Or old people. The ones it really knocks out are the healthy prime-of-lifers, like you." He got up. "I'll be back in a while, Horny, and we'll have you out of here in a day or two. But right now," he said, nodding to the orderly, "no visitors."

"Yes, doctor," said the orderly, closing the door behind him and turning toward Hake, and then Hake took a closer look at the hairy, lean man wearing those whites. It was almost not a surprise.

"Hello, Curmudgeon," he said.

"Not so loud," said the spook. "There's no bugs in the room, but who knows who's walking down the corridor outside?"

He pulled some newspapers out of the bedside table. "I just wanted to give you these, and let you know we're thinking of you. The Team's got a new assignment for you as soon as you're well enough."

"New assignment? Cripes, Curmudgeon, I haven't even done the first one yet. Why would you give me another assignment when I screwed this one up by getting sick?"

The spook smiled and unfolded the papers. Several stories were circled in red:

NEW VIRUS CUTS PRODUCTION
40% IN SWEDISH FACTORIES

said the *New York Times*, and

DANES GRIPE,
GERMANS COUGH

said the *Daily News*, over a picture of long lines of men
waiting to get into a public lavatory in Frankfurt.

"What makes you think you screwed up?" asked Curmudgeon.

V

Every priest has someone to confess to—a rabbi has
another rabbi, even a Protestant minister has some
ecclesiastical superior. H. Hornswell Hake had no one like
that. He was a Unitarian, as alone in command as any
ship's captain on the high seas. The idea of laying his
problems on Beacon Street would have struck him as
ludicrous if it had entered his mind at all. And so, without
a wife or steady lover, without parents, not actively in
psychoanalytic therapy and even (he realized with some
concern) lacking in really close friends, he had nobody
to talk to.

And he wanted to talk; God, how he wanted to talk! It is
not an easy thing for a man to discover that he has in-
fected half a continent. It clawed at his mind. Hake's life
agenda was not clear to him, but parts of it were certain.
Most certain of all, that his goal was not to make people
sick but to make them well. Jogging, stretching-and-bend-
ing, working out with the weights, he kept thinking about
Germans and Danes red-eyed and sneezing. Flat on his
back, he saw himself as a Typhoid Mary on a continental

scale. He was flat on his back a lot, too. The disease Hake had spread through Western Europe was what the Team called a Three-X strain, which meant only that it had so high a relapsing rate that the average sufferer could count on three recurrences of fever, trots and miseries. Hake received the best medical care and achieved five. Weeks passed before he was ready for duty again.

Not that he was either idle or alone. When he was relapsing, Alys Brant, Jessie Tunman and half a dozen others rallied round with soup and solicitude; when he was up and about, Jessie was there with concerns about the Carpet Caper and the next budget meeting, his LRY director with plans for the Midsummer Magic Show benefit and worries about which teenagers were into what drugs, Alys Brant with her own inevitable self. Alys had had only the lightest touch of the sickness, but it was enough to give her strong sympathy with Hake's bouts, and that was more sympathy than Hake felt able to deal with. He kept her at bay by sending her off on library-research jobs for him, and by the time he was well enough to get back to church for a Sunday morning sermon he had decided what he wanted to do. Like many a minister before him, he was going to work out his problems on the congregation.

The weather had turned hot. Hake walked slowly over to the church before the service, pacing himself to keep from working up a sweat or increasing his respiration—he did not want to breathe in any more of the smoggy air than he had to, especially with the special tinctures of the pizzeria next to the church. In this kind of weather he either ran at daybreak, when it was still cool, or gave up running entirely. He unlocked the church door and propped it wide.

It was an old church and a small one, but it was Hake's own. His heart lightened as he went inside, studying the worn carpet, neatening the racks of name badges waiting for the congregation. The paint was chipping on the ceiling again. Hake frowned. The Team had been spendthrift in providing luxuries for his own use—the wind generator, new office furniture, beautifully functioning fittings in the bathroom, even a redone kitchen when bachelor Hake almost never cooked a meal. It was time they put a little of that money into the church. Perhaps new floor coverings so that they could give up the fund-raising Carpet Capers. Next time he talked to Curmudgeon— But when would that be? And maybe—maybe, after this morning's sermon, there would be no handouts from Curmudgeon ever again. That would be a pity, perhaps. But it would be better than living with guilt.

"As most of you know," he began, "I spent several weeks in Europe last month, and it has made me think about the world. Some of what I'm thinking I don't like. I look at the world, and I see a crazy kind of race where the way to win isn't to run faster than the other guy but to trip him up. It isn't war. But it isn't peace, either, and it is degrading the quality of life for everybody, for ourselves as well as for the rest of the world." Because of the warm spring weather, there were only about thirty-five people in the church, cross-legged on the floor, slouched on beanbag pillows or sitting properly erect at the benches along the sides of the room. They were all listening attentively—or, if not attentively, with that polite expression of passive acceptance that he had seen most Sunday mornings of his life from this pulpit. "Some of it is economic," he said, "so that we play games with each others' currencies, raiding the pound and speculating on the mark; dumping gold on the market when the dollar softens, and buying it up to hoard when the Russians or the South Africans or the Indians start to sell. Some of it is mercantile. We sell wheat for less than it costs to raise, to countries that ship us TV sets for less than they cost to make. And some of it—" he hesitated, looking at the words he had written down, looking for the courage to go beyond them—"some of it is psychological. We censure the Spaniards for not giving freedom to the Basques, and we snub the rest of the world for interfering with our own dealings with the Navajos."

The eyes were glazing now, as he had known they would be, but doggedly he went on reciting statistics and explaining policies. Even Ted Brant, lying back against the beanbag, knees up, one arm possessively around Alys's shoulder, the other hand resting on Sue-Ellen's knee, was no longer looking hostile, only bored, while Alys was nodding at every point. It wasn't agreement, really. She was just acknowledging the use Hake was making of the information she had supplied him. Hake went on with his catalogue: aid to defectors, support to dissidents, jamming of broadcasts, dumping of pollution—"those thousand-meter stacks get rid of our own pollution," he said, "but only by throwing it up high enough so that it comes down on London and Copenhagen." Allen Haversford was no longer glassy-eyed. The director of International Pets and Flowers was listening with full, if noncommittal, attention, and so, surprisingly, was Jessie Tunman.

Hake rounded into his moral. "What I have come to believe," he said, "is that it is not enough not to be at war. We need more. We need tolerance and caring. We need to give credit to those who disagree with us for being perhaps wrong, but not villains. We need to accept diversity and encourage individuality. We need to abandon suspicion as a way of life, and turn away from either preemption or revenge. And we need to find within ourselves the solutions to the problems we make, instead of trying to make our own condition relatively better by making someone else's relatively worse. And now," he said, "Ellie Fratkin and Bill Meecham will entertain us with one of their lovely cello and piano duets."

To the strains of Schubert—or maybe it was Kabalevsky, he had misplaced his notes and when Bill and Ellie played, all the selections sounded about the same—he sat on the platform and looked out over his congregation. To the extent that Hake had family, they were it. He knew them from the inside out—inside best, as he knew his adopted Uncle Phil not as the steely-eyed IRS examiner but as the hiccoughing and amiable drunk who showed up at one of his hospital stays with a wetting, weeping baby doll as a get-well present, having forgotten what sex his sister-in-law's stepchild happened to be. Bland Teddy Cantrell, squatting like a Buddha and nodding to the music, would always be the tearful suicide-attempter who had set fire to Hake's study with a starter's pistol when his wife left him. One of the times his wife left him. The two gay

Tonys, the stablest and most dignified couple in the church as they leaned shoulder-to-shoulder against the wall, had blubbered their hearts out to him while deciding to come out of the closet. How many of them had he reached with what he had had to say? And as the coffee came out and the parishioners drifted around, he listened to the comments. "Really elevating," said the tall Tony, and the plumper, younger one said, "You always make me feel good, Horny." Jessie Tunman: "I only wish you were that open-minded about other things, Horny." Elinor Fratkin, hissing into his ear the moment she caught him alone: "I'm simply *ashamed*, Horny! How can I face William when you didn't say that what we were playing was his own transcription of the Bach partita?" Frail old Gertrude Mengel, tottering to him on a cane: "Oh, Reverend Hake, if only my sister could be hearing you! It might have kept her off drugs." Alys Brant, lingering next to him while Ted clutched her hand and stared resolutely away, "I loved the way you put it all together. When are we going to New York to finish the research?" Teddy Cantrell: "You've given us a lot to think about." And just behind him, Allen Haversford, eyes hooded, stiffly shaking Hake's hand: "You certainly have, and I want to talk to you about it at some length, Reverend Hake, but not just now."

Did that sound like a threat? At least a warning? For better or worse, it was about the only sign he had that anyone had really listened to him. He went back to his home, spent the day fiddling with filing sermons and putting together reports for the Monday Board meeting, watched television for a while and decided to go to bed early; and when he flushed his toilet that night it spoke to him in Curmudgeon's voice.

The essence of comedy is the incongruous thwarting of expectations. Hake saw his life as taking a comic turn. Kidnapped by a girl who had tried to lure him into a toilet. Funny! The real guns didn't make it less funny, they only turned the humor black. Sneezing western Europe into an economic tremor, what could be funnier than that? And now being given cloak-and-dagger orders by another toilet, that was hilarious—after it had stopped being startling, anyway.

When you looked at the appliance itself there was nothing particularly funny about it. Squat, solid and almost majestic in heather-blue ceramic, it looked like a superbly engineered device for exporting a person's excretory by-products as decently and as rapidly away from the person himself as anyone could wish. And nothing more. And in fact it was all of that, but something more. The bottom of the flush tank was four inches thick. Whatever was inside was concealed by the seamlessly molded ceramic, but from a palm-sized metal grille underneath the tank the voice came. The flushing lever was resilient black plastic, attractively scored with a moire surface. It did not look as if it could recognize Hake's thumbprint. But it could. Hake experimented in fascination. Flush with his finger, flush with his fist, nothing happened—except that the water in the bowl quietly scoured and drained itself away. Flush with his thumb, as the design invited one to do, and he had established contact with Curmudgeon himself.

It was only his own thumb that would do it. He proved that with accommodating—but faintly uneasy—Jennie Tunman the next morning, when he lured her into the new bathroom on a ruse: "Flush that for me, will you? I want to see if I can hear it out here."

And she did, grinning skeptically and a little nervously, and he couldn't—neither the sound of the water nor Curmudgeon's recorded voice. Only Jessie herself. "We've sure come up in the world, Horny. And now—" fleeing—"I'd better get back to the correspondence."

It was not quite true, Hake saw, that his life was turning funny, because funny was what it had been for some time. He would not have lasted through those flabby decades in a wheelchair if he hadn't seen the humor of it. Raunchy young male lovingly tended by the sweet-limbed girls the jocks envied him, football coach who could not totter the length of the field alone, religious leader who had never for one moment considered the possibility of the existence of a supernatural god—or any other kind, either. Spiritual counselor who eased three hundred parishioners' sins and temptations, that he had never had the chance to experience himself. Oh, yes! Funny. Funny as that thing must be at which you must laugh, so that you won't cry. Exactly as funny as, and funny in exactly the same way as, what was happening in his life now. Being talked to by a toilet was ludicrous, but so was most of the life story of Horny Hake.

What his toilet had said to him was:

"Horny! If you are not alone, flush the toilet again at once!"

There was a short pause, presumably while the toilet satisfied itself it was not immediately to be reflushed, and then Curmudgeon's voice said more amiably, "After all, old boy, you could have been into some peculiar customs we didn't know about. If you are, practice them in some other john. In this one, when you press the lever down you will get any messages from me that have accumulated. Do it at least three times a day—when you get up, around mid-afternoon, just before you go to sleep. If there aren't any messages, or when the messages are over, you'll hear a four-forty A beep. That means you can reply, or leave a message for me if you have one."

There was a pause, but as Hake did not hear a 440-hertz tone he assumed that Curmudgeon was marshalling his thoughts. When the toilet spoke again it was crisp and clear:

"So here are your instructions, Hake. First, keep on building up your strength. Second, report to IPF tomorrow afternoon for a physical—just go over there, they'll know what to do. Third, flush three times a day. Whether you need to or not. And, oh, yes, that sermon was a smart move, but don't overdo it. It's all right for your congregation to think you're a woolly-headed liberal, but don't go so far you talk yourself into it. We're pretty pleased with you right now, Hake. There's a nice little report in your promotion package. Don't spoil it."

The toilet beeped, and then returned to being only a toilet again.

* * *

Riding over to Eatontown the next day, Hake investigated the inside of his mind and found only a vacuum where his moral sense should be. Curmudgeon was *so* sure that his orders would be obeyed and his cause was just. Was it possible that it was? But surely it couldn't be right to make people sick who had done one no harm! But surely a man like Curmudgeon could not be so self-assured and still be as wholly wrong as he appeared. But surely— There were too many sureties, and Hake didn't really feel any of them. How was it possible that everybody in the world seemed absolutely sure they were in the right, when they all disagreed with each other, and when Hake felt nothing of the sort? Maybe the thing was to go with self-interest? Hake's self-interest seemed to lie with Curmudgeon, exempter from laws, provider of new bathrooms, balancer of the budget. If he stayed with Curmudgeon, he had no doubt, he would find some pretty nice fringe benefits. He might not have to ride around in this sort of smelly, choking charcoal-burning cab when he went out. Electrocar, inertial-drive, even a gasoline Buick like that of the person who had first summoned him to this exercise, they were all within his reach.

At IPF he didn't see Allen Haversford, only a pretty young nurse who took his vital signs, turned her back while he undressed and got into a cotton smock, X-rayed him through and through, slipped him three painless spray-injections (for what? what plague would he be spreading now, and where?), pronounced him fit with her eyes as well as with the signed report she Xeroxed for him to keep, and turned him loose. After he shook her hand and was already on his way to the gate, Hake came to a sudden realization. Old Horny was horny! And he had been given an invitation, and had let it slide.

With so many of the women he encountered a protected species, not to be touched, and with so much of his adult life spent under circumstances in which sex was only an abstraction, Hake knew he was pitifully unworldly. No other man in New Jersey would have left that office without trying it on, especially with the kind of encouragement he had no doubt he had observed. This needed to be thought out. He dropped the afternoon's meeting with the school administration from his thoughts, crossed Highway 35 and ordered himself a beer in the lounge of an air-conditioned motel.

It was all part and parcel of the same thing, he told himself. Who the hell did he think he was, some kind of saint? Why shouldn't he have a few vices? Why was he running away from Alys Brant, and why shouldn't he let Curmudgeon make his life easier? He had another beer, and then another. Because he was in the best of health, three beers didn't make him drunk; but they did make him lose sense of time. When he made up his mind that he would go back and see if that clean-featured young nurse was as interested as he thought, he discovered that it was past seven, the gates were closed. He had not only missed the meeting with the school but he had not even had time to get back home for his afternoon flush before getting over to the Midsummer Magic Show. Too bad, thought Horny, striding out into the highway and commandeering a cab, but tomorrow was another day, and she'd still be there then!

The Midsummer Magic Show was the church's big fund-raiser. It took place in an old movie theater at a traffic circle near Long Branch. In high-energy days the theater had sucked audiences away from the downtown houses, kids with their dates, young marrieds with their kids, senior citizens destroying one more day. Now the flow was seeping back to the cities, and the highway audiences had drained away. The theater kept going with classic movie revivals at a dollar a head, and now and then a concert. Nothing else would draw enough to pay the costs of keeping the theater alive. Mostly those didn't, either, so that the manager was thrilled to rent it for one night each year to the Unitarian Church. Hake got there just as the magician, The Incredible Art, was setting up his effects.

Alys Brant saw Hake walking down the aisle and waved the fingers of one hand. That was all she could wave; she was strapped into one of Art's illusions, rehearsing to be The Woman Sawed in Half, and her hands were crossed

tightly on her breast to stay as far as possible away from
the screeching, spinning buzz saw that seemed to be slicing
through her belly. When The Incredible Art saw whom she
was greeting he stopped the saw, levered it up and away
from her and began to extract her. "Hi, Horny," he called.
"Help me get this thing back of the curtain."

Art was built to be a magician, or to look like one: six
foot three and weighing a fast hundred and forty-five
pounds, narrow face, piercing eyes. He wore his blond hair
in General Custer flowing waves, beard and mustache the
same; he looked like a skinny Scandinavian devil and had
cultivated a voice an octave below Mephistopheles'. Wraith-
thin, he was astonishingly strong. The prop weighed as
much as a piano, and although it was on rollers Hake was
puffing by the time they had it out of sight, while The
Incredible Art was incredibly not even sweating. "Hate to
have to do that by myself, Horny," he observed, wrapping
his long arms around one end of it and tugging it a few
more inches out of the way. "Guess I'm ready for 'em
now."

Alys returned, slinky in diaphanous harem top and
pants. "That saw always makes me have to pee," she confided. She was braless under the filmy bolero, Hake saw—
and, he was pretty sure, pantyless below, too, although the
way the gauze draped around her it was hard to be sure.
He found the illusion both exciting and uncomfortable. His
glands had not yet resigned themselves to missing out on
the nurse, and when Alys began admiringly to trace his
pectorals with one hand and his latissimus dorsi with the
other they stirred with new hope. The woman's signals
were maddeningly contradictory! Hake formed phrases in
his mind, like, If you're so horny for Horny, honey, where
were you in Europe? But, fairly, he admitted to himself
that his signals to her had to be equally contrary and
obscure, because his drives and prohibitions baffled them.
He escaped when the theater began to fill, helped by the
fact that among the earliest arrivals were the other three
from Alys's family, Ted Brant looking annoyed, Walter
Sturgis worried, Sue-Ellen reproachful. Hake took a seat as
far from them at the opposite end of the first row as he

could manage. It would have been better to sit naturally and suspicion-allayingly next to them. But he didn't feel up to it.

The Incredible Art's performance included all the standards Hake remembered from every other magic show he had ever seen, from vanishing billiard balls to producing live pigeons from Alys's bodice, after he had finished sawing her in half. The audience was half children—and the other half grownups volunteering to be childish again for one night—and they ate it all up. As they always had. Six thousand dollars in admissions had funneled into the church treasury, the people were having a ball, and Hake allowed himself to feel good.

And therefore unwary; and when The Incredible Art began calling volunteers up from the audience for his last and greatest feat, Hake allowed himself to be swept with the flow.

"And now," the magician boomed compellingly, "for a final demonstration of The Incredible Art of The Incredible Art, I am going to try an experiment in hypnotism. I have here thirty volunteers, selected at random. I ask you, ladies and gentlemen, to tell the audience: Have any of you been rehearsed, coached or instructed in any way as to what you are supposed to do up here?"

All thirty heads waggled "no," Hake's among them.

"Then I want all of you to let your heads hang forward, chins on your chests. Close your eyes. You are growing sleepy. Your eyes are closed, and you feel sleepy. I am going to count backwards from five, and when I say 'zero' you will be asleep: Five. Four. Three. Two. One. Zero."

Hake was not sure he felt sleepy, but he did seem to be comfortable enough as he was. He heard sounds of movement on the stage, and peered through a slitted eye to observe Art quietly shepherding half a dozen of the volunteers back into the audience; evidently they had looked up and shown they were awake. "Now the rest of you," Art rumbled. "Keep your eyes closed, but raise your heads. Do not open your eyes until I say 'open.' At that time you will be fully aware of what is going on, but you will not remember any of it after you leave this stage. Now, open!"

Hypnosis, Hake thought, was not all that different from the rest of life. He didn't feel changed, but he found himself compliantly raising an arm, then squatting on the floor, then performing a little dance. It was as easy to do what he was told as to break the pattern of obedience. So why not do it? Still, it was strange. He tried to remember what being hypnotized had felt like, back in the hospital when his whole chest and torso were flaming with pain after surgery. Not much. Not anything, really, except that after the anesthesiologist had made her passes the pain had seemed a little less important. It was . . . strange. So he went on doing what The Incredible Art told him to do, along with the other survivors on the stage, his mind and senses open to taste this new experience, until Art began pairing them off into waltzing couples. That Hake perceived as somehow threatening. He broke stride, and Art waved him off the stage. Of the original thirty, only six people stayed there through the end. Somehow, Hake was not surprised that one of them was Alys.

At the party afterward, The Incredible Art was riffling cards in a series of buck-eye shuffles for some of the kids. Hake, drink in hand, drifted over to him. "I was never hypnotized that way before," he offered, still trying to analyze his feelings about it.

"You weren't then either," said Art, tapping the deck and popping all four aces into the hands of a ten-year-old girl.

"I wasn't? But— But I found myself doing things without any real control."

"Did you?" Art fanned the deck, displaying fifty-two cards neatly ordered into suits and denominations, and then put it away. "I don't know what you did do," he admitted. "I've done that show a hundred times. If I get enough people up on the stage, a few of them will do everything I tell them to. The rest I lose."

From behind Hake, Jessie Tunman said triumphantly, "Then it's just a trick!"

"If you say so, Jessie." The Incredible Art grinned like a tiger behind the blond mask of hair. "But I think what you mean is when *I* do it it's a trick, when somebody else does it it's science, right?"

"The phenomenon of hypnotism is well established in psychological literature," she said stiffly. "There's a point at which being a skeptic betrays simply an unwillingness to accept the evidence, Mr. Art."

"Now you're talking about flying saucers," he said. They had had this argument before. "You're going to tell me that with all the recorded sightings only a prejudiced bigot would say they don't exist, right?"

"No. I wasn't going to tell you anything, Mr. Art. It's no concern of mine what you believe in or don't believe in. But there are things your much vaunted rationalism just can't explain. UFOlogy went through all this in the Sixties. One guy said the UFOs were weather balloons, another said meteorites. People said any crazy thing that came into their heads, rather than accept the reality of visitors from some other place in the universe. Dust devils, the planet Venus, even swamp gas! Nobody could face up to the simple facts."

"What are the facts, Jessie dear?" Art inquired softly.

She scowled. "You exasperate me!"

"No, really. I want to know."

She said, "I don't think you do. But it's simple. It's the law according to Sherlock Holmes. 'After you eliminate the impossible, the explanation that is left, however improbable, must be right.' You might choose to believe that fifty thousand responsible observers are all crazy or liars. To me, that is impossible."

Hake put down his glass. "Nice talking to you," he said, and made his escape. He didn't want to be in that argument, and the party showed signs of breaking up anyway. A family who lived in Elberon offered him a lift back to the rectory, and he squeezed into the back seat of their inertial two-door, with a sleeping three-year-old in his lap and the whining flywheel tickling the soles of his feet through the floorboards underneath, and when he entered his bedroom he heard a sound from the bath. The toilet was making a little whining sound as it leaked water.

Guessing correctly that it was demanding attention, he

flushed it at once. An instant voice barked, "Stay right there, Hake!" A moment passed, then the same voice, Curmudgeon's voice, with a tiny difference in quality that made him realize it was not a recording but the man himself direct, snarled, "What the hell, Hake! You didn't report in for your afternoon message."

"I'm sorry, Curmudgeon. I got busy."

"You don't *ever* get that busy, Hake! Remember that. Now, I want you in New York tomorrow, two P.M., in the flesh."

"But—I've got appointments—"

"Not any more, you don't. Call them off. Take down this address and be there." Curmudgeon spelled out the name of what sounded like a theatrical casting agency in the West Forties and signed off.

Thoughtfully, Hake used the toilet for its alternative purpose, and then shrugged. As with The Incredible Art, it seemed as easy to obey the command as to rebel against it. He put on his pajamas and a robe and walked out into the office to get Alys's phone number.

To his surprise, the light was on. Jessie Tunman was there, writing rapidly in her shorthand notebook. "Oh, hello, Horny. I didn't mean to disturb you."

"You didn't. That's all right." He looked up the Brant-Sturgis number and touched the number-buttons. It was answered at once, and by Alys. "Hello, Alys. Horny Hake here. I just realized that I have tomorrow free. I know it's short notice, but would you like to do that library bit with me? You would? That's great, Alys. All right, I'll be ready at nine, and thanks." He hung up, pleased with his cleverness. Using Alys as a front, no one would think that he was going to the city for some hidden reason; at most, they would think his hidden reason not hidden at all. He said benevolently to Jessie, "Working late, are you?"

"I just wanted to remind myself of some things I have to do tomorrow, Horny. And, to tell the truth, since we've got the air-conditioning and all—well, I like to be here. It's pretty hot in my room." Jessie lived in what had once been a beach motel, now more or less remodeled into one-room apartments. Its one significant advantage was that it was cheap. "Horny? I didn't mean to eavesdrop, but are you going to the library in New York tomorrow?"

"Yes. I've been promising myself that I would for a couple of months, and I just decided to do it."

"Can I go along? There's—" She hesitated. "I know you don't believe in it, Horny, but there's some new material on UFOs out, and I'd like to look into it. I won't be in your way."

Hake said, "Well, I'd certainly be glad to have you, Jessie, but it's not my car."

"Oh, I'm sure Alys won't mind. Matter of fact," she said archly, "I bet she'll be glad for a chaperone, you know, so Ted and Walter won't be worried. That's wonderful, Horny! I'm going home right this minute, so I can get in early and take care of everything before we go."

As it turned out, Alys didn't mind at all, or said she didn't, and all the way into New York Jessie Tunman primly rode the mother-in-law seat in the back of the little charcoal-generator. It was a two-hour ride, the three-wheeler barely crawling as it climbed the long bridge ascents and the occasional hills; but on the level it chugged along at the double-nickels, and downhill it took off at terrifying speed. As they whined down the ramp into the Lincoln Tunnel, Alys slipping wildly between the sectional buses and the fat tractor-trailer trucks that were inching along, Hake was glad they were almost there, prayerful that their luck would hold out a few minutes more.

It had been smuggy-hot all the way in, and the tunnel itself was a gas chamber. "Roll up your windows," Alys gagged. It didn't help. By the time they broke into open air, even the open air of midtown Manhattan, Hake's head was pounding and Alys's driving had become even more capricious. They drove down to the Village, parked the three-wheeler in the three-deck parking garage that surrounded the arch in Washington Square and walked over to the library. It was bloody *hot*.

A drama was being enacted in New York City that day; dressing while watching his TV news program, Hake had seen shots of a tank-trucker from Great Kills, perched over

the discharge hose of his gasoline truck with a lighted
Davy lamp in his hand, holding Rockefeller Center hostage
in the cause of returning Staten Island to the state of New
Jersey. Ringed by police sharpshooters who dared not fire,
giddy in the fumes of the gas that vented up past the wire-
screen around his candle, the man had been haranguing
twenty terrified captives, as well as the millions beyond
who listened safely through the networks' parabolic microphones. Breathing shallowly of the hot, carbonized air,
feeling the asphalt suck at his shoes, stepping around dog-
turds and less identifiable gobbets of filth, Hake understood
how the man had gone mad, how a thousand city-dwellers
a year raped, crucified, leaped from windows or set fire to
themselves. It was an environment to madden anyone, especially in weather like this.

And when they walked in through the double revolving
doors of the library, it was into dry, sweet spring. A room
five stories high, and air-conditioned to perfection! "Power-
pigs," snarled Hake, but Alys laid her hand on his arm.

"It isn't just for people, Horny, dear, it's for all the
computers here which would break down if they didn't
keep the air just right. Come on, we sign in here, and then
they'll give us a terminal."

The library gave them more than that. They gave them a
room to themselves, glass-walled on three sides, looking
out into the five-floor atrium on the fourth, with comfortable chairs, a desk, ash-trays, a thermos flask of ice-water
. . . and the one thing that made it all real: a computer
terminal. Alys escorted Jessie Tunman to her own cubicle,
a few doors down the corridor, then came back and closed
the door. "Now I've got you, Horny," she said, touching
her palm to his cheek. And passed by him, and sat down
before the terminal. Expertly she punched in her signature
number, taken from the card issued at the desk, and a
series of codes. "I've ordered a citation index search for
starters, Horny, keyed to any three of six or more subject
phrases. You'll have to tell me what the phrases are. Did
you know you're a very sexy man, Horny?"

Starting to ask what she meant by the first part of what
she had said, Hake jumped the tracks as he tried to switch

to the second. "Alys," he said, "please remember that I'm your marriage counselor, as well as, I hope, your friend."

"Oh, I do, Horny, I do. Now, the kind of phrases we give the computer are whatever subjects interest you. For instance," she tapped the keys, "some of the things you were talking about in your sermon, like so." The screen on the terminal typed out the words:

1. Major strikes.
2. Exotic plant and animal pests.
3. Currency manipulations.

"Got it?" she asked. "What else?"

"I could answer that better if I knew what you were doing."

"Sorry, Horny, I thought I explained all that. You were real cute at the magic show."

"Please, Alys."

"Well, you were. It's a real kind of turn-on, being hypnotized, isn't it? Back at college we all took the psych courses just for kickiness. My goodness, Horny, the fun we had hypnotizing each other! . . . Oh, you want to get on with this, don't you? Well, it's simple. Once we program searches for six or eight subjects, the computer selects some basic sources in each of them—say, a newspaper story about the bus strike in London, or the police in New York, and one on those water-lilies you were talking about, and so on. Then it starts searching for works that cite sources from any three of those subjects. If you find somebody's written a book that includes material on three of the things you're interested in, then the chances are pretty good you'll be interested in the book, right? Funny thing. When we were in Europe, the way you were being Big Daddy to those kids, it turned me right off. Did you know that?"

Half laughing, and half of the laughing from embarrassment, Hake said, "Let's stick to one thing at a time, okay? I'm also interested in fads that keep people from working. How do you say that?" He was thinking of the hula-hoops, of course; and when they found a generic term for that, and for terrorism, and for filthy cities, and for dumping commodities and despoiling natural resources and two or three other things, Alys punched an "execute" code and they watched the screen generate titles, quick as a zipper, laying them line by line across the tube:

AAF Studies World Events, monograph, U.S. Govt. Prntg. Offc.

AAAS Symposium on Social Change, Am. Acdy. Adv. Sci. proceedings.

Aar und das schrecklichkeit von Erde, Der, 8vo, von E.T. Gründemeister, Köln.

Aback and Abeam, A Memoir, by C. Franklin Monscutter, N.Y.

Abandonment of Reason, by William Reichsleder, *N.Y. Times* Sun. Mag., XCIV, 22, 83–88.

Abasing the Environment—

"No good," said Alys, leaning forward and hitting the switch that stopped the quick-time march of titles up the screen. "At that rate we'll be here till winter and still in the As. I like *manly* men, Horny, that's why I sometimes get just smothered with Walter and Ted, they're so *kind.*"

"Alys, damn it!"

"Well, I just want you to know. So here's what we'll do. First, I'll kill all the foreign-language entries; should have thought of that in the first place. Then I'll set it to look for citations in five categories instead of three, how's that?"

"You're the expert," Hake said. "What would happen if you programmed it for all, what is it, all nine?"

"Why not?" She tapped quickly and sat back. Nothing happened.

"Shouldn't you start it?" he asked after a moment.

"I did start it, Horny. It's sorting through maybe a thousand works a second, looking for one that has all the things you want. There can't be very many, you know. You're a lot different now than you were in Europe."

"Oh, God, Alys," he said, not looking away from the screen. But that was not very rewarding. They sat for a full moment, and there was no flicker at all.

"I have a friend," said Alys thoughtfully, "who has an apartment not far from here. I have a key. There's always

something in the refrigerator, or I could pick up some kind
of salad stuff and maybe a bottle of wine——"

"I'm not hungry. Listen, suppose we do find something.
What do I do then, read the whole book here?"

"If you want to, Horny. Or if you want hard copy to
take home, there's a selector switch on that black thing
over there, it'll make microfiche copies for you. Or you can
order the book itself on inter-library. Usually takes about a
week to get them. I'm really disappointed."

"Well," he said, "it isn't that I don't *like* you, Alys,
but——"

She laughed affectionately. "Oh, Horny! I meant the
way we're not getting anything. Let me cut back to six
items, and see if we come out with a manageable number."

And in fact they did. Eight books, about fifteen magazine and journal pieces—and real pay-dirt. A dissertation
by a political-science Ph.D. candidate called *The Mecha-
nisms of Covert Power*. A Johns Hopkins conference on
"External Forces in National Development." And three or
four theses and monographs, all right on Hake's target.
"What I really need," he said, surveying the mounting
stack of microfiche cards, "is one of these computers for
myself. I'll be a year reading all this."

Alys leaned back, stretched and yawned prettily, covering her mouth with the back of her hand. Hake averted his
eyes from the deep-necked peasant blouse with its white
lacing, and remembered to look at his watch. He was due
at Curmudgeon's in forty-five minutes, and how was he
going to get rid of Alys? It was a convenience to have the
question posed to him in that way, because it spared him
the necessity of considering whether he really wanted to
get rid of her. Wine, salad and a friendly apartment
sounded actually pretty nice.

"Oh, hell," said Alys crossly, bringing her arms down.
"There's Jessie."

Hake leaped to his feet. "Come in, come in," he said,
astonishing Jessie with his cordiality. "Alys has been showing me how to work this thing and, I must say, she's really
been marvelous about it. How are you doing, Jessie? Need
any help? I'm sure Alys will give you some pointers. As for

me, I've got a couple of errands to run. Suppose I meet you back here at, let's see, say three-thirty? That way we can miss most of the rush hour. . . ."

The building was fifty stories tall in a block of smaller ones; the elevator was high-speed and did not rattle, and the name on the door of the suite of offices was

Seskyn–Porterous
Theatrical Agency
"Through These Doors Walk Tomorrow's Stars"

The waiting room had seats for twenty people. All were full. A dozen other prospective stars of tomorrow were standing around, pretty dancers and bearded folk singers, nervous comedians and a lot of other people who did not look like performers at all. Hake didn't have to wait. He was shown at once into a corner office with immense plate-glass windows, and Curmudgeon was sitting at a tiny, bare, glass-topped desk, his hands folded before him.

He got up and shook hands silently, shaking his hairy head as Hake said hello. "Just a minute," he said, walking to the windows and turning on a strange little buzzer device that rattled irregularly against each of them, and then switching on a radio behind his desk. Just loudly enough to be heard over the classical-rock music, he said, "You're punctual, and that's a good way to be. Your physical came through, four-oh; you're in as good shape as you've ever been in your life. What do you say? Are you about ready for an assignment?"

"Well," said Hake, "I don't know—"

"Course you don't know. I haven't told you yet. Let me read you something."

He unlocked one of the desk drawers and took out a single sheet of paper in a sealed folder. "Subject, H. Hornswell Hake," he read. "Blah, blah, blah, physical status excellent, blah, here we are. 'Subject has displayed commendable initiative and resourcefulness. He is rated superior in the performance of his duties, and will be recommended for promotion at the first opportunity.'" He dropped the sheet into a metal wastebasket, and watched as it abruptly sprang into flame and consumed itself. Stirring the ashes, he said, "What do you say to that, Hake?"

"I guess I say thank you. What does that mean about a promotion?"

"What it says. You do good work, we reward you. Simple's that. Is there anything you want?"

"Well— New carpets for the church," Hake said, remembering. "Maybe a little car. And, yes, I'd like a computer terminal of my own, if that's not too—"

"Forget the computer," said Curmudgeon. "For now, anyway. Car, all right. Carpets, sure." He made a note for himself on the palm of his hand. Craning to see, Hake observed that the whole left palm was covered with cryptic scribbles. "Anyway," he said, "you won't be needing any of that right away. The church is going to close down for the summer in a couple of weeks." He didn't put it as a question; he knew it as a fact. "I'll see that the carpets are ready before Labor Day. About a car, get it yourself. Whenever you want to. I'll arrange for financing. But right now you're going on a vacation to a dude ranch."

"I am? Why am I?"

"Because you've been given it as a ministerial perquisite," Curmudgeon explained. "Actually, you won't be lounging around the swimming pool and making out with the divorcees. It's basic training for future missions. You'll like it; you're a health nut anyway. You report to Fort Stockton, Texas, a week from Monday for three weeks. Bring jeans, shorts, hiking clothes; bring whatever you like to make it look good, but you won't have much need for neckties or dancing shoes. Any questions?"

"Well—"

Curmudgeon stood up. "It's good you don't have any questions," he said, "because I've got another appointment in two minutes. Watch your mail for tickets and travel information—and when you find out you've won the trip, be sure you act surprised. Meanwhile— *What the hell?*"

There was a muffled thunder-roll outside the windows, which rattled in a more somber rhythm than that of the buzzers at their bases. Curmudgeon sprang to look out, Hake right behind him. East and north, a dozen blocks away, tiny black things were sailing through the sky, followed by a ropy cloud of black smoke shot through with flame.

"Christ," said Hake. Some of those black things looked like bodies!

Curmudgeon stared at him narrowly, then relaxed. He took his hand away from the .45 at his hip, where it had flown at once, and said, "See what we're up against? That was the guy with the gas truck, I bet. He was one of the New Dorp Irredentists. And that was Madrid money that got them going, you know. We'll fix the sons of bitches when that Dutch-elm beetle Haversford's got gets into their— Well, never mind that. Just remember what you just saw. It'll do more for your morale than fifty lectures Under the Wire."

New Dorp Irredenists? Dutch-elm beetle in Spain? "Under the Wire"? But before Hake could ask about any of these confusing things he was out in the anteroom again, threading his way through the starlets and tap dancers, with all the questions unasked; especially including that central question that went, *What made the gas-truck driver do it?*

VI

WHEN Hake emerged from the slow-jet at Fort Stockton the heat wrapped itself around him at once. He was sweating before he got to the bottom of the ladder, panting as he walked the twenty yards from aircraft to the opening in the fence marked "Gate 1." (There was no Gate 2.) He was met by a young black woman—black as to ethnicity, not skin color, which was a sort of sunny beige. There was no exchange of recognition signals. Clearly she had been briefed with description and photograph, perhaps also with fingerprints, genetic code and retina-prints, for all Hake knew. There was also the consideration that no one else got off the slow-jet. She came up to him unhesitatingly and said, "You're Hornswell Hake and I'm Deena Fairless. Let's go to the plane." Also unhesitatingly, he went along. She didn't ask if he had checked any baggage. She knew he had not. He had been instructed to take only toilet articles and personal items not to exceed four kilograms, and she assumed he had complied. Fairless pointed to the passenger side of what looked like an old electric golf cart, got in on the driver's side and was in motion before Hake had fully settled himself in. There was no top. The drive to the end of an auxiliary runway, where a small plane was waiting for them, was only about two minutes, but it was long enough for Hake to think of sunstroke. He followed the woman up a retractable ladder into what he recognized as some sort of old military plane; he did not know enough to be sure of model or function, but it seemed to be one of the vertical-takeoff counter-insurgency gunships that had been popular in the old brushfire wars.

Hake's guide turned out to be Hake's pilot as well. She checked Hake's seat belt, spoke briefly into the radio, went through a thirty-second checkoff against a printed list, and launched the plane in a climbing turn that made no use of the runway at all. It was a brute-force takeoff in a brute-force kind of airplane, and Hake knew that the fuel that got them into the air would have been enough to have kept his rectory warm all the last winter.

It stuck in his craw. He leaned over and yelled in the pilot's ear, "Isn't this a terrible waste of fuel?"

She looked at him with mild astonishment. "You mean this SHORTOL? Depends on how you look at it, Hake," she yelled. "These are the planes we've got."

"But a lighter plane—"

"Sit on it, Hake," she yelled good-humoredly. "I knew

you were a conscientious type the minute I saw you, but you haven't worked out the figures. How much energy do you think it takes to build a plane? Don't guess. I'll tell you. Quarter-million kilowatt-hours or so, so if we junk this to get a little one it's like peeing away ten thousand gallons of fuel. Anyway," she finished obscurely, "every now and then you need what this plane can give you. Now shut up and let me fly."

It was clear that Deena Fairless didn't want conversation, so Hake forbore to ask her where they were flying. He knew that it was generally southwest, at least. Fairless hadn't said, but Hake could estimate direction well enough from the position of the sun. They flew low, under ten thousand feet, and updrafts from the dry mesas kept them in bouts of turbulence. Fairless didn't talk, or at least not to Hake. She kept moving her lips into the radio; he could not hear what was said, but granted it enough importance to refrain from offering conversation. Only as they began to climb over a ridge of hills she leaned toward him and said, "Have you got a lot of fillings in your teeth, Hake?"

"No. Not too many."

"Lucky," she said, looking over the hills. "There's the Wire."

There was something there to look at. He could not identify it, was not even sure he was seeing what he saw. It looked like pencil-thin searchlight beams winking on and off, tinged with color, one red, two bluish-green. The beams were very faint except for high patches where they impinged upon wisps of cirrostratus, and even there they existed only as split-second impressions. As they topped the hill he saw what looked like a tilted plain of chicken wire sloping away on the far side. But he had only a glimpse, and then they were dropping to a short, black-topped landing strip next to a cluster of buildings. Painted on the roof of one low, long shed were the words HAS-TA-VA RANCH. He saw what looked like a row of small and unprosperous motel cabins, a corral with a clump of horses milling around one end, a few stables. The horses did not even look up as the plane screamed down to a rolling stop

on the airstrip, which was the only indication in sight that
the place was anything other than an attempt at a tourist
attraction, rapidly going broke.

"Welcome to your new home," said Deena Fairless, un-
strapping herself and flipping switches off. "You'll love it
here."

Hake didn't love it there. He didn't hate it, either; he
didn't have time. Or energy. Up at 4:45 A.M., and a quarter-mile run before breakfast, snaking among the supports
for the wire-field overhead. Ten minutes to go to the toilet,
and then out again. Sometimes for an hour's hand-to-hand
combat instruction, flinging each other into hillocks of
sand or clumps of buffalo grass—the buffalo grass was
softer, but once in a while there was a snake in it. Sometimes for calisthenics. Sometimes for scuba-training, practicing clearing the mask, practicing snatching the mask
away from each other—those were good times, because
with water-discipline enforced it was about the only time
any of them got an all-over bath; but not so good, because
with water-discipline a necessity the pool was never
changed. Then something sedentary for half an hour's rest:
learning to use bugging equipment, learning to know when
it was being used on themselves. Making repairs in equipment. Morale—over and over, morale. Then lunch, twenty
minutes of it. Then more. And more and more. Hake had
tucked a dozen microfiches into his "personal effects" bag,
but he never learned if there was a viewer on the premises,
because he never even found time to ask.

Hake's fellows included three dozen persons, most of
them new trainees like himself, a few old-timers being
brought back on line for reassignment, a cross-section of
humanity. Hispanic teen-aged boys, a glowingly long-
legged California blonde, one elderly black professor, a
nun. They all shared the same bunkhouse, tucked in the lee
of a dune Under the Wire. They all, somehow, kept up.
The only thing they seemed to have in common was that
they had little in common—beyond, of course, the purpose
of their presence here. If Hake had looked around his
commuter bus one morning and seen all of them there he

would have considered them a perfectly normal busload of average Americans. The group changed. Some came, some went. The San Diego blonde was the first to go, to Hake's regret, but a day or two later a New Orleans brunette turned up, along with two middle-aged Japanese ladies from Hawaii. The only constants were the instructors: a one-legged youth for surveillance and debugging, a whipcord and vinegar senior citizen for hand-to-hand and physical training, Deena Fairless for scuba and instrument repair, all of them, taking turns, for the morale lectures. In the first ten days Under the Wire, Hake never did the same thing twice, and never came to the end of a day without falling instantly into exhausted sleep, regardless of hunger, pains, itches or the occasional mad singing of the wire overhead.

He had not, as it turned out, stayed at Has-Ta-Va Ranch any longer than it took to get into a truck and bounce half a mile under the power rectenna that he had glimpsed from the air. By the time he had been dropped off and set about drawing two sets of underwear, ten pairs of socks and the stoutest hiking boots he had ever had on his feet, he had figured out both what he had seen and why he was there.

The training base was hidden under the microwave receiver that supplied most of three states with electricity. The power came from space. Twenty-two thousand miles straight up from the equator a magnetohydrodynamic generator hung in geosynchronous orbit, sucking electrical energy out of plasma, transmuting it into microwaves, pumping five gigawatts of it down to the Ok-Tex-Mex grid. The trouble with a "stationary" orbit is that it can only be stationary directly over some point on the equator, so the rectenna had to be tilted toward the south: thus the slope of the hill. At 30° North Latitude the tilt did not have to be extreme. And, as a valuable by-product, there was all that land under the wire that was, if not immune, at least resistant to airborne or satellite inspection. Some was used for grazing forty-acre cattle, or the three-five buffalo hybrids that survived better and gained faster, if you could get used to the gamey, sweetish taste of the meat. Some was used, or was sometimes used, for irrigated crops—soy, sorghum or alfalfa. (But not this year, with the water tables sinking.) And some was used by Curmudgeon's people, for the purposes that brought Hake there. Ok-Tex-Mex was not the only huge rectenna bringing down MHD power to pop American toasters and light American homes. SCALAZ, on the Gila River, handled more energy. Three or four others were the same size, and the new one in the Gulf of Mexico off Cape Sable was much larger (when it wasn't being ripped up by tropical storms). But Ok-Tex-Mex had a special advantage. It was a long way from anything more populous than a dude ranch. There were reasons for that. That part of Texas, south of the Permian Basin, had never had much to make anyone want to be there, at least above ground; and the stuff that had been below ground had long since been pumped into the tanks of American cars and burned away.

Being Under the Wire was not so bad, once you got used to a couple of things. The Wire itself was not your average snow fence. It was three hundred square kilometers of dipole elements, each with its own filter, gallium-arsenide Schottky barrier diode rectifier and bypass capacitor. Put them all together and they were supposed to be something over eighty percent efficient at sucking in low-density microwaves and spitting out 10,000-volt DC into the Ok-Tex-Mex power grid. It was eight percent transparent to sunlight, and a hundred percent leaky to rain—when there was any rain. It was also hot and noisy. Most of the eighteen percent loss came off as heat, and convected harmlessly away into the Texas air. Most of what was left appeared as a dull, faint hum, like a toy-train transformer spread out over the sky. Living Under the Wire meant that where the Wire came down low to the ground you felt its radiance like a toaster element overhead; where it was high, the convection sucked in surface winds; and always it droned at you. It did other things. The support columns got in the way of moving around. And there was the little problem with the microwave energy itself. There was a good chance it damaged DNA. The cattle grazing under it were raised for slaughter, not breeding; there was some question about what sort of descendants they would have. (And the people in the camp underneath? No one seemed to want to discuss it.)

The satellite transmitter was constantly locked onto a corner-reflector at the center of the rectenna's spread. Ninety-nine-plus percent of the time it stayed centered there, or no farther from it than the wire could accommodate. The average power density of the beam was comfortably low. Unfortunately, it didn't always stay average. Atmospherics intervened. The interface between air layers became lenses. Focusing one way, the beam spread over more area than the rectenna accepted, and some of the power was lost. Focusing another, the power density climbed. That was when dental fillings became significant. In a dense beam, the result was the damnedest toothache anyone could have. For this the management of the training camp offered aspirin, or even rough-and-ready extraction if desired, and nothing else. (The good part was that the worst lumps in the beam seldom lasted more than an hour or two. Only enough to drive a sufferer out of his mind for a while. Not enough to interfere with his training.)

What was left of Hake's convalescent frailty was sweated out of him in running, knee-bends and hand-to-hand combat, an eclectic discipline that seemed to include judo, *la savate,* sapping-and-stabbing and the dirtier kinds of Saturday-night punchups. *That* wasn't bad. Hake hadn't had his strong male body long enough to take it for granted, and when he sent the Louisiana charmer flying and dropped one of the professors to the ground, his knee on the man's throat, two seconds after they had jumped him from behind, he heard himself growling with pleasure. There was a session on how to make plastic explosives on a base of Vaseline, with ingredients purchasable in any drugstore, and one on the use of Blue Box and Black Box penetration of telecommunication networks. They weren't bad, either. The technology was fascinating to the MIT dropout who had not thought of any of those things for years. They trained with a large selection of electronic cameras and microphones, and each of the trainees in turn took the equipment to spy on the others. The prize was when the nun came up with a two-minute sniperscope tape of one of the teen-agers masturbating behind a cluster of yucca. Hake was impressed. Not so much by the nun's technical skill as by Tigrito's energy. Hake did not seem to have the energy left after a day to think of sex. (Or not in the first week; but then, Tigrito had been there for four.) When Hake thought of sex, or indeed when he let his mind drift in any direction at all away from remembering to spit into his facemask and rehearsing the nomenclature of the parts of the rifle-microphone, was only during the indoctrination lectures. Sprawled out on the sparse grass, the sun beating through the wire overhead, they listened to Deena or Fortnum or Captain Pegleg going on and on about their purpose in being there:

"The United States is threatened as never before in its history—" Pegleg drumming on his outstretched artificial limb with the fingers of one hand, while the words droned out of him as if he were himself a tape—"by a world in which our rightful defense forces are stymied by red tape and international agreements, any questions? Right." There weren't any questions. There was a difference of viewpoint, to be sure, but Hake did not feel a necessity to air it, and besides Mary Jean was stretched out before him with her hands folded behind her head and he was enjoying what he saw.

Or, "Under the constitution and laws of our land—" this was old Fortnum, who stood up when he talked to them and insisted on alert posture from his audience— "we are charged with securing the blessings of democracy to ourselves and our posterity, which we got to do by keeping our nation strong and secure, any questions?" There weren't any questions for Fortnum, either. He was the only one of the instructors who had the habit of imposing extra duty for misdemeanors. Attracting his attention was usually a misdemeanor.

Deena Fairless was the only one who held Hake's attention as a speaker. For one thing, she didn't sit or stand but moved around among them, sometimes rousting them awake with a toe when the after-lunch heat began to put one or another of them away. For another, she talked about more interesting things. "By presidential directive, we are limited to covert, non-lethal operations on foreign soil only. All three things, remember. Covert. Non-lethal. Foreign. Now, if there are no questions—" she barely paused, but there weren't any questions then, either—"let me explain some of the things you've been seeing around here."

And that was how Hake found out that agent training was only one of the functions of the installation. There was a research-and-development underground—literally underground, dug into the side of the slope itself—a few miles away, and that was where things like the IR spectacles and the foamboats came from. There was a place euphemistically called "debriefing." None of them were *ever* to go near it. Nor likely to, since it was constantly patrolled with attack dogs. Deena Fairless didn't say who was "debriefed," but the trainees formed their opinions; and if any of them happened to be taken out by the Other Side, decided they could expect to wind up in some other "debriefing" place at some other point on the surface of the Earth. There was even a small writers'-colony place—that was the one that was actually housed at the Has-Ta-Va Ranch itself—where psychological warfare texts were prepared.

And then, when God was kind, they were permitted to watch films. They saw notable agency triumphs of the past, the counterfeiting operations that broke the Bank of England and the price-rigging that bankrupted ten thousand Indian, Filipino and Indochinese rice growers. Those, they were given to understand, were only a tiny fraction of the successful ventures of the agency. Those were the blown ones, where the Other Side, or more often the Other Sides, knew what had happened. There were still huger projects that had never been detected. And that, they understood, because they were told so day after day, with relentless insistence, was the Optimal Project: to do something that weakened some part of the rest of the world relative to the United States without ever being found out.

And, of course, at the same time the Other Sides were doing all they possibly could to the United States. The water lilies that were choking out every slow-moving stream in the Northeast, the "Hell, No, I Won't Mow!" revolt of condominium owners in Florida, the California stoop-labor strikes and the truckers' go-slow that jointly had kept fresh vegetables rotting in the fields and warehouses while consumers paid triple prices for canned goods —all had been traced to foreign intervention, playing the Team's game from the other side of the board. They were doing it now. Even under the microwave antenna, even fresh and new to the Southwest as he was, Hake could see that the sparse grass was browning and dying. The Other Side, they said, was cloudnapping again, projecting bromide smoke into the big cumulus over the Pacific and stealing their rain before it ever reached America.

Perhaps Hake's microfiches could have told him when the game had begun, if he had had time to read them. Peer as hard as he could into the future, he could not see where it all would end.

Even Southwest Texas got cold at two in the morning. Surprising cold, mean cold. Overhead the ten thousand Texas stars winked through the moaning wire, and the north wind that strummed the rectenna froze Hake at the same time. And froze Tigrito and Mary Jean and Sister Florian and the two Hawaiian ladies; they were worse off than Hake, not being New Jersey-bred. Deena Fairless seemed comfortable enough, but then she was the one who had rousted them all out of bed at midnight for this training exercise. She had had time to prepare for the night march—including, Hake was pretty sure, wool socks and thermal underwear.

Mary Jean, propped against the same three-cornered pillar as Hake, wriggled closer to him. He did not suppose that it was affection. She was a long way from Louisiana. What she was after was warmth. Nevertheless he glanced at Deena, who said, "Stay awake, that's all." But Hake's problem was not sleepiness. Hake's problem was that Deena had shattered one of the truly fine erotic dreams of his recent memory when she came in with her flashlight and twisted him awake by the toe. He still wasn't quite out of it. Mary Jean certainly did not smell like a dream girl—

more like a real one who had been worked hard and bathed insufficiently—but some synapse, cell or process in his brain unerringly identified a yin for his yang, and the real person drowsing against his shoulder merged with the dream one he had abandoned so reluctantly.

"Stay awake, I said!"

"Sorry, Deena," Mary Jean apologized, shifting to a more alert posture. "When are we going to get moving?"

"When it's clear."

"When will it be clear?"

"When Tiger comes back and tells us so." Deena hesitated, then said, "Move around if you want to. Keep your voices down." They were in an arroyo that bent sharply just ahead of them; good cover from sight, as the sighing wire overhead was good cover for sound. At this point the antenna was at least seventy feet above them, but Hake could see it as a winking tracery of scarlet spiderwebs, faint but clear, as it reflected the pulse of the radar corner beacons. In fact, it was astonishing how much he could see by starlight, now that his eyes had had two hours to adapt. Deena Fairless was unscrewing what looked like a huge tube of toothpaste, head cocked in concentration, squeezing out a dab of what it contained onto her finger.

"What's that?" asked Beth Hwa, sitting cross-legged, spine straight and alert.

"That's what we're going to stick up a cow's ass," said Deena. There was the sort of silence that follows a wholly unsuccessful joke, until Deena said, "No kidding. That's the job for tonight. We're going to move in on the three-five herd, locate the heifers and smear some of this on their, excuse the medical terms, their private parts. I don't mean rectums, I mean vaginas. But if you can't figure out which is which you have to do both."

The silence protracted itself, but changed in kind; now it was the silence that surrounds a group of persons wondering if somebody was playing a very bad joke of which they were the butt. Deena chuckled. "It's a simulation," she explained. "Represents an actual operation, of which you may, or may not, hear more before you leave here."

"Some operation," snarled Sister Florian.

"Well, you're excused from that part," said Deena. "You're going to be our lookout."

"I don't need to be excused from anything," the nun said angrily. "I'm only saying I hate it."

"Sure you do. But you'll thank me for it some day. Why, the time will come when you'll all look back on these good times Under the Wire and say— Hold it!"

A loose stone slid down the arroyo slope, followed by Tigrito, sulking back from his patrol. "No cowboys anywhere I could see," he reported. "Hey, man. Let me get some of that heat." He sat down next to Mary Jean on the other side, and put his arm around her.

"What about the herd? Did you find them?"

"Oh, sure, man. Nice and sleepy, 'bout half a mile away."

"Then we go. You too, Tiger. On your feet, Mary Jean, and from now on no talking. Tiger leads, I go last. When he has the herd in sight he stops and you all take a handful of this gunk and start smearing."

"How do we tell which is a heifer? In fact, what's a heifer?"

"If you can't tell you just do them all. Move out, Tiger. Glasses on, everybody."

Through the IR spectacles Hake saw the scene transformed. There was residual heat in the slope of the hill, so that they were moving over dully glowing rocks; Tigrito, ahead of him, was bright hands and head moving around a much darker torso, and the wire overhead was a dazzle of bright spots, obscuring the stars. He could not even see the red and blue-green laser beacons through it, and when he took his eyes away it took some time to adjust to the relative darkness. It was a long, hard downhill crawl, then a harder uphill scramble. There the top of a ridge had been shaved away to accommodate the rectenna and the wire was no more than ten feet above the ground. They all walked stooped and half-crouched across the ridge and didn't straighten out until they were sliding down the loose fill the bulldozers had pushed onto the other side. It was said that touching the rectenna might not kill. None of them wanted to find out.

The three-eighths buffalo–five-eighths cattle hybrid herd was resting peacefully at the bottom of the slope, uninterested in the human beings creeping toward them. The three-fives were bred for stupidity as well as for meat and milk, and the breeding had been successful all around. What they liked to eat was the blossom from yucca—which is why, Hake learned, the yucca's other name was "buffalo grass"—and on that diet they fattened to slaughter size in three years.

Deena gathered the troops around her and, one by one, squeezed a sticky, oily substance into each palm, and waved them toward the herd. They picked their way down the sliding, uneasy surface. Hake slipped and fell, and as he recovered himself he heard Tigrito whine, "Hey, man! You wasn't here before!"

A bright light overwhelmed the IR lenses—Deena's; it showed a man in a stetson and levis, pointing a gun at Tigrito. "Got ya," the man crowed. "Y'under arrest, ever' one of you, get your hands up!"

Mean rage filled Hake's skull. The bastard had a gun! If Hake had had one of his own— He didn't finish the thought, but his fingers were curling around a trigger that wasn't there. And he wasn't alone. Tigrito, still whining and complaining, was moving slowly toward the man; and behind the cowboy, Sister Florian reached out for his throat. Not quietly enough; the man half heard her and started to turn, and Tigrito launched himself on him, bowled him to the ground. The gun went flying, Tigrito's hand rose and fell.

And it was all over. Tigrito rose to his knees, still holding the rock he had caught up to bash the man's skull with. "Did I kill the fucker?" he demanded.

Deena was bending over him with the light. "Not yet, anyway. Hellfire. All right, let's get on with it. Sister, you stay here and keep an eye on him. The rest of you, go get those cows!"

What Hake retained longest of the incident was a startling fact. He had been willing to kill the cowboy. If he had been asked the question as a theoretical matter, before the fact, he would have denied the possibility emphatically. Ridiculous! He had no reason. He had nothing against the man. There was no real stake riding on the incident. He was certainly not a killer! But when the moment came, he knew that if he had had a gun he would have pulled the trigger.

Actually, the man had not died. They had gone about their farcical task of slapping goo under the cattle's tails, and then taken turns to carry the still unconscious man all the long way Under the Wire to the barracks. As far as Hake knew, he was alive still; at least he had been when the truck from Has-Ta-Va carried him away with a concussion and possible skull fracture, but breathing. The six of them looked at each other in the barracks, hands, faces and clothes smeared with green paint—it was not until they reached the lighted dugout that they knew what Deena had spread in their palms. As Hake fell into bed, for the forty-five minutes before reveille, he thought there might be repercussions. He also thought he knew what had been so strange about the expressions on the faces of all his comrades. They had all been very close to grinning.

But in the morning, when Fortnum fell them out in the pre-dawn light, no word was said about the incident. They ran their mile, swilled down their breakfast, spent their hour on the obstacle course and showed up for Deena's class in computer-bugging. After ten minutes of drill on the nomenclature of the machine Hake could not stand it any more. "Deena," he said, "how is the guy?"

She paused between "bit" and "byte" and looked at him thoughtfully. "He'll be all right," she said at last.

"Are we in trouble?"

"You're always in trouble until you get out of this place," she said. "No special trouble that the Team can't handle. It's happened before."

The whole group knew about what had happened, and one of the ones who had stayed behind put his hand up. "Deena, what the hell were you-all doing out there, anyway?"

Deena glanced at her watch. "Well— Tell you what. Pegleg's off with the plane, Fortnum's gone to pick up supplies and I have to make a report. I'm going to leave you on your own for, let's see, ninety minutes. Only, so you shouldn't waste your time, you've got two assignments, with prizes for the winners. First, see if you can figure out what the exercise was last night. Second, I want each one of you to think up an Agency project. You'll be judged on originality, practicality and effectiveness, and so you'll know it's fair I'm going to let Fortnum do the judging."

"How do we find out about the exercise?" asked Beth Hwa.

"That's your problem," Deena said agreeably.

"What are the prizes?" Hake asked.

"That's easy. Everybody but the first prize-winner in each category gets punishment duty. So long; you've got eighty-eight minutes left."

They had never been on their own before in the middle of the day, were not sure how to handle it. A dozen of the group drifted toward the scuba pool, Hake included; included also, most of the six who had gone on the exercise. The reasons had nothing to do with the problems. It was a way of getting some of the paint residue off, and a way, too, of waking up that underslept part of their brains that wanted more than anything else to crawl back into the bunkhouse. They stripped down to the all-purpose underwear and quenched themselves in the tepid and stagnant water.

Then the guessing began.

"Maybe we were practicing how to immobilize, I don't know, cavalry or something. With like sleeping drugs."

"Shee-it, man! What cavalry?"

"Well—race horses, maybe. Sometimes they give you anesthetics through an enema, don't they?"

"Or maybe it was going to be some kind of poison, to kill off somebody's beef supplies."

"Come on, Beth! You think the Team'd send people around to massage ten or twenty million cows' asses? Wait a minute. Maybe in a real job it wouldn't be paint but—I don't know. Honey? And it would attract flies, and they'd spread disease—?"

Fanciful ideas. The group seemed to generate a lot of them. Sprawled in the sun, under the shadeless wire, Hake's tired brain was not up to the task of trying to guess whether any of those ideas were more fanciful than what he already knew the Team had done. Sitting near him, Mary Jean leaned over and whispered in his ear. "You got any better ideas?" He shook his head. "Then maybe we should start on the other project, I mean thinking up a real job. Wait a minute, I've got some paper."

While she was rummaging in her shoulder bag Hake leaned back and closed his eyes, letting the talk drift over him. Some of the things they had guessed as explanations for the mission last night might work as project proposals, he thought. They were still going at it avidly—as though each and every one of them had taken it as a personal challenge. How had they all become so bloodthirsty?

"—some kind of irritating acid, make them stampede—"

"—constipate them till they bloat up and die—"

"—smells bad to the bulls, or, hey! Maybe bulls get turned off by green paint!"

"No, wait a minute, Tigrito. Look at it the other way. Suppose it was some kind of chemical that interfered with intercourse. Maybe made the bull lose its, uh, erection."

The Hawaiian woman sat up straight. "Better idea!" she cried. "Why waste it on bulls? I'm going to try that out for the other assignment: some kind of chemical that you give women, I don't know, put it in their food maybe, that sterilizes them. Or makes them unattractive to men."

"Or it wouldn't have to be a chemical, Beth," said the black professor. "Subsidize the fashion industry, get them to go back to the bustle or the maxiskirt or something like that."

"Or better! How about starting a back-to-religion thing? Get all the women to become nuns."

The professor said thoughtfully, "That actually happened, you know, back in the Middle Ages. So many people taking vows of celibacy that the French kings got worried about the population drop. Only that would take pretty long to be effective—twenty or thirty years before it mattered much, and who knows what the world would be like then?—Oh, hi, Sister. We were just talking about nuns—"

Sister Florian sat down, looking pleased with herself. "I heard what you were talking about." Her usually severe face was conspicuously good-humored.

"Okay, Sister," said Tigrito. "You got something goin' for you. What is it? You figure out what we was up to last night?"

"No," she said cheerfully, "I didn't figure it out. I *found* it out. You all took off and left me alone with the computer. I gave it the unlock command and ordered it to look up Team projects involving large-mammal genital areas."

"Come off it, Sister! How'd you do that?"

"Well, I set up a matrix of large-mammal genitals, chemical or biological agents, Team projects—"

"No, no! I mean about the unlock command."

She smiled sunnily. "I watch what she does, Tigrito. She types out the date of the month, plus two, and then her own last name. Then it's open. So I did exactly the same thing. It took it a little while to hunt, but it came up with equine gonorrhea."

"Equine gonorrhea?"

"There was an epidemic of it in America back in the 70s. Now there's a new strain that's infectious for all large mammals, and antibiotic-resistant, too. I guess what we're going to do, some of us, sometimes, is infect breed cows, so that they'll infect stud bulls, so we'll knock out a big chunk of a cattle-breeding program. Somewhere. My own guess is maybe Argentina. Maybe England or Australia? Could be anywhere. Anyway," she said, "I wrote it all down and time-stamped it and left it on Deena's desk, so that's that." And she folded her hands in her lap and beamed around at them.

But Hake was no longer listening. A chain of associations had formed in his mind. Nuns. Convents. People flocking to religious orders. A back-to-religion movement. He began to write quickly with the stub of a pencil Mary Jean had provided him: "Religious leaders like Sun Myung Moon, Indian gurus, Black Muslims and others have effectively taken significant numbers of persons out of the work force in America. Proposal: Charismatic religious leaders be identified and evaluated. Where they may be effective they can be subsidized or—"

He pulled his feet back just in time to avoid having them stepped on as Tigrito, stalking furiously around the scuba pool, stopped in front of him. The youth grinned down at Mary Jean. "Hey, let's pick up where we left off," he said, clumping himself down between them. Hake instinctively made room as the boy took Mary Jean into his arms.

"Watch it," Hake said irritably.

"Oh, man! I *am* watchin' it, been watchin' it a long time, now I'm ready for touchin' it and squeezin' it— Shit, lady!" He went sprawling into Hake's lap as Mary Jean's elbow, traveling no more than eight inches, got him just under the ribs. Hake shoved him away.

"Fuck off, Tigrito," said Mary Jean.

"Yeah," said Hake. The youth glared at him, then rolled to his feet and came up with his arms spread and curved.

"Lady tells me to fuck off, that's her business," he said, moving toward Hake. "Ain't yours, mother-fucker."

Hake was on his feet by then too, his arms automatically responding by coming to the grappling position, but he took a shuffling half-step back. It wasn't really his fight, he told himself. If anyone's, Mary Jean's, who could handle it fine by herself.

"Chicken-shit too," jeered Tigrito, and feinted a kick at Hake's belly.

Hake had an immense respect for Tigrito as a brawler, having lost a dozen falls to him in the ritualized hand-to-hand on the training field. But the part of his mind that evaluated and weighed was not operative then. When Tigrito's foot came up Hake sidestepped and caught it; as Tigrito spilled backward he gripped Hake's arms and pulled him over his head, flying; Hake twisted in mid-air and kneed the boy in the chin. In ten seconds it was all over, Hake kneeling on the boy's chest and lifting his head to thump it on the rough cement.

"Dear God," came Deena's voice from behind. "Leave you guys alone for a few minutes and what do I find? Hold it right there, killer. Fight's over. You're all on punishment detail tonight."

When he finally reached his bed that midnight Hake was so exhausted that sleep was out of reach. He tossed for a while and then stumbled into the latrine to write his compulsory postcards. One for Jessie Tunman, a picture of a gorge on the Pecos River: *Having a fine time, getting a lot of rest, see you soon.* One to go on the church bulletin board: *Miss you all, but will be back full of energy for the church year;* that was a picture of a herd of three-five hybrids, with a cowboy in a helicopter moseyin' them along. They were each supposed to send three postcards a week, but Hake had fought it out and got the number reduced. He didn't have three people to send postcards to. Apart from the church, he hardly had anybody.

Crawling back to his bed, he wondered what the church would have thought of their battling minister that day, street-fighting with a barrio kid. Alys, at least, might have been delighted. And it would be very nice to have Alys delighted, in some ways, he thought, tossing angrily and very aware of Mary Jean's tiny snores two bunks away. He counted up. He had been Under the Wire for eleven days. It seemed longer. He was not exactly the same person who had flown west from Newark. He was not at all sure what person he was, but the old Reverend Hake would not have brawled over a woman.

And the twelfth day, and the thirteenth day, and the fourteenth day came and went, and everything outside the state of Texas receded farther and farther from his thoughts. The people who mattered were Deena and Tigrito and Beth Hwa and Sister Florian and Pegleg and Mary Jean, especially Mary Jean. On the fifteenth day, behind the bunkhouse, they kissed. There was no conversation. He simply followed her around the building. When she turned, his hands were on her. For three or four minutes their tongues were wild in each other's mouths; and then he released her and they trotted to the lecture on *ChemAgents, Use of.*

Hake's glands were aflame, and concentration on Pegleg's drone wasn't easy. When Hake became conscious of the youth's suspicious glower he sat up straighter and tried to get Mary Jean (not to mention Alys and Leota and the nurse from International Pets and Flowers) out of his mind. "You got these agents," Pegleg droned, staring at Hake while he drummed on his artificial limb, "and you will be conversant with your use of them when you leave here, any questions? Right."

Thankfully, one of the others was smothering a yawn and Pegleg's glare was diverted. Hake listened, trying to square what the instructor was saying with what he had been told was basic gospel. The Team's charter did not permit the taking of human life. All the instructors had emphasized that. Other kinds of life, though, were not protected, and Pegleg seemed to be giving them guidelines for extermination. "You take your agent V-12," he was droning, "along with your Agent V-34 and you dump them in a pond, any questions? Right. Next day you have a solution of your O-ethyl S-diethylaminoethyl methylphosphonothiolate, what you used to call your Agent VM, any questions? These here quantities are adjusted to your average barnyard pond of 100,000 gallons and produce your concentration of zero point two parts per million, which will kill your fish and your frogs and your small mammals, any questions?" He gazed challengingly at them, drumming on his leg. "Right. Your concentration increases with time," he said, "and so after the first day it becomes toxic to your larger mammals as well."

He rose painfully to his feet and limped over to the blackboard. "That's for your what you call your aqueous dispersants," he said, beginning to draw what looked like a bowling ball, pierced on either side with fingerholes. "Now this here," he said, "is your schematic of these here little things in the dish. Come up one at a time and take a look." When it was Hake's turn, he saw half a dozen tiny pellets in a glass petri dish. He had to squint to see them; they were no more than a sixteenth of an inch in diameter. He could not see the holes at all. "These here," droned Pegleg, "are your pellets for your spring-loaded or your carbon-dioxide-propelled devices, like your Bulgarian Brolly and your Peruvian Pen. Your pellets are platinum. Each of your little holes—" he pointed to the diagram on the blackboard—"will take two-tenths of a microliter of Chem-Agent, whatever you put in them. Anybody want to guess what that is?"

Tigrito waved a hand. "Arsenic?" he ventured.

Pegleg gave him a glare of contempt. "Arsenic! You got to have a hundred milligrams anyway to do any good with *arsenic;* you got two hours' latrine duty for dumbness. No. There's three things could go in there. You can use your biologicals, like germs. Or you can use your plutonium-239, only then they can find your pellet easy with a radiation detector. Best thing is one of your neurotoxins in your phosphate-buffered gelatin, any questions?"

"How do you get anyone to swallow it," Beth Hwa asked uncertainly.

"You got two hours too, who said anything about swallowing it?" Pegleg reached under the table and brought out what looked like an ordinary brightly colored woman's umbrella. "This is your Bulgarian Brolly. There's a spring-loaded gun in the shaft. You put your pellet in, load the spring, point it at the, uh, the subject and push the button. If you poke the, uh, animal with the Brolly while you push the button all he feels is the poke from the umbrella.

"Or," he went on, stooping to pick up a large ballpoint pen, "this here is your Peruvian Pen. It's gas loaded. You charge it with your ordinary CO_2 soda-water capsule. It hasn't got the range of a Brolly. And it won't go through, like, clothes, unless you give it a double charge, and then it makes more noise. It takes your average, uh, subject about four or five days to die, because the stuff has to get out of the pellet and into his bloodstream. So you can be long gone. Other side of it is, it's no good to stop anybody fast, any questions?"

Hake raised his hand. "I thought the charter of the Team didn't allow killing human beings?"

"You got two hours too. Who said anything about human beings?"

"You said it would go through clothes."

"I meant like a horse blanket," the instructor explained. "Or like fur. But that's not to say," he went on darkly, "that the Other Side wouldn't use these same things on *you*. It was the Bulgarians invented the Brolly in the first place, and they didn't use it on no Airedales. You stick around, Hake. I got some little jobs for you besides the latrines. Any questions?"

But even the little extra jobs passed, and on the sixteenth day the whole crew was assigned to spraying defoliant on the three-five pasture—the animals cropped the yucca so heavily that every once in a while the inedible plants had to be killed off, to give the "buffalo grass" a chance to come back. By the time they came back Hake had solved his sexual problem, and so had Mary Jean. Wolfing down their food that night they sat touching on the wooden bench. Deena was amused. Sister Florian was tolerant. Tigrito was sulky. And Beth Hwa, that quiet, middle-aged wife of an avocado shipper from Hilo, intercepted Mary Jean on the way out of the mess hall and handed her something. Mary Jean showed it to Hake, grinning; it was a pillbox. "In case we got caught short," she explained.

The remainder of the three weeks began to look more attractive. But on the seventeenth day Fortnum told them the Congressional Oversight Committee was coming around for its annual inspection, and they all better look sharp, and that night everything was changed. Pegleg tucked them in with the news that there was going to be a special assignment for the morrow, and in the morning he told them what it was:

"This is not, repeat not, a training mission," he singsonged. "This is the real thing. You will be given full gear for an extended stay in the open, and the whole class is going to participate. Five of you will go by plane to Del Rio. The rest will be trucked to Big Bend National Park. We gonna have ourselves a wetback hunt!"

"Wetbacks?"

"Hell, yes, Tigrito! You ought to know what a wetback is. Got too many Mexes coming in and taking our jobs, you know? And it's up to us to stop them."

Hake said, "Wait a minute. I thought the presidential directive limited us to actions outside the United States."

"Shit, man. They *come* from outside the United States, don't they? You're never gonna get anyplace on the Team, you keep coming up with stuff like that. Now, you listen to me. We're going to go down to the border and we're going to make friends with the wetbacks. Then we're going to track back to find out where they're coming in, and track forward to where they're going. Any of you do good, you'll likely get yourselves sent to St. Louis and Chicago and maybe even New York to find where they're going there. There's not going to be no direct action against them, that's for the Immigration. We're just going to locate them and get the evidence. That's good duty. So don't fuck it up."

Ten minutes to pack. They looked at each other, and Tigrito announced that he was going to get to Chi if he had to kill for it, and Sister Florian suspected that it was all just a scheme to get them out of the way while the Oversight Committee inspected the installation, and Hake and Mary Jean tried to estimate their chances of being on the same truck. Or plane. But, in the event, Hake never saw the wonders of wetback life in the big cities. Just as the trucks were about to leave he was pulled off the detachment and ordered to the office of the training director and there, sitting on a wicker chair on the second-floor porch of the main building of Has-Ta-Va Ranch, talking on a hush-phone, was hairy, fidgety Curmudgeon, his gun strapped to his side.

"I didn't expect to see you here," said Hake.

"Course you didn't," said Curmudgeon, putting down the phone. "You're going back to Europe."

"I am? Why am I? What have you got for me to spread this time, leprosy?"

Curmudgeon looked at him thoughtfully. "Leprosy? Oh, no, Hake, that wouldn't be any good. Hard to infect anybody. And the incubation period's much too long. That job you did last month, that was the kind of thing. Did you know German absenteeism's up eighty percent for the month? And, naturally," he said, "our laboratories have just announced a real breakthrough in immunization. We've got enough material for sixty million shots right now. We're selling it all over the world, and making a nice few bucks for the balance of payments. But anyway, that kind of thing was only your first mission, Hake. You couldn't really be expected to do anything independently. No. But now we think you're ready for the big time, and I really liked your religion proposal."

It took Hake a second to remember the project he had been outlining next to the scuba pool, just before his fight with Tigrito. He had turned it in and heard no more about it. "I—I didn't think anyone paid any attention to it."

"Hell, yes, Hake! It's a fascinating idea. If we could find a European Sun Myung Moon, or even some good messianic leader, why, we'd back him to the hilt. There are new sects springing up in Europe all the time. The important thing is somebody who has enough personal charisma to make a good pitch. Any thoughts on what sort of thing we should look for?"

"Well— Actually," Hake said, warming up, "I did think more about it. It would be good to find someone with a special appeal to industrial workers. Or miners."

"That's the idea, Hake!"

"Of course, I'd need some research facilities, to look up proselytizing religions—"

"Sure you would, but not now. You won't have time. You've got to catch a bus out on the highway in two hours. Then you'll fly to Capri."

"Capri? What the hell do I want in Capri?"

"That's what the orders say," Curmudgeon explained. "You'll be met. When you get there they'll tell you why that has to be where you're going."

"But— My books, for research! I'll need them. And clothes. I'm not dressed for a trip to Italy."

"The clothes are all taken care of, Hake. There's somebody in Long Branch packing a suitcase for you right now—we've, you know, arranged a letter with your signature for your housekeeper. The clothes'll be waiting for you when you get there."

"But my church is expecting me back next week! And what about the rest of the training course here?"

"You'll probably be there in a week," said Curmudgeon. "Two or three at most, probably. And as to the course— why, you've just graduated."

VII

Bus to Odessa; prop plane to Dallas-Fort Worth; jet to Rome (where Hake spent ninety minutes racing back and forth on the back of a moped to collect a suitcase); jet to Capodichino Airport; monorail to the Bay; hovercraft to Capri. Hake had left Has-Ta-Va Ranch at two in the afternoon. Fourteen hours and eight time zones later, he was bouncing across the Bay at what local time said was noon but what his interior body clock could not identify at all. What he was sure of was that he was very, very tired. He was also rather close to being seasick. He had not expected a hovercraft ride to be so choppy. Each wave-top slapped fiercely against the bottom of the vessel, and his queasiness was not helped, as he landed, by the fact that the hovership terminal stank of rotting fish.

As promised, he was met. A young woman in a black ruffled shirt and black velvet cut-offs pushed her way past the would-be guides and the vendors of Capri bells and said, "Father Hake? Yes? Give me the ticket for your bag, please. I will meet you at the car park."

Her voice seemed familiar to Hake, and so did her soup-bowl hairdo. But in his precarious condition he could not identify her. When she arrived at the car park it was in a three-wheeled electric scooter, open to the air, and any impulse toward conversation was quelled by the noise of the traffic. Capri was hot. Steamy hot and smoggy hot. The fish smell was from tens of thousands of dead little fingerlings floating belly-up in the Bay or washed on the sand, and it stayed with them all through the drive up a precipitous road. Then, at the top of a bluff, they reached a pink stucco hotel, and the smell was less fish and more oil.

The woman marched Hake through the lobby and into an elevator, shushing him until they got to the fifth floor. A Chinese couple was just coming out of a room across from the elevator, and evidently having trouble with the lock. The woman leaped to help them, closed it securely, rattled the knob, returned their key and accepted their thanks, and then let Hake into the room next door. "Get some rest, Father Hake," she advised. "I will call for you in the morning."

She gave him his key, and closed the door behind her.

Hake found himself in a room roughly the size of his parsonage porch in Long Branch, long enough for two normal rooms and with a balcony stretching out into the Italian sun to make it longer. Piggery! It was more luxury than Hake had ever been used to. He detected a faint twinge in the place where he kept his social conscience, while another part of his conscience was telling him that he really should be getting down to thinking about the question of proselytizing religions. But he also found that it was not hard to convince himself that, after more than two weeks Under the Wire, a person was entitled to a little comfort. He kicked off his shoes and explored the room.

The bed was oval, and covered with tasseled red velvet. When Hake sat on the edge of it to rub his feet it gave his bottom no resistance. A water bed! He wound up with his posterior at about ankle level and a rigid board under his knees, and the returning ripples dandled him up and down for minutes. Next to the bed was what looked like the instrument panel of an airplane: buttons, dials, switches. Some were clear enough. The sunburst was for the lights. The stylized figures of a maid and a waiter for calling service. The remote control was for the television set. Others were opaque to Hake's perceptions. But there would be time for that. He switched on the television and lay back on the rippling bed, gratefully chill beneath him after the hot ride from the hoverport.

At that moment the lights and TV went out.

It was not just his room. The liquid-crystal illuminated hotel sign over the reflecting pool was out, too; so was the golden glow-panel over his balcony that recklessly had been going even in the middle of the day. There had been a power failure.

Since power interruptions were so familiar a part of Hake's everyday life he began at once to catalogue what problems it might bring. Lack of heat, not a problem. Lack of reading lights—well, apart from the fact that it was broad daylight outside the window, he was starved for sleep anyhow. Lack of air-conditioning? Maybe that would be a problem. He opened the French doors to the balcony, just in case. Elevators, TV, telephones were no immediate concern of his.

So there was, really, no problem. It seemed a heaven-sent injunction to catch up on his rest. He threw his clothes off, stripped back the velvet spread and summer-thin blanket and in a moment was wholly unconscious on the delightfully cool and quivering bed.

He woke up with the sound of an angry Italian voice bellowing at him, and discovered at once that the cool was no longer delightful.

It was the middle of the night. The lights were on, in his room and outside. The voice was from the television set, which had come on along with the lights and air-conditioner. The breeze outside had turned cool, and the air-conditioner was making it cooler still. In fact, he was freezing. He fumbled the sound of the TV down, and the voice of the Italian man in the commercial, who appeared to be enraged because his wife had put the wrong brand of cheese on his pasta, dwindled to a furious whimper.

Hake puzzled over his watch—the bedside clock was of course useless—and decided that he had slept the clock around. It seemed to be about two in the morning, local time. He did not feel rested, but he was awake and, worse, shivering cold. He managed to get the air-conditioner turned off and the window closed, then climbed back on the bed with thin blanket and stiff spread pulled around him. It was not enough. The water under him sucked the heat away, and there was no heat in the room. Not surprising. Who would have expected to need central heating in Capri in the summer? He told himself that his body warmth would soon enough make the bed comfortable, and to distract himself he tried to decipher what was happening on the television set. It seemed to be showing straight commercials: cheese, wine, then a sports car, then the national lottery; a deodorant, an aphrodisiac (or perhaps just a perfume; but the bulge in the trunks of the handsome male model was pretty explicit), and then what appeared to be an institutional propaganda piece. It showed a young Italian youth, clearly stoned out of his mind. A sad baritone voice-over sighed, *"Ecco, guaio perchè fare così?"* The youth shrugged and giggled. The scene dissolved to the great cellar of a winery. In the vaulted room plastic kegs of wine were tumbling majestically off a conveyor belt, while at the far end of the chamber was a loading dock with a waiting and empty truck. The camera's eye narrowed down on an abandoned forklift truck, alone in the middle of the room. Hake could not understand the sorrowful Italian-language voice-over, but the message was clear enough. The forklift operator was away from his post. The wine was not getting onto the truck. The deduction that the missing operator was the blind-stoned kid was confirmed at once, as the scene changed to the following morning. The young man, no longer stoned, now repentant, stood humbly beside a white-haired man carrying a clipboard. Hake recognized the man at once, him or his double. He had seen him a hundred times on American television, tapping his glasses on a desk as he sold everything from stomach-acid neutralizers to hemorrhoid salve. By the end of the commercial the prodigal forklift operator had cleared away the backlog, the trucks were loaded and rumbling away, and the conveyor belt once more brought in its endless chain of kegs. *Marijuana sì—PCP no*, said the fatherly baritone, as the same legend appeared on the screen.

Interesting enough, but Hake was still freezing. His body warmth was not up to the demands imposed on it by the heat-sink of twelve hundred liters of cold water.

He was still exhausted, but he accepted the fact that there was no way for him to get back to sleep without Something Being Done. He got up and dressed. By and by he began to feel less chilled, but no less sleepy. And every time he lay down on that bed, even through clothes, spread and covers, he could feel the heat soak right out of him into the water.

It was no good.

He turned on the light and opened his bags. The little shoulder-carrier he had brought from Under the Wire had a sweater in it, but as neither it nor he had been washed for some time when he last wore it he was not anxious to put it on. The suitcase Curmudgeon's minion had packed for him in Long Branch had nothing at all. Almost nothing he could wear, in fact. The Agency expediter had packed as full a Capri wardrobe as Hake's closets permitted, but unfortunately had not known that his measurements had changed. No doubt it was Hake's own fault for not throwing out what he could no longer wear. But the shorts, tank tops and sports jackets that had served him well enough as a 145-pound weakling in a wheelchair would no longer go around him, and the few newer garments were not warm.

Still, as long as he was up and moving about he was warm enough. And as long as he was awake he might as well be doing something.

Among the other things he had brought from Under the Wire were his microfiches—musty, dinged at the edges, but no doubt still serviceable if he could find something to read them with. Was there a fiche scanner on the television set?

There was. The instructions varnished to the top of the set were unfortunately in Italian, but the mechanism looked simple enough. What he also found was that the television set was a lot fancier than any he had seen in Long Branch. There was also something described as *Solo per persone mature—film interattivo.* It appeared to have a handset controlling it, but it did nothing at all until he realized that the coin slot next to it needed to be fed. It was just the right size for a *cinquenta lire nuove* piece, and immediately he had inserted the coin the broadcast channel disappeared and was replaced by an extremely good-looking Oriental girl reclining in the pose of the Naked Maja.

Technically the set was astonishing. Hake by trial and error found that the handset would let him view a whole catalogue of nude women, and men, too; that another control on the set allowed him to rotate the figure and zoom in and out on any desired part; and even that he could bring two figures together and manipulate them around each other. While he was trying to discover whether the picture showed them actually in contact or merely superimposed photographically his coin ran out and the screen went dark.

That had been interesting, also somewhat unsettling. Hake got up and explored the rest of the room's facilities. Under the TV was something called *Servizio,* which turned out to be a little refrigerator and bar stocked with whiskey, wine, fruit juices and beer. He thought for a moment of getting drunk enough to supply French central heating and going back to sleep; but that way, he suspected, lay pneumonia. Still, one beer wasn't a bad idea. Carrying it, he checked out the bathroom. The toilet seat vibrated on command, he found. The shower head pulsed, and so, he discovered, did the spray in the bidet. Behind a panel near the door was a coffee maker and a bun warmer, and when he sat on the edge of the still chill bed to drink a cup of hot coffee he kicked something and found that the bed, too, could be made to ripple rhythmically by pushing a switch. Quite an inventive room.

It was not, however, a room to be alone in. Everything urged company, and Hake didn't have any.

What was worse, one of the girls on the television had reminded him of Mary Jean. He sat daydreaming of Mary Jean as a possible subject for *film interattivo,* and then of Alys, and of Leota, and realized he had a problem. It was a problem most men face, some of them very often, but

Hake growing up in a wheelchair had learned to sublimate and to repress that problem, and the new Hake, the muscular Hake of the barbells and the two-mile runs, the action-oriented Hake from Under the Wire—that Hake was a different person. That Hake wanted a different solution, and there was none in sight.

He dumped the rest of the coffee, put his clothes on and ambled out of the room.

The long and silent hall was empty, the ceiling lights economically dimmed down. There was a dank, musty smell that he had not remembered, and a large, semicircular water stain by the Chinese couple's door that he had not noticed before. Rather poor management, he thought; would there be anyone in the lobby? Maybe an all-night coffee shop to get something to eat?

The lobby was also dimmed-down and silent, but he managed to wake the desk clerk long enough to get change, and from the automatic vending machines he got candy bars, a Rome *Daily American*, and even an Arabic-language daily published in Naples. Then he returned to his room.

Reminding himself that he was not in Capri for pleasure, he pulled the covers off the bed and spent the next hour reading and eating candy bars, lying on the floor. After an hour or so he made the trip down to the lobby again for some fifty-lire change and ultimately fell asleep, with the light on, on the floor.

At ten the door buzzer woke him.

The room was now intolerably hot, and his bones ached from the floor, but he opened the door. It looked like the girl who had met him at the hoverport, but was not. It was male. "Mario?" he guessed.

The youth smirked. "Yes, of course Mario," he said. "But you did not recognize me as a signorina, did you? We must not often be seen together, you see—Hake! What insanity have you been up to?"

"What? Oh, you mean why the room is this way. Well, we had a power failure. And I nearly froze to death on that bed."

Mario's eyebrows rose. He switched on the air-conditioner and said, "Why did you not use the bed heater? What heater? Oh, Hake, you are such an innocent! Here, this switch on the side. You set it to whatever temperature you would like. Thirty-five if you want it, or even more."

"Oh, hell." Now that it was explained, it was perfectly obvious. He dialed it to forty degrees, promising himself at least a nice warm nap. As he straightened up, Mario was approaching him with what looked like an elaborate silver-filigree bracelet. "Hey, what's that for?"

Mario snapped it on his wrist. "So that you may enjoy that bed with the companion of your choice, or with none at all," he said good-humoredly.

"It's a sexual-preference thing? I've never seen it."

"A local custom," Mario explained. "If you wear this it indicates you do not wish anyone to inaugurate a sexual approach to you. See, I also wear one. Without it on, you would be kept quite busy and it would perhaps interfere with your duties. You will find that such bracelets are quite scarce on Capri, for after all why else would anyone come here?"

"Well—" said Hake.

"Oh, do not fear, when you are off duty you may remove it! Now, do you wish to shower, or at least dress?"

"I suppose so. Oh, and listen," Hake said, "I haven't been wasting my time. I managed to get a couple of papers last night, and checked all the stories about religion."

"Very commendable, Hake," Mario said, glancing at his watch.

"There wasn't an awful lot, but there was one stroke of luck. I found an editorial in something called, what is it, *Corriere Islamica di Napoli* about an interesting youth cult. There's this fellow in Taormina—"

"That is splendid, Hake, but please, your shower. We must hurry. Of course you will want a coffee? Then you can tell me all about it. But the taxi is waiting, and my expense account—well, you know what it is like with one's expenses!"

Actually Hake did not know. He had never had an expense account from the Team. But if what Mario had meant to imply was that his expenses would be scrutinized it seemed to Hake strange that they should take a taxi all the way to Anacapri to sit and drink morning coffee in an open-air restaurant exactly like twenty-five others they had passed on the way; and then to take another taxi all the way back to a restaurant that turned out to be a block from Hake's hotel, for the lunch Mario insisted he had to have at the stroke of twelve. It seemed to Hake that Mario was not a very efficient secret agent. In fact, flaky. The Mario of Munich and the rest of the flu-spreading trip had been subdued and deferential; this one was more like a plumbing salesman on a tour.

And when the lunch came Mario picked at it. He was obviously much more interested in the nearly nude dancers in the floor show than in eating. He divided his time between staring at them as they whipped off their peasant skirts to reveal nothing much beneath, and nudging Hake and peering at his face excitedly. Hake felt distinctly uncomfortable. Mario had been much the same on the patio at Anacapri, where bar girls in bikinis had served them their cappuccinos. In neither place did he seem very interested in the Islamic youth cult Hake had boned up on out of the Arab-language newspaper and a few discreet questions to the Lebanese night porter at the hotel.

It all seemed like an awful waste of time to Hake, and the situation did not get better. After the lunch Mario had barely picked at, he said, "Well, perhaps it would be as well for you to rest this afternoon. I will meet you for dinner. And then we will plan our activities for tomorrow."

"What activities? Look, Mario, I came here on a specific mission, and Curmudgeon said it was of the highest priority."

"Ah, Curmudgeon," said Mario, shrugging easily. He took a nail-clipper from his pocket, signaled for the check and began manicuring his already perfect nails. "At Headquarters what do they know of us in the field, eh? You are doing very well, Hake. There is no need to try to impress the home office with your diligence. In our work it is always essential to move with precise knowledge, according to a plan. Speed? Yes, sometimes. But caution and precision, always."

"But—"

"Hush!" Mario gestured at the waiter, coming to bear away check and credit card. "Have the goodness to postpone this conversation to a more opportune time," he said coldly. Then he dropped his napkin—on purpose, as it appeared to Hake—and bent down to retrieve it. There was a quiet but definite sputtering sound from under the table. The lights went out, and Mario sat up, rubbing his fingers.

Hake stared. "Mario! What the hell did you do?"

"I warn you again, Hake, not here! Have they taught you nothing in Texas?" Mario whispered furiously. They sat in angry silence until the waiter returned, carrying check and card, his expression embarrassed. Hake could not understand a word of the Italian, but the sense was clear enough. Due to this wholly unforeseeable interruption to the electricity, the computer was unable to process the credit card.

Mario held his hand up forgivingly. *"Capisco,"* he said. *"Va bene. Ecco—due cento, tre cento, tre cento cinquenta, e basta. Ciao."*

"Grazie, grazie, tanto, arrivederla," said the waiter, clutching the wad of lire gratefully.

And walking along the crowded street, on the short block back to the hotel, Mario said, "Yes, of course it was I. Why do you think I selected that table? There was an electric outlet beneath it for the cleaning. Have you not been taught, it is the little things that add up?"

"And last night in the hotel. Did you do that, too?"

"Of course I did, Hake. Both the electricity and the flooding. I wedged the lock in that room door, and when I left you I turned on their taps, just a trickle, with a washcloth stuffed in the drain. Were you not taught such things?"

"Christ, no." Hake thought silently for a moment. At the steps to the hotel he said, "You know, all that seems pretty chicken-shit to me. You're just annoying people. You're not doing any real damage."

"I see! And that is not worthy of your efforts, Master American Spy? What a pity! But it is exactly this that we must do, on a small scale or large! The lit match in the mailbox. The phone off the hook. The emergency cord pulled in a tram at the rush hour. Each is tiny, but together they are great!"

"But I don't see—"

"But, but, but," said Mario, "always there is a 'but'! I have no time to explain these simple things to you, Hake. I have much to do. Go inside. Swim in the pool, meet some signorinas—you may take off your bracelet, and then you will see! And I will meet you tonight for dinner—and," he twinkled, "perhaps I will have a surprise for you! Now go, I do not wish to be seen too often in your hotel."

But when they met later, Mario's mood had changed again. He drove the three-wheeled Fiat-Idro vengefully along Capri's narrow roads. After ten minutes of it, Hake asked, "Are you going to tell me what you're angry about?"

"Angry? I am not angry!" Mario snapped over the noise of the wind. And then, relenting, "Well, perhaps I am. I have had sad news. Dieter is in jail."

"That's too bad," Hake said, although in his heart he was not moved. "What's he in for?"

"For the usual thing, of course! For doing his job."

Mario drove in silence for some minutes, and then, surprisingly, his face cleared. Hake stared around to see why. They were passing through an olive grove, where crews of Ethiopian laborers were cutting down trees, stacking them and burning them. The smoke drifted unpleasantly across the road. It was a hot evening anyway; the wisps of steam from the Fiat's exhaust vanished almost at once into the air, and the laborers were glistening with sweat. But Mario seemed pleased. "At least some things go well," he said obscurely. "Now observe, we are almost there."

Their destination turned out to be an open-air *trattoria* on the brink of a precipice. They drove under a vine-covered arch, atop it a bright liquid-crystal sign that showed what looked like an ancient Roman peasant being shampooed with a huge fish. The name of the place was *La Morte del Pescatore*. Mario tossed the Fiat's keys to a parking attendant, and led the way between tables and waiters to a banquette overlooking the cliff.

And there, beaming at them, was Yosper.

"Well, Hake!" he said, rising to shake hands from the meal he had not waited to start, "so we meet again! Are you surprised?"

Hake sat down and spread his napkin on his lap before he answered. When he had seen Yosper last it had been in Munich, along with Mario and Dieter and the other two young thugs who had accompanied him; and none of them had responded by word or hint to any of his overtures about the Team.

"Not really," he said at last.

"Of course you weren't," Yosper agreed heartily. "I knew you understood we were part of the gang in Germany."

"Then why didn't you say something?"

"Oh, come on, Hake! Didn't they teach you anything in Texas? All information is on a need to know basis, that's doctrine. There was no need for you to know; you were doing fine without it. And declassifying is *always* contra-indicated when it might jeopardize a mission. Which it could have; who knew what you might take it into your head to do? The whole point of what you were doing was that you were a simple man of God, doing the Lord's work in Europe. What better cover could you have than to believe it yourself?" He raised a hand to forestall Hake. "And then, of course," he said, "that was just your first training mission. We all do a blind one first. That's doctrine, too. Can't expect special treatment, can you, Horny?"

"Can Dieter expect special treatment?" Mario put in sullenly.

"Oh, Mario, please. You know that Dieter will be taken care of. A few days, a week or two at the most—we'll have him out of there. Don't we always?"

"We don't always get put in a Neapolitan jail," Mario responded sulkily.

"*That's enough.*" There was a distinct silence, and then Yosper continued on sunnily, "Now, as I'm well ahead of you, why don't you both order? There's excellent seafood here. Though not, of course, local."

After a moment, Mario began ordering methodically from the most expensive items on the menu. He did not meet Yosper's eyes, but the old man was only looking amused. Hake settled for a *fritto misto* and a salad, unwilling to load his stomach in the heat. When the waiter had gone, he said, "Is it all right to talk here?"

"We have been, haven't we? Don't worry. Mario will let us know if anyone is pointing a microphone at us."

"Then let me tell you what I've done about our project. I told Mario that last night I found some interesting leads in the newspapers. This afternoon I went to the American Library and did a little research. There's useful stuff. The most interesting is a new Islamic cult that preaches a return to purity, no intercourse with infidels, four wives to a man, instant divorce—for men, of course—and all the rest. Just like Mahmoud himself. It's not here on Capri. It's mostly in a place called Taormina, but there's also a center in a town named Benevento. According to the map, that's up in the hills, not very far from Naples."

Yosper nodded judiciously, mopping up his *salsa verde* with a chunk of bread. "Yes, that sounds promising," he conceded.

"It sounds like just what I'm supposed to be looking for!" Hake corrected. "Or almost. I'm not sure that Curmudgeon wanted me to get involved with Islam. I got the impression that he was thinking more of some fundamentalist Christian sort of sect— What's the matter?"

Yosper had put down his bread and was scowling fiercely. "I don't want to hear blasphemy," he snapped.

"What blasphemy? It's the operation I'm assigned to, Yosper. My orders are—"

"Fuck your orders, Hake! You are not going to despoil the word of God. Stay with your Mohammedans, who the hell cares about their false idols? Don't mess with your sweet Redeemer!"

"Now, wait a minute, Yosper. What do you think I'm doing here?"

"Following orders!"

"Whose orders?" Hake demanded hotly. "Yours? Cur-

mudgeon's? Or am I supposed to make up my own little
trick-or-treat pranks like Mario, blowing fuses and setting
fire to mailboxes?"

"You are supposed to do what you're told to do by the
officer in charge, which in this case is me."

"But this mission—" Hake stopped himself as the waiter
approached, wheeling a table with a solid-alcohol lamp
under a huge chrome bowl. By the time the waiter and the
maître d' had finished collaborating on Mario's fettuccine
Alfredo, Hake had a grip on himself.

"All right," he said. "How about this? Suppose I found
some Christian revivalist to preach abstinence, to cut the
population down? I know it would be slow, but—"

Mario chuckled. "In *Italy?*"

"Yes, in Italy. Or anywhere. Perhaps it shouldn't be
abstinence but birth-control, or even homosexuality—"

Mario was no longer laughing. "That's not funny."

"I don't mean it to be funny!"

"Then," said Mario, "it's funny. Grotesque, even. Not
the homosexuality, but your bigoted, out-of-date attitude
toward male love." He had stopped eating, and the look on
his face was hostility and wrath.

Yosper intervened. "You two quit fighting," he ordered.
"Eat your dinner." And after a moment he began a conversation with Mario in Italian.

Hake ate in silence, averting his eyes from both of his
table companions. They did not seem to mind. Their conversation appeared to be about the food, the wine, the
models who moved around the restaurant displaying furs,
jewels and bathing suits—about anything and everything
that didn't include Hake. It was a lot like it had been in
Germany, and Hake was beginning to have a bad feeling.
What was going on? Once again, the situation did not add
up. The mission that had been top-priority urgent in Texas
did not seem to matter at all on Capri. What was he carrying this time?

For that matter, what was he doing in Italy at all? He
did not fit into this expensive restaurant filled with the idle
rich, or with the rich corrupt: Ex-oil sheiks in burnooses,
black American dope kings, Calcutta slumlords and East-

ern European film stars. Hake had not realized there was so much money in the world. Mario's fettuccine cost as much as a week's shopping at the A&P in Long Branch, and the bottle of Château Lafite he was washing it down with would have made a sizeable down payment on repainting the parsonage porch. Not just the money. Energy! He had become calloused to power-piggery, with all the jet fuel he had burned for the Team, but this! The illuminated sign outside the restaurant alone would have kept his heater going for weeks. And it was not even in good taste. The liquid crystal display showed a man in Roman peasant costume either trying to snap at a huge fish or trying to avoid it: the fish moved in toward his face, the man's head bobbed away, and back and forth again.

Yosper leaned over and said, "Got over your bad mood?" He didn't wait for an answer. "There's a story behind that sign, you know."

"I was sure there would be," Hake said.

"Oh, come off it, will you? We've got to work together. Let's make it easy on ourselves."

Hake shrugged. "What's the story?"

"Um. Well, one of the Roman emperors used to live around here, and he took walks along this cliff. One day a fisherman climbed up from the beach to make his emperor a present of a fish he had just caught. It didn't work out very well. The emperor was pissed off at being startled, so he ordered his guard to rub the fish in the man's face."

"He sounds like a mean son of a bitch," Hake observed.

"That's about the nicest thing you could say about him, actually. That was Tiberius. He's the one who crucified our Lord, or anyway appointed Pontius Pilate, who did. There's more to it. The fisherman wasn't real smart, and when the guard let him up he wised off. He said, 'Well, I'm glad I tried to give the fish to you instead of the other thing I caught.' 'Let's see the other thing he caught,' Tiberius said, and the guard opened up the bag, and it was a giant crab. So Tiberius had the guard give him a massage with *that*, and the fisherman died of it."

"Nice place," Hake said.

"It has its points," said Yosper, eyeing two models displaying lingerie. "I hope you've been paying attention to them. Well! How about a sweet? They do a beautiful crêpes suzette here."

"Why not?" said Hake. But that wasn't the real question; the question was *why?* And how? What was the purpose of this silly charade, and where did the money come from? Especially bearing in mind Mario's remarks about his expense account, what could possibly justify the tab they were running up in this place?

And would continue to run up—until the night ran out, it began to appear. Neither Yosper nor Mario seemed in the least interested in leaving. Finished with the crêpes, Mario proposed brandies all around; after the brandies, Yosper insisted on a lemon ice "to clear the palate." And then they settled down to drinking.

Toward midnight their waiters went off duty and were replaced by bar girls, a different one with every round and all pretty, and there had been a sort of floor show. The comedians had been pretty much a waste of time, being obliged to operate in half a dozen languages, but the stripteasers were handsome women, a regular United Nations of them in a variety of colors and genotypes, and so were the models, hostesses and hookers who continued to stroll through the room. Hake provisionally decided that his guess about Mario's inclinations had been wrong, judging by the way his attention came to a focus every time a new girl came near, but he was losing interest. He wasn't just sick of being in this restaurant, he was pretty sick of Mario, too. The youth felt obliged to point out each celebrity and notoriety he recognized: "That's the girl who played Juliet at the Stratford festival last year. There's Muqtab al'Horash, his father owned thirty-three oil leases. He comes here to buy things for his harem off the models. Now and then he buys a model. There's the President of the French Chamber of Deputies—" Hake felt he had been condemned to spend his life in this gaudy, raucous room that he was sick of, with Mario, whom he was sick of, and especially with Yosper, of whom he was sickest of all. The man just did not stop talking. And he was not your common or garden variety of bore, who will keep on regardless of blank expression or eyes darting this way and that, seeking escape; Yosper wanted full attention, and enforced it. "What's the matter, Hake? Falling asleep? I was telling you that this is *Italy*. The national motto is *Niente è possible, ma possiamo tutto*. Everything's illegal, but if you have the money you can do what you like. 'S good duty, right, Mario? And heaven knows we're entitled—"

But to what? To this endless ordeal of squirming in a shag velour armchair, while beautiful women kept bringing drinks he didn't want? Hake had the Munich feeling, the conviction that a script was being played out that he had had no part in writing, and in which he did not know his lines. In Germany the feeling had been uncertain and only occasional—until that woman, what's her name, Leota, had turned up and made it all concrete. Here it was real enough, but he did not understand what was going on.

Yosper was back on the subject of the emperor Tiberius, and growing argumentative. It was not the drink. He had been drinking three Perrier waters for each brandy, Hake had observed, but he was warming to his subject. Or subjects. All of them. "Come right down to it," he declaimed, "old Tiberius was right about the fisherman. Asshole had no business coming into a restricted area, right? You can't exercise power without discipline. Can't enforce discipline without a little, what you might call, cruelty. Study history! Especially around here, where it all happened. When the Christians and the Turks fought naval battles over this part of the world they didn't fool around with compassion. Turk caught a Christian, like enough they'd stick him assdown on a sharpened stake by the helm, to keep the steersman company. Christians caught a Turk, same thing. And you know, those poor impaled buggers used to laugh and joke with the helmsmen while they were dying! Now, that's what I call good morale."

Mario staggered to his feet. "Excuse me," he said, heading for the men's room. Yosper laughed.

"Good kid," he said, "but he has a little trouble confronting reality now and then. Symptom of the times. We all get taught that it's bad to hurt anybody. 'S what's wrong with the world today, you want my opinion."

"What's wrong with the world *tonight*," Hake said recklessly, "is I'm really tired of this place. Can't we go?"

Yosper nodded approvingly and signaled for another round. "You're impatient," he said. "That's the same as eager, and that's a good thing. But you have got to learn, Hake, that sometimes the best thing you can do is just sit and wait. There's always a reason, you know. Maybe we don't know it, but it's there."

"Are you talking about God or Curmudgeon?"

"Both, Hake. More than that. I'm talking about duty. My family's duty-oriented. It's what I'm proudest of. We paid our bills. My Dad, he was gassed at Verdun, did you know that? Burned him right out. After that it took him twelve years of trying before he could knock Mom up, so I could be born. But he made it. I'm right proud of Dad. No, listen to me, Hake, what I'm saying's important. It's *duty*. That means you have to pay your dues on demand. Maybe it's a Roman short-sword in the guts, or an English cloth-yard arrow at Crécy. Molten lead. Pungee pits. Flame throwers—you'd be amazed how much fat'll come out of a human body. Why, when they opened the shelters in Dresden after the firestorm, there was an inch of tallow on the floor all around."

"Or maybe," snarled Hake, "it's just sitting in a gin-mill on the Isle of Capri, listening to somebody trying to turn your stomach."

Yosper grinned approvingly. "You've got it, Hake. That's duty. Doing what you're told."

He held up, while the cocktail waitress brought them their new drinks. Behind her was another woman, slim and tanned, wearing an assortment of mood jewelry and not much else. "Speak English?" she inquired. When Yosper nodded she handed them each a card, then gracefully displayed her wares. She was more interesting than the things she had to sell; they were out of any sex shop in America. Marriage ring, divorce ring, open marriage ring; a "try it on" mood brooch in the shape of a bunny's head, eyes dilated when the wearer was available, contracted when not; vasectomy badge, laparoscopy bow-knot choker, fertile period locket; gay shoulder-knots and SM leather wristlets. There were very few sexual interests you could not be outfitted for from her selection. She showed them all before leaving with a smile and a trail of familiar perfume.

" 'Spalducci's Bottega,' " Yosper read from the card. "Works of the devil, those places, but I have to admit the girl herself has the look of something from a better Maker. Oh, I'm not one of your religious bigots, Hake. I can understand temptation for the sins of the flesh. Didn't Our Lord Himself stand on that mountain, while the Devil offered him all the treasures of the earth? And He was tempted. And——"

His voice stopped. He sat up straight, peering across the tables. Mario was hurrying toward them, buttoning and zipping as he came, his face agitated. As soon as he was in earshot he called something in Italian, tapping his silver bracelet; Yosper asked a sharp question in the same language, and the two of them sped for the doors.

Hake sat there, watching them go. When they were out of sight he turned his card over. There was a message penciled on the back:

> Meet me
> Blue Grotto
> 0800 tomorrow.

It was no more than he had expected when he saw that the model had been the girl from Munich and Maryland, Leota Pauket.

It was three A.M. before he got back to his hotel. Yosper and Mario, sitting grim-faced and silent next to him, refused to answer questions, curtly ordering him to stay put until called for. He didn't need answers, or at least not from them.

And he did not stay put. He set his alarm and by six was on his way down to the waterfront.

The only words Hake had to discuss his intentions were "Blue Grotto" and *quanto costa*. They would have to serve. There was no difficulty finding the right quayside. All quaysides were right. Wherever he looked were signs in every language, urging tourists to the Blue Grotto. The difficulties were the weather, which was wet and gray, and the time of day, which was a lot too early for your average Capri boatman to be ready for a customer. The big party boats inshore were still under canvas, and deserted. Farther out on the catwalk were a cluster of smaller ones, propelled by the stored kinetic energy of flywheels; a few of them had people working around them, but none seemed up to speed. If the *signore* would wait just an hour, perhaps at most two. . . . If the *signore* could only defer his desires until the time when the tour buses began to arrive. . . . But Hake did not dare wait. If Leota wanted to see him in private, she would be gone by the time the traffic grew heavy.

It took time and patience. But Sergio suggested Emanuele, who thought Francesco could help, who directed Hake to Luigi, and at the end of the list Ugo had just unclutched his flywheel. They were off.

The diamond-shaped craft whirred down the coastline, with surf pounding the base of the cliffs a few hundred yards to their left. The flat flywheel amidships was not merely the power source for the screw. It served as a sort of gyroscope as well, leveling out some of the rock and pitch of the waves. That was not altogether a good thing, as Hake perceived as soon as the first chops began to splash over the coaming. By the time they turned in toward the steep cliffs around the Grotto, he was drenched with salt water and a fairly high amount of floating oil.

Ugo explained, by signs and gestures, that as the only entrance was by sea they would now moor the power vessel to a buoy and transfer to the rubber raft they had been towing behind. "No, Ugo, not so fast," said Hake, and began signs and gestures of his own.

When the boatman realized what Hake wanted, he exploded into Neapolitan fury. Hake did not need to understand a word of Italian to comprehend both the premises and the conclusion of his syllogism perfectly. Major premise, timing the waves and judging the currents at the cave entrance required every bit of the skill and training of a master boatman, such as himself. Minor premise, the *turista* clearly didn't have the skill to navigate soap out of a bathtub. Conclusion, the best that could come of this mad proposal was that he would lose fee, tip and an extremely valuable rubber boat. The worst was that he would be sentenced for cold-blooded murder. And the whole thing was out of the question. But money talked. Hake handed over enough lire to arrange for the boatman to expect him in an hour, and he entered the rubber boat.

The raft had no draft, and thus no consistency of purpose. Hake had no skill, and so entering the cave became a matter of brute force and persistence. On a negligible ledge near the cave two slim young men were sunning their already dark bodies, and Hake's flounderings took place under their amused and interested eyes. A powerful little hydrogen-outboard was bumping against its moorings just below them. Hake wished he could borrow the boat, but saw no way to accomplish it. In any event, he was committed. The rock ledges of the low cave entrance looked seriously sharp. Avoiding puncture, Hake almost lost an oar. Reclaiming the oar, he misjudged a wave and crunched the side of his skull against the low roof of the cave. But then he was through . . . and suspended in space.

From the outside the Grotto had looked neither blue nor inviting, but inside it was incredible. The sun that beat through the tiny entrance came in by a submarine route. By the time it illuminated the interior of the cave all of the warm frequencies had been trapped underwater, and what glowed inside the Grotto was pure cerulean. More. The light was all below the surface. Oil slicks marked the interface between air and water, but where there was no oil there seemed to be nothing below the level of Hake's boat: he was floating in blue space, topsy-turvy, disoriented—and enchanted.

He was also alone.

That was not a surprise in itself; it was far too early for the tour boats. But it was already past eight o'clock. Finding the boat and arguing with its owner had taken longer than it should, and where was Leota?

A string of bubbles coming in from the cave mouth

answered him. Under them was a wavery pale shape that could have been a large fish, began to resemble a mermaid and then became Leota, air tanks strapped to her back and breathing gear over her face. She moved upward through the bright water and surfaced a few yards away. She pulled the face mask off and hung there for a moment, regarding him, then swam to clutch the end of the raft. "Hello, Hake," she panted, her voice tiny in the huge wet space.

Hake looked down at her, almost embarrassed. Apart from the straps for the air tanks, the woman was wearing very little—*la minima*, it was called—a brightly colored triangular scrap of cloth below her navel, held by thin cords, and nothing above. "Get in, for God's sake," he said.

"I'll get you all wet and oily."

"Get in, get in!" He leaned to starboard while she climbed in from port, and they managed to get her aboard without tipping over. They regarded each other silently for a moment before he demanded, "What are you doing in Italy?"

She threw her hair back and wiped oil from her face. "Better things than you are, at least. I never thought you'd be pushing drugs."

"Drugs?" But even as he spoke, he knew he did not doubt her.

"That's right, Hake. That's what your bunch is up to. I'm willing to believe," she conceded, "that you didn't know it, because I don't think it's your style at all. But there it is." She turned to study the empty cave entrance for a moment. "I have ten minutes, no more," she added. "Then you stay here for a while and I'll go. Don't try to follow me, Hake. I have friends—"

"Oh, for God's sake. Look, first things first. Are you sure about the drugs?"

"Bloody damn sure," she said. "The Italian cops put one of your boys away for it yesterday. Stopped him in that galleria in Naples, with a satchel full of Xeroxed directions for making angel dust."

"I never heard of angel dust!"

"What they call pay-chay-pay. PCP. It's an old drug,

comes back every twenty years or so—when a new generation comes along that doesn't know what it can do to you. One or two shots can screw up your head forever. Thing is, it's the easiest thing in the world to make. Any high-school kid can put it together in Mom's kitchen if he has the directions. Your boy was selling the recipe to all the *ragazzi* in Naples—until one of them finked to the fuzz."

They were drifting close to the wall of the cave. Awkwardly Hake sculled them a few yards farther away, while Leota watched with amusement. He said doggedly, "I don't want to call you a liar, but I didn't think the, uh, the group I'm involved with would do anything like that. How do you know this person worked for us?"

"Oh, I know. Who do you think alerted the Italian narcs to plant the kid in the galleria? You want the details?" She leaned back against her air tanks and recited: "Dietrich Nederkoorn, comes from a little fishing village in Holland, deserted the Dutch Army three years ago, worked for your boys ever since at one crummy thing or another. About twenty-five. Gay. Beatle haircut. Blue eyes, black hair, freckles, medium height."

"Yeah," Hake said slowly. "I saw him in Germany. But why would we do a thing like that?"

"What I've been asking you all along, Hake. I don't mean why they would. I mean why you would. For the gorillas you work for, sure, it's tailor-made. Very cost-effective. It's like a bite of the apple from the Tree of the Knowledge of Good and Evil. Once you get it started, it runs itself. By now there must be a million of those circulars in Italy. If Nederkoorn weren't such an asshole he wouldn't be in the slammer now. The process was already on the way. There's no way in the world the Italian narcs, or anybody else, can catch up with all those leaflets and all the copies that are being made. So there goes a whole generation of Italian kids. Thousands of them, maybe millions, are going to be showing up for work stoned out of their heads from something they scored two weeks back—if they show up at all. It's a big success, Hake. The government's got an all-out drive against it right now, school assembly programs, TV commercials, rock stars traveling the country to campaign against it—for all the good that's going to do," she said bitterly. "What kind of human being does a thing like that?"

"I wish I could tell you," Hake said unhappily. Well, part of it he could have told her. The obsession that caused Mario and the others to practice their petty harassments with fuse-blowers and tiny floods was enough to explain Dieter's being unable to stop. But— "But I don't know what I'm doing in this," he said. "All I've done is sit around."

She stared at him. "You didn't know? Oh, Christ, Hake. The reason they brought you over here was to put the finger on me."

"I never said a word!"

"No, Hake," she said, with no anger in her tone, "I'm sure you didn't. I wouldn't be here if I weren't. You're dumb, yes. But not treacherous. You didn't have to. Your tickle-taster took care of it for you."

"What the hell's a tickle-taster?"

"You're wearing it right now, Hake." She pointed to his silver wristlet. "Works sort of like a polygraph; it monitors your pulse and blood levels. All they had to do was wait until you went *boing* on the taster, and then see who caused it. Which was me. I knew they were close. They could figure I had to be working at one of three or four places on Capri, and all they had to do was plant you in them one after another until I turned up. Oh, Hake," she said, actually smiling, "don't look so *guilty*! They would've got to me sooner or later."

Hake stared at the judas on his arm, shining cold blue in the diffuse light. "I'm sorry," he said.

"Yeah. Well. Listen, there's not much they can do to me. I'm on Italian territory. I haven't done anything against the law here, or anyway not much. Besides, I helped the Italians find Nederkoorn."

Hake said, "I think the way I was looking wasn't so much guilty as just plain foolish. What will you do now?"

Her expression became opaque. "That much I don't trust you, Hake." And then she added, "Actually, there's not much I can do. I'm blown, for here and now. I'll move to another place. There are others who will stay and carry on—" She hesitated, glanced at her watch, and then said more rapidly, "And that's what I wanted to see you for. Will you join up?"

"Join what?"

"Join on the side of the good guys! What the hell do you think? You can make up for a lot of crumminess if you've got the nerve to take a stand now."

Hake brought his open palm down flat on the water, splashing the girl and startling her. He said furiously, "God *damn* it, Leota! How do I know your stupid games are any better than theirs? This whole situation is *sick*."

"Then don't make it sicker! Come on, Hake. I don't expect you to fall into my arms now. I just want you to think about it. I've got to go, but I'll give you time. Overnight. I'll call you at your hotel tomorrow morning. Early. I'm sure they're bugging your wire, so I won't say anything. You speak. Just say hello. Say it once for yes, twice for no—three times for maybe. Which," she added irritably, "is about what I'd expect from you. Then I'll get in touch, never mind how. And, Hake. Don't try setting any traps or anything. I'm not alone, and the other people on my side right now play rougher than I do."

She picked up her face mask, but paused before putting it on. "Unless you'd care to say yes right now?" she inquired.

He didn't answer, because there was a sound like a tiny rapid-fire cap pistol from the mouth of the cave. They both turned. The little hydrogen-powered outboard came bouncing through the opening and then arrowed straight toward them, looking as if it were suspended in blue space.

Hake grabbed an oar. He didn't know the two men coming toward them, but it was a good bet that they worked for Yosper. "Get out of here, Leota!" he cried. "I'll see if I can keep them busy—"

But she was shaking her head. "Oh, Hake," she said sorrowfully, "no, they're not yours. They're a lot worse than that."

Hake held the oar before him like a quarter-staff, but it was apparent that it would not be much use. The two men were not very big, and certainly not formidably dressed. Like Leota, they wore *i minimi*. But unlike Leota, they carried guns. The one at the motor had a pistol, the other what looked like a rapid-fire carbine, pointed directly at Hake. It was now obvious that they were the two who had been lounging on the ledge outside; more than that, they had a somewhat familiar look—like someone he had seen somewhere before, and a lot like each other.

"Put your oar down, Horny," Leota said. "I didn't mean for this to happen, at all."

The two men did not only resemble each other, they were almost identical. They had to be twins: tiny dark bodies, no more than five feet three, long straight black hair, neat short beards, black eyes. From under the tarpaulins Hake could see them sitting in the bucket seats on either side of the chattering outboard, Leota draped across the coaming on one side of them. Two well-to-do Eastern gentlemen enjoying the Mediterranean with a pretty girl: there was nothing in that spectacle to attract anyone's attention. He could hear the first of the party boats arriving with its tandem flywheels whining away, but one of the men had his foot on Hake's neck. "Easy, cock," he said, grinning conventionally. "Don't try to sit up. You'd just get all those nice people killed."

"Do what they say, Horny," said Leota. Hake didn't answer. With a foot on his windpipe he couldn't. And what was there to say?

They bounced over the gentle swell for twenty minutes or more. Then the machine-gun sound of the motor slowed, one of the men wrapped a cloth around Hake's eyes, he was kicked in the small of the back, the tarps were dragged off him and he was prodded up a rope ladder. "Stay on deck, sweetie," said one of the men in his high, accentless voice—to Leota, Hake assumed. Then one on each side of him they shoved him through a door and down a steep companionway. He heard a door close behind them, and one of the men said: "You can take the blindfold off now. And sit down."

Hake unwrapped the rag from his face and blinked at

them. He was in a low-ceilinged room, bunk beds at either end and a padded locker along the wall, under a porthole covered with a locked metal hatch. There was barely room for all three of them at once. He sat on the locker less because he had been told to than because it was the best way he had of establishing distance between them. But one of them pulled camp chairs from under a bunk, and they drew them up one on each side, facing him.

Then he remembered where he had seen them, or one of them, before. "Munich! When I was sick. I thought you were a doctor."

"Yes, Hake, that was me. I am Subirama Reddi," said the one on the left, "and this is my brother Rama. You can tell which is which because I am left-handed and my brother right. We find this useful. Also Rama has a scar over his eye, do you see? He got that from an American in Papeete, and it makes him mean."

"Oh, no, not mean!" said Rama, shaking his head. "We will get along very well, Hake, provided that you do exactly as we say. Otherwise——" He shrugged, with an expression that was somewhere between a smile and a pout. They spoke perfect English, colloquial and quick if sometimes odd. It was not quite true that they had no accents. The accents were there, but they were not identifiable. To Hake, they sounded vaguely British, but he thought that to a Brit they would have seemed American—as though they had come from somewhere along the mid-Atlantic ridge, or perhaps from Yale. Their voices were as high and pure as lead tenors in a boy's choir, though what they said was not childish. "What you must do," Rama Reddi went on, "is to tell us completely and quickly all of the names of the agents you have worked with, and what you know of the operations of your agency."

This was not going to be a pleasant time, Hake realized. And it was all foolish, because he knew so little! He turned to Rama and began, "There isn't much I can tell——" The next word was jolted out of his mouth as Subirama's fist hit his ear. Hake turned toward him in rage, and Rama's fist clubbed him on the other side. It was now clear why their opposing handedness was useful.

Subirama moved his chair back a few inches, and switched the gun he had been holding in his free hand to his good one. He spoke rapidly to his brother, who nodded and produced a rope. While Rama Reddi was tying Hake's hands, Subirama said, "You Americans are very confident of your size and strength. I do not, actually, think you could prevail against either one of us in bare-hand combat, much less two. But I think that you might attempt something which would make it necessary for us to kill you. So we will remove temptation." He waited until his brother had finished with Hake's hands, and then drove his fist into Hake's stomach. "Now," he said conversationally, "we will start with the names of the persons you have contacted in Italy so far."

Before they were through Hake had told them everything they asked for. He did not try to resist, after the first few minutes. As long as they confined themselves to beating him he might survive, and even recover; but they made it clear that if he held out it would cost him his fingernails, his eyes and his life, in that order. He gave them names he didn't know he remembered. All four of Yosper's helpers. Every member of his class Under the Wire. He even gave a physical description of the woman who had led him to his first interview at Lo-Wate Bottling Co. and the sheepherder who had driven him to the airport bus. He could not tell which parts interested them. When some name or event led them to demand more information, he did not see why. Why would they care about a Hilo avocado-grower's wife? But they questioned him endlessly about Beth Hwa. He told them what he knew, everything he knew, some of it four and five times. Then they let him rest. Hake didn't think they were being considerate. He thought their fists were sore.

He would have resisted more, he told himself, if he had had anything to resist for. But the talk with Leota had shaken him again: what was he doing working for the Team in the first place? Why had he left a perfectly comfortable, personally rewarding and socially useful life as a minister in New Jersey to involve himself in these desperate adolescent games? He climbed into one of the bunks, hungry, exhausted, feeling sick and in pain. He could not believe sleep would be possible, his head pounded so. Then he woke up with Leota sitting on the bunk beside him and realized he had been asleep after all.

"These are aspirins, take them," she said.

He pushed her away and himself up, his head thundering lethally. "Get lost," he snarled. "This is the bad-cop and good-cop routine, right? I saw it on television."

"Oh, Hake! You are so terribly ignorant. The boys *are* bad, bad enough to kill you, more likely than not. And I'm good. Mostly good," she corrected herself, holding out the pills. She put an arm behind his head while he drank the water to swallow them, and said, "You look like hell."

He didn't answer. He sat on the edge of the bunk for a moment, then tottered to the tiny toilet and closed the door behind him. In the mirror he looked even worse than he felt. His face was puffed out from chin to hairline; his eyes were swollen half shut, and his ears rang. He splashed cold water on it, but when he tried drying his face with a scrap of towel it hurt. He moved his lips and cheek muscles experimentally. He could talk, and maybe even chew; but it was going to be some time before he could enjoy it.

When he came out Leota was gone, but reappeared in a moment with a tray. She closed the door behind her, and Hake heard someone outside lock it. "Your friends are taking good care of me," he said bitterly.

"They aren't friends of mine, only allies. I told you I didn't mean for this to happen." She put the tray down and sat next to him. "I brought you some soup. After you eat I've got an ice bag for your face."

He could not bring himself to say thank-you. He grunted instead, and allowed her to feed him a couple of spoonfuls of the thick soup. The rocking of the boat dumped half of each on his lap, and he took the spoon and bowl away from her. The soup was a minestrone, no more than luke-warm but not bad; and he was famished. He emptied the bowl while she talked. "I'm not responsible for the Reddis! Sometimes we work together, sure. But they're mercenaries.

They'll kill. They'll do anything they're paid to do. And they scare me."

"What have you paid them to do to me?"

"Not me, Hake! *We* don't pay them. They're working for—" she hesitated, glancing at the door. "Never mind who they're working for," she said, but on her bare thigh, below the short terrycloth beach robe, her finger traced out the word *Argentina*. "Your own boys have hired them from time to time, I would guess. Right now, somebody else. What does it matter? But when my group needs help, sometimes they give it. If they hadn't taken out your friend Dieter's bodyguard, he never would have been arrested. So with their help we stopped your people from killing kids."

"And how did they take out the bodyguard?"

She flinched. "He was a mercenary, too. What does it matter?"

"You say that a lot," he commented. "It matters to me."

"Well, it matters to me, too," she said sadly. "But what's worse, Horny? What kind of people pass out poison dope?"

He took the ice bag from her and gingerly applied it to his jaw. His head was still hammering, but it was a slower, less shattering beat. "Well," he said, "I'll grant you there are faults on both sides. Just for curiosity, what did you *think* was going to happen in the Grotto?"

"I thought I'd try to recruit you to our side," she said simply. "Don't laugh."

"My God, woman! What do you think I've got to laugh at?"

"Well, that's it. I wanted to talk to you. The Reddis were just supposed to stay outside and warn me if your boys came along, or if—excuse me, Horny—if you tried to bring me in, or anything like that."

"Um." Hake transferred the ice bag from right cheek to left thoughtfully. What she said made sense, but did not change the fact that he had spent three hours being beaten and was now held captive, with a future outlook that at best was not to be called promising. "I guess I know what an innocent bystander feels like," he said resentfully.

"*Innocent?*" Leota closed her mouth to cut off the next

words, and then, carefully, said, "I wouldn't exactly call you innocent, Horny."

"Well, all right! I made some mistakes."

She shook her head sorrowfully. "You don't really know what's happening, do you? You think all this has happened at random."

"Hasn't it?"

"Random as a guided missile! Your boys go straight for the jugular every time."

"No, that's ridiculous, Leota. I've been with them often enough to know! They're the most bumbling, incompetent—"

"I wish you were right!"

"Really! They picked me out just by chance in the first place. No reason."

"You mean you don't *know* the reason. There was one, believe me. They probably had you under surveillance for months before they pulled you in. Somebody spotted you as a likely prospect—"

"Impossible! Who?"

"I don't know who. But somebody. I know how they work. First they pulled your records, then they did a full field check. You must have looked okay, but they had to be sure. So they called you in. You could have told them to get lost—"

"No, I couldn't! I was in the Reserves. They just reactivated me."

"Oh, yes, you could, Horny. You could always have just said no. What would they have done, taken you to court? But you didn't. So you passed the first test, and then they slipped you a few bucks and gave you a dumdum assignment to try you out. Don't look at me like that, Horny, that's what it was. A two-year-old child could have done it, and probably better than you. But you did it, so you passed that test too, and when you found out what it was all about you passed another. You didn't blow the whistle on them."

"I couldn't!"

The girl looked away. "Well, no, you couldn't, Horny, because you probably wouldn't have lived to get to a reporter. Somebody would have seen to that. Whoever fin-

gered you in the first place probably had an eye on you.
But, Horny, you didn't know that. You didn't even try; so
you passed. Next stage: they send you to training camp.
You pass with flying colors. They send you here to fink on
me— Don't tell me again you didn't know you were
doing it. If you'd thought at all you could have figured it
out. Some kinds of coincidences can't be coincidences.
When you saw me you should've got suspicious."

"By then it was too late."

Long pause. "Yeah," she said, and began to cry. "It's a
lot too late," she managed to say.

It took some time for her meaning to penetrate.

When Leota had left him alone again Hake sat on the
edge of the bunk, staring at the red denim coverlet of the
upper bunk across the stateroom. He did not see it. His
mind and his whole body were in standby mode. It was
almost a kind of paralysis. In all the long years in the
wheelchair he had never been so little in control of his own
fate as he was now.

If indeed he had ever been in command of his fate.
Everything Leota had said rang true. He had followed
along a course that he could not believe had been of his
own choosing. Passive. Obedient. Even cooperative. A willing accomplice of people he despised, doing things he
loathed. Hake was not sure who he was. The brawler who
had exulted in the fight with Tigrito was a person he could
not recognize as himself.

It was murderously, densely hot in the little stateroom,
and with the portholes sealed shut there was no air. At
least the pain in his battered head was less. It was even
bearable; Leota's aspirins had worked. Or the bruises had
dwindled in his consciousness in comparison with the implications of what she had said. Hake allowed out of his
mind the thought that this smelly, steamy room might be
the last place he would ever see alive, and studied it. It was
not exactly frightening, but it was paralyzing. Once again
he could see no handle to grip his life by, nothing he could
do to change his state.

When Leota had left, responding to three sharp raps on the door, she had gathered up bowl, tray, spoon and even the ice bag to take away. If she had left even so much as a table knife— But there was nothing like that. There was nothing in the room that was not either securely fastened down or harmless.

He wiped sweat from his face, stood up, pulled off his shirt, kicked off his shoes, and was still sweltering. He could not even tell whether it was day or night. The questioning and beating had seemed endless, but might really have been only for an hour or two; the brief sleep could have been minutes, or could have been anything. No light came through the sealed hatch over the portholes. He did not even know whether the little ship was moving or bobbing somewhere at anchor.

He threw his pants across one of the far bunks and stretched out. There was a quality that was almost satisfying about the total impotence of his position. As there was nothing at all he could do, he was permitted to do nothing. Even the faded pounding in his head, the tenderness of his face and the ache in his gut became only phenomena to be observed. He was very nearly at peace as he drowsed there, one arm behind his head, and he was amused to find that his impotence did not extend to all of his person. In all the time he had been talking to Leota one part of him had been very aware of her round, tanned legs and the gentle feminine smell that came from her. He could smell it now; and that, and perhaps the rocking of the boat, and perhaps some unidentified personality trait in the new Hake combined to make him want very much to make love. And when after a time Leota came in again, bearing fresh ice bag, water and aspirin, and the door was locked behind her and she sat on the edge of the bunk, he reached up toward her. Startled, she said, "Heeeeyyy—" And then, pulling her lips away from his, "At least let me put down the glass." It was like making love in a dream, easy, unhurried and sure, and he was not even surprised to find that she was as ready as he.

When they were apart he traced the gentle edge of bone

before her left hip with his fingers and said, "You know, I didn't really expect this, but I'm awfully glad about it." Their eyes were only inches apart, and she looked into his carefully, then kissed him, shook her head, sat up and glanced at her watch.

"Take your aspirin," she said, "and then let's talk. I've got twenty-five minutes left to turn you."

"Turn me into what?" he asked, swallowing obediently.

"Turn you into a double agent, Horny," she said.

He slid to the edge of the bunk and sat next to her. He brushed her bare shoulder with his lips thoughtfully. "Oh, yes," he said. "My little problem."

"It's actually our problem, Horny. But that's the deal they'll give you. If you'll work with them they'll let you go. They've got a plan. They're going to ransom you—exchange you for somebody the Team's got hidden out in Texas. Don't ask me who; I don't know."

Hake said consideringly, "I don't really know how high a price the Team puts on me."

She said, "Well, to be frank, Horny, the twins don't really think it's very high. They'll let themselves be bargained down—of course, assuming that you go along. Otherwise there's no deal for you. Or maybe for me, either," she added. "If they, ah, dispose of you I really don't think they will want me to be around as a possible witness to murder."

That was a new thought, and a soberingly unwelcome one to Hake. He put his arm around her warm, damp waist, but she did not yield. "So we have to talk, Horny. I don't think there ought to be any *moral* question for you. I can't believe that you want to be loyal to a bunch of destructive lunatics. It's not just the PCP, or bribing half the disk jockeys in Europe to play narco music, or counterfeiting the pound, or jiggering everybody's computer nets. Or spreading disease, or insect pests, or allergenic weeds, or—"

"I didn't know about the narco music," Hake said. "And what's that about the computers?"

"All the time, Horny. How do you think they finance

themselves? Or, for that matter," she added honestly, "how do you think I do? I'm not saying I really like the way my side operates. They spy on you, we spy on you. They trick you, I trick you."

"I like the way you do it better," he observed. "What do you mean, you spy on me? Is that how you knew I was going to the Team in the first place?"

"Certainly. We don't have the resources the Team does," she said bitterly, "but we do what we can. I have an old school friend who—no, never mind who she is. We don't have time. I have to persuade you to turn around."

"Oh," said Hake, "I thought you knew that. I'm turned."

She looked at him. "You're sure?"

"Sure?" He laughed. "What I'm sure of is that I'm getting real tired of being *used*. But I'm willing to try it your way."

She studied him carefully, then shook her head. "All right," she said. "Now all we have to do is hope the Reddis don't change their mind. And—" she glanced at her watch— "we still have twenty minutes."

He pulled her toward him, but he had misunderstood her meaning. She resisted. "Wait a minute, Horny. Now it's time for me to ask you the question."

"What question?"

"The one I told you I was going to ask: Why did you do all this?"

He said peevishly, "I thought we'd just been over all that. *I* don't know."

"But maybe I do. I have a theory. Don't laugh—"

He was a long way from laughing.

"I have to start from the beginning. What do you know about hypnotism?"

Hake took his arm away from her and said, "Leota, I'm not an impatient man, but if you've got a point I wish you'd get to it."

"Well, that is the point. You act hypnotized. Do you understand what I'm saying? Whatever anybody tells you to do, you do. You're suggestible. Just like someone in a hypnotic trance state."

"Oh, hell." He was exasperated. "I can't be hypnotized to do things I wouldn't do otherwise—that's a fact! Everybody knows that."

"They do? How do you know it? Have you made a study of hypnotism?"

"No, but—"

"No, but you sure as hell act as if you were! Don't give me knee-jerks, Horny. Think about it."

"Well—" He thought for a moment, and then said cautiously, "I admit that I don't altogether understand what I've been doing the last couple of months. I've wondered about it. I went along with any lousy thing they suggested quick enough—as you point out."

"I don't mean it critically, Horny. The opposite of that. You couldn't help yourself, if you were hypnotized."

He looked at her. "How sure are you of any of this?"

"Well, not very," she admitted. "But it makes sense, doesn't it? Is there any other way to explain it? You can't even call it reflex patriotism. You went along with me, too, when I told you not to report me."

He looked up with a spasm of hope. "But—that was *against* the Team!"

Leota shook her head. "Men! That's male ego for you. You'd rather believe you were a skunk of your own free will than a helpless dupe. But the fact is, that's a strong sign of the trance state. It's called a tolerance of incongruities. It means you act as though mutually conflicting things are both right, or both true."

He protested, "It's all impossible! They couldn't hypnotize me without my remembering it!"

"How do you know that?"

"I don't, but—"

She said, "It could have been a post-hypnotic suggestion to forget. Or you might not have been aware of it in the first place. They could have slipped you a drug. Planted a tape under your pillow. *I* don't know. All I'm sure of—"

She was interrupted by the sound of the door being unlocked. The Reddi with the scar over his brow looked in on them, his right hand resting on the holster of a pistol. He smiled.

"Ah, I see you are making good progress, sweetie," he observed as Leota grabbed for her beach dress and held it before her.

She said coldly: "We've made the deal, Rama. Now it's up to you to work out an arrangement for a trade."

"I see," he said, studying them in amusement. "Yes, perhaps something can be done. When my brother returns we will speak further. But how can we know that Reverend Hake will keep his word to us?"

Neither Hake nor Leota answered; there was no obvious answer to give. The Indian nodded. "Yes, that is a difficulty. Well, I had thought that you might wish to come on deck, my dear, but perhaps you prefer to remain here?"

He smiled—it was almost a friendly smile, at least a tolerant one, Hake was astonished to discover—and closed the door behind him.

Hake and Leota looked at each other. Hake said, "Ah, about what he was saying. How do you suppose they're going to make sure I keep my bargain?"

"I don't have a clue, Horny, except that it probably will be in a way you don't like. The easiest thing would be to kill you if you don't. If the Team can plant somebody who can get at you when they want to, and I can, then it's a real good bet that the Reddis can, too. Or it might be something a lot worse."

"Such as?"

She said angrily, "The worst thing you can think of. Or worse than that, the worst thing either of them can think of. Addict you to a drug? Give you a fatal disease that they keep providing you the medicine for? I don't know. They'll think of something."

The future began to look rather dubious to Hake. "But maybe it won't be that bad," she added, trying to reassure him. "There's nothing you can do about it anyway, right? Whatever it is, it's better than floating up on the docks of the Bay of Naples."

"Why Naples? I thought we were around Capri?"

"You'd have to ask them why. Last I saw, we were tied up to some industrial dock. If you listen, you can hear trains in the freight yards."

He listened, putting his arm around her again, but heard nothing he could identify. "Well," he said, "as it looks like we still have some time—"

"Wait a minute, Horny." She was still listening, with an expression of puzzlement. There was a faint, rapid patter of feet on the deck outside, and then something that was almost a splash.

She stood up, pulling the dress over her head. "Something's going on," she announced, and opened the door a crack. There was no one outside. "I'm going to take a look. You'd better stay here."

"No. I'm coming too."

"Then stay back." She crossed to the deck door, which was slid fully open, and looked around. Hake came up behind her and peered over her shoulder. They were moored to ancient wood pilings, alongside a bulkhead. Greasy water lapped against the wood, and beyond the bulkhead were bulbous, immense tanks of some sort. It was night time, but the tanks were brightly lit, and around and among them Hake saw figures moving cautiously closer. There was no sign of either of the Reddis.

"Oh, Christ!" she whispered. "It looks like your boys are coming after you. Or, more likely, after the Reddis and me. Rama must've seen them and taken off!"

"What will happen to you?" Hake demanded.

"Nothing real good," she said worriedly. "Hake, I'm going to get out of here. You stay. You'll be okay. If you can, stall them." She ran into the cabin and came out again, strapping the scuba tanks on hurriedly.

"Wait!" he protested. "I want to see you again!"

She paused for a second, regarding him. "Oh, Horny," she said, "you are so bloody *naive*." She kissed him hard and fast, and lowered herself over the far gunwale. Minutes later, when the first of the approaching men had reached the short gangplank, Hake came out of the cabin with his hands up.

"It's me!" he cried. "Thank God you got here! They've all taken off that way, not more than five minutes ago—if you hurry you can catch them!" And he pointed down the waterfront toward the likeliest, darkest spot.

VIII

YOSPER was having a high old good time. He took command of the little ship like a corsair, dispatched his pirate crew in all directions, himself straddled the quarterdeck and strutted back and forth. He did not neglect the perquisites of conquest. He found three bottles of Piper-Heidsieck nicely chilled in the cabin aft and shared them with Hake while they supervised the search.

The pursuit on land came up empty. Dietrich, fresh out of a Neapolitan jail, reported that there was no one in sight; he had paid off the hired hoods and sent them away, and the quarry had escaped. I'm glad, Hake thought; one out of three glad, anyway. But Yosper's bright old eyes were on him. "Don't look so happy," he said. "You've got a lot of explaining to do. D'you know what we had to do to get you out of this? First we had to find you. Tracked down the boatman, located a witness in the tour boat outside the Grotto. Then we had to message back to Washington for spy-satellite photos to track this ship. Then we had to hire half a dozen muscle to come in after you."

"I'm sorry to have put you to the trouble."

"Sure you are. Dietz! Go on below and give Mario a hand checking this ship out, then we'll all celebrate."

Hake wasn't listening. He was calculating. The worst thing about owing somebody your life was that it became difficult to be rude to him. But for how long? A week?

Well, two or three days, anyway. At a minimum, for longer than would help him now, when he urgently wished for license to tell Yosper to piss off, and didn't have it. The man was an arrogant ass, and was repetitively proving it.

"—give it back now."

Hake woke up. "What?"

"I said, you might as well give us back the bracelet now," Yosper repeated, pointing to the silver bangle on Hake's arm. "We won't need it any more on you. Served its purpose. We knew you'd go off to see her, long's we didn't catch her at the *Pescatore.* So we kept you tagged. You didn't move ten feet without registering. But the boat was a surprise, and by the time we could follow you were out of range."

Silently Hake unstrapped the band and passed it over, as Mario and Dieter came up from the hold. The Italian was carrying a flat metal box, and they were both looking worried. Yosper scrambled to his feet.

"It's defused," said Mario, breathing hard. He handed it to Yosper, who accepted it with care.

"Yeah," he said. "It would have blown this ship up easy enough. And then—" He gazed out at the spherical tanks, only yards away, and Hake was astonished to see that the old man was grinning. "Fifty thousand metric tons of liquid hydrogen!" he breathed. "Man! What a blowup that would've been! You see what kind of people your girl friend's mixed up with, Hake?"

"Smart, though," said Dieter. "It's one of ours."

Yosper frowned, then shook his head. "They're a crafty pair. You're right. If the Eye-ties had found pieces of this, we would've taken the rap, and, man, we all would've been in the soup! They must've got it when they were working on the North Sea job."

Hake sat up. "Hey! Are you saying they worked for you?"

"Not any more. They take their work too seriously, Hake. Killing's against our charter," he said virtuously, "except in unusual circumstances. But they *like* it. You're lucky to be alive. If you hire them and don't want killing it costs extra, would you believe it?"

"I don't understand you people," Hake said.

"Because we use mercenaries? Grow up, boy! Don't get means mixed up with ends. We're doing *right*. The Reddis are only tools we use when we have to. You don't ask a gun if it believes in democracy. You just want to know that when you pull the trigger it'll go off." He handed the box back to Mario. "In the old days," he went on severely, forbearingly, "we understood that. I don't blame you for getting mixed up now. How can you give it all you've got when you're told we must never drop a bomb or fire a rocket or kneecap an enemy or blow up a bridge? But those are the rules. We don't make them. We just do what we're told—and we use what we have to to do it."

Hake sat back, letting the words wash over him. Yosper's morals were not a concern of his, he told himself. He had other concerns, and he was not in the least sure of how to handle them, or how they were going to come out. He found himself studying Mario and Dieter, who sat in rapt attention to the old man. Precisely as if they hadn't heard all this before, as they surely had; exactly as if it were worth hearing at all. It was very strange that everyone he met—Yosper, Dieter, Mario, Leota, even Jessie Tunman, even the Reddis—behaved as if they were all quite sure of their role in the world and the righteous necessity of getting on with it. While he wasn't sure at all. And Yosper kept right on talking:

"—old days at the United Nations, shee-it! We knew who was who! Knew how to handle them, too. Get a Rumanian chargé d'affaires in bed with a nigger boy and show him the photographs, then he'd come along! Or hook a Russian code clerk on heroin and hold his supply up. World was a lot simpler then, and if you want my opinion better. We were doing God's work and we knew it. 'Course, we still are, but sometimes— Ah, well," he twinkled, "you're getting tired of hearing me, aren't you, boy? And those lumps on your head probably don't feel too good, and you're likely getting hungry. Dietz, you get rid of that thing—" he nodded toward the bomb— "and, Mario, you bring the car around. Champagne's all gone, and it's about time we ate."

The questions in Hake's mind all wanted to be central, and all kept colliding with one another. How seriously, for instance, should he take his deal with the Reddis to "turn"? They hadn't actually released him; he had been rescued. But still they might have their ways to enforce cooperation. And before he had that one even properly sorted out, much less solved, there was another: Had Leota really gotten safely away, and where was she now? And that was nudged away by, What about the Team project for supporting messianic religions? What about for God's sake his *church*? Was it getting along without him? How much reality was there in Leota's crazy conjecture about being hypnotized? And back to wondering if Leota was safe.

The advantage of a head full of unsorted thoughts and problems was that it kept his mind off Yosper's interminable chatter. Which went on as they moved between the great double-walled spheres of hydrogen, became louder as they cut between the thumping compressors that kept the hydrogen liquid, recessed briefly as they stood by the immense hot-air vents that roared 150-degree waste heat into the already sultry Italian sky—there was some risk that one of the not very alert fuel-depot guards might hear—and resumed full momentum in the Cadillac that Mario steered athletically along the waterfont, up through a tangle of climbing, narrow streets and into the parking lot of a huge hotel atop the Vomero. Hake was given twenty minutes to clean himself up, pat water on his bruises and change into fresh clothes out of the bags that Mario had obligingly brought from Capri, and then it was a reprise of the night before at *La Morte del Pescatore*. They had, again, the best table in the house. It looked out over the Bay, with Vesuvius's cratered peak illuminated in red, white and green searchlights a dozen miles away, and Yosper was saying, "Veal, Hake! If you don't want fish, take veal; it's the only kind of meat the Italians understand, but they know it well." The pills that Leota had given him had long since worn off. His jaw and belly felt as if cattle had stampeded over them. He was exhausted—it had been a shock to him to find that it was still only nine o'clock at night by the time they reached the hotel—and he felt as if he were running a temperature. But the thing he was sickest of was the sound of Yosper's voice. The old man was engaged in a lengthy debate with the waiter on what proportion of Parmesan cheese should go into the softer base in his *scaloppine alla Vomero cordon bleu,* and with the wine steward on whether the Lacrima Christi really came from the vineyards on Mount Vesuvius, or was something their *bottiglieria* cooked up out of grape husks and hydrochloric acid that afternoon.

Hake ordered at random, wanting nothing more than to get it over and get to bed—and, as soon as possible, back to Long Branch, New Jersey. When Yosper tried to guide him to a specialty of the house, he snarled, "Anything! I don't care. I didn't come here to spend the taxpayers' money on gin mills!"

Yosper gave him a level stare and sent the waiter away. When he was gone, the old man said, "Hake, two things you should remember. First, you don't talk about working for the government when anybody you don't know is listening. Second, this isn't costing the taxpayers a dime. Not ours, anyway. Dieter, who are we sticking with this one?"

"I was going to use my Barclay card," the Dutch boy said. "It goes to KLM."

Yosper nodded, grinning. "That gets charged to the airline, who charge it to a special account that turns out to be unauditable funds for the Dutch spooks. There's no way they'll trace it to us. Let's see, on Capri I think we used the Banco di Milano credit, which goes through the Italian hydroelectric syndicate to their Air Force Intelligence. You know how to handle the computers, you can get anything you want—and the enemy pays for it! So eat hearty, boy. Every lira you spend takes one away from the other side."

He paused, and said to Dietrich, "That reminds me. Will you check on that other matter?" The boy nodded and slipped away, as the waiter came back with platters of raw vegetables and antipasto.

Chewing the crunchy celery and hearts of palm turned out to be an ordeal for Hake. Half of his molars felt loose in their sockets, and protested the force of his jaw. He ate sullenly, doggedly, staring out across the gentle bay. With the festooned lights of the cruise ships at the docks, the cars along the waterfront, the distant villas on the Portici and Torre del Greco shore it was both lovely and awful—so terrible a waste of energy that he could not understand why it was tolerated, or how it failed to sink the Italian economy. To be sure, the farms and peasant villages were practicing stricter economies than anything in New Jersey, he knew. But that made this prodigious waste even more immoral. There was something very sick in the world he lived in. And if the healers, or the people who thought they were healing it, were all like Yosper, what hope was there for even survival? The old man was holding forth on religion again. It was God's plan for the world, he was saying, that the righteous should survive and conquer; and the words beat against Hake's inner thoughts confusingly. Then he did a double take on a phrase of Yosper's and demanded, "What did you say?"

"You should pay attention," Mario said accusingly. "Yosper is a great man and he saved your life."

The old man patted Mario's arm tolerantly. "I was saying that I don't hold with Darwin."

Hake goggled. It was exactly as if he had said he thought the earth was flat. "But— But you just said you thought the fittest should survive."

"I said the righteous, Hake, but I'll agree it's the same thing. God gives us the strength to do His will. But that's nothing to do with your Darwin. It's against the Bible, so it's wrong; that's all there is to it. And," he added, warming up, "if you look at the whole picture with the eyes of understanding, you see it's against science, too! Real science, Hake. Commonsense science. Darwin just doesn't add up. Heaven's name, boy, just open your eyes to the marvelous world we live in! Electric eels. Hummingbirds. Desert seeds that are smart enough to pay no attention to a shower, but sprout for a real rain—are you telling me that all happened by *chance*? No, boy. Your Mister Darwin just can't cut it. Just look at your own *eye*. Your Mister Darwin says some pollywog sixteen billion years ago started out with some scales on its skin that responded to light, am I correct? And am I supposed to believe that for all those years it just kept on trying to turn those scales into something that'll read a book, or watch a TV screen, and turn with the most beautifully designed muscles and nerves you ever saw, and weep, and magnify, and— Why, your scientists can't even *build* a machine as sensitive as the human eye! And you want me to believe all that happened by chance, starting from some fish's scales? That's as crazy as— Wait a minute."

Dieter had come back, followed by a waiter bearing a telephone. While the instrument was being plugged in the Dutch boy whispered in Yosper's ear. "Uh-huh," said Yosper, looking satisfied. "Well, let's drop this argument, as it's making our friend uncomfortable. I think that wine's breathed about long enough now, let's get the waiter to pour it."

Hake shook his head unbelievingly. But what was the use? His chicken Marsala was arriving; he waited impatiently for the waiter to finish boning it before his eyes, and then ate swiftly. "I don't want any dessert," he said, finished while the others were still savoring the best parts of their meals. "I think I'll go to bed."

"Sure," said Yosper hospitably. "You've had a rough day. Let's get straight about tomorrow, though. You're on an eight A.M. flight to Leonardo da Vinci. When you get there, go in to the depot in Rome, the place where you got your clothes on the way down here. They'll fix you up with the right documents and tickets; I think it's a two P.M. flight to New York—you'll sleep tomorrow night in your own bed—but they'll straighten all that out for you. Leave a call for six. Mario'll pick you up at six-thirty and take you to the airport."

"I will have a coffee sent up to you before we leave," Mario said agreeably. "If you wish something more before your flight, we can get it after you check in at Capodichino."

Hake stood listening. And fidgeting. His instincts wanted

to say something his mouth was reluctant to speak. Finally
he managed to say, "Anyway, thank you. All of you. I
guess you did get me out of a tight place."

"No more than was coming to you, dear boy. You were
a great help to us. Your nut-lady and the wogs were a
considerable annoyance, and now they're taken care of."

"But they got away!"

"The wogs did, yes. But that's not all bad, Hake. They
are an unpleasant pair, and catching them is like catching
rattlesnakes in a net. Besides, dear boy, it's nothing *personal* with them. I didn't want to punish them. You don't
punish a bomb, you just make sure it doesn't blow you
up."

They were all smiling at him, Yosper still eating, the
boys leaning back and holding hands. Hake waited for the
other shoe to drop. It didn't. He said tightly, "The girl got
away too."

"Not far, boy," said Yosper pleasantly.

"What are you talking about?"

Yosper sighed. "Well, let's see if we can find out," he
said, and picked up the phone. He spoke for a few seconds
in a language Hake did not know and then put it down,
beaming. "She's in Regina Coeli right now, Hake. She'll be
out of circulation for a while."

"Jail? For what? She didn't break any law here!"

Yosper shook his head, chuckling. "She broke the most
basic law of the land. You see, her little bunch of amateurs
pulls the same trick we do, only they're not as good at it.
She was operating on forged identity and credit. But once
we tracked her down to the *Pescatore* and dear Mario
turned her room—why, we knew what she was using. The
rest of it was easy. We blew her credit. She got as far as
Rome, and they picked her up for using phony cards. She's
a bankrupt, Hake. They'll auction her off in the Rome
slave market to pay her bills. It'll be a good long time
before she bothers us again."

Twenty-one hours later Hake jumped out of a taxi on the
Trastevere side of the Ponte Sant'Angelo. He had not
wasted his time in Rome. The training Under the Wire,

and the on-the-job skills he had acquired in the last few days, had all found a use. From the Team's safe depot in Rome he had secured his new passport and his return ticket to America, along with a few items of standard equipment he had requisitioned on the spot—one of them being the inks and papers to change his ticket, and the cards to finance a few extracurricular activities. The rest of the day had been spent finding out what he needed to know. He set his walking stick and "satchel" on the sidewalk under the looming layer-cake of Hadrian's Tomb and paid the driver carefully, adding coins according to volume and pitch. When the words dwindled away and the tone dropped back down to tenor he turned away, picked up his gear and crossed to the parapet near the bridge. The Tiber River at that point was a gently meandering stream, between grassy banks, here widening into a pool, there narrow and swift. It did not look artificial. It looked as if it had been there forever.

"*Siete pescatore?*" Hake had not noticed the approach of the Roman policeman. "*Pesce,*" the man repeated, demonstrating a rod and line with his electric baton. "Feesh? You feesh? Have license?"

"Oh," said Hake, enlightened. "No, I'm not going to fish. No fish. Just look. *Voyeur.*"

"Ah, *paura!*" said the patrolman in sympathy, touching Hake's shoulder before moving on. Hake leaned idly on the balustrade, giving the policeman time to get out of sight. It was true, what he had been talking about. There were anglers on the Ponte Sant'Angelo, dangling hooks into the stream as it flowed under the bridge, even at this hour. And in the stream itself, elderly women in hip-length waders were whipping the shallows with fly rods. Hake could not see whether they were catching anything. But he wished them luck, for it took their attention off him.

He walked quickly twenty yards out onto the bridge and there, just as the map from the depot had said, was an iron disk set in the sidewalk. Using the walking stick as a crowbar he levered the cover off and peered in. It was totally dark, and it stank. That was as expected, too, if not very attractive. He dropped the knapsack in and heard it hit a cement landing a few yards down; he followed, climbing down a slippery metal ladder and lowering the cover back into place above him.

As soon as it was closed the stench became abominable, and the absence of light was total.

He was in Rome's greatest and oldest sewer. Was the Tiber polluted? *Va bene!* Roof it over. Let it fulfill its function! And now the river was in fact a sewer. It rolled under a grassed and gardened parkland strip with a new, and artificial, stream running its length to justify the maps and the bridges. Waste disposal was benefited. Esthetic appeal was maintained. And *la cloaca maxima nuova* flowed untroubled to the sea.

Untroubled? Yes, perhaps, but not untroubling. The stink was at least of an order of magnitude worse than anything Hake had previously experienced in his life. Hastily he fumbled around on the slimy cement to find the knapsack, located the ripcord and popped it open. It made a sharp rush of sound, like a tire abruptly going flat, and unfolded itself. In ten seconds it had sprouted prow and stern, stretching itself into the form of a kayak. He fumbled around to orient himself and found what he was looking for. Inside the well for the paddler was a plastic pouch which, opened, produced flashlight, folded paddle and a breathing mask.

When Hake had the mask on, he took the first full breath he had allowed himself since entering the manhole. It was bearable. Barely bearable. It was like being downwind of an ill-kept abattoir, where before it had been like being one of the beeves.

He thumbed the light on and looked about him. The Tiber water did not look bad. Things were floating in it, and the stench was undeniable, but it looked, actually, merely cool and wet—until he held the light at arm's length out away from the cement landing, and saw the oily iridescence shining up. The roof was steelwork with a courtesy patching of plaster, most of which had peeled away. Under it the river moved more briskly than it appeared. When Hake was in the kayak he found that paddling was hard work.

It would have been intelligent, he realized, to have let himself in upstream of his destination, rather than down. He had not been that intelligent. Each stroke moved him a yard forward, and while he was bringing the paddle up for the next stroke the current slid him a foot back. It was complicated by the need to change sides from time to time, and still more by the fact that he had to use care; he did not want the sewer sloshing over into the kayak, because the smell would be certain to make him conspicuous where he was going. Even so, he could not avoid a certain amount of dripping. Within a minute he had begun to sweat, and no more than two or three minutes later he was panting for breath. If there had been anything to Leota's talk about hypnotism, he thought grimly, he could have used a little of the trance state now. Anything—anything that would take his mind off the smell, and the heat, and the fatigue that was beginning to burn his already sore muscles.

He had expected it to take ten minutes to paddle the four hundred yards up the underground Tiber. It took half an hour, and by the time he found the landing he was looking for he was spent. Stench or none, he pulled the mask off to allow his lungs more air.

But he was there. He was under the great pavilion that had been built to straddle the river, for music and dance and other special functions. And if his information was correct, Leota was somewhere overhead.

There was a lock on the door but once again the training Under the Wire proved itself. He was through it in a minute, emerging into a steel-staired cement shaft. After climbing six short flights he found a door and, opening it quickly, slipped through.

He was in a round chamber, not very large, that looked like a surgical amphitheater. The center was a sort of pit, like an orchestra hall set up for a pops concert. It was surrounded by circular, rising tiers of benches; and for some reason it looked reminiscent. But not familiar. Scattered around the pit were cloth-draped wooden stands, like the ones animal trainers use to put their lions through their paces, but they were not occupied. He had cut it close, but the auction had not yet begun. A few dozen persons were strolling about the pit, others seated on the benches above. Waiters in smoking jackets and waitresses in tiny cocktail skirts were passing among them with trays of wine and orange juice, and no one had observed him as he entered. He reached for a glass at random and realized what non-memory had been trying to assert itself as he tasted the orange. The place was exactly as he had imagined Shakespeare's Globe Theatre to be. A woman in a long dress and corsage approached him. *"Il programma, signore?"* He took the program and thanked her, and then, when it appeared more was expected, gave her a hundred-lire tip. She was looking at him curiously, and he turned away as if urgently in need of a place to set down his orange-juice glass.

Half the crowd on the floor seemed to be Western businessperson types, both male and female. The others wore burnooses, a few dashikis, and Hake caught phrases of old, familiar tongues. He did not pause to listen. He felt out of place, and was anxious to avoid attracting attention. The sunglasses covered his two still black eyes, but the bruises on his face were visible and he was aware that he carried with him a faint smell of the sewer. He was also younger than almost any of the other men, and far less expensively dressed. But as he looked closer he revised his opinion. It would not be easy to be out of place in this group, they were too disparate among themselves. The sheiks were not all Arab, and probably not sheiks. Hake recognized Bedouin and Turk as well as the familiar Palestinian and Lebanese of his childhood. Some of them were black, and broader-featured than any of those—perhaps Sudanese, perhaps anything at all. Or anything that had money. That was the unifying characteristic of them all, whether they wore burnoose or open-necked sports shirt, or, like the woman who snapped at Hake in French when he bumped into her, a velvet pants suit. Some of them were worse dressed than Hake. But there was about them an air that said that, if so, it was because they chose to be; and they all had the look of persons who acquired what they liked.

Hake reached out for another glass—this time making sure that it was wine, not a fruit juice, that it contained—and retired to the edge of the pit to study the *programma*. It was not exactly a program. It was more like a catalogue. A soft, matte-paper cover enclosed a four-page, neatly photocopied listing of the fifteen indentured credit-fraud criminals who were to be sold off that evening.

He had taken an Italian-language copy of the insert, which perhaps was why the program-vender had looked at him that way. Leota's name was not on the list. Well, of course, it wouldn't be. He searched carefully and decided that *Joanna Sailtops, signorina di 26 anni, degli Stati Uniti, L2 265 000* must be she. And if the two-million-lire-plus figure represented her selling price, it would be well within the limits of the credit cards he had forged.

There was nothing else in the insert that seemed helpful, but inside the matte cover was some material repeated in eight languages, including French and German and Japanese, but also in English and Arabic. They all said the same thing, and were descriptions of the conditions of sale. The contract conformed to Italian law, which meant, at least, that Leota would be somewhere in Italy until it expired; outside, it automatically went void. Each of these persons had pleaded guilty to credit fraud and accepted indentured service in lieu of prison terms. Proceeds of sale would go to repay the losses sustained, and to post bonds; a percentage was deducted to cover the expenses of the State in the conduct of the trial and the auction. Each person was fully guaranteed against any permanent damage. Each had been given a full medical examination that afternoon and the records would be kept; a similar examination would be performed upon conclusion of the term of service, and if any lasting harm had been inflicted the indentured person would have the right of suing for damages, as well as a possible criminal action against the purchaser. It was not quite slavery, Hake conceded to himself. But close enough, close enough!

He looked up. Something was happening. The prospective buyers who had seated themselves were leaving the benches and coming down into the pit, and in a moment he saw why. Attendants in the smoking jackets of waiters were leading in a procession of persons wearing thin cloaks and *i minimi*. They were the subjects of the auction. And the fifth to enter was Leota.

The costume that had seemed a little extreme, but highly attractive, in the Blue Grotto struck Hake as appallingly scanty here. Even covered by the clinging, but nearly transparent, cloak. Hake did not like the way the other customers looked at her—they were not all studying her, to be sure, but even the fact that the other fourteen items of merchandise drew attention, some of them a good deal more than Leota, seemed to him demeaning. He pushed his way past a cocktail waitress and a slight, dark man in a kepi and a tailored shorts-suit to reach her. Her eyes widened.

"Hake! Get the hell out of here!"

He shook his head. "I'm going to get you out. I'll pay your bill—"

"Piss off!" she hissed, staring around. On the covered drum nearest hers one of the attendants was demonstrating the muscles of a teen-aged peasant boy with macho gill-wattles carved into his neck. Only the Arab in shorts was watching them. And he was smiling. The fact that Leota had a friend present made her more interesting, Hake realized angrily. She leaned close and whispered, "You can't afford this. And I'll be all right. If you want to do something to help, remember what we were talking about on the ship."

"I remember. But I'm going to buy you free, Leota. I've got the, ah, the price."

"Idiot! You use phony credit and you'll find yourself up here too! Horny, you can be so *stupid*. If I go out of here with you, how long do you think it'll be before your buddies come after me?"

While he was trying to think of an answer to that, she added: "It's only going to be thirty days or so. They bid on per-diem contracts, and I ought to be good for sixty or seventy hundred thousand lire a day." She glanced at the

Saudi, who was strolling closer, studying the shape of her body under the cape. "Now get lost! I—I appreciate the thought, Horny, but I don't need your help. I'll be a lot safer if some pasta manufacturer takes me home for a while, until things cool off."

"Excuse me," said the Saudi politely, moving past Hake to peer into Leota's face.

Hake felt himself trembling. The notion of Leota being sold into—into what was, after all, prostitution! like some Minneapolis teen-ager shagged into the stable of a Times Square pimp!—stung him in nerves he had not known he possessed. He was conscious of an unusual squirming in his groin. It was not figurative, but a physical fact, as if his testicles were responding to the threat to his manhood by trying to creep up out of sight. And at the same time he was conscious of a strong desire to punch the Arab out.

And all this was as astonishing to Hake as it was unpleasant, because he had never known himself as a beaugallant. I'm a God-damned *anachronism*, one part of his mind was telling another, I belong in the court of Aquitaine! And quite separately, another piece of his mind—or perhaps a piece of Horny Hake that lived nowhere near his mind—tensed the muscles and worked the tendons and moved the joints that stiff-armed the Saudi, grabbed Leota by the arm and dragged her across the clearing floor, toward the exit— The exit where one of the attendants was picking up a phone, while three others moved menacingly toward him. One caught at each of Hake's arms. The third shook a fist, hissing furiously in Italian. From behind, something struck Hake's shoulder; he craned his neck, and saw that it was the Saudi, thin lips pouting under the raptor nose, ivory swagger stick raised to hit him again. One of the attendants moved diplomatically between them. The Arab drew back, suspending the attack in preference to being touched, and declared in particulate Oxonian English, "This common creature—has had the impudence— to ruffianize me."

"I didn't!" The attendant twisted his arm, but Hake blazed, "He's lying! At most, I brushed him aside!"

"I suggest—" shrilled the Arab—"that we permit the authorities to deal with this gangster!" And it was only then that Hake saw that a pair of *carabinieri* had appeared behind the attendants. One of them, whom Hake had somehow seen before, was speaking sorrowfully and judgmentally in Italian, while the attendants nodded.

"He says," translated the other policeman, "that you have already confessed yourself to be a sexual pervert—do you deny it? for shame!—a voyeur! And you trespass here, offending our guest, Sheik Hassabou."

Hake's diminishing rational self possessed enough jurisdiction still to cause him to say, quite reasonably, "I see there may be some sort of misunderstanding here." But at the same time the non-rational one was swelling against thinning control. The Arab thoughtfully lifted his swagger stick again. Analytically, Hake might have perceived that it was unlikely he meant to strike. Why should he? Right was on his side, along with the majesty of the law. Analytical Hake was not involved. Glandular Hake and machismatic Hake and the ensorceled Aquitainian Hake outnumbered and overwhelmed the analytical one. He flung the policeman's arms away. Alarmed, the Saudi struck at him with the baton while his other hand went instinctively to the hilt of the ceremonial dagger at his belt.

And, of course, beyond question the Arab would not use it to kill. And when Hake instinctively grabbed for the dagger and it came away into his astonished hand, he would not have used it to kill either. But reflexive Hake did not know the first, nor reflexive Arab, police and attendants the second; and all at once he was the very picture of mad pervert at bay with naked blade in his hand. "Oh, Horny!" wailed Leota's voice, "you should have listened—" And they all moved in at once, and clubbed him to the ground.

IX

WHEN I was a ballsy boy like you," said Yosper, swirling the whiskey around his glass as they waited for Hake's plane, "I was as shit-stupid as you are, or, no, not that stupid, but stupid enough. I could've aced myself over any dumb, dirty pretty-puss that lifted a leg on my fireplug, same's you. 'Course, I didn't. Even then, I had some smarts. But I could have, yes." And it was as if they were playing the same scenes all over again. The sets were a little different; they were in the sky lounge at the Rome airport instead of a Vomero restaurant or Capri night club or the Munich pension. But the actors were the same, and playing the same parts. Only the one supporting actor who was Hake himself was made up in a different way: he had a compression bandage over his left ear to protect the new stitches that held it on. The rest—the black eyes, bruised jaws, the stiff and uneasy way he moved—they were the equivalent of the lettering on an easeled poster, *Some Time Later*, which he himself did enact. But the play was all reprise, Yosper's monologue attended by the chorus, brave Mario, sweet Dieter, even laughing Carlos, who had just flown in from heaven knew where, to join Yosper for heaven knew what. "—of course, there are some brutes that I personally would not touch with a borrowed, ah, thing. Not now. Not even when I was a great deal younger than you, Hake, and almost as dumb. Were you balling her?"

Hake glared at him through swollen eyes. The old man waved a hand. "I guess you were, and you got your *cojones* misplaced to where your brains belong. Foul, foolish business, Hake, but it's happened to better men than you, and I won't hold it against you. Looks like you're home free. Not counting a few aches and pains, of course. The cops dropped charges, fair enough; figured they got their jollies kicking you around on the way to the *questura*. So there's nothing on the record, and won't be unless you pissed the sheik off worse'n I think you did. But that I doubt, because he's gone. So—no report, no problem. The boys and I won't say anything. And, man! You're some mean hand at a bar-room brawl, Hake, you know that? Seven against one, and you wade right in! Wouldn't've thought it of you."

"Stop now," Hake said clearly.

Yosper was brought down, disconcerted, in full flow. "What?"

"I said stop for a minute. Please," he added, pro forma. "I want to know what happened to Leota."

"Why, she's gone, Hake. The Sheik of Araby took off for his desert tent off in the Sahel or someplace, and naturally he took her along to give him what he wants. You know," he said scientifically, "from what I hear, those sheiks want some freaky fixin's when they go to it. Too bad you can't ask her about it sometime, Hake. Be interesting to learn something, you know?"

"Yosper, God damn you—"

Around the table the three young men shifted position slightly, without either menace or anger, simply entering the "ready" mode. Yosper raised his hand. "Hake here isn't going to do anything, are you, Hake? No. You shouldn't take the name of the Lord in vain. But He's got as much sense as I have, and He knows you're just pissed off." He paused for a second, looking at Hake with sharp blue eyes that, for a wonder, had something in them Hake could only recognize as compassion. "Get over it, boy," he said.

"You'll never see her again. Listen. Likely as not she'll come out of it smelling of roses. Old Sheik Hassabou gives his ladies emeralds and rubies—maybe a few little scars too, of course. Don't get sore, boy."

Hake said bitterly, "Of course I won't get sore! Why should I? All you've done is get a girl's life wrecked, and involve me in dope selling, and—"

"Shu, shu, boy. There's important reasons for all this."

"I can't wait to hear what the important reason for addicting kids to dope is," Hake snarled.

"Hake," Yosper said kindly, "dope's not that bad. I been there. You ever hear of Haight-Ashbury?"

Hake shrugged. "Some place in California? A long time ago?"

"I was there," Yosper said proudly. "It was all love and sharing, and dope, and nobody got hurt. Much. 'Course, it didn't last. The rich ones went to Napoma. The rest of us tried the East Village, and the caves on Crete, and Khatmandu. I did every bit of it, boy, and I thank my Lord Savior I don't have to do it again." He stared into space, his lips working as though he were tasting something he liked. "Good dope in Nepal," he said at last, "but it's against God's commandments. Now they're all off around the Persian Gulf, old bastards like me that haven't learned their lesson and kids that don't know the score yet."

Carlos grumbled, "Yosper, why do you waste your time with him?"

"It's no waste," Yosper said earnestly. "The boy's got good stuff. He justa has a few wrong ideas, like about dope. Why, look at it the righta way, we're doing those wop kids a favor."

"Us too," Dieter grinned. "We make even more from PCP than we made from selling Ku Klux Klan nightshirts in Germany."

"But the kids get the most out of it," Yosper insisted. "Dope separates the men from the boys, and it teaches you a lot about just plain living. Why," he said earnestly, "wasn't for my time in the Haight and Khatmandu I wouldn't be half this honest and open and compassionate."

X

HAKE flew back to the United States in far grander style than he had left it. Not merely was he in the first-class section of the Trans-Pam jumbo, marinated in wines, cosseted with cushions, but the seat beside him was paid for and empty. The stewardesses made it up into a little bed for him. The Team rewarded its members.

But Hake's question was how he could best reward the Team. He began to think of it while the jet was lunging up into the yellow-gray Tyrrhenian sky and the oily beach at Ostia was dropping away beneath. He did not sleep, even though one of the stews brought him hot milk and another sat beside him, to stroke the poor bandaged head of the man who had been so brutally attacked by *ragazzi*. He wished they would leave him alone. He was busy scheming.

At Kennedy the chief flight attendant hurried out the gate to speak to the customs agents and a stewardess found him a wheelchair. He went straight to the head of the line, and when he got through Immigration a Trans-Pam courier was waiting to conduct Reverend Hake to his waiting limousine. Hake was aware of what was happening. Part of it was only that Yosper had whispered a word in the purser's ear, to say that this poor man's very life was at risk because of a mugging in the shadow of the Colosseum itself. But part of it was more. The invisible embrace of the Team never let him go.

One of Yosper's boys had even phoned ahead. It was ten at night before the limo reached Long Branch, but Jessie was warned and waiting. She peered into his ruined face. "Oh, Horny! They said you might need a wheelchair, but I thought we could just use your old chairlift. Then you can lean on my arm—"

"I can walk, Jessie." He waved the driver away—let the Team tip him, if a tip was what he was waiting for.

She clucked despairingly. "You look really terrible, Horny."

"I appreciate your telling me that, Jessie." He proved his ability to walk by limping heavily past her into the house. All of the cuts and stabbing pains had turned into sullen sore aches and stiffnesses, and walking was no fun. He didn't want to discuss it. Knowing she had followed him into his room he dropped his bag and said over his shoulder, "And for the next few days I don't want to see anyone but you."

"Well, I don't blame you there, Horny."

"Except," he said, "first thing tomorrow I want you to get an IBM representative in to see me, and a car dealer. And, oh, yes, while I think of it, a carpet salesman. And day after get me on an early flight to Washington."

"You mean the Metroliner, right?"

"I mean a flight. On an airplane, and now I'm going to take a hot bath and go to bed. Good night, Jessie."

As soon as she was out of the house, clucking and fussing, coming back twice to tell him that she had left him a pot of chicken soup on the stove and that she wasn't really sure she could get all those people in but would do her best, Hake spilled his battered bag onto the bed. He dumped the filthy clothes, some of them still from the unwashed weeks Under the Wire, into a hamper and hesitated over the rest. Lock-pick, garroting wire, circuit testers. Telecommunications codes and Blue Box pitchpipe. At the bottom were the tapes and fiches The Incredible Art had given him so long ago, and for them he could see no immediate use. For the other things—yes, no doubt. He was not yet sure what the use would be but he would find one. He stripped off his clothes and limped to the full-length mirror in the bathroom door.

He was, in fact, a mess. The old network of scars on the left side of his chest, where his ribs had been spread and respread with tools like car jacks, were almost lost under the greater, newer marks. He had green-gray bruises all over his body. Both eyes were black. Under the adhesive dressing, the squashed sides of his nose were purply red, and the bandage over his ear was stained with blood. He studied himself appraisingly and nodded. Nobody trained Under the Wire could have done a more thorough job.

Remained to see what he was going to do about it.

He ran hot water prodigally into the tub and, while he was waiting for it to fill, experimentally flushed his toilet. It did not speak to him, not even a "hello." Apparently he had been given the evening off.

Hake lowered himself into the steaming tub, so sore and so troubled that he was almost at peace. Inside his head was a solid and well-defined lump of cold anger. It was not mere helpless rage and frustration, not any more. It had been transmuted, and the transmutation occurred as Yosper and his boys were walking him through the perfunctory Roman passport control. They ambled in military formation, Yosper on his right side, Dieter on his left; Carlos followed a few paces behind and Mario took the point; it was exactly as if they were patrolling some not quite secure area, and as Yosper waved genially to the boarding clerk and led Hake past her into the waiting plane, he stopped and said, with real emotion, "You're a good man, Hake." He patted Hake's shoulder awkwardly, and then amended himself. "Too shitfired headstrong, sure. Get you in trouble one of these days, boy, real trouble, mark my words. But you got a lot of Moxie. I want you to know I'm sending a commendation in for your promotion file. And next time I have a job you can help in, I'm going to ask for you *by name.*"

"Thank you," said Hake, and at that moment he made his resolution.

In his own bathtub, staring up at the green mermaids on

the plastic shower curtain, he was calculating ways and means.

They would forgive you anything, he thought. Just so you got the job done. More so if you showed balls enough to run a game of your own now and then. Leota had been quite right; they were grooming him for a big one, and evidently they considered he was coming along just fine.

Very well. He would accept their trust. He would play their mad macho games, and do his best to earn more trust. It was a good thing to be trusted, because without the possession of trust you did not have the power to betray.

This time the receptionist at the Lo-Wate Bottling Co. was a slim middle-aged Oriental male instead of his first visit's guardian of the gate, but he gave Hake the identical loathsome stare. "Do you have an appointment?" he asked, as if it were a foregone conclusion that Hake did not.

"I am the Reverend H. Hornswell Hake, to see Curmudgeon at once, and I don't need one. Tell him I'm here."

Hake sat down and opened a magazine without waiting for an answer. He had no doubt that he would get past the receptionist. If his name or the lumps on his face were not passport enough, his arrogance would be. Hake was far from sure that arrogance would melt all difficulties in dealing with the Team. But it was the best tool he had in his chest to use at that moment. And, besides, it gave him pleasure.

When he finally was led to the remembered office Curmudgeon's scowl was black. "You jerked me out of a planning meeting!" he barked. "Man, you got a lot to learn. *Never* come here without orders, do you understand?"

"I understand," Hake nodded, "and will comply, provided you cut out the chickenshit. Don't give me any more missions where I don't know the score. Not any. Otherwise I make a lot of trouble. Do *you* understand?"

"Now, listen—"

"Not yet. First take a look at my face. I'll grant you that half of it is my own fault, but the other half isn't. I got these lumps because the Team let me down. That's not going to happen again, and the way we're going to keep it from happening is I'm going to get a full briefing before I ever lift another finger for you. More than that. I'm going to have the right to accept or decline, whatever it is." He stopped and leaned back. "I hope you understand and will comply," he added mildly.

Curmudgeon glowered silently for a moment, one hand combing its fingers through his dense beard while the other hovered nervously near the butt of his .45. Then, surprisingly, he shrugged and relaxed. "Maybe Jasper Medina's right about you," he said.

"Depends on what he says."

Curmudgeon said thoughtfully, "Says you're a lot tougher than you look. Well, that's what we need. But that doesn't mean you can pull a stunt like this again! Once, *maybe*. Twice and you've had it, Hake, you really have!"

"I understand and will comply," Hake said, "provided some dummy doesn't do something that leaves me no choice. Now, what I came down here for. I've ordered some stuff for myself—a car, a computer terminal, some odds and ends for the church—"

"Computer! Not a chance, Hake. Grade Three field agents don't rate personal computer terminals, do you have any idea what those things cost?"

"Charge it to KLM."

"No computer! It isn't just a question of the money. You'll make yourself too conspicuous. No."

Hake scowled, then decided to pass it. If he decided he really needed one he would get it anyhow, and figure out how to pay for it with the skills learned Under the Wire. "Then one last thing. I want Team help to get Leota Pauket out of that sheik's harem."

Curmudgeon grinned. "There you went too far. You go near him, or her, and you're dead, Hake."

"But I'm responsible for her being there!"

"Why, sure you are. What's that got to do with it? No way. Sheik Hassabou's a significant contact and not to be endangered. Don't knock it, Hake. Outside of Jasper Medina's commendation, about the only thing you've got going for you is that you facilitated making that contact. You didn't plan it that way, but we hit lucky."

"Him? What's he good for? He's a played-out oil sheik, nothing left but money."

Curmudgeon shook his head. "That far you can't push me. I'll tell you this much. The Team has a major objective, and we needed someone to help. He's it. When Medina contacted him to drop the charges against you it gave a chance for certain other topics to be raised—and they were. That's it, Hake. You can have all your other toys."

"But Leota—"

"Knock it off, Hake! We've got no reason to do that woman any favors. I'll tell you what," he said, relenting slightly. "She's only got thirty days to do there. Then I'll see. Maybe we can clean her slate for her."

Hake had a sudden preview of what Leota would say if he told her the Team had offered to clean her slate. Still, he had found out more than he had known when he got here, and the most he had really expected was a crumb or two of information.

"I'm waiting, Hake."

There was such a thing as pressing your luck too far. Unwillingly, Hake said, "I understand and will comply, but—"

"No but. No more conversation," said Curmudgeon. "Good-by, Hake."

When Hake got back to Long Branch his new car was waiting at the curb. It was a Tata three-wheeler, hydrogen propelled, and Jessie Tunman came out on the porch to get a look at it. "Why yellow?" she sniffed.

"It was what they had in stock," Hake said.

She shook her head disapprovingly. "After all the things you've said about power-piggery," she remarked. "And with the balance of payments going crazy with these new hydrogen imports—well, it's your life. Are you going to be able to take care of any business now, Horny?"

"What kind of business?"

"Well, some parishioners want to talk to you—"

"No counseling until my face heals up."

"All right, but Alys's husbands have been on the phone, twice each."

"I don't want to hear."

"And that windmill makes a *terrible* racket sometimes, Horny. I've called the construction people three times but they never do anything about it."

"Tell them," he said, "that if they don't get a man down here today I'm going to rip it out and buy a new one from someone else."

"Horny!"

"Tell them. Now I'm going to take my new car for a spin."

"Drive it in good health," she sniffed.

That was far from certain, he thought, wincing at the pain of unfamiliar muscles as he stepped on the unfamiliar accelerator and clutch and brake. But this was not a joy ride. It might even be rather essential to his life. It had occurred to Hake in Curmudgeon's office that it might be easy to overplay his hand, with possibly very unhappy results. On the other side, there was a way to improve the cards he had been dealt. What he was after now was a new hole card; so he drove down to Asbury Park, stopping at a discount store along the highway to buy a new cassette recorder and tapes.

The beach was full of bathers, of course, but only a few surf-casters were out on the rock jetties; there was not much to be caught any more in the sludgy New Jersey Atlantic. Painfully Hake climbed the rocks past them, to a place where wind and surf and distance blanketed his voice. He sat down, put a new tape in the machine and began to speak.

"My name is H. Hornswell Hake, pastor of the Unitarian Church in Long Branch. I was first contacted by the spy and sabotage group called 'The Team' on March 16th, when a person I suppose to have been a Team agent, representing himself to my secretary as an IRS man and to me as a senator's administrative assistant, came to my house to order me to active duty. . . ."

By the fourth day after his return Hake did not look much better, but some of the aches were dwindling. In a way, the beatings were an asset. They had made Jessie Tunman willing to keep everyone away from him, though she expressed herself baffled that he was continually inventing excuses to go out: to the supermarket, to get a morning paper, to mail a letter, to drive his new car for fun and practice. "I can do all that for you, Horny," she protested. "All but drive that silly yellow car, anyway, and that's wasting power!" When he replied that he needed the exercise or wanted the fresh air she gave up, unsatisfied and unreconciled. It didn't matter. He had to get out to do what he needed to do.

And when at last, on the twentieth try, each one from a different public phone, he finally found The Incredible Art at home, he cried, "Thank God!"

"Who is this? Horny? What's the matter?"

"Nothing's the matter, Art—well, it's complicated. Are you alone in the house? Good. I'll be over to see you in five minutes." And actually he made it in three. The tapes he had made on the jetty in Asbury Park were burning holes in his pocket.

The home of The Incredible Art was almost invisible from the street—not much less so when you walked up to the front door, for Art had built it into the side of a hill. A concrete casting in the shape of a magician's peaked hat was beside the door, and when Hake pressed the bell it lit up and croaked, "Who dares approach the sacred cave of The Incredible Art?" Hake didn't have to answer. The door was open before the tape recording finished, and Art's skinny, blond face was peering worriedly out. "My God, Horny," he said.

"I had an accident," Hake said. "I've been thinking about printing up cards to give out."

"I never thought you'd turn into a brawler at your age. How about a cup of tea?"

"Maybe later." Hake pushed past Art into the house and closed the door. He reached into his shirt and pulled out the sealed packet of tape cassettes; he had not wanted to be seen carrying them inside. "I want a big favor, please, Art."

The magician pursed his lips, looked at the sealed packet. "I bet that isn't home-made cookies."

"It's something I want you to keep for me. In a really safe place. If you hear I'm dead, or if I don't come back and ask for them in thirty days, then open up these tapes and play them. And please don't say anything about this, don't even say you saw me, to anybody at all."

"Oh, wow." Art sat down, tugging at his blond beard. He looked at the package of tapes without taking them. "Horny, what are you into?"

"I just can't tell you, Art. Of course—" stiffly—"if you're afraid of trouble—"

"It ain't the trouble, Horny, it's the curiosity." The magician leaned forward to take the package from Hake's hand. He shook it, listened to it, then tossed it back and forth from hand to hand, watching Hake's face. "You know," he mentioned, "you're an amateur at sealing up packages. I could get into this and reseal it and you'd never know the difference."

"Just please don't, Art."

The magician nodded. "One question. Why me?"

"Because I trust you. Also because you're always doing TV and radio appearances; you'll know how to use the tapes if you have to. I should tell you that it might not be—" He hesitated. He had been going to say "easy." Candor made him finish, "safe."

Art whistled thoughtfully. He stood up and began to walk around the room, juggling the packet. "What about that cup of tea?" he asked over his shoulder.

"All right, but please don't drop them."

Art put a kettle on the stove and then turned around, spreading empty hands. "Drop what?" he grinned.

"Where—"

"They're where they'll be okay for a while. I'll find a better place, but even you won't know where it is. Are you sure you can't give me even the teensiest hint?"

"I'm sure, Art. And I'm not finished, I'm sorry to say. I need to find somebody, and I'm hoping you can help me with your computer."

"Oh?"

"It's a woman. Her name's Leota Pauket. P-A-U-K-E-T."

"Uh-huh. Of course you can't tell me much about her?"

"Well, last I saw of her she was in Rome, but she's an American. From somewhere in the midwest. I think."

"Splendid, Horny!" Art thought for a minute. "As I see it, you have two ways to go. First we could try telephone listings. I can start a search program to query every exchange in the midwest for a listing for this Leota Pauket. Figure fifteen seconds a directory, maybe a couple thousand directories—you could complete it in a day or so. Wouldn't cost anything, which is a big advantage—information queries are free. But it doesn't work if she doesn't have a phone."

"What's the other way?"

"That's harder. You have to get into the memories for Social Security or the Bureau of the Census, something like that. I can't do that, but I've got some slippery friends. They might help."

"As far as that's concerned," Hake said cautiously, "I think I could handle that part."

"You what?"

Hake said defensively, "I'm sorry, Art, but that's part of what I can't talk about. However. I'm not real sure she's anywhere near America; last I heard she was in the, uh, entourage of a sheik named Hassabou."

Hake's expression cleared. "Why didn't you say so in the first place? All you need is celebrity service—come on, I'll set it up." Hake followed into another room, where Art sat before his computer terminal, typed rapidly for a second and then sat back. "How much of this stuff do you want?" he asked. "Here, sit down. Slow it down with this thing here if it's going too fast for you." And it was; the machine was racing through line after line of printout, far more information than he could actually use. The sheik's name was Sheik Badawey Al-Nadim Abd Hassabou, and every directory of the rich and the famous had something about him. The sheik's wealth was estimated at more than three hundred million dollars, exclusive of family holdings. The sheik's home was in Rome, Wad Madani, Beverly Hills, Edinburgh, a place called Abu Magnah or his yacht—depending on the season, and on the sheik's mood. The sheik's interests seemed to be the three S's: sex, surfing and sports cars. The sheik's family, like the families of most of the oil Arabs, had long since left the Persian Gulf, no longer held the worthless oil leases, had their money in Argentine cattle ranches and Chicago real estate, but saw no reason to spend much time in those places when the fleshpots of Europe and California were so much more fun. The sheik was fifty-one years old, but in astonishingly good health. Hake gloomily accepted the truth of that part of it. The man in the auction room had obviously kept fit.

The information came from gossip columns, financial reports and various who's-who directories. None of it mentioned an acquisition of the sheik's named Leota Pauket, of course. Hake had not expected it would.

He sat back. "Enough," he said. "Does it mention where he is right now?"

"Hold on." Art punched out orders, and the machine typed out: Presently in Abu Magnah.

"Abu Magnah?" Hake tried to place the town and couldn't. He got down the old red atlas and looked for Abu Magnah. It was not on the map. It took Art inquiries to the information services of three Arab consulates, the National Geographic Society and the cartographical division of the public library before he was able to locate it. Armed with latitude and longitude Hake carefully marked a cross on the map and sat back to regard it. Squarely in the Empty Quarter. Hundreds of miles from anything more metropolitan than a flock of sheep. Hassabou liked his privacy.

"You want that cup of tea, Horny? You wouldn't want to tell me what this is all about?"

"Well—she's a girl I know, Art. I'm a little worried about her."

"I can see that you might be."

"You mean because she's in this guy's harem? Well, sure." He grinned suddenly. "Sometimes I think I should've married somebody like Jessie—younger, of course—when I was still in the wheelchair. Then I might not have these problems."

He peered around the room, wondering where Art had

managed to hide the tapes. Then he said, with some embarrassment, "Art, I can't tell you how grateful I am——"

"Why should that worry you? You can't tell me anything else, either, right?" The magician was smiling, but the smile leaked away as he said, "Look, Horny. You're into some kind of spy thing, aren't you?"

"Would it make a difference, Art?"

"Not to whether I do what you want, no. But it would make a difference." Art hesitated. "No offense, Horny," he said, "but spies are a sad lot. They're not only immoral, they're incompetent."

"Oh, I don't know if I agree with——"

"I'm not talking about you personally, Horny. I mean the whole industry. Look. I'll give you a quick test question. Name three cases where any nation in modern times gained anything by spying."

"Are you serious? Come on, Art! I could name hundreds!"

"Oh? All right. Go ahead."

Hake frowned. After a moment, he said, "Well, I've never taken any special interest in the subject of spying. . ."

"All right, let me suggest a couple of examples to help you out. For instance, what about World War II? Russian spies told Stalin when Hitler was going to attack. British intelligence learned a panzer division had moved into Arnhem just before they jumped. Hitler had the time and place for D-Day. The British broke the Luftwaffe code, so they knew their bombing targets twenty-four hours ahead. The Americans broke the Japanese Code Purple, so they had three days' warning of Pearl Harbor——"

"There you are!"

The magician shook his head. "Uh-uh. Not one of them used that information! Sometimes they just didn't believe it, like Hitler and Stalin and Montgomery. Sometimes they believed it, all right, but they were afraid if they acted on it they'd give away their sources. That's why the Americans got creamed at Pearl, and that's why Churchill let Coventry burn. So tell me this, Horny. What's the use of having spies in the first place?"

"Well, there must be other examples!"

"If you come across very many, please be sure to tell me, all right? And that's only talking about plain spying. If you get into the cloak-and-dagger stuff, the CIA sort of thing, bumping off one foreign politician and starting a revolution against another one, it gets even worse."

Horny flushed and changed the subject; it was getting a little too close to his own private space. "You keep on surprising me, Art," he said. "I didn't know espionage was one of your interests."

"The totality of human experience is my interest," the magician said seriously. "Especially when it affects friends of mine."

"I do appreciate that," Hake said awkwardly, "but—"

"But you can't talk about it. Right. So what else is new? Have you had a chance to look over that stuff I gave you a couple months ago?"

"What stuff? Oh," Hake said, remembering the fiches and cassettes that had been rattling around his bag all over the world, "you mean on hypnotism. No, I'm sorry. I just haven't had a chance."

"That I can believe," Art grinned. "No matter. They're copies, take your time. More tea?"

It was still daylight, but there was not so much of it left that Jessie wouldn't notice how long he had been away. Given any choice at all, Hake did not like to lie. He decided to make it possible to tell a misleading and incomplete truth instead by stopping by his church. It wasn't just for the sake of the cover story. The church was important to Horny, was very close to being his whole life. Being in it gave him a welcome feeling of refuge.

On a hot July afternoon the church was of course empty. The grass needed cutting and the windows were dusty, but there was enough activity in the pizzeria next door to make the whole block seem alive. Cars were whining in and out of the drive-in, and dozens of others were parked—a lot containing couples, one that seemed to contain a birdwatcher, or at least someone who was studying everything around, Hake included, through field glasses.

Hake drove gingerly through the erratic kids and into the church lot. Between his car and the front door he paused every few steps, to pick up empty Coke cartons and wedge-shaped pizza containers.

After the spicy smells from the pizzeria, the interior of the church smelled strongly of must and dust, but it was looking good. The First Unitarian Church of Long Branch now had a new green and gold nubbly carpet down its main hall, in a pattern guaranteed to drink up spilled wine and hide cigarette burns, and the contractors swore that its roof would no longer leak. So the Team was continuing to reward him and his. He eased himself stiffly and painfully into the torn leather chair in his study—that was another part of the payoff, to be sure—and began to make notes for the Buildings and Grounds Committee:

1. Cut lawn.
2. Prov. wst bskts nr pzria (worth trying?)
3. Check roof for leak after next rain.
4. Carpet gntee in safe dep box?
5. Plants watered? Lawn? Shrubs?

He had a list of fifteen items before he was done, and another of ten for Decorations and Special Functions. They were something to give Jessie to show where he had been, anyway. More or less content, Hake got up to prowl the church. All was in order. The familiar rooms were neat, if dusty. The main meeting hall, of course, was not. Social Action had been meeting there again. As he was pushing the chairs back into position and dumping ashtrays he heard a shrill peep-peep-peep from the parking lot.

He stopped and frowned. Was there another Tata in the neighborhood? Or another car with the same waspy, petulant horn? He finished quickly and locked up behind himself.

There stood his Tata, crystal bubble and bright yellow paint. But as he slid under the bubble he saw a note pinned to the steering wheel:

Our bargain still holds. Get out of this car at once.

It wasn't signed, but it didn't have to be. It was one of the Reddi brothers, of course. He sat paralyzed for a moment, and then it penetrated his mind that "at once" might very well mean "at *once*." He slid out from under the bubble and stepped back, looking around for someone to talk to about this unexpected problem.

There was a faint hissing sound from the car, a little like the buzz of a young rattlesnake.

Hake had learned something Under the Wire. He dropped flat on the damp asphalt. There was a blast of white fire and a crack like a giant whip. The shattered crystal bubble flew into the air; the yellow chassis of the Tata peeled outward, and it began to burn.

It was not a very big explosion. The hydrogen fuel was mostly in solid suspension in metal, and it burned rather than blowing up. But it was enough to destroy the car, and it surely would have been enough to destroy Hake, too, if he had been inside it.

When he was through with the police, and the firemen, and when the wrecker had come to tow what was left of his three-wheeler away, one of the policemen walked him to the door. He didn't need it; he wasn't hurt. But he was glad enough for it, except for the cop's conversation, which was about how unsafe your hydrogen cars were compared to your good old gas-burners—

"Have there been a lot of, uh, accidents like this?"

"No. But it stands to reason."

At his door, Hake thanked the policeman and headed for his bedroom. To his surprise, Jessie Tunman was there before him. She was in his little private sitting room, not the one he used for counseling, studying the tool kit he had brought from Under the Wire. "Those are my personal possessions!"

She blinked up at him, startled but self-possessed. "What in the world happened to you?"

He said, "My car blew up. Total loss."

"Well, I sent off your check for the insurance, so I guess you're covered. Those things aren't safe, you know."

He said, "Thank you but, Jessie, I'd prefer you didn't touch my possessions."

She nodded noncommittally. "Sure have been a lot of changes around here, Horny. Car blowing up. You getting yourself all beat up. All this new stuff—"

"And here's another change. Please don't come into my part of the house when I'm not here."

She stood up, skinny legs unwinding. She was taller than he was, but she seemed to be looking up at him. "As a matter of fact," she said, "that's one of the changes. You wouldn't have spoken to me that way six months ago."

As the door closed behind her Hake debated getting up to lock it. It seemed too pointed, at least until she was well out of hearing. He didn't need Jessie to tell him how he had changed. He was aware of all the many ways in which the present H. Hornswell Hake D.D. was utterly unlike the one she had come to work for, just a few years before.

He kicked off his shoes, pulled the shirt over his head and felt at least a little cooler. It occurred to him that he could easily be as cool as he chose. With the new dispensation, why not an air-conditioner? The Team would pay for one if he ordered it, and the overhead wind generator, whose constant ratchety whine was beginning to get noisy again, could power air-conditioning enough for ten houses like this. If he wanted it. If he were that much of a power-pig.

If he had changed that much.

He sighed and pushed the heap of burglar tools to the back of his dresser, and there were the Incredible Art's neglected tapes and fiches.

Well, why not? He had nothing more pressing.

The difficulty was that there were so many of them. But they were all marked, and one, bearing the note "Short course on the basics," looked like a good place to start. This one, Hake observed, was a video cassette. Easy enough. He slipped it into the tape deck of his bedside TV set, and leaned back on the pillow to watch.

It seemed to be a slide talk prepared for college freshmen, but held his interest as he watched all the way through.

If you jab a person with a pin, you expect him to hurt. If he doesn't hurt, or says he doesn't, his behavior is contrary to expectation. If you are of an inquiring turn of mind, you try to understand why he is behaving that way, and when you know the reasons the behavior is no longer contrary. It is now what you expect.

If Harry is walking across a room which he can plainly see contains an obstacle, we expect him to avoid stumbling over it.

If Jacqueline attempts to unclench her fist, we expect her to succeed.

If Wilma cannot remember the color of her kindergarten teacher's hair, we expect the memory to stay lost; and if all of these expectations are defeated we ask why. Is Harry blind and Jacqueline paralyzed and has someone just shown Wilma a Kodachrome of her kindergarten class? Say, no. But say instead that we discover that someone has suggested to each of these people that they behave as described. Now we are on the track of a solution to these puzzles, and we learn that the solution has a name. It is called "hypnosis." And there is a theory. In fact, Hake discovered, there were God's own quantity of theories, all the way back to Franz Anton Mesmer's own in the year 1775.

Mesmer was a doctor, and he thought he had found a way to cure some kinds of illnesses without nostrum or knife—considering the state of medicine at the time, a very good way to go about it. It rested on what he called "animal magnetism." If he made certain mysterious passes with his hands near a subject's head, and then commanded the subject to do certain things, the subject would do them. Even if they were quite strange. Even if what he was told to do was to get well. Even when, you would think, they would normally be impossible. He could command the subject to go rigid, and get him stiff as a board. He could command the subject to feel no pain. Then he could pinch him, poke him, even burn him.

All that was well reported, and seemed to be objectively true. The patients said it was true. Observers said it was true. Dr. Mesmer himself said it was true. He then went on to say he knew *why* it was true. He said there was a magnetic fluid—he even allowed it to be called a "mesmeric fluid"—which surrounds everyone, and the passage of the hands through the fluid rearranges it to change the state of animal magnetism in the subject, thus producing the effects described.

That's where he made his mistake, because scientists then went looking for the fluid. There isn't any. It doesn't exist.

Denials and objections flew, and continued to fly for more than two centuries, but, whatever you called it, the thing did just what Mesmer had claimed for it. Even more. People had their teeth filled under hypnotic commands to feel no pain, and got up from the dentist's chair smiling and grateful. Women had babies with no other anesthesia, and laughed and chattered through the delivery.

There were, to be sure, a few little anomalies.

As electronic technology began to invade medical, experimenters reported some puzzling results. If they measured the electrical potential of the nerves affected, no matter how comfortable the subject said he was, those nerves were twanging. And if they got the subject into automatic writing, his mouth might say, "Gee, no, that doesn't hurt," but his hand would be scribbling, *"Liar."*

And all that was very interesting, Hake thought when he had finished, but what did it mean? If it had anything to do with his behavior, or Leota's, or the Team's, he could not detect the relationship.

He realized his feet were getting cold. He put his slippers on and padded into the bathroom to make himself a glass of instant coffee. While he was waiting for the water to run hot he peered at himself in the mirror, absently aware that the nose looked almost human and the bruises were beginning to fade, half listening to the whir of the ventilator and the diffident gurgle of the john, his mind full of hypnotism.

He now knew more than he had ever wanted to know about the subject, but not the thing that would clarify the world for him. Maybe he was looking in the wrong place? Maybe he should have been reading *Trilby* instead of listening to Art's tapes?

And tardily he realized that the toilet was still running. Not only that, but splashing and gurgling louder than ever.

"Oh, cripes," he said out loud. He had forgotten to check for messages.

He pressed his thumb onto the pattern-recognizing moire of the flush lever, and Curmudgeon's voice snarled gloatingly, "Got yourself in the soup again, didn't you, Hake? Maybe it'll teach you a lesson. You're fooling with some dangerous characters, and right now I can't spare much Team cover for you. So lay low. Stick with that bunch of pagans you call your congregation. Talk about the whooping crane and the sanctity of interpersonal relationships and stay off the hard stuff, you hear me? That's an order. Do you remember what you're supposed to say when I give you an order?" There was a tiny beep, and then only the faint whisper of the running tape, waiting.

Hake remembered. "I understand and will comply," he said reluctantly. A moment later the tape sound stopped, and the toilet was only a toilet again.

Thoughtfully, Hake used it for the purpose for which it was intended. The team's communications were astonishingly quick; he was being more closely watched than he had realized. Of course, the blowing up of the car had attracted attention. It was not the sort of thing that would not be noticed. But still—how had they known so fast?

He washed his hands and went back into his bedroom, and Alys Brant said sweetly, "Hello, Horny. I hope you're glad to see me."

Hake stopped cold. Alys was propped on his bed, feet demurely tucked under her. She had done something new to her hair, but it had not made her less attractive; the way she looked was sweet and trusting. Nevertheless! "What the hell are you doing here?"

"Please don't be angry, Horny, dear. I need a place to

stay. Just for a night or two, until I can get to my aunt's place."

"Alys," he said, "for Christ's sake! Don't you know Ted and Walter already blame me for taking you away from them?"

"Oh, them," she said. She shrugged and stretched. "They'll get over it. You have nothing to do with it. I made up my mind to leave them long ago. I just need to be free—good heavens, you know all that; you listened to us complain and fuss and go over the same thing over and over again in counseling. So now I've moved out. I've been staying with—a friend. But that got impossible, too, so I came here. I just don't have any other place to go, Horny."

"It's completely out of the question, Alys!"

She sat up, covering a yawn. "Nobody's ever going to know. Except Jessie, maybe. But she's very loyal to you. Horny? Have you got anything to eat? I've been walking for hours, and carrying those bags." She looked toward an overnight case and a plastic shopping bag, neatly tucked by Hake's dresser. "Not much, are they? But all my worldly goods."

Angry, Hake walked over to it and threw a sweatshirt over the pile of burglar tools.

"I already saw that stuff," Alys pointed out. "And I was listening to you in the bathroom while you were getting ready to tinkle. You were talking to somebody. And I've been meaning to ask you for some time what you were into with dear old Leota Pauket. It's some kind of spy thing, isn't it, Horny? Would you like to tell me all about it while we eat?"

He sat on the edge of his bedside armchair and regarded her. The woman was full of surprises. "How do you know Leota Pauket?"

"Went to school with her. I hadn't seen her in years— then, last spring, I just bumped into her on the street. Right outside the rectory here, as a matter of fact. We had a few drinks, she wanted to know what was happening in my life. Well, we had just been through one of those long, stupid sessions with you, and I told her all about it, and you seemed to fascinate her. She wanted to know all about you.

Do you remember that really nasty weather we had, just before we went off to Europe with those kids?"

Hake nodded. "When you were here for counseling." It wasn't hard to remember; that was the session that had been interrupted by his summons to the Team.

"Well, that was when it was."

"You didn't say anything to me."

"Well, really, Horny! Why should I? I had no idea you knew her—in fact, I guess you didn't. But then in Munich, she was the one who brought you back to the hotel. She was wearing a wig, but it was Leota, all right. As soon as she saw me getting out of the elevator she ducked out. And then I got a note from her. Real spy stuff: 'Please don't mention me, ever. I'll explain when I see you. It's important.' Something like that."

Horny Hake sat thoughtful for a moment. At least that explained how Leota had turned up on the bus to Washington. She must have known he was being drafted into service as soon as he did.

But it didn't change the present realities. "Notwithstanding all that, Alys, you've got no business here now. What's going to happen if your husbands find out?"

"We'll just have to make sure they won't find out, right, Horny? I mean, it looks like you're pretty good at keeping secrets. You surprise me, honestly you do."

He groaned. "Alys, I give you my word, you're getting into more than you can handle. Is there any possible way I can believe that you'll forget all this?"

She shook her head. "Huh-uh."

"This isn't any game! How do you think I got these lumps? People get killed!"

"It sounds really interesting, Horny."

"This room could be bugged right now. If Curmudgeon finds out you're involved I don't know what he'll do."

" 'Curmudgeon.' That's a name I hadn't heard before." She stood up. "Let's go in the kitchen and get some dinner started, and then while we're eating you can begin at the beginning and tell me all about it. You can take your time. We've got all night."

XI

HAKE woke up from a profound and actively dreaming sleep, and did it instantly.

In the split second between the moment he realized he was awake and the moment he opened his eyes, he achieved a synoptic flash of memory. It took in everything. It included finding Alys in his room, talking to her, eating with her and, by what had seemed at the time a logical and inevitable progression, going to bed with her; and he even knew at once what and who had awakened him.

The figure standing beside his bed, tall, skinny and silent, was Jessie Tunman. Her eyes glittered, and she was soundlessly shaking his shoulder. She glanced contemptuously at the nude and sleeping form of Alys Brant, and retreated to the door.

Hake pulled his robe on and followed her. He whispered savagely, "You have no right coming into my room!"

"Her? I don't care about *her*." The glitter in her eyes was triumph. "Orders from Curmudgeon. Get yourself dressed and come out into the office."

He stopped with the sash of his robe half knotted. "What do you know about Curmudgeon?" he demanded.

"Just do it." He had never heard that tone from her, a senior-citizen gloat over the smart-assed kid. She did not linger to explain. She turned and marched down the hall, and even the way she walked was smug.

Of course, he thought, Jessie was the one! She had spied him out for recruitment to begin with. Her previous career had been "government employee." She hadn't lied on the job application, she had merely failed to say what part of the government she had worked for. And no doubt she had been observing him carefully all the while she typed his sermons and filed his mail, judging from arcane clues (whether he took the liverwurst on rye or the cheese on a toasted roll) what his performance would be in the field. He had had no privacy at all! Jessie checking him out for the Team. Alys reporting to her old school chum, Leota. He might just as well have lived his life in Macy's window.

The way that Alys lay, curled comfortably in one undemanding corner of his bed, was exactly as she had been when he woke. Her eyes were closed. There was no doubt in Hake's mind that she was wide awake behind them. Shaved and showered in less than five minutes, he pulled on his clothes without speaking to her. It was convenient for both of them that they should agree to pretend she was still asleep. For her because she did not have to take a part in this scene; for him because he was not sure what he wanted to say to her. Not until he found out what Jessie had to say, at least. Not even then, most likely, though there was no doubt that he would have to say something anyway.

In the office, Jessie had turned on the heater against the morning damp, and swept the collating table clean. She was laying out a kit of tools and gadgets Hake had seen before, but not here: an instant camera, a box of various printed forms, bottles of inks, soft cloth pads. One of the instructors had run through them for the class Under the Wire. It was strange to think of Jessie being there, no doubt many years before him.

She glanced up. "You look all right to have your picture taken," she observed.

"Are you going to tell me why?"

"Of course I am, Horny, only now hold still a minute. No, not there. Move away from your diploma. I don't want to have to bleach out anything on the wall—there." Jessie's little camera clicked, and in a moment she spun out half a dozen passport-sized photographs. "Bruises show," she said critically. "Can't be helped. Now you do me." She looked around for a different bare wall, found one and handed him the camera. "I fooled you, didn't I?" she said.

Hake got her in the viewfinder and waited till her expression was at its smuggest before pushing the lever. "Well," he said, "if I'd used my head I would have figured out you were the one who recruited me. I knew you used to work for the government."

She retrieved the camera and sighed, studying the pictures. "What a youth-oriented culture we live in, Horny. They retired me six years ago—of course, you never really get out of the Team; you'll find that out. But they put me on inactive status, except for odd jobs now and then. Like checking you out." While she talked she was trimming the edges of the pictures. "We've been promised an age of enlightenment, you know, when we show we're worthy— but it seems a long time coming." Mournfully she rummaged around in envelopes of printed forms. Then she brightened. Nothing could permanently dampen her mood. "Anyway, I've got one good mission left in me! And we're going to do it."

" 'We?' "

"You and me, Horny—and others. This is a big one. I got my orders by pouch, six o'clock this morning."

She was so very *pleased* with herself. As she trimmed and pasted and stamped, every movement as sure and easy as turning the church mimeograph, from time to time she broke into an uncharacteristic grin. "Get a haircut, Horny," she advised. "All these pictures look too much like you, it's not convincing." She chuckled reminiscently. "First covert operation I went on," she said, "they gave me a picture of the wrong woman! Curmudgeon was my case officer then, new on the job, and he screwed it up. Big mission, too. Actually," she said, peering at him over her glasses, "it was a little like yours in Germany, you know? I was targeted against this fellow in South America. We wanted to get him in trouble with his wife, so my job was to give him a little something to take home to her that she wouldn't like. . . ." She bit off a piece of magnetic tape and rubbed the end smooth, smiling to herself.

"Did you have trouble?"

"Oh, you bet I did! Six months taking the cure myself when I got back."

"I mean for having the wrong picture."

"Oh, no. Tell the truth, I don't think he even looked at my face. Of course," she added seriously, "it's not all fun and games, Horny. The sooner you learn that the better off you'll be. This new one could tilt the whole balance of payments back where it belongs! But it's good to be *alive* again!"

And that was something they shared, Hake thought; he had been as dead as old Jessie in his wheelchair, and this new life, with all its adolescent agonies, was an unearned rebirth.

She looked up with a sudden frown, back in character. "But you watch yourself, Horny! The Team is a little worried about you, you know. Can't blame them. Getting yourself involved with that woman, getting your car blown up by terrorists— Oh, you better get out of here while you can, Horny. Let things settle down. You'll thank me in the long run. You were dying on the vine in this dump. Sign here," she added, handing him an Illinois driver's license made out to "William E. Penn." She said, "That's you, for the purposes of this mission. Practice signing a couple of times first so you'll get it the same on all of them."

"All of what?"

"All your ID, dummy! Passport. Social Security card. Credit cards. Visas for Egypt and Al Halwani. Then go eat. By the time you've had your breakfast I'll have all your documents ready, and mine too. So open the church safe before you go. I can't take this stuff back to my room— and you don't want me to leave it out here for anyone to see, do you?" Picking up a new set of forms she said, "And get rid of that girl right away."

He was thinking about Al Halwani—wasn't that the place Gertrude Mengel had mentioned in the hospital?— but he flared up. She stopped him. "It has nothing to do with your sex life—badly though you handle it. That's orders."

"Why?" he demanded.

"So you can flush your toilet in private. There should be instructions for you on the tape by now."

He didn't have to get rid of Alys. She was nowhere in sight.

He made sure of it by looking in every closet and behind every door, but she was gone. No doubt she had left by the back way. It wasn't a permanent solution; her bags were still present.

Alys intended to return, and it was evident that she had no doubt he would let her in. She had had no doubt the night before, either, and she had been right; why, Hake demanded fiercely of himself, why is it that everybody else in the world knows exactly what they want of you and knows you will give it to them?

He had no answer. So he did what Jessie had wanted of him, and had known he would do. He retired into his bathroom, placed his thumb on the lever and flushed the toilet.

"Well, Hake," said Curmudgeon's curmudgeonly tones from the hidden speaker under the flush tank, "must be getting a little hot for you in Long Branch, eh? All right. You're leaving in three days. We've arranged your substitute, same guy as last time, and Jessica Tunman will provide you with documents. Take this down. Friday, fly to Egypt with Tunman. Reconnoiter the installation marked on the map in Al Halwani. Then proceed surface transport to Al Halwani City. Once there you will apply for a job at Al Halwani Hydro Fuels at 1500 hours on the 23d. When hired, start work; your language skills will give you priority. You will be contacted with further instructions. . . ." There was a long pause. "I'm waiting," said the recorded voice.

Hake said quickly, "I understand and will comply." The tape shut itself off, and there was silence in the bathroom.

It was still a dangerously silly way to conduct the business of a spy agency. But his orders were clear.

Al Halwani.

And Leota would be no more than a thousand or so miles away.

The day dragged past. His mind was on the other side of the ocean, but he managed to get through the round: the two-mile run, the barbells, attending to correspondence with Jessie (her eyes glittering with joy, her pencil dawdling as she took his dictation, but insisting nevertheless that they had to continue with their regular duties until it was time to leave). She went home early. "Woke up before my time this morning, Horny. I need to catch up some sleep."

He changed quickly into the sweatsuit and jogged his remaining mile on the beach in the dwindling daylight. Al Halwani Hydro Fuels. The balance of payments. What payments ever went to Al Halwani? For hydrogen, just a trickle. That's all hydrogen amounted to.

Oh, sure there was a time when there was a constant torrent of gold flowing into the Near East, Al Halwani included. But that was when oil flowed out. When the Israelis blew out the oil domes and set fires raging out of craters a half-mile across, oil stopped. Not all of it. But only a trickle survived. So the oil sheiks had gone to where their Swiss bank accounts were, and the fraction that survived, unburned and undamaged by radioactivity, was now operated by whoever remained on the scene to operate it—sometimes quite strange people. It was not enough to affect anyone's balance of payments.

And who would you pay it to? Oil had been the only reason there was for cities in places like Al Halwani, Abu Dabu and Kuwait. When the reason disappeared the cities died. The nomad people became nomads again. The buildings were still there, and the hotels, and the museums and concert halls and hospitals. But there weren't any jobs, were there? He tried to remember the postal cards he had seen. That didn't suggest a thriving metropolis. A few tourists to keep the hotels scratchily alive. And, yes, over the years immigrants had come to the Persian Gulf—the kind of kids, like old Gertrude Mengel's sister, that had once been called "hippies," political refugees, writers, people who did not hold regular jobs but could subsist almost anywhere that was cheap. Al Halwani was a little like Paris in the 1920s, and a lot like the Greek islands in the 1960s. Part Greenwich Village. Part Haight-Ashbury. And if they were managing somehow to squeeze out a few dollars by making and selling liquid hydrogen to the more prosperous countries, who would begrudge them that?

By the time he trotted back up the beach it was dark. In the street lights he saw Alys Brant, peering curiously into a car parked near his door. The car turned on its lights and whined away as he approached, and Alys greeted him by handing him a sack of groceries. "Do you like chicken à l'orange, Horny? And you do have a wok, don't you? Or a big frying pan will do."

"I thought you didn't like to cook," he said.

"I want to earn my keep." She took the key out of his hand, unlocked the door and preceded him inside. "Just for a little while, you know, Horny. And I'm really awfully grateful to you for putting up with me."

He really ought to get her out of his life once and for all. But the damage was done. Anyway, he would be off on another mission in a few days. Anyway—anyway, Hake admitted to himself, the idea of letting somebody else cook his dinner again was not unattractive. He postponed conversation and headed for the shower. The hot water felt good. The toilet was only a toilet, with no new confusion to add to his life. And by the time he was dressed again Alys had dinner waiting.

She seated him, flushed and smiling. There were candles on the kitchen table, and a bottle of white wine. "Don't you want to know what I've been doing today, Horny?"

He cut into the chicken, which was in a soupy, sticky sauce. "I guess so."

"Of course you do. I spent the whole afternoon at a travel agency, looking at South Seas folders. Tahiti! Bora Bora! Don't they just sound marvelous? How do you like your chicken?"

"It's very fine," Hake lied gallantly. But at least the stir-fried vegetables were edible. "I thought you were going to your aunt's."

"Oh, she's as much of a drag as Ted and Walter. She'd just tell me I belong with my husbands. I don't have to go to New Haven to hear that. But at least I'll be out of your way before you go to Cairo."

Hake dropped his fork. "How the hell do you know I'm going to Cairo?"

"The tickets were in your pocket when I hung up your coat, dear. Is that all you're going to eat? I didn't make any dessert, but we could just have some more wine. . . ."

Hake said tightly, "Those tickets belong to a friend of mine. Old Bill Penn. We were, ah, in seminary together."

"The passport was there too, dear, and it had your picture on it." She smiled forgivingly.

"I don't want to discuss it," he said. He doggedly bent to his food.

They ate quickly, and after Alys cleared the plates away she stood behind him, her fingers on his neck muscles. "Poor old Horny," she said, "all tensed up. You're like *iron*."

It was true enough. He could feel the strain in the shoulders and arms, across the chest, even in the abdomen. All the muscles he had painfully built up since the days in the wheelchair were now turned against him. "I could make all that go away," she said softly.

"I'm not in the mood."

"Silly! I didn't mean sex—although that's always good, too. And I'm just not strong enough to massage you when you're like this." She was kneading his shoulders very agreeably, but now she stopped, just resting her hands on him. "No, we'll just relax you, Horny. We're going to relax every muscle of your body. You're going to be all relaxed, and we'll start with your feet. You can feel your toes relaxing now, and—"

He sat bolt upright. "What are you doing?"

"I'm just relaxing you, Horny," she said sweetly. "I learned it in college. It's not really hypnotism, just a kind of suggestion. Do you feel your toes relaxed? And your

soles of your feet, they're getting all comfortable and relaxed too, and your ankles—"

"I don't want to be hypnotized!"

She let go of him and sat down again at the table. "All
right, dear," she said. "Let's try something else. Maybe you
should just let it all out. Tell me what's getting you all up
tight."

Hake swallowed the rest of his glass, reached for the
bottle and then checked his hand. "I don't want any more
wine. I want some coffee."

"It'll just get you more tensed up, Horny."

"I *need* to be tensed up! And you're leaving here toni—
tomorrow morning at the latest," he added.

"Whatever you say, of course, dear," she said, heating
water for his coffee. "Well, if this is to be our last night
together, let's make it pleasant, shall we? Do you want to
look at my travel folders?"

"Not a bit," he said.

"No, somebody else's trip is never very interesting, is it?"
She poured coffee and brought it to him. Determined to
make conversation, she said, "Is Art coming over tonight?"

"No."

"Oh. He's good company for you, Horny. You really
should have more friends." When he didn't respond to that,
she tried again. "Do you believe in teleportation, Horny?"

"Oh, God. I get enough of that from Jessie."

"Well, it's just funny. I keep seeing this same man all
over. He was outside this morning, and he was sitting on a
bench on the boardwalk when I came back from the gro-
cery store, and then he was in a car right outside the house
while I was waiting for you. Now, he really couldn't have
done that, Horny. There just wasn't time for him to get
from one place to another."

"You weren't watching, probably. No reason you should
be."

"Yes, I was. I can even tell you what he looked like.
Some kind of Indian, or maybe Pakistani. Young. Rather
good-looking, in a way—"

Hake put his coffee down. "Did one of them have a scar
on his face?"

"Why—maybe. I didn't look that closely but, yes, I think he did. What's the matter?"

"Just stay there," said Horny, standing up. "I want to take a look outside."

But there was no sign of either of the Reddi twins anywhere outside the parsonage, front or back. Hake stood quietly in the darkness of the porch for a long time, watching everything that moved on the avenue. Cars, some high-school kids, a couple of elderly people tottering toward their senior-citizens' rooming houses. Nothing that looked like a conspirator.

When he came back into the house Alys was standing in his private sitting room, looking puzzled. "Horny! Do you *mind* telling me what is going *on?*"

"Sit down, Alys. I mind. But I'm going to do it anyway."

He went into his bathroom and turned on the shower, closing the door behind him. Back in the sitting room, he took a seat facing her. "You have to do one of two things right now, Alys. You have to promise me that you'll keep your mouth shut about everything I'm going to say. Or you have to leave here this minute."

"Oh, Horny!" she gasped, obviously delighted.

"Damn it! I'm serious."

"I promise!"

"You used to teach the sports-and-art classes in Sunday school, didn't you? So you can help me. First off, that wasn't one man you saw, it was two. They're twins, and they're the ones who blew up my car. They don't fool around. They gave me most of these bruises, and if they know what I'm doing they'll probably give me worse."

"Horny!"

"Second," he said, "your friend Leota. She's not as free and easy as you might remember her. In fact, she's a slave."

"A *slave?*"

"In the harem of an Arab sheik."

"In a *harem?*" Alys's eyes were bright as stars.

"Now, that might sound romantic to you—"

"Oh, boy, does it!"

"—but it's no joke. I'm going to rescue her. You know I'm mixed up in some secret stuff. You're better off if you don't know any more than that. But I'm going to take a chance and go from Cairo to Al Halwani by way of the sheik's palace, and on the way I'm going to get Leota out of there."

"Horny! You're such a nerd. How are you going to do a thing like that?"

"I don't know. But I'll do it. Maybe I can even do it legally. Hassabou had no right to take her out of Italy, that was part of the contract, so he's violating the law. Anyway —I'll do it. But I need to doctor up some documents before I do, and that's where you come in. I don't have much artistic talent. So please, come in the office with me."

As he was opening the church safe, he called over his shoulder, "You don't have to do any of this. Outside of the Reddis, there are other risks. You might get in trouble with—the people I work for."

"You mean the government," she said, nodding. "Tell me something. Why won't you get in trouble yourself?"

"Maybe I will. But I'm going to call up on my toilet— oh, never mind that part, Alys. I'm going to put in a message saying that I left early because the Reddis were threatening my life. I think that might cover me—anyway, it doesn't matter a hell of a lot." He had laid out the little forger's kit. He said, "Let's see. I need to change the date on the Egyptian visa. Call up Trans-Pam and get the first flight to Cairo. Should I change the passport to a different name? Maybe I should. Or—"

Alys took his hand. "Horny?"

He looked around, irritated. "What?"

"Take me along."

He was so startled that he forgot about being irritated. "That's ridiculous, Alys!"

"No, it isn't ridiculous."

"It's impossible."

"It isn't impossible, either. If you can cook up documents for yourself, you can cook them up for me, too. And Leota was my friend longer than she was yours."

"Just forget it, Alys. It's dangerous."

She leaned forward shyly and rested her cheek against his. "It's also *thrilling*, Horny. Do you know what you're talking about? Just my lifelong secret dream, that's all. Sheiks that carry their women off on white steeds. Real men!"

"More likely to carry somebody off on a hydrogen buggy," he snarled. "And those real men do funny things to their real women."

"Oh, Horny." She moved back and looked at him fondly. "Dear Horny, is it possible that you don't think I can handle a man? Trust me in that, if in nothing else. So I regard the matter as settled. I'll give you a hand with the documents . . . only, Horny? There's one thing about the class I taught in Sunday school. Jim Tally taught the art. I was their judo coach. But if Jessie Tunman can forge a passport, I can too."

XII

THE elderly Egyptian pilot twisted in his seat, bawling something. He was pointing down at the desert, and, although Hake's rusty Arabic had been coming back to him, most of what the man said was lost. "Drive the airplane," Hake ordered. From the way the Egyptian handled the little prop-jet Hake suspected he had got his first flight training in MIGs, from Soviet advisors before the Yom Kippur war.

"What's he trying to tell us?" Alys asked in Hake's ear.

Hake shrugged. "Something about the wind being bad. I think it's about that stuff down there." They both craned to look down. The Empty Quarter was empty, all right: rocky desert, not even a herd of goats or the black tents of a Bedouin camp. But parts of the ground were queerly colored, brownish green and strangely out of focus, as if an oily fog lay over the scraggly bushes.

"I wish this plane had a bathroom," Alys said irritably. She was playing the part of a bored American tourist extremely well: pretty; well dressed, in her three-piece gray shorts-suit with a puff of scarlet silk at her throat. It was a wholly unsuitable costume for the Empty Quarter, but for that reason all the more suitable for someone who wanted to look like a tourist.

Her fidgety boredom probably was not altogether an act, Hake thought. Likely enough, she was having second thoughts about this adventure. The night before in the Cairo hotel, both of them out of it with jet-lag and fatigue, she had lain rigid beside him in the immense king-sized bed. When he had moved to touch her, more out of compassion than lust, she had jerked angrily away. He could understand her qualms. The closer they got to Abu Magnah, the more his own qualms surfaced. What had looked easy from half a world away looked more and more daunting at first hand.

"What's that idiot doing now?" she demanded.

The pilot had unstrapped himself, leaving the controls untended, and was staggering back toward them. In Egyptian Arabic he shouted, "The oasis is coming up in just a minute. Did you see the locusts?" Hake turned to peer back along their course, but the sweep of the wing blocked his view. "Too bad you missed it," grinned the pilot. "Now fasten your seat belts. If God wills it, we are about to begin our descent into the landing pattern." He returned to his seat and a moment later, as he took over from the autopilot, the plane dipped one wing and began to circle to the left.

As the undercarriage rumbled and locked in the landing position, Hake got his first glimpse of Abu Magnah. It was much more than he expected. It looked like the interlocking-circles symbol for the Olympic games, but on a huge scale—immense disks as much as a mile across. They were irrigation circles, and where they interlocked was no cluster of tents and palms but a city. Wide roads threaded in between the farm plots, almost bare of traffic.

It had been Hake's notion that Abu Magnah was a private pleasure dome of Sheik Hassabou's. It was bigger than that. At least fifty snow-white, dome-shaped buildings were laid out in city blocks; minarets and mosques in white and gold and darker colors; a sprawling building like two dominoes joined together with a hotel sign on top of it, and, out in the farm circles, surrounded by walls, two or three story-book palaces, with pools and gardens. All in all, it was daunting. And quite new. There were few trees, because Abu Magnah was not yet old enough for trees, though a bright green pattern of seedlings showed where pine groves would be one day, and a scattering of gray-green promised olives. At the edge of one huge circle north of the city, dark brown and damp earth only lightly flecked with the beginnings of a crop of some kind, there was a rectangular tower taller than any of the minarets. Scaffolding showed that it was still under construction. Then the airplane dipped and twisted, and a runway was rushing up to meet them.

They went through the haphazard customs formalities, and the pilot was waiting for them at the hotel van. "Pay me now, please," he said.

"No. Why?" asked Hake. "You still have to take us south."

"But if you pay me here with your credit card it will be in the sheik's currency, which is tied to the Swiss franc. Besides, how do I know you will not go off without paying?"

"Well—" said Hake, annoyed, but Alys Brant moved in between them.

"Not a chance," she said firmly, and tugged Hake into the van. "Oh, Horny," she sighed, settling herself, "you do let people impose on you. You must have a lot of personal charm, why else would I have let you talk me into this crazy scheme?"

With an effort, he didn't answer. He clamped his jaw and stared out of the van window. There was not much traffic apart from themselves—none at all to pass, except for a huge machine that looked like a snow-removal truck but turned out to be a sand-sweeper. But the wide road was banked like an autostrada. If it was not used often, at least it was used when drivers wanted to go fast. And as they passed one of the walled compounds, borne on the hot wind through the open windows of the hotel van, Hake heard what sounded like rushing water. A waterfall? How preposterous, in the middle of the Empty Quarter!

How formidable, too. He was surrounded by evidences of wealth and power, and who was he to oppose them? Not to mention that formidable power he worked for, with whom he would sooner or later have to reckon.

"*Ahlan wa-sahlan*," said the formally dressed clerk at the registration desk, offering a pen.

"*Inshallah*," responded Hake politely. He signed in, one eye on the signature on his passport to make sure he had it right, and they were conducted to their suite. They had three bellmen to carry their four small pieces of luggage— "I must do some shopping," Alys whispered in the elevator —and all of them fussed about, opening and closing drapes, trying gold-plated taps in the bath, adjusting the air-conditioners until Hake handed them each a fifty-riyal coin. He closed the door behind them, stood thoughtfully for a moment, and then began to rummage in bureau drawers until he found, first, a copy of the Q'ran, and then what he was looking for: a leather-bound, gold-stamped little volume that was the telephone directory for Abu Magnah. The curlicued script was easy enough to read, surfacing in his mind out of childhood memories as he needed it. But he wasn't actually reading it. He didn't exactly know what he was looking for, and what he was mostly seeing was the tenuousness of his plans. 1, go to Abu Magnah. 2, rescue Leota. 3, figure out what to do next. Even as an overall strategic intention it lacked focus. And tactically . . . where did one begin with step 2? The rescue had seemed even possible, back in Long Branch, as if all he would have to do was go to the local police station and report a kidnapping. But in this oasis town, fiefdom of Hassabou and his relatives, that was not even a hope.

Alys emerged from the bathroom, smiled at him and began to unpack: her cosmetics in a row on the mirrored dressing table, her toiletries in the bath, her clothes in the top drawers of the largest chest. "If you'll give me one of your credit cards," she said, "I'll get whatever else I need this afternoon. You can put your own stuff in that other bureau."

"Don't get settled in," he said. "We're only going to be here three days at most."

"But we might as well be comfortable while we're here. Don't worry, Horny. I can whisk all this stuff back in the bags in two minutes—after you figure out what we're going to do, I mean."

"Fine." He got up and gazed out the window. Hot as it was, the streets were full of people, a League of Nations of the Arab world. Some of them might help, mightn't they? A little baksheesh, a clever play on old blood feuds—he could see Jordanians and Yemenis, even an Ait Haddibou Berber in white burnoose and headdress. All he had to do was figure the right ones to approach. His previous experience as a spy-saboteur was not much help; it had led him to a sort of James Bond conviction that somewhere along the road from the airport, or in the lobby of the hotel, some swarthy Levantine merchant or deferential tiny Annamese sailor would beg a ride, or ask for a light, and turn out to be an ally. It had not worked out that way. He was on his own.

"What's this stuff, Horny?" Alys had finished her own unpacking and started on his. She was investigating the jumble at the bottom of the bag, lock pick and electronic teasers, code books, the rest of Art's tapes, a stiletto.

"Tools of the trade. Just leave them."

She sighed with pleasure. "You do lead a fascinating life." She put them in a drawer, hung up his shirts and sat down to regard him brightly. "Let me see," she said. "Since you're the expert spy, I'm sure you've got a plan all worked out for what we're going to do next but, just for practice, let me see if I can figure it out. Since we're pretending to be tourists, we'd better tour. We can look this place over, and that way we can see how to get at Leota. They must have some nice picture postcards in the lobby. Maybe a map. I'll bet we can piece together quite a lot of information, just by sightseeing and so on. And then, by tonight, we'll be in a position to make a plan. Am I right?"

Hake studied her innocent face for a moment, then grinned. "My very thoughts," he said. "Let's go."

Where the two wings of the hotel joined, the architect had placed a revolving roof dining room. They ate in the turret that night, and as the restaurant turned Hake could see the sheik's palace, floodlit in pink and blue under the bright desert night sky. Now that they had seen it close at hand, it looked more formidable than ever . . . but maybe, Hake thought, he was just tired.

It had been a tiring day. Alys had found postcards and maps easily enough. After ten fruitless minutes talking about tour buses with the concierge—none of them went to the right places, and Hake could not find a way of explaining what the right places were without giving away more than he wished—they had walked out the hotel door and been besieged by taxi drivers, thrilled with the notion of being hired for an afternoon's sightseeing. Hake picked a displaced Moslem Armenian named Dicran (least likely to notice anything strange about his Arabic, while he was still practicing it), and they had driven around for three hours. Dicran's over-the-shoulder commentary was a gloss of what he considered the romantic and strange—white Mughathir camels swinging along, ridden by the local police; mosques for Sunni, Shiite and Alawaite Moslems, churches for Druses, Dervishes and, yes, even Christians. And he had been proud to show them Sheik Hassabou's palace on request. They drove along the farm highway that ran past its walls, and Dicran confided in them, smirking, about the electrified fences inside what looked like green hedges around the harem. Not to mention infrared alarms and armed guards at all the entrances. He had insisted they visit an *aipursuq*—Hake had puzzled over the word for a while, then laughed as he recognized "supermarket"—to buy local cucumbers, pomegranates and figs, and they had picnicked on real grass, just across the road from the palace itself. Dicran had been a mine of information. But, when you put it all together, how much closer were they to rescuing Leota? Or even to making a plan?

Not much.

But here, in public, with the headwaiter bringing them immense old-fashioned menus, they couldn't talk about it anyway. And there was always the chance he would think of something. As the waiter strolled gracefully away Alys giggled and leaned closer to Hake. "He's wearing eye shadow!" she hissed.

"That's kohl, Alys. It doesn't mean he's gay. They need it to protect their eyes from the sun."

"At night?" She winked and returned to the menu.

She at least was having a good time, especially when she glanced up over the menu at Hassabou's pink and blue palace, and seemed almost to stop breathing. It wasn't fear. It was excitement. There was something about the idea of being held so closely that thrilled her. He almost thought she envied Leota; but, as she turned back to the menu, all she said was, "Do you suppose the trout is fresh?"

It was, and could not be from any place closer than the Pyrenees. And so was the Iranian caviar they began with; and the wines were château-bottled Graves.

Alys ordered with the precision and arrogance of a well-practiced tourist. Calculating the cost of the meal in his head, Hake thanked his one-God-at-the-most that he was not going to have to pay for it.

He understood at least that reason why Yosper and the others so enjoyed their work. It was difficult to remember that thrift was a virtue when you didn't have to pay the bills—when, in fact, with their complicated juggling of computer programs and credit cards, each charge was paid unwittingly by an enemy, so that each extravagance was a blow struck against the foe.

Living like a millionaire was a new experience for Hake, and quite an immorally pleasant one. But it shriveled in contrast with the lifestyle of Sheik Hassabou. Abu Magnah was not his personal possession, but it was, every inch of it, his family's. Their palaces were the dozen others scattered around the irrigated areas, but his was the largest, the principal, the one from which the power flowed. And what power! He had created a world, where nothing had been before but a silty, salty camel-wallow and a few dwarf trees.

The irrigation circles that gave Abu Magnah life could have been created at any time. But no one before Hassabou had been willing to pay the price. Under the scrub and rock was an ocean of fossil water—faintly brackish, yes; but cool, ample for irrigation, even drinkable if one were not fastidious. But it was nearly half a mile down. Every pint delivered to the surface represented 2,000 foot-pounds of work. Power-piggery! And on a vaster scale than Hake had ever dreamed. The sheik had found the old oasis, and bought it, and tapped its underground sea to recreate in the Empty Quarter those Al Halwani courts and palaces he had played among as a child. All it took was energy. Energy took only money. Money enough to buy his own plutonium generator—soon to be replaced, Dicran had said, by the new solar tower going up north of the city— and pump the water up from the sea beneath the sands. Money to distill the water to drink, and to spread it in the irrigation circles around the desert, so that the great rotating radii of pipe could make the desert bloom. Money to track-truck in the marble and steel to build his palaces; to subsidize and house the Palestinians and Saudis and Bedouins who farmed his circles and staffed his city; to buy his own muezzins to call out the hours for prayer, and to build the towers they called from. Money to buy a woman he fancied, and to bribe the police to look the other way when he abducted her here. One woman? Perhaps he had a hundred. Dicran's winks and leers were ample for a thousand.

And the money was there. For more than a generation all the gold of the Western world had sluiced into the Near East to pay for oil. Oil became capital. Capital bought hotels and auto factories and publishing companies and thousands of square miles of land, some of it in building sites in New York and Chicago and Tokyo and London. Even when the oil was gone, the capital remained and replenished itself, and kept pouring money into their treasuries.

That was what Hake was challenging.

Against that, what forces could he muster?

There were some. The pick-lock and martial-arts skills he had learned Under the Wire. The codes and cards that would let him draw on the secret funds of half a dozen major industrial powers. His own determination.

The forces were not even, but for this limited objective, the rescuing of a single prisoner—maybe they were even enough. If he was general enough to know how to deploy them.

With all that money, could he not buy himself an ally or two? A corruptible cop? A Palestinian with relatives still stuck on the West Bank? Maybe even one of Hassabou's guards?

But how, exactly, did you go about that?

And there were only two days left.

They took their after-dinner coffee and brandy on the roof terrace, just outside the rotating turret. They were the only ones at the tables around the swimming pool, and the barman obviously thought they were crazy. The night wind was still hot. The sand made the surface of their table gritty however many times he wiped it away. But at least they could talk freely.

Alys was not in a mood to conspire. "You'll work it out, dear," she said, stretching languorously and gazing out toward the dark desert, "and, oh, Horny! Doesn't this beat the hell out of Long Branch, New Jersey?"

Well, in a way it did. In some ways Hake was still very young, freshborn out of the wheelchair. But the darkness under the horizon's stars struck him as less glamorous than threatening.

Alys lifted her snifter to her lips and then jerked it away. "What's the matter?" Hake demanded.

She was laughing. "Parts of this place are a lot like Long Branch," she announced. "There's a bug in my brandy."

Hake woke up with a flashlight shining in his eyes. A voice he had not expected to hear said, "Don't move, don't touch anything." A rough hand patted his body and explored under his pillow. The light circled around the bed and did the same for Alys, who woke with a gasp. Then the light retreated. Hake could not see past it, but he remembered the voice.

"Hello, Reddi," he said. "Which one are you?"

The wall-bracket lights came on, revealing the slim, dark man with the small, dull gun pointing at them. "I am the one who is quite ready to kill you, Hake. I do not like having to follow you all over the world."

"Well," Hake said, "I really didn't want to put you to the trouble." He rubbed his eyes and sat up. Beside him Alys was awake but silent; she was watching the entertainment with great interest, waiting to see what would come of it.

The gun was in the Indian's right hand, and there was a scar over his eye: this twin was Rama Reddi. "How did you find me, Rama?" Hake asked conversationally.

The Indian said, "It was not hard to guess you would be coming to see Leota. Especially as you took her old school chum with you. I caught up with you in Cairo, and beat you here in a private jet; I was in the airport when you arrived."

"I didn't see you." Hake didn't expect an answer to that, and got what he expected. He rolled his feet over the side of the bed and said, "Do you mind if I get up and make myself some coffee before we continue with this? I have instant in the bathroom."

"Yes? And what else do you have there, Hake? I am more comfortable to keep you where you are."

Alys stirred. "Suppose a person has to tinkle? As I happen to."

Rama Reddi studied her for a moment, then went to the bath. He peered inside, entered, rummaged among the pile of towels, opened the medicine chest. He did not leave the door, and the gun remained fixed on them. "All right, Miz Alys Brant," he said. "Keep in mind that this gun does not make any noise, and I have no special reason not to kill you both, since Hake has chosen to cheat my brother and me on our agreement."

"Now, wait a minute," Hake said. "I haven't broken our agreement. If anybody has a right to be pissed off, it's me—why did you blow up my car?"

"Then our agreement is in force? You will work with us?"

Hake rubbed his chin. "Well— Will you help me get Leota out of the harem?"

"Certainly not. Have you not understood that my brother and I are not amateurs, or patriots? We have no client for this."

"I'll be your client. I'll give you information—for a starter, I'll tell you about the mission I'm on now. It's big. It involves at least twenty Team personnel—"

"In Al Halwani, yes, to sabotage the solar power installation," Reddi nodded. He paused, watching Alys carefully as she came out of the bathroom. She was holding a glass of instant coffee for Hake, a towel wrapped around it to save her fingers from the heat. When Reddi was sure there were no surprises in the towel, he said, "I have no client for that either, Hake. It does not interest me."

"I didn't know you knew about that," said Hake, dampened. "But it's got to be pretty valuable. I have a map of it—I can get plans, even bring you with me, maybe. Surely you could sell the secrets to somebody."

The Indian looked at him incredulously. "If I wished to do that, why would I go so far? And we still have no client."

Alys said suddenly, "Horny offered to be your client."

"Do not interrupt unless you can say something intelligent, Miz Brant. How would he pay?"

"He can get money out of the computer system. *Lots* of it. Can't you, Horny?"

"Sure I can, Reddi. I'll give you a—a hundred thousand dollars!"

Reddi crossed to a chair by the bed and sat down, the gun now in his lap. "That at least is a new idea. Perhaps it is worth discussing." He sat silently for a moment, then produced an envelope from his pocket and tossed it to Hake. "Here," he said. "I will go this far for you now."

The envelope contained three photographs of a woman in harem dress and face-veil. It was Leota!

Although the thing Hake most remembered about Leota was that she was a different woman every time he saw her, this was a new variety of different. She wore gold arm-bangles, tight vest and baggy, gauze pants, and she seemed to be wearing curiously patterned stockings beneath the pants. Two of the pictures showed her getting out of a huge old gasoline-burning Rolls-Royce, one of them in heated argument with a black, liveried driver who carried a dagger. The third— Hake studied it carefully. It showed Leota sitting at a table with another woman, and behind them was a familiar window opening on a rooftop view. "That's right here in the hotel!" he cried.

Reddi nodded. "I too found it amusing that she was here, while you were looking for her all over town. I took it this afternoon. She comes here sometimes for tea."

"You mean she can get out?"

The Indian said, "Do not assume that means she is free, Hake. There are bodyguards always. And the bracelet on her left arm is a radio. Because of it she can be traced at any time, and they listen to her conversations. However," he went on, "I permitted her to see me. She is therefore alert, in the event that I elect to assist you in this."

"The price is a hundred thousand dollars," said Hake.

"Oh, at least that," the Indian said, studying Hake. After a moment he said, "You are puzzling, Hake. You have become a great deal more sophisticated since Munich. You miss much that is obvious—for example, you must have seen the solar facility that Sheik Hassabou is constructing here as you flew in, but you did not recognize what you saw. But you are using your government's facilities for purposes of your own, and on no small scale, either. This implies to me that you have a means for breaking computer net security. I will have to talk to my brother but— Yes, *that* would be worth something to us, Hake."

Hake glanced at Alys, and picked his words carefully. "Supposing," he said, "that I could tell you where to find the code words and programs to break into the Team computer net and help you, ah, steal them."

"You cannot give them to me yourself?"

"I don't have them. But Yosper and Curmudgeon do, and they'll be in Al Halwani."

Reddi rubbed his right hand along the barrel of his gun contemplatively. "I think," he said, "that you are lying to me."

"No! Why would I do that? Talk it over with your brother, we can make a deal."

"Oh, I will talk to him, Hake. But now I want both of you to lie face-down on the bed."

The hairs at the back of Hake's neck prickled erect. "Listen, Reddi—"

"*Now.*"

Hake set the coffee down and, unwillingly, joined Alys on the bed. They heard Reddi move across the room. The light went off. The door opened and closed.

Alys sat up immediately. "Horny, what the hell are you doing, lying to that man? You trying to get us killed?"

Hake breathed hard for a moment, trying to accept the fact that they were both still alive. He said, "I'm trying to prevent it. Figure it out, Alys. Suppose I gave him the code words and cards and told him my thumbprint opens a channel. What do you suppose he'd do after he got them?"

"Why—if he'd made a bargain with us—"

Hake shook his head. "He wouldn't have anything more to gain. He'd take off with the cards and the codes—and my thumb."

"Horny! He wouldn't!"

"He would. Go to sleep, Alys. We're going to need our rest, because we're going to have to do this alone."

But he slept poorly. Twice he woke up to the sounds of distant sirens and what sounded like fire-engine hooters, and the second time thought he heard the patter of rain against their window. Rain! Of course not. It was still dark, and he forced himself to keep his eyes closed.

Until Alys whispered softly in his ear, "Horny? Horny. Wake up and tell me what's going on."

It was barely first light. She was pointing to the window, which seemed to be covered with great oily drops of black-

ness. The sirens were still going, and a distant *hee*-haw
hooting that sounded like an air-raid alarm. He got up and
approached the window.

The oily raindrops were not drops of water. They were
insects. Hundreds of them, rattling against the window and
dropping to the little ledge below. All the ornamental plantings on the window were covered with them, the flowers
invisible under a hundred insect bodies apiece, the stems
bending to the dirt beneath their weight. "Locusts," breathed
Hake.

"How awful," said Alys, fascinated. "Are those the same
ones we flew over?"

"I expect so." She was standing beside him, shivering
with excitement. Looking out the window was like looking
through one of those snowflake paperweights, except that
the flakes were dark browny-green. They drowned the
desert view with their bodies. Hake could see the buildings
across the street and, dimly, a minaret a few hundred yards
away. Beyond that, nothing, only the millions and billions
of insects.

Out in the hall the hotel's piped-music speakers were
muttering in several languages. Hake opened the door.
Alys listened and said, "It's French. Something about the
main body of locusts being on the radar—two kilometers
north, approaching at twenty kilometers an hour. But if
this isn't the main body, what is it?"

"Don't ask me. We never had locusts on the kibbutz."

The speaker rattled, and began again. This time it was in
English. "Gentlemen and ladies, we call your attention to
the swarm of locusts. They are in no way harmful or
dangerous to our guests, but for your own comfort you
will please wish to remain inside the hotel. The main
swarm is approximately one mile away, and will be here in
some five to ten minutes. We regret that there may be
some interruptions in serving you this morning, due to the
necessity of employing staff in protecting our premises
against the insects."

"I bet there may," said Hake, staring out the window.
Past the thousands dashing themselves against the window,
through the dung-colored discoloration of the air, he could

see turbulent activity in the streets below. Women were streaming out toward the farms, carrying nets, that looked like wicker fish traps and wire-screen cylinders, while hydro-trucks of men with heavy equipment were threading past them. Farther out, the sky was black. There appeared to be two layers of clouds, the rust of the swarm beneath, the red-lavender of sunrise on the wisps of cirrus higher up.

"Oh, Horny, let's go outside and see!"

Hake tore himself away. "We might as well, I suppose." They dressed quickly and took the elevator. The lobby was full of guests, milling around far earlier than most of them had intended to rise. By the time they reached the sidewalk the sun was above the horizon, but it was still twilight—a green-browny twilight that rustled and buzzed. The fountain outside the door was already crusted with a skin of drowning insects, and a porter was setting up an electric fan to blow clouds of them into a net sack. As they stepped off the curb, bugs crunched under their feet. Alys stared around, thrilled, oblivious of the insects that drove against her face and were caught in her hair. "How exciting!" she said. "Do you suppose they do this often?"

"If they did there wouldn't be any farms," Hake said. "They call them 'seventeen-year' locusts, but I don't think they come even that often. And time's running out for us."

"Horny! You can't be thinking of going after Leota in *this*. We don't even know where she is."

From behind them, Rama Reddi said, "She is in the gardens at the palace."

Hake spun. "How do you know that?"

"Oh," said the Indian, "it is not only her jailers who can track her electronically. Do you want to talk or get on with the project?"

Hake hesitated. "Why did you change your mind?"

"I did not change my mind. It is the circumstances that have changed." Reddi waved an arm at the locusts. "There is much confusion because of this, and the odds become better. I don't promise. But I have a car; let's go see."

*　*　*

The air was filled with insects now. To supplement the dull, dingy sun the Land Rover's headlights were on, and their beams painted two shafts of insect bodies ahead of them. Reddi drove carefully through the hurrying farm workers, circling around trucks on the shoulder of the road; it was not far. They crossed a bridge over a rapidly flowing river, with what looked like a waterfall just below —no, not a waterfall; it was a hump in the river itself. And past the bridge, in a field that had once been barley and was now green-brown insects, shadowy figures were scattered by great fans. From what they wore Hake knew they were women; he could not have told in any other way, because what they wore was flowing robes and the head-dress and scarf—the *hatta w-'aqqal*—that was meant to protect against desert sand, and worked as well against locusts. Across the road a line of men was moving away from them, beating at the plants and forcing the locusts into flight again. Hake could not see what purpose that served, until he saw that the insects in flight were being sucked through the fans into wire cages. It was not just the fans. Hake became aware of a pungent, cockroachy smell: pheromone attractants.

At a turning, Reddi stopped the car and turned off the headlights.

"What's the matter? Why don't we go find Leota?"

The Indian said, "She is the third one in line back there. Did you not see her? But her little bracelet is still broadcasting, and my device located her." He stared around, scowling. "However," he said, "there are problems."

"What sort of problems?" Hake demanded.

"You see them!" He gestured at the men across the road. "They have radios too. And it is probable the sheik himself is wandering about. He enjoys adventure— Hell!" He stared in the rearview mirror, then jumped out of the car and held up a warning hand.

One of the women was walking toward them. At Reddi's signal, she stopped. It was impossible to make out her face, but Hake had no doubt who she was.

"She saw us pass," said Reddi. "But it is too dangerous."

He tugged at his scant beard, and then shook his head. "We will go on and try again, later."

"The hell you say! This is the best chance we'll ever have, Reddi!"

"It is no chance at all. If there were no men near— But there are, and the guards are always monitoring. We cannot even speak to her, or they will hear."

"We can just take the radio off her—"

"And do what? They are all around. If they look to where she is supposed to be and see no one, what will they do, Hake? Say, 'Oh, perhaps my vision is blurred, I must be mistaken'? No. They will investigate. Then they will search, and if they search they will find us. And if we take her in the car, even if we do not speak, they will hear the sound of the car over the radio, and will locate her with the direction-finders. No. It is impossible. A little later—"

"I don't believe you'll do it later," Hake said. Alys put her hand on his arm.

"Mr. Reddi? Why can't I take her place?"

"What?" Hake cried. "Don't be insane! You don't know what you're saying."

She leaned to kiss his cheek. "Dear Horny," she said, "Leota is my friend, too. And anyway—it does sound interesting. And when you come right down to it, men always liked me better than Leota, back in college, and I don't think Sheik Hassabou will mind too much."

She jumped out of the car. The Indian glanced once at Hake, then followed. Hake started after them, then stopped himself; it was out of his hands; if he said anything, it would be heard and they would all be caught. He squinted through the blur of locusts as Reddi produced wire cutters and expertly snipped the golden arm-bracelet. It was soft, easy to remove, easy to bend onto Alys's willing arm.

Almost at once a voice came from it. "What is happening, Leota?"

"Nothing," said Leota, chin on Alys's shoulder. "I just tripped and bumped into something." She hesitated. "I'm getting tired of being out here," she complained. "I'm going back to my room to sleep for a while, if His Excellency doesn't require me."

The voice laughed. "His Excellency will surely wake you if he does."

Alys touched the bracelet, then smiled at them. She formed with her lips the words *Get out of here!* as she turned to move slowly toward the distant loom of the palace. Hake stared after her as they turned and retraced their path, until Reddi snapped, "Eyes front! Don't attract attention! That's the sheik." They were crossing the bridge, and down the stream, on the permanent hump of water, someone was standing on a surfboard, moving back and forth across the standing wave. He did not look toward them, and in a moment the locusts hid him from view.

XIII

Having stuffed herself, gauze pants, harem vest and all, into one of Alys's baggier suits, Leota was now trying to make her face look more civilized in Alys's mirror with some of Alys's cosmetics. Rama Reddi, in the copilot seat, was busy with a notebook, studying what and writing what Hake did not want to imagine. The pilot was obviously consumed with curiosity. He had put the plane on autopilot long since and was trying to strike up conversations with the passengers.

At least he had gotten over being indignant at being forced to take off in a locust swarm, but now he wanted to chat. "It was quite exciting, was it not, effendi?" he called to Hake, enunciating each syllable with care for Hake's practicing ear. "But what a pity! These people know nothing of locusts. They will capture only a few. The rest will fly on. If it would rain— Then they would stay on the ground and could be scooped up. But it will not, I think."

In spite of himself, Hake was intrigued. "Why do you want them to stay on the ground?"

"Why does one want to eat? They are excellent protein. And nearly gone, like your whooping crane. This pitiful remnant! In the time of my father the swarms would blacken the sky for days, horizon to horizon. When they alighted they would break the limbs of trees. Then the Europeans came with their insecticides, and our children fall to kwashiorkor for lack of protein."

He would have chatted on forever, but Reddi snapped his notebook closed and fixed the pilot with his stare. "Now you will shut up," he said. "Here. These are coordinates for where you are to land. I will then go on with you, while these two remain." When the pilot looked stubbornly blank, Reddi added, "Hake, translate."

Hake scowled. "Why do you want to split up? Why are we going there instead of Al Halwani?"

"Because I wish it." He did not wait for a reply, but straightened up and fastened his seat belt again. Only the top of his head was visible over the seat-back, shiny black hair slicked straight back, and it did not invite discussion.

Hake recognized the wisdom of at least part of what Reddi had said—the pilot had already had to be taken into their confidence far more than was reasonable, for what was supposed to be a super-secret operation. But he didn't like it. He leaned to Leota's ear. "Do you know the bit about Mahomet and the camel?"

She looked at him. "He let the camel's nose into his tent, and the rest of the camel followed? Yes, that's the way it is with the Reddis, Hake. I thought you found that out in Italy."

"Well, I did. But I didn't have much choice—"

She grinned suddenly, the first smile he had seen from her since her rescue. She leaned forward and kissed him quickly. "I'm not complaining!"

She dabbed at her face once more with a wet-packed tissue, then sighed and gave up. Putting the cosmetic case away, she said, "I was real ready to get out of there,

Horny. Mean bugger, that old sheik. Do you know how he got me out of Rome? With one of his boys holding a knife at my throat as we went through the port at Ostia. He had me believing he would have used it, too." The smile was completely gone now. She said, "I hope Alys is going to be all right."

"She said she could handle any man alive, Leota."

The girl looked at him. "Yeah. That sounds like her."

The pilot looked around, having returned to indignation. "Effendi, you and the woman should now have your safety belts secured," he pointed out in Arabic. He did not wait to see that they complied, but slammed the plane into a tight turn.

Twisting to keep his seat while fastening the belt, Hake could get only glimpses out of the tiny window: sand and wide, empty roads; dunes, and the broad sea beyond them; a cluster of one-story buildings that looked as though they had been put together out of used gasoline tins. They bounced in to a rough and ill-kept runway, and the pilot swerved off it at high speed toward a small building next to the stilted control tower. He cut the engines and turned around. "Now what?" he demanded. "If you wish me to take off, we must do it within a half-hour. This pig-pen is not equipped for night operations."

"How lawful you are," Reddi commented, when he understood. "Have the kindness to bring the luggage in— all but my own bag, the brown one." He opened the door and crawled out over the wing, gave one contemptuous glance at the airport structures and then ignored them. When the pilot was safely away on the far side of the nose of the plane, grumbling as he pulled the baggage out of the compartment, Reddi said, "I will leave you here. I will take the plane; please pay the pilot whatever is necessary, including an extra three hours of flying time."

"For God's sake, why?" demanded Hake, managing not to add that it was, after all, his plane.

"You and Pauket will go to the city by ground. There are buses, but perhaps you will want to walk; it should take you no more than a day, and you can purchase hiking equipment at the hostel here. This is best. First, because your objective is along the coastal road and you can study it. Second, the customs will be far less thorough here than in the city airport, and I do not suppose Pauket's credentials are in very good order. Third, I have arranged to meet my brother there, and it is not desirable that you be present."

"And, fourth," said Leota, "you want a chance to conspire with him in private."

He glanced at her. "Do you blame me? I have done as I undertook, and I have not been paid. My brother and I must make arrangements to be sure we are not cheated."

"I'd give something to know what those arrangements are," she said.

He was silent for a moment, regarding her. Then he sighed. "In spite of our occasional association, Ms. Pauket," Reddi said, "you have learned very little. Would you have four of us go in with guns? It would not succeed. But much can be done. Persons the Team considers their own are not. Parties of opposed interest may be induced to work together. This is where I am in charge, and when it is necessary you will be told what to do. Of course," he added, "all depends on my brother's decision."

"The hell you say, Reddi!" Leota flared. "A lot depends on what *we* decide."

"No. Very little. What choice do you have?" He waited for a moment, then nodded. "Very well. I will be in the Crash Pad tomorrow night—"

"Crash Pad?"

"The hotel," Reddi said impatiently. "The sign on it says *Intercontinental*, but ask anyone for the Crash Pad and they will direct you to it. Do not ask for my room. Go to it. It will be high up, on the top floor if I can arrange it, otherwise as close as possible to the top. You will know the room because it will have a *Do Not Disturb* sign on the door with the opposite corners bent back. Is that understood? Good, now pay the pilot."

Hake looked at Leota, who nodded. He shrugged and moved to intercept the Egyptian as he returned from dumping the luggage at the door marked, in several languages, *Customs and Passport Control*. They haggled for the obligatory few minutes, then returned to the plane. Hake was beginning to feel actively good. The desert afternoon air burned his lungs and throat, but it was a good heat, familiar from his childhood; and Leota was beginning to seem more at ease.

Reddi was already standing on the wing of the plane, impatient. He said, "Are you quite sure that the pilot understands he is paid in full and that there will be no gratuities?"

"He understands," snarled the pilot, adding a sentence in Arabic that Reddi did not comprehend and Hake tried not to. He had no desire to learn of the pilot's sudden death.

The hostel had probably once been something else; at least, it was not very good as a hostel. Its advantage was that neither the veiled Bedouin woman who showed them their room nor anyone else seemed to care much about IDs. It had very few other advantages. Two cots with Army blankets. Bare walls. Two sand-frosted windows that did not open. Signs in ten languages—not all of them repeated in all the languages: "No Alcoholic Beverages" was only in three Near Eastern languages and, curiously, in German; "No Smoking in Bed" was only in English.

Leota gathered up an armful of clothes and headed for the showers, pausing only because Hake insisted on taking her photograph first. He heard the distant tinny rattle of the pipes as he laid out the rest of the contents of Jessie's do-it-yourself ID kit. Passport and visas, no problem; he sealed the photographs on them and added appropriate stamps. He assembled metal type to read JFK-CAI and CAI-KWI, added airline and flight indicia, tapped the type into alignment and pressed them onto a ticket form: result, a perfect ticket showing that one Millicent Anderson Selfridge had flown from New York to Kuwait; he then threw away the ticket itself and left the used carbon copy to add to Leota's documents. For the sake of completeness he made her a set of credit cards, a Massachusetts driver's licence, a Blue Cross card and one for Social Security. It took three-quarters of an hour to finish it.

And Leota was still in the shower, the water gurgling

intermittently. What was taking her so long? Didn't she know the concierge would be raging at the waste of water —if, that is, the concierge was bothering to listen?

He rubbed the cards between his palms to age them, bent a few corners artistically and studied the result. They looked good to him, for a first effort; he hoped they would look as good to any inquiring official.

He had stowed away the blank cards and kit, undressed and lay back on one of the bunks, almost falling asleep, before Leota returned. Her hair was wrapped in a towel. She wore Alys's familiar long print housecoat and, queerly, heavy knee-length socks; as she moved, he caught a glimpse of thigh and discovered that she still seemed to be wearing the embroidered stockings beneath them. He said, "Welcome back, Millicent."

"Millicent?" Her expression was calm and detached as she put the traveling bag down and began to towel her hair.

"That's your new ID," he said, getting up to show her the documents. She inspected them carefully, and then said:

"You do good work, Horny. Horny? Alys must have a blow-dryer somewhere in those bags. See if you can find it. And tell me what we're doing now."

Hake did his best to fill her in, aware that he knew less than he needed to know. Leota listened abstractedly, her expression remote, as she dried her hair, and brushed it, and began to sort out the contents of Alys's baggage. She asked a few questions, but did not press when Hake's answers were unsatisfactory.

She seemed, in fact, to be moving in a dream. When she had all Alys's possessions laid out on the cots—two long dresses, five pounds of cosmetics, even a titanium-rutile tiara among them—Hake saw that her eyes were filled with tears.

He said awkwardly, "You've had a pretty hectic time. Maybe I should just think about getting you back to America, or wherever. I can deal with this alone."

She looked up at him. "Hell you can, Hake."

"Well. . . . I guess you're worried about Alys. But I think she'll be all right. She was looking for an adventure."

"Adventure!" she exploded. "What do you know about adventures?" Then she calmed, and the glacial, detached expression returned. "Well, actually," she said, "I suppose Alys is better suited to that life than I was. He's an interesting old bastard, the sheik. Very artistic. And very technological. And if it gets too bad, she can always get out of it, sooner or later—she's in a better position to yell for help than I was. But still—"

Hake was finding the conversation uncomfortable. He wanted to know. He did not want to ask. He could feel a queasy pelvic sensation that he did not like, and did not even want to allow himself—after all, he pointed out to himself, Leota's sexual activities were not any of his concern. As she herself had told him. He was, however, entitled to feel compassion, surely. He said, stumbling over the words, "Was it, ah, really bad?"

She looked at him in silence for a moment, and then said only, "Yes."

He could not think of a response, and after a moment she said, "Or, actually, no. I haven't got things sorted out yet, Horny."

He nodded without saying anything—it did not signify understanding, only acceptance. He stood up, helped her repack Alys's bags, and began to get ready for bed, all in silence. And then, as he was taking off his shirt, Leota touched the great broad welts on his chest.

"Horny? Those are your scars, from something that almost killed you."

"Yes?"

She dropped her robe. What he had thought to be embroidered stockings were tracings in blue, green and yellow on her legs, and they covered her entire body, a tattooed explosion of surreal color. She said, "These are mine."

Before dawn they were on the road, the rented A-frame awkward on Hake's shoulders. The "objective" was four miles down the road, and it would be hot, broad daylight before they reached it; now there was a faint slipperiness of dew on the paved road and the occasional greenery. For most of these plants, most of the year, that would be the only water they saw. Or needed.

Neither Hake nor Leota spoke much. For Hake, he had too much on his mind—or none of it really on his mind, because he could not keep his attention on any one question. There were a dozen trains of thought slithering inconclusively around his head: the Team; what the Reddis were up to; the broad sand hillocks to one side of them and, now and then, a look at the sea to the other. And, over and over again, Leota. None of them came to a climax, and perhaps he did not want them to; they were less uncomfortable where they were.

When the oil sheiks owned this part of the world, they had climbed to the top of their mountain of petrodollars and looked toward the west. What they saw, they copied. Hospitals and libraries. Museums and shiny convention hotels. Beaches, with marinas that now rotted empty. Roads that would have done credit to Los Angeles, divided by parkway strips that would have graced Paris. The plantings along the parkway strips were dead now, because no one had chosen to spend the money to bring them water. But the long, wide, silent highway itself stretched endlessly along the sea.

It was not quite deserted. As it came near to daylight occasional traffic shared it with them. A bus like the Metroliner, whispering past a train of camels—not like the Metroliner, because its exhaust was only a thin plume of steam, that disappeared almost at once in the morning light. Hydrogen-powered. Reasonable enough, here where it came from. Hake felt a moment's envy. And some worry, too, because there were signs along the road with troublesome implications. Bleached old metal ones in Arabic, with messages like:

Military Reservation
Keep to Road
Passage Prohibited After Dark

And one in English, carelessly lettered on a painted-out road-traffic sign, but quite new:

HAUL ASS
If you can read this,
you don't belong here.

No one challenged them. No one seemed to care. But Hake was glad when the sun was up, at least, even though the heat began at once.

They walked on in silence through the morning, the heat building up with every hour. When the sun was directly overhead they paused in the ruin of an old bus stop and drowsed for an hour or two, drinking sparingly from their canteens, and then moved on. A few minutes later Leota broke the silence. "Have you been thinking about my question?"

Hake had been thinking about everything but—more than anything else, about the implications of Leota's body paint. It took him a moment to remember what question she had asked him. "You mean about why I do all this? God," he said fervently, "have I not!"

"And?"

He thought for a moment. "If you mean am I aware of ever being hypnotized into being a spook, no. I did some reading up on hypnotism, and none of it seems to fit. In fact, I've still got some stuff in my bag."

"But you aren't convinced. You don't believe anybody did this to you. You'd rather think you were a villain than a dupe."

He looked at her sharply, but her tone was not contentious, only thoughtful.

"I'd *rather*," he said, "know exactly what is going on. In my head, and in my life. Whichever way it came out. But I don't."

She nodded and was silent, eyes fixed on the empty road ahead. The highway was bending away from the coast now, and the dunes between them and the sea were higher.

Leota said something, so faintly he could not hear it against the hot on-shore wind and had to ask her to repeat it. "I said, do you know, I almost didn't go with you when you turned up?"

"For God's sake, why? Did you *like* it in the harem?"

She looked at him quickly—not with anger, he saw. She said placatingly, "I don't know why. But when you and Reddi and Alys turned up, you looked like—invaders. You didn't belong there. I did, and it felt wrong for me to let you capture me."

"*Capture* you!"

"I know, Horny. I'm telling you the way it was in my head. You were on the other team. And I don't think I was hypnotized, either—just kidnapped at a knife-point," she said bitterly. "I don't know how I could have escaped from the harem. But I didn't even try."

They drew off the road to let one of the tandem buses whine past, the passengers half asleep in the heat, paying no attention to them. Hake studied the map thoughtfully for a moment. "We've only got a couple of miles to go, near as I can figure it," he said.

"Shall we get on with it?"

"I've got a better idea. If we're going to snoop, I'd rather do it at night, and it'll be sundown in a couple of hours. Let's go for a swim."

"Swim?"

"Up there." He pointed to the now distant dunes, a few hundred yards ahead. There was a sand-covered side road leading between two of the larger ones. "Let's take a look."

The quarter-mile of coast behind the dunes had once been developed as a beach; there were abandoned cabanas and dressing rooms and the wrecks of refreshment pavilions. And no human beings in sight. They dropped their packs and their clothes in the shade of what had once been a lifeguard tower and ran down to the bright blue water. There was no surf to speak of, only gentle foot-high waves moving diagonally in from the sea, but the two of them splashed the water into foam. Leota's painted skin made her look like a naiad in the crystal sea, and Hake could feel his parched tissues soaking up moisture as they floated and dove in the shallow water. They did not go out far, or stay in long. But when they returned to the lengthening shade and sprawled out, their bodies drying almost at once in the hot breeze, Hake felt a hundred times better, and Leota dropped off to sleep.

He let her rest for an hour, and then they dressed, resumed their packs and started off again, with the sun now low behind them. Before they had gone a mile it set, quickly and definitively. There was a minute when their shadows were long and clear before them, and another minute when the shadows had gone entirely. The darkness did not hinder their walking. There was a more than half-moon already in the sky, ample to see where they were going. As the dry earth gave up its heat the night wind began to blow toward the sea and the temperature dropped. They stopped to add sweaters to their covering, and pressed on, with the moon bright before them and the dunes interrupting the spread of stars to their right. There was no one else on the road now, not even the occasional bus or truck.

But when Leota spoke it was almost in a whisper. She tugged Hake's arm. "What's that up ahead?"

Hake had been more intent on her than on the road, but he saw at once what she was pointing to. The old road ended only a few hundred yards ahead. It seemed to be swallowed up in an immense dune; and before the dune there was a wall of waist-high concrete set with reflectors, leading to a newer, far less elaborate detour that struck off at an angle into the desert. The dunes that covered the old road did not seem to be there by accident. They were buttressed by cement and faced with stone. They had not blown there at the whim of the winds. Someone had put them there.

"I think that's it," he said.

"This place? I don't see any kind of generating plant."

"It's got to be on the far side of the dunes." He hesitated. "We're going to have to climb them. It'd be easier if we left the knapsacks here—"

"All right."

"—but we might want to take pictures or something when we get to the top."

Leota stopped, with the A-frame straps half off her shoulders. "Make up your mind, will you, Hake?"

"We'll take them," he decided. "But it's going to be a tough climb."

And it was, harder than any climb Hake had made in his post-invalid life. Even harder than the grueling exercises Under the Wire. The sand slipped away under their feet, so that they were constantly sliding back at almost every step, and where there was rock or concrete there were few footholds. To Hake's surprise, however, the going became easier as they neared the top. The sand was firmer and more cohesive, and there was even a growing scatter of vines and stunted plants. There was a smell in the air that Hake could not identify. Partly it was the sea. But part of it was like the church lawn new-mown in the early spring: the smell of cut grass and stalks of wild scallions. And there was also a pungent, half-sweet floral odor that he had experienced somewhere before (but where?), which seemed to come from the scraggly volunteer growth. He did not understand these plants. They were oddly succulent for this arid part of the world. Parched and half-dead, they still seemed improbably frequent on the dune; were they some sort of planting designed to keep the dune from moving in on the road?

And then they topped the ridge and looked out on the moonlit sea.

Panting from the climb, Leota found breath enough to whisper, "What's *that*?" Hake did not have to ask what she meant. The same question was in his own mind. A quarter-mile out to sea, rising from the water and braced with three moon-glittered legs like one of H. G. Wells's Martian fighting machines, a tall tower rose. Its head was a squashed sphere, and it shone with a sultry crimson, like the heart of a dying fire. It was not only light that came from it. Even at the top of the dune, they could feel its heat. Around its legs were a cluster of metal domes, awash in the sea, and what looked like barges moored to them.

Hake stood up for a better look around. Below him, the reverse slope of the dunes made an immense open bowl facing the sea. It could not have been all natural. Bulldozers and blasting had helped that shape along. It was more ovoid than spherical, and not entirely regular, but a mile-long bite had been taken out of dunes seventy feet high. And the seaward face of the dunes was no longer barren. It looked like an abandoned suburban yard, with the honeysuckle gone wild. Here and there along the slope shrubs and bushes were scattered. Hake was no gardener, but he could not have identified them anyway. They were choked under coils of ropy vine. The vines were everywhere, glossy leaves, gray-green in the moonlight, furled flowers, vines that were thinner than wire or thicker than Hake's forearm. The mown-grass smell came from them. It was stronger now, and with a smoky aroma like marijuana burning, or candles that have just been blown out.

The logic of the design spoke for itself. As the Texas Wire sloped to face its geosynchronous satellite, this receptor cupped to confront the sea. "It has to be solar power," said Leota, and Hake nodded slowly.

"Of course. But where are the mirrors?"

"Maybe they take them in at night? For cleaning?"

He shook his head. "Maybe," he said. "But look at the way this whole area is overgrown—it's almost as if they used to have something here, and then abandoned it."

Leota said simply, "That thing out there doesn't look abandoned."

Hake shrugged, and then came to a decision. "The best way to look at a solar power plant is when it's working. I'm going to stay here till sunrise and see what happens."

Leota turned to look at him. "Wrong, Hake. *We're* going to stay."

"What's the point? You'll be more comfortable down by the road. And maybe safer. If this thing is operational, there are bound to be crews putting up the mirrors and so on—it's easier for one person to stay out of sight than two."

She did not answer, only began pulling the thermal sleeping bag out of her pack. "It's too cold to argue," she said. "And this thing is big enough for two. Are you going to join me or not?"

Hake gave in. Leota was right—right that it was too cold to argue, and right that the sleeping bag was big enough for two. Inside the bag it was no longer cold at all, as soon as their combined body heat began to accumulate. They wriggled out of their sweaters, then squirmed out of their pants and then, without transition, found that they were beginning to make love. In the absolute silence of the Arabian shore, with the bright moon peering through the vines over their heads and an occasional star, it seemed a very good place for it. They remembered to be hungry, afterwards, and divided a couple of chocolate bars, and then rested, sleeping and waking, with no clear distinction made between the states.

The only way Hake was certain he had been sleeping was that he woke up, with Leota tense in his arms. She had said something. He was no longer warm. The bag was wet and chill, soaked with cold water; and the silence was gone, replaced by a distant thumping sound of a pump and a slithering, creeping sound like a forest in a gentle wind. He blinked and beheld Leota's face peering out toward the sea, lighted with a strange violet radiance. "It *hurts*," she complained, squinting.

It was almost dawn. The moon and stars were gone, and the sky had turned blue, with a rosy aurora toward the east. The sullen red glow from the top of the tower was gone now; obviously it had cooled through the night, and was now only a black ellipsoid, no longer radiating. But something new was in the sky. A poorly defined, purplish splotch of light hung above the horizon. It was not bright, but as Hake looked at it his eyes began to ache. "Don't look that way!" he ordered, clapping a hand to his eyes, then squinting between his fingers.

"What is it, Horny?"

"I don't know! But I think it's ultraviolet, and it'll blind you if you let it. Look around you, Leota!"

The slithering noise came from the myriad tangled vines. Their furled flowers were opening and turning themselves toward the sea. Amid the glossy, green-black leaves, pearly white flower cups were swelling and moving, new ones smaller than his thumbnail and huge old ones the size of inverted beach umbrellas, and each pearl-white cup, tiny or immense, was pointing the same way.

Hake and Leota stared at each other, then quickly

crawled out of the sodden sleeping bag and began to dress, careful not to look toward the spectral violet glow. The reason for the wetness revealed itself; under the vines there was a tracery of plastic tubing, squeezing out a trickle of water to irrigate the plants. None of this was accidental. A great deal of design and an immense effort of work had gone into it. "Good God," said Hake suddenly. "I know where I've smelled these flowers before! IPF had some of them in Eatontown."

But Leota wasn't listening. "Look," she said, barreling her fingers to make a fist-telescope and peering out toward the sea. The sun had come up, as abruptly as it had set the night before, and it was blindingly bright. But it was not alone! It had two companions in the sky, the purplish glow, now comparatively fainter but no less painful to look at, and a tinier and fiercer sun atop the metal tower. Careful as he was, Hake could not avoid an occasional split-second glance at one or another of the three suns. Even with eyes closed the after-images were dazzling in green and purple.

"The flowers are the mirrors!" he cried. "Like morning glories! They turn toward the sun, and reflect it to the tower!"

"But what's that purplish thing?" Leota demanded.

He shrugged. "Whatever it is, we'd better get away from it. But—but this is perfect! You hardly even need machines —just the tower, to generate electricity, or hydrogen, or whatever. Why is it secret?"

"Because we don't have it ourselves," Leota said bitterly. "Because your friends don't want to give foreigners credit for it. Because they're pathological liars. What difference does it make?" She squinted down toward the base of the tower. "Regardless," she said, "there are people working down there now. I move we get out of here and see if we can catch the morning bus to the city."

They made their way to the highway nearly blind, and even hours later, when they had succeeded in stopping a bus and were looking for the hotel called The Crash Pad in the city, Hake could still see the after-images, now blue and yellow, inside his eyes. They had come within measurable distance of blindness, he realized. If Reddi had known where the installation was, he had known enough to warn them of the danger, too. And he had not elected to do so. Which said something about their relationship with the Reddis.

The hotel was the only one available for transients in the city. It was set back from the roadway in a little park (now bare, because unwatered), and the entrance was behind a three-tiered fountain (now dry). The lobby was a ten-story-high atrium, with its space filled with dangling ropes of golden lights (now dark) and with a pillar of outside elevators at one side, only one of which seemed to be working. They used their faked passports to register for a room and were relieved to find that the desk clerk did not seem to care that they were in two different names. There was no bellboy to help them with their baggage, but as their baggage amounted only to the two knapsacks the problem was not severe.

Hake's notions of luxury had been formed in Germany and on Capri, and they added up to a really large room with an auto-bar. This was a suite. There was no soap in the bathroom, and the ring around the bidet suggested that someone, sometime, had mistaken its purpose. To offset that, it had its own kitchen (not working) and dressing room; and if the bed was bare, it was also oval and a good ten feet across. Its sheets and covers were stacked on top of it, along with half a dozen huge towels, and when Hake knelt on it to reach them he was surprised to find that it gave gently under his weight in a fashion quite unlike anything he had ever experienced before. "Silicone foam," Leota explained. "Like Silly Putty. I've seen them, but I've never actually slept on one."

It was clear that the hotel was willing to allow them whatever luxury they liked, as long as they didn't expect any of the hotel staff to provide it. Hake carried towels to the bathroom and checked out the kitchen. A strange fermenting odor led him to the refrigerator which turned out to hold two half-gallon jugs of fresh orange juice, fresh no longer; he dumped them down the sink and discovered it was plugged up. The twin TV sets on either side of the immense bed didn't work, either, until he crawled behind the head of the bed to plug them in. The room had been neither dusted nor swept in recent times, but there was a vacuum cleaner with attachments at the bottom of one of the immense closets. There Leota drew the line. When she had finished making up the bed she said, "That's good enough. We're not going to be living here forever, after all. I saw some shops in the lobby; are any of those credit cards good enough to get me some clothes of my own?"

"Let's hope so," Hake said grimly; and while Leota was re-outfitting herself he prowled the top three floors of the hotel, looking for the room with the bent *Do Not Disturb* sign on the door.

There wasn't any. The Reddis either had not yet arrived or did not choose to be contacted.

When Leota returned Hake was sitting on the edge of the bed, watching an old American private-eye movie on the television. "Are you having a good time?" she asked.

He looked up and switched the set off. It was no loss; he had not seen any of the last twenty minutes of it. "I've been thinking," he said. "I'm not sure I want to contact the Reddis. They're pure poison."

"And your friends on the Team are better?"

"No, they're not. I should be applying for a job at Hydro Fuels right about now, and I'm not sure I want to do that either. Do you want to know what I am sure of?"

She sat down and waited for him to answer his own question. "I'm sure I like *this*. Being here. With you. And I'd like it to go on."

He stood up and paced to the window. Over his shoulder, he said, "I'm willing to do what's right, Leota—my God, I *want* to. But I don't know where right is, any more, and I guess I understand how people give up. Take what they can get for themselves, and the hell with everybody. And we could do that, you know. We've got unlimited credit. Anywhere in the world. We can do anything we like, as long as the credit cards last. We could catch a plane to Paris tonight. Or Rio de Janeiro. Anywhere. We can milk the cards for a million dollars in cash and put it in a Swiss bank, so if they ever catch up with us we can go right on with real money."

She said thoughtfully, "The Reddis wouldn't let us. We owe them. They'd find us, even if your friends didn't."

"So we give the Reddis what they want. The Team—" Hake shrugged. "I guess they would catch us, sooner or later," he admitted. "But what a great time we could have until they did!"

"Is that what you want to do?"

Hake said slowly, "Leota, I don't *know* what I want to do. I know what would be nice. That would be to marry you and take you back to Long Branch, and get busy being minister of my church again. I don't see any way to do that."

She looked at him appraisingly, but did not speak.

"Even better. We could change the world. Get rid of all this crumminess. Expose the Team, and put the Reddis out of business, and make everything clean and decent again. I don't see any way to do that, either. I know how all that is supposed to go, I've seen it in the movies. We defeat the Bad Guys, and the town sees the error of its ways, and I become the new marshal and we live happily ever after. Only it doesn't work that way. The Bad Guys don't think they're bad, and I don't know how to defeat them. Mess them up a little bit, sure. But sooner or later they'll just wipe us out, and everything will be the same as before."

"So what you're saying is we should have a good time and forget about principle?"

"Yes," he said, nodding, "that seems to be what it comes down to. Have you got any better ideas?"

Leota sat up straight in the middle of the bed, legs curled under her in the half-lotus position, looking at him in silence. After a long time, she said, "I wish I did."

Hake waited, but she didn't add anything to what she had said. He felt cheated, and realized that he had expected more from her. He said belligerently, "So you're giving up too!"

"Shouldn't I?" She was beginning to cry. Hake moved toward her but she shook him away. "Give me a minute," she said, drying her eyes. She gazed out at the bright harbor, marshalling her thoughts. "When I was in school," she began, "and I first got an idea of what was going on, it all looked simple. We got our little group going, the Nader's Raiders of international skullduggery, and it was really exciting. But the whole group's gone now. I'm the only survivor. Some got scared off, two wound up in jail, and it isn't fun any more. Sometimes I get help from volunteers. Sometimes I work with people like the Reddis. Usually I'm all by myself."

"Sounds like a lonely life."

"It's a *discouraging* life. The world isn't getting any better from anything I do. Mostly it seems to be getting worse. And every time I think I get a handle on the roots and causes of it all, it turns out wrong. Like hypnotism. I thought that might account for it and, do you see, if it did, then there might be something I could do. But it doesn't. It doesn't even account for the way I acted in Hassabou's harem."

Hake got up awkwardly to stare out the window with her. He was pretty sure he didn't want to hear any details of how Leota had acted in Hassabou's harem. He said, "Why didn't you go public?"

"Aw, Horny. First thing I thought of."

"So did you try it?"

"Ha! Did we not! My PoliSci professor had a friend on a TV station in Minneapolis, and she got us a five-minute spot on the news. We taped it. Everything we knew, or deduced—but it never got on the air. And the Team got on us. The professor lost tenure—for 'corrupting a student'— me! And I took off. The trouble was the station wouldn't believe us, and the people who did believe us called Washington to check." She moved restlessly around the room; then, facing him, "For that matter, why didn't you?"

He said, "Well, I thought of it. As a matter of fact, I left some stuff in New Jersey—a complete tape of everything I knew up to the time I got back from Rome." He told her about International Pets and Flowers and his visits to Lo-Wate Bottling Co., and about The Incredible Art. She listened with some hope.

"Well, it's a try at least," she conceded. "Is there anything in the tape that you could call objective proof? No. Well, there's the rub, Horny. Of course," she said thoughtfully, "this fellow's in entertainment, so he's got more media access than you or I. Maybe somebody might listen —especially if it comes out the way you told him, and you get killed or something."

"Now, that's a cheerful thought." They were both silent for a moment, thinking about that cheerful thought. "I told him about you," he mentioned.

"Oh? Saying what?"

"Well, not about you personally, so much, but I asked him about hypnotism. He knows a lot about it. In fact, he gave me some tapes. Do you want to look at them?"

"What good would they do?"

"Maybe none, how do I know? But we don't have an awful lot else to do, do we?"

She sighed, and smiled, and came over to kiss him. "Sorry, Horny. I guess I'm still up tight. Let's see if that TV set has a viewer."

It did—for, Hake thought, the primary purpose of displaying the equivalent of filthy postcards. But it would work as well for Art's tapes and fiches. He pulled them out of the bottom of his knapsack and stuck one at random into the scanner.

The first panel was a page of a technical journal, with a paper by two people on the resemblance between sleep and hypnotism. It seemed that people who napped easily were, by and large, also easily hypnotizable.

Hake looked at Leota. Leota shrugged. "I don't take naps very often," she said. "I don't see what that has to do with anything, anyway."

"Let's try another," Hake said, and dumped the rest of the microfiches on the floor. Among them was a cassette, home-made by The Incredible Art. Hake clicked it into the player and turned it on, and Art's voice came to them.

"I don't know how much of this stuff is going to be useful to you, Horny," it said, "but here's the whole thing. What I started with was my own magic act. You remember how I did it. I get maybe thirty people to come up on the stage and I give them the usual 'you are getting sleepy-

sleepy-*sleepy*' stuff. Most of them will act as if they're really going to sleep. The ones that don't I scoot right off stage, so I have maybe twenty left. Then I command them to try to raise their arms, but I tell them they can't. The ones that don't respond, off. So I have about a dozen. I keep going until I have maybe half a dozen that will do any damn thing I tell them to.

"Now, are they hypnotized? Beats me, Horny. I wondered about that, so I looked in the literature and this is some of the stuff I found. The key papers are, hold your breath, *Hypnosis, Suggestion and Altered States of Consciousness: Experimental Evaluation of the New Cognitive-Behavioral Theory and the Traditional Trance-State Theory of 'Hypnosis'*—that's in quotes, quote Hypnosis unquote—by Barber and Wilson, and *Hypnosis from the Standpoint of a Contextualist,* by Coe and Sarbin.

"Read them if you want to. I'll tell you what they say— or, anyway, what I think they say. The Barber and Wilson paper is about an experiment they did. They took a bunch of volunteers and divided them up into three parts. One third they did nothing special for; they were controls. One third they hypnotized, putting them into trance state in the good old-fashioned way and giving them suggestions. The last third they just talked to. They didn't hypnotize them. There was no trance state. They didn't even ask them to do anything. They just said things like, 'Have you ever thought of what it would be like to not feel pain, or to remember your first day in school, or to be unable to raise your arm? If you want to, maybe you'll think about these things.' They call it 'thinking with.' So then they did the experiments. Arm heaviness, finger anesthesia, water hallucination—I think there were ten different things they tried. And then they matched the responses of the three groups, scoring them so that the highest response—the 'most hypnotized,' you would call it—would be 40, and the total bomb-outs, no response at all, would be zero. No group came out with zero, in fact no individual did. They took a score of 22 as the cut-off point, and this is what they found out:

"For the control group, 55 percent of the subjects scored

23 or better—so even if there isn't any preparation at all, a lot of people will act as if they're hypnotized anyway.

"For the hypnotized, trance-state group, 45 percent scored 23 or better. *Forty-five percent!* Less than the controls.

"And for the thinking-with group, you know how many scored 23 or better? A hundred percent. *All* of them."

The voice on the tape paused for a moment, and then continued. "Ah, here it is. So then I did some more reading, and I came across the Coe and Sarbin piece. They have a theory about hypnotism. They call it the 'dramaturgic' view, *i.e.*, hypnotic subjects are acting out a part. You ought to read the paper, but, here, let me just read what it says at the end. 'We underscore the proposition (long overlooked) that the counterfactual statements in the hypnotist's induction are cues to the subject that a dramatistic plot is in the making. The subject may respond to the cues as an invitation to join in the miniature drama. If he accepts the invitation, he will employ whatever skills he possesses in order to enhance his credibility in enacting the role of hypnotized person.'

"Get it? They're playing a part. And what makes me think there's something to it is, I know that's what I do when I get up on a stage. I play a part. I'm not me, the fellow who lives in Rumson, New Jersey, and keeps parakeets. I'm The Incredible Art. If you look at it in one way, I'm sort of hypnotizing myself into behaving, what do they call it, counterfactually. And not just me. All actors. They get up there night after night. The corns don't hurt, the cough doesn't hack, whether they're exhausted or not the step is spry—until the curtain comes down, and that glorious, radiant creature schlumps away to the dressing room and the Bromo-Seltzer and the Preparation H."

He was silent for a moment. Then, "Well, there it is. I hope you find the stuff interesting. If you ever get through all this, come by the house and have a drink and we'll talk it over."

"The more I try to understand what's really happening in the world," Hake said, getting up to click off the player, "the more I find out I don't know *anything*. The hell with it."

Leota curled her legs under her on the bed, straightened her back and stared him down. "What do you mean, the hell with it?"

"I mean I get lost in the complications. And I don't have time for them. I was supposed to apply for a job two hours ago."

She flared, "Do you think I'm going to marry a *nincompoop*?"

"Who said anything about getting married?"

"You did! Just a few minutes ago. And I even thought about it, but I made that mistake once and I'm not going to do it again."

Hake was getting angry, too. "I'm Hornswell Hake, minister," he snarled, "and I do the best I can. I can't do everything. I don't *know* everything. I wish Art were here —he knows more about some of this stuff than I do. I wish I could see what's right and best—but I can't. If that makes me a nincompoop I'll just have to live with it."

Leota stood up for emphasis, moving toward the window. She said, "Anybody can do the right thing when it's perfectly clear what the right thing is! But how do you ever know that? You don't, and you have to act anyway."

"I know that."

"Then—"

"Then," he said, "I do what I can see I damn better do, which is to get my tail over to the place I was supposed to be at two hours ago and apply for that job."

They stared at each other for a moment, then Leota broke eye contact. She turned and gazed out the window.

A sudden rigidity in her stance, the way she held her head, the set of her shoulders, alarmed Hake. "What's the matter?" he demanded.

She said, "Did I ever tell you how we left Rome?"

"What's that got to do with what we're talking about?"

"Hassabou wouldn't live in a hotel. Not him. He had his yacht at Ostia. One day we just went for a sail—and didn't come back. When the yacht got to Benghazi his boys took me to the airport. With a knife at my throat. Come look."

Hake peered out the window, past the bright gold mosque and the minarets toward the harbor. "See the sailing yacht out there, the big one? That's the *Sword of Islam*. It's Hassabou's yacht."

XIV

ONE more complication was not even important in Hake's head; there were so many, too many, already that it didn't matter. Obviously Leota was at risk in one additional way. Hake had no way to solve that problem, but he could ease it. He left Leota in the room just long enough to buy her some new clothes. In cloak, ankle-length skirt and *hatta w-'aqqal* she was stifling in Al Halwani's noonday heat, but not recognizable.

They did not speak as they strolled toward the employment office of the hydrogen-power company. Leota walked a traditional two paces behind him, head demurely down. Hake, in burnoose and caftan, was almost as hot as she, but would have been no better off in any other costume— the desert people, or the men among them anyway, had long since found that loose, enveloping garments were more protection against the heat than exposed skin. And there was no cultural prohibition against Hake's looking around him as they walked—for people from the Team, for the sheik's men, for the Reddis, and even just to sight-see.

The surprising thing, once he saw it, was that Al Halwani had no fire hydrants. It had no sewers and no water pipes, either, though that was not as apparent. Fat electric tankers carried drinking water to each building's cisterns from the distillation plants outside the city, and the sewage went right into the thirsty ground. There were spots of green near some of the older buildings, where the outflow from the plumbing nourished growth.

Three hundred years ago this whole part of the world had been uninhabited, bar an occasional wandering tribe or caravan of traders. Then the droughts and famines of central Arabia drove some of the nomads south, just in time to be on the scene when Europe bestirred itself and reached out for colonies. There were no national boundaries. There were no nations, or not until the British named them and drew lines on maps for the convenience of the file clerks in Whitehall. High Commissioners like Sir Percy Cox decreed this patch of sand for Kuwait, and that for Ibn Saud, and these arguable patches in between for no one, or for both neighbors in common; and so it was.

Then oil came, and those extemporized lines became intensely important. A quarter of an inch this way or that on a map meant a billion dollars in revenues.

Then the Israelis came, with their shaped nuclear charges. And no one cared any more.

The cities that had bloomed overnight into Chicagos and Parises became ghost towns. Abadan and Dubai, Kuwait and Basra began to dry up again. The shiny western buildings with their plate-glass walls and ever-running air-conditioners stood empty and began to die. The traditional Moslem architecture, thick-walled, pierced with ventilating slits, survived. And the migrants from all over the Arab world began to move home. Or move on. What was left was a hodge-podge of tribes and nationalities; and then the westerners began to move in, the hippies and the wanderers, the turned-off and the dissatisfied, the adventurous and the stoned. The American colonies had been built out of just such migrants two centuries before. Al Halwani was the Philadelphia or the Boston of the new frontier, crude, unruly, polyglot—and promising.

In order to get to the sand-colored headquarters of Al Halwani Hydro Fuels, Ltd., Leota and Hake had to walk along the esplanade, with the narrow beach to one side and, beyond it, the indigo bay and the stately *Sword of Islam* at anchor a quarter of a mile out. Leota did not look up. Hake studied the yacht carefully. Although it was a three-masted schooner, with gay flags in the rigging, he knew that inside the narrow hull were engines and enough technology to exempt it from any problems of wind or currents. He could see the big globe of hydrogen fuel. He could also see figures moving about on its decks, but there was no way of telling which was who. Whether they could see him was a whole other question. He did not really think they could, or not well enough to identify either him or Leota under the headdresses. But he was glad enough to push through the revolving door and enter the Hydro Fuels waiting room.

The employment office was almost empty, and the elderly woman at the desk handed them applications. They sat down at a plastic writing desk and began to fill them out.

The questions on the forms were in four languages, and fortunately for Leota English was one of them. Hake took pride in filling his own in Arabic, drawing the flowing curlicues as neatly as the lettering on an engineering sketch. There were not very many questions. Hake copied the details of his fictitious biography out of the Xeroxed resume Jessie Tunman had made for him—how long ago was that? Only four *days*? And then the intercom on the receptionist's desk rattled. "Send them in, Sabika," said somebody's voice, and they got up to be interviewed.

The personnel director was male, young and one-legged, and the name-plate on his desk said *Robling*. He hopped around to get them seated, grinned at them as he propped his crutch on the edge of his desk, and studied the forms. "Nice to see a couple of Americans here, Bill," he said, "but what are you doing in those getups?"

"We, uh, converted," Horny Hake said, after realizing that "Bill" referred to the name on his papers. "We're not real religious, though," he added.

"None of my business," Robling said cheerfully. "All I do is match people to jobs, and looks like you've got some good experience. Not too many people show up here with a hydrogen-cracking background."

"Uh-huh," Hake said, and recited the invented information on the documents. "That was in Iceland, three years ago. It's geothermal there, but I suppose it's pretty much like solar."

"Close enough. We have a lot of turnover here, of course. People come in, work a while, build up a stake. Then they take life easy for a while. But something ought to open up for you. Maybe in two, three weeks—"

"No sooner than that? I really need a job now," Hake said.

"Like that? Well—there's no job right this minute, but if you're short of money maybe I could help out."

"It's not the money. It's just that—" It's just that I have to start work on your project so I can wreck it for the Team; but Hake couldn't say that. "It's just that I want to get to work."

The personnel director's eyebrows went up; evidently that was not a common attitude among the drifters. "Well, that's a good trait, anyway up to a point. But the only vacancies we have at the moment are pushing a broom."

"I'll push a broom."

"No, no! You're overqualified. You wouldn't be happy, and then when something did open up it'd make trouble to jump you over the others. Still—" Struck by a thought, the man picked up Leota's questionnaire. He scanned it and nodded. "We could put your lady on the payroll for that. *She's* not overqualified." He glanced at the form again and snapped his fingers. "Penn," he said. "Yeah. Did you look at the bulletin board outside? Because I think there's a message for you."

"Who from?" Hake asked, off balance.

"Well, I don't know. We get all kinds of drif— all kinds of transients coming through here, and people leave messages. Only reason I noticed yours is that it's kind of a famous name. William Penn, I mean." He was nice enough not to smile. "So what do you say?"

Hake opened his mouth, but Leota was ahead of him. "I'll take it."

"Right. Uh, you said you weren't real religious, but does that mean you can take the veil off? Because we'll need a picture of you for the ID."

"That'll be fine," Leota said, loosening the headdress. "Do you want to take it in here? All right. Honey? Why don't you check the message board and wait for me outside?"

There was no one in the waiting room but the receptionist and a skinny old Yemeni, with crossed (but empty) cartridge belts across his blouse, absorbed in an Arabic-language crossword puzzle. Hake moved toward the pinboard behind the receptionist's desk and scanned the tacked-up messages. *"Milt and Terri, Judy and Art were here and are heading for Goa." "Patty from South Norwalk, call your mother."* The one that was meant for him was a small envelope with the name "William E. Penn" neatly typed on the outside. Inside, it said:

You are invited for cocktails aboard the *Sword of Islam.* The boatman will furnish you transportation as soon as you get this.

Hake folded the note back into its envelope, thinking grim thoughts. Whatever else might happen, he was not letting Leota back on that yacht.

He turned as the door to the personnel office opened, and there was Leota, standing in the doorway. She stopped in the open door, hesitated and then beckoned to him. He could not see her expression through the headdress.

As he approached, she caught his arm, drew him inside and closed the door. "There's another exit past the camera room," she said. "I'm sure Mr. Robling won't mind if we use it?"

The personnel director looked them over for a moment, then shrugged. "Why not?"

Down a cement-tiled hall, out through a metal door, into the stark sunlight. "What's the matter?" Hake demanded.

"Don't linger, Horny. That fellow in there is one of the Reddis. I don't think we want to talk to him."

"Christ." They hurried around a corner, then paused where they could see the Hydro Fuels building. "If we go back to the hotel he'll find us. He must have followed us from there." He handed her the note. "This was what was waiting for me."

She read it quickly, and then said, "Wow."

"That's about the size of it, yes," he agreed. "We can't go back to the hotel because of the Reddis, and we can't go to the yacht because of the sheik. You know what, Leota? We don't have a lot of options."

She stared through the veil at the building. Apparently Reddi was still inside. "Horny?" she said.

"What?"

"You got your pronouns wrong. It isn't 'we.' It's *you* that can't go back to the hotel, and *me* that doesn't want to go to the yacht. The other way around, there's no problem."

"What do you mean, no problem? Those guys are mean, Leota. I'm not letting you face up to them by yourself."

Her eyes were on him, and once again he wished he could see her face. She said sharply, "I've told you before, Horny, I don't play this big strong man and little weak woman game. I was dealing with the Reddis when you were still running covered-dish dinners in New Jersey. You go on to the yacht. Call me at the hotel when you get a chance."

"And what do you think you're going to do?"

"I'm going back in the waiting room and talk to Reddi. And you can't stop me." And he couldn't, because she picked up her skirts and ran, the intricately decorated backs of her legs flashing under the flopping hem of her gown.

There wasn't just one boatman, there were five of them, and they were armed. Desert Arabs often carry rifles for decoration, like a walking stick or a rolled umbrella. Hake did not think these rifles were ornamental. He paused on the broad, dead esplanade, but there were no more alternatives in sight than there ever had been. He handed over his letter and got into the covered launch. None of the few strollers on the boulevard paid attention as the high whine of the inertial drive changed pitch when the helmsman clutched in the propellor. Two of the other boatmen cast off the moorings, and they pulled away from the little floating dock.

As they approached the yacht, it began to look like a battleship. Its sides towered twenty feet over them as they approached the gangplank, the masts far higher still. Curmudgeon was standing at the rail and looking down, his face granite. Hake hesitated and looked back at the waves. These waters had a reputation for sharks. But what was he going to face on the yacht?

"Move him on," Curmudgeon called testily, and one of the boatmen prodded Hake with his rifle. "You took your time getting here," he said, as Hake came up level with him. Nothing could be read in his expression as he stood with one hand on the rail, open shirt, yachting cap, white slacks, rope sandals. Behind him two more crewmen stood, representing, with the five behind him, a great deal more overkill than Hake thought necessary. Their presence was a threat. But Curmudgeon didn't threaten. Or even reproach; all he said was, "The others are waiting for you below."

Hake had never before been on a centimillionaire's yacht. There was less opulence than he might have guessed, no swimming pool, not even a shuffleboard court on deck. But he could not see most of the deck, only a small portion, deck-chaired and awninged, at the stern, and the short foredeck with hoists and coiled cables; most of the deck space was out of sight on the levels above him. Inside there were no murals or carved panels, and the rails were only brass. But they passed an open doorway, with a sirocco of engine heat coming out of it, and Hake caught a glimpse of pipes and stacks going down, it seemed, indefinitely. *Sword of Islam* was a sailing yacht. But its auxiliaries looked big enough to drive an ocean liner.

Curmudgeon had told the truth, the others were waiting for him, in a lounge with windows looking out the stern of the yacht. There was more opulence here than in the passages—potted palms, a wall of tropical fish tanks, bean-bag pillows thrown about by the chairs and couches—but it looked more like some Short Hills playroom than a sheik's tent. Jessie Tunman looked up from a gin-rummy game with one of Yosper's youths—Mario?—and snapped, "You'll get yours, Horny. You had no right to take off with that chippy!"

"Hello, Jessie." There were a dozen people in the lounge, and he recognized most of them—Yosper and his boys, the young Hispanic called Tigrito and Deena Fairless, the instructor from Under the Wire. They did not look welcoming.

Yosper hopped off a chair and advanced, his bright blue eyes regarding Hake steadily. Then the old man laughed. "You always were a ballsy boy, Hake. Remind me of myself, before I discovered our Lord Savior—and the Team."

Hake nodded and sat down, trying to look relaxed as Yosper studied him. "What's it going to be, Hake?" the old man demanded. "You part of the operation, or are you going to go on being a pain in the ass?"

"I've carried out my assignment," Hake said.

"Oh, sure, Hake, I expect you have. And we're going to take your report, and then we'll know for sure. I was asking about from now on."

Hake hesitated. "If I complete this operation, can I retire?"

"That what you want, boy? Why," Yosper said easily, "that's not up to me, but we all got to retire sometime, so why not? I guess it depends on how good your report is, and what you do over the next couple of days. Where's your lady friend?"

"Leota's out of it!"

"No, Hake," the old man said earnestly, "I have to disagree with you on that. She's not out of it, unless old Hassabou says she is. Right at the moment I think he considers her a piece of his property that got misplaced, and he's not too fond of you about it."

"Why do you care what he thinks, for God's sake?"

Yosper said, "Watch your language. We care a lot, dummy. Hassabou used to own this whole country. And after they're bankrupt he's going to sell it to us. You going to tell us where she is?"

"No!"

Yosper grinned. "Didn't actually think you would, but that's no problem. Al Halwani's not that big a place. Jessie? Give us those maps, will you? And now we want your report, Hake, starting with reconnoitering the solar-power plant."

Jessie picked up the cards and slid the cover off the table, revealing a back-projected screen. As she manipulated the keyboard at the side of the table it displayed a satellite-reconnaissance photograph of the coastline, with map outlines superimposed on it in red. She zoomed it up to a close view of the tower and the ridge of flowering dunes, and then handed Hake a light-pencil.

"Pull back a little," he said. "It doesn't show the roads." Greenish dots flickered and swarmed into a new focus, and he nodded. The squat, rectangular spot in the middle of the bay was the solar tower itself. The crescent beach was a mosaic of green and white, the sunplants half open and facing to an afternoon sunset. The roads were darkened by shadow, but they could be made out.

"That's the main guard shack," he said, pointing the arrow of the light-pencil to a blotch atop the dunes. "They were in there all night. I don't think they patrol—anyway, we didn't see any signs of them along the road. There's a path up from the highway. There's cover most of the way, but not much right around the shack."

"You listening, Tiger?" Yosper demanded. "That's your job. Take your position; then when we move, you cut communication and immobilize the guards. What about the beach side of the dunes, Hake?"

"They're completely covered with the plants, all the way down to water's edge. There's something down there that looks like a building—" he pointed with the pencil—"but I don't know what it is."

"Control center for the tower. Keep going, Hake."

"That's about it, as much as I could see. I don't know why they're so important—they could just use mirrors."

"You don't know cowflops from custard, boy," Yosper explained kindly. "You use live plants, you don't have any problem of guidance for mirrors—the plants aim themselves. Keep themselves clean, too, as you ought to know. Or didn't I read your 201 file right?"

"I did clean mirrors one year in New Jersey, yes."

"So why don't you understand more of what you see? What about the tower?"

"It's tall and isolated. A few boats around it. No connection to the land that I could see."

Impatiently, "There's a tunnel. Keep going."

"That's it. I couldn't see much—except that purple light. That I don't understand at all. It hurt my eyes to look at it. It just appeared in the sky."

"Hellfire, Hake, that's a hologram. That's the beauty part of the whole scheme. Didn't they teach you any geometry in school? If they bred the flowers to point directly at the sun, they'd reflect directly right back *at* the sun, and what would be the good of that? So they breed them to respond to high UV—good thing you didn't stare at it real long, because most of the radiation's out of the visible spectrum. Then they generate a spinflip laser hologram in the right UV frequencies and just move it where they want it in the sky, halfway between the sun and tower. Draw yourself a diagram when you get a chance, and you'll see that all the reflectance has to go right to the tower every time."

Hake stared at the tabletop, calculating angles in his mind. "Why, that's brilliant, Yosper." He shook his head. "Damn it! Why kill them off? Why don't we just let them go ahead and make hydrogen for us?"

Yosper was scandalized. "Are you crazy, Hake? Do you know how much of a drain on the balance of payments you're talking about? We'll make a deal, all right, but we'll make it with the sheik. *After* we take these hippies out. Blow up the tower. Kill off the plants—we've got a great little fungus specially bred by our good friends in Eatontown. They've borrowed beyond their means to get this thing going, and when we're finished with them they'll be bankrupt. Then old Hassabou comes back to power, and we make a deal."

"Let's get on with it," Jessie Tunman complained. "Did Horny get the job on the tower so he can let us in?"

Hake glared at her, then admitted, "Well, actually, no. I mean, they'll give me a job, but not for a couple of weeks. They hired Leota right away."

"Hake!" Yosper exploded. "You failed your assignment!"

"I couldn't help it! They said I was overqualified—whose fault is that? I didn't make up the cover identity!"

"Boy," said Yosper, "you just lost most of your bargaining power, you know that? We spent five effing months getting you ready for this because you spoke the languages, could get by with the locals—and now you're no place!"

Jessie Tunman looked up. "Maybe it's not so bad," she said.

"Don't talk foolish, Jessie! If we wanted to storm the tower we wouldn't have bothered with lover-boy in the first place."

"He's still here. He just doesn't have an ID to get into the tower."

"That's right, but— Oh," Yosper said. "I see what you mean. All we have to do is get him an ID." He beamed at Hake. "That shouldn't be too hard, considering our resources, at that. You got anything else to say, boy? No? Any more questions about what this mission is all about?"

"I do have one. Why do we have to destroy it? Why don't we just steal the plants and build our own?"

Yosper shook his head. "Boy, don't think. Just do what you're told. We've had the plants for three years. They're no good to us."

"Sure they are. That coast looks a lot like Florida."

"Hake," the old man said kindly, "Miami Beach is in Florida. All that land's built up, or didn't you notice? God has chosen to give these creeps just what you need for this kind of installation—sunlight, water, port facilities. Most of the U. S. of A.'s too far north. Even around Miami you'd only be getting forty or forty-five percent yield in the winter. Get it up to where you really need it, around New York or Chicago, not to even think about Boston or Seattle or Detroit, and you just don't have power to speak of at all for three or four months of the year."

"Yosper," Hake said, "doesn't that suggest to you that maybe God is telling you something?"

The old man cackled. "Bet your ass, boy. He's telling me that we've got to use the gifts He gave us to do His will! And that's just what we're doing. If God wanted the Persian Gulf to have our power, he would have put Pittsburgh there. Oh, maybe we could use it around Hawaii—or even better, like Okinawa or the Canal Zone, if we hadn't given them away when we didn't have to. You got to figure the useful areas are between twenty-five north and twenty-five south, and in God's wisdom He has seen fit to put nothing but savages there. Switch that thing off, Jessie." He stood up. "I got to go talk to Curmudgeon and the sheik," he said. "You people just take it easy for a while. You, Hake? I think you better stay in your stateroom till we need you. Tiger'll show you where it is."

As it began to grow dark they fed him. A very young black child in a tarboosh knocked on the door and passed in a tray. *"Bismi llahi r-rahmani r-rahim,"* he piped politely. Hake thanked him and closed the door. The polite form was an invocation of the compassionate and merciful Allah, and Hake could only hope that the sentiments were shared by the members of the crew whose voices had finished changing. The food was lamb, rice and a salad, all excellent. Hake ate cheerfully enough. He was getting used to the patterns of working in the cloak-and-dagger business, long periods of waiting for something to happen without knowing what it was going to be, long periods of doing something without quite knowing what it was for. And now and then, for punctuation, somebody hitting him or blowing up his car.

He had not only got used to it, he was almost coming to accept it. At least for himself. For Leota— That was something else, and worrisome. Neither Yosper nor Jessie Tunman had said where they proposed to get an ID to copy, but Hake was far from sure they would not think the one Leota had been given a good source.

No one had told him he was a prisoner, and nothing stopped him from opening the door and joining the others.

He didn't want to. Watching them play their silly spy games was unappealing. They acted like—

They acted like half the world, he told himself, playing a role. Dramaturgy. "Thinking with."

As The Incredible Art had said, if you looked with open eyes, that explained so many of the fads, lunacies, causes, passions, meannesses and incongruities of human behavior! It even explained Hake himself. It explained why he had played the game of being a minister so long . . . and then the game of cloak-and-dagger spook . . . and then the game of rebel against the skullduggery. It explained why Yosper played Christian and criminal at the same time, why Leota played revolutionary and harem slave; and it explained how the world got into such a mess to begin with. Because we all play roles and games! And when enough of us play the same game, act the same dramaturgic role, at one time—then the game becomes a mass movement. A revolution. A cult. A religion. A fad.

Or a war.

He put his tray outside the door and leaned back on the neat, narrow bunk. There was an important piece missing in all of this. The cause. How did all these things get started?

The question was wrong. It was like asking why the locusts came to Abu Magnah. No individual locust had made the decision to attack the city, there was no plan, there was not even a shared genetic intent. If one examines the fringes of a locust swarm, what one sees is a scattering of individual insects flying blindly out, twisting around in confusion and then flying back in to join the cloud. What moves the locust swarm from one place to another is the chance thrust of wind. The swarm has no more volition than a tumbleweed.

And he, and Yosper, and Leota, and everyone else— what were they doing, if not devoting all their strength to being a part of their particular swarm? Causes and nations moved where chance pushed them—even, sometimes, into a war of mutual suicide, when both sides knew in advance that neither winner nor loser could gain.

Exactly like locusts—

Someone tapped at his door.

Hake sat up. "Yes?" he called.

It opened on the child who had brought his dinner, looking fearful. In barbarous English he said, "Sir, I have brought you tea, if God wills it."

Hake took the tray, puzzled. "It's all right," he said kindly, but the boy's fright did not diminish. He turned and bolted. Hake sat down and put the tea on the night table, his train of thought shattered. Not that it mattered. None of it was really relevant to the present problem, which was pure survival, his own and Leota's.

Something rolled across the floor as he shook the napkin open. When he retrieved it, it was a double golden finger-ring.

There was no note, no word of any kind, but he didn't need one. On this yacht at this time it was not likely that there was more than one person with the double-ring of an American group marriage. So Alys was aboard.

"Wake up now, Mr. Hake. There is to be a briefing."

Hake staggered to the door and opened it on Mario, looking sleepy but oddly pleased with himself. "Now? It isn't even five A.M.!"

"Not just at this minute, no, but soon. Immediately after the sheik's morning devotions. However," he smirked, "there is an interesting development which I think you will wish to see."

Hake groggily pulled on his shoes. "What is it?"

"Hurry, Mr. Hake. See for yourself." The youth led the way back as they had come, to the aft deck. It was just sunrise, and the slanting light laid long shadows across the city of Al Halwani, and on the launch that was whining toward them. "They radioed that they were bringing some-one," Mario said over Hake's shoulder. "There, do you see? She is sitting by herself, just inside the canopy."

"Leota!"

"Yes, Mr. Hake, your dear friend, for whom you risked so much. So now you will be together again—or, at any rate, not more than a few hundred feet apart. I don't suppose Sheik Hassabou will invite you to his harem."

"How did you catch her?"

Mario frowned. "It was not difficult at the end," he said. "She was simply strolling down the esplanade by herself. The boatmen recognized her, and she offered no resistance."

Hake leaned over the rail to watch, as the launch came up to the float. A woman in veil and headdress was waiting; it was only from her wrinkled and age-spotted hands that Hake could tell she was ancient. As Leota came aboard she shrank from the old woman, who angrily thrust her inside.

"Mario— Mario, I want to talk to her. Just for a minute."

"Why, Mr. Hake! What a ridiculous request! Of course that is impossible—and now," the youth said merrily, "if you do not come quickly you will miss your breakfast." The confused baying from across the water was the muezzins' calling for five-o'clock prayers. Down on the landing stage the boatmen were dropping to their knees, and on deck those of higher status were spreading their prayer rugs, checking the built-in magnetic compass for proper orientation, before doing the same.

Hake followed Mario to the dining salon. He did not eat, did not join in the conversation, accepted only coffee. His mind was full of quick plans and instant dismissals, and when the Team members got up for their briefing he trailed after them silently. Only when they passed an arms locker, with one of the armed boatmen standing silent before it, did he hesitate. For just a second. He could overpower the guard. Seize a couple of the rapid-fire carbines and a dozen clips of cartridges. Shoot up Yosper, Tiger, the crewmen and everyone else. Find the harem. Arm Leota. Make a run for the launch.

And what were the chances of getting away with it? At the most hopeful estimate, one in a million? Something in Hake's upbringing had taught him to risk anything to save a woman from debauchery . . . but did Leota share his view?

A crewman with an actual scimitar pulled back a gold cloth curtain, and they were in the sheik's private salon.

If opulence had been missing below decks, it was all concentrated here. Iced fruits in crystal bowls, tiny coffee cups and squares of sweetmeats on hammered silver trays; chests of glazed tile, covered with rugs that had not been woven to rest on any floor. Even the gold cloth drapes were not cloth at all; as the yacht moved, the way they swung showed that they were actual gold.

The sheik was already present, sitting above the others in a cushioned chair. He was older than Hake had remembered, and better looking: olive skin and nose like a bird of prey, the eyes brilliant within their circle of black kohl. Next to him, half a foot lower down, Curmudgeon was sitting erect and impatient. The meeting was short. There was little discussion and, to Hake's surprise, not even any recrimination. Even Jessie Tunman confined herself to glaring poisonously at him from time to time. Curmudgeon spelled out the plan, pausing to defer to the sheik every time Hassabou stirred or cleared his throat, and it was all over in fifteen minutes.

Hake's part was simple. He was to report to the control shack with his fake ID and the story that he had been assigned as a sweeper. It would be too late for them to bother checking up at night, even if they became suspicious, and by the time the personnel office opened in the morning it would be all over. Hake would remain in the tower at sunrise—there was some danger there, Curmudgeon noted grudgingly, but he would simply have to take his chances. Yosper, his boys and others would come to the tower in scuba gear, and he would let them in. They would be armed with sleep gas, missile weapons and canisters of fungus spores. The sleep gas was to knock out the people in the control shack when they came to it through the tunnel under the bay. The guns were in case the sleep gas didn't work. The fungus was to destroy the sunflowers. Another party was to take out the guard shack on the dunes, and when all was secure they would blow up control shack and tower—having first photographed everything and taken off any interesting-looking equipment. The yacht would pick them all up, and then—

No one said anything about "then" as far as Hake was

concerned. It was as if his life had been programmed to stop when the tower was destroyed.

Ten minutes after he was back in his cabin the twelve-year-old, trembling, brought him an unordered bottle of mineral water. "I will be back in half an hour," he whispered, and disappeared; and when Hake picked up the napkin, he found a tiny cassette recorder, with a tape in place.

Leota!

But it was Alys's voice that came to him from the tape. "Keep the volume down!" it ordered at once. Then, "Horny, Leota came aboard wired. God knows how long it will be before they find the radio, so don't waste time. Tape all the information you can, put the recorder under your pillow and go for a walk. Jumblatt will get it when he cleans up your room. Don't talk to him. Don't try to see either one of us." Then, incredibly, a giggle. "Isn't this *fun?*"

An hour later Hake was back in the lounge, looking as much like a loyal member of the Team as he could. That involved some sacrifice. Yosper was holding court, explaining to Jessie Tunman that men were better than angels ("The Lord never picked no *angel* for our Redeemer, did he?"), offering to bet Mario and Carlos that they could not find any reference to the Trinity anywhere in the Bible, informing Dieter that, whatever he'd seen in medieval religious paintings to the contrary notwithstanding, neither he nor Albrecht Dürer nor anybody else knew what the face of Jesus looked like: "It's right in the Bible, boy! His face was like unto the face of the Sun! You see any blue eyes and scraggly blond beard on the face of the *Sun?*" Having settled that, he looked around for someone else to instruct, but Hake had had enough. He got up and joined Tigrito at the pool table. They were all up, all their glands flowing, ready for adventure, like kids on the way to Disneyland; even Jessie Tunman was flushing and giggling like a teenager. Hake was up in a different way. He knew, without question, that the next few hours were going to make a change in his life, and part of him was terrified. When at last he became aware of stirrings outside he dropped his cue and ran to peer over the railing.

The landing stage was packed with penguins. It was the women of the harem, all in long black gowns and headdresses, stepping clumsily into the launch. One looked up toward him, but he had no way of telling who it was.

From behind him Tigrito said irritably, "Come on, man, take your shot!"

"Sure. What's happening?"

Tigrito glanced casually over the side, then grinned. "Going into battle, you know? They send the women and children to the hotel, get them out of the way. Don't worry, old Hassabou will bring them back tomorrow morning."

"I wasn't worried," said Hake, coming back into the lounge to take his shot, but it was a lie. He was worried about a great many things, not the least of them whether the tape he had just made had had time to reach Leota.

XV

HAKE took the afternoon bus back along the coast, got out at the path to the guard shack, climbed the dune and presented himself to the guards. The noise from the solar tower was immense, even at this distance, rumble of pumps, roar of gas and steam, scream of tortured molecules ripped apart. The rifleman sitting on a canvas chair outside the shack took a plug out of his ear, yawning and scratching. He glanced uninterestedly at Hake's forged identification badge and made a coarse remark about male scrubwomen. "Too bad you're a man," he said. "You can't go down for an hour yet, and if you were a woman we could pass the time more interestingly."

"Not very many trespassers to keep you busy?" Hake offered conversationally.

"Trespassers? Why would anyone trespass? All we do is keep silly people in boats from coming too near the tower. Go, sit in the shade. When the noise stops, you can go down to the control."

So Hake sprawled out under a clump of sunflowers, fingering the badge that had once been Leota's, his mind clear and almost blank. He could not plan very far. All he could do was go through with his orders until he saw a chance to do something else. When the sun set the guard waved him down. Actually the noise had not stopped. There was still plenty of heat in the receptor cavity at the top of the tower, and the turbines continued to roar.

Scrambling down the path in the dusk, Hake remembered the summer's moonlighting—he had still been in the wheelchair—when he held a part-time job cleaning heliostats for Jersey Central Power & Light. The big, jointed mirrors were stowed shiny side down to keep dust from coating and salt spray from pitting their surfaces. Even so, Hake, or someone like him, had to get out and spray them clean once a month—a job that never ended, because by the time the last sector was detergented the first was beginning to cloud up again. But the sunplants cleaned themselves.

Going inside the control dugout was like entering the bridge of a ship. CRTs glowed in a rainbow of colors at half a dozen monitoring stations, displaying a hundred different kinds of data about temperature, pressure and every other transient state at every point in the process. One set monitored the air as it was forced through its tiny pipes across the heat receptor. Another tracked the expanded air as it turned gas turbines to generate electricity. Others reported on the sea-water as it was boiled into steam, the splitting of the steam into its elements, the exhaust of waste brine back into the ocean, the pumping of hydrogen and oxygen to the liquefaction plants beyond the end of the cove. Hake knew this was so, from knowing how the plant worked, but he could read none of the indicia. They were only glowing masses of colors and symbols to him.

A short, dark woman looked up from one of the screens to glance at his credentials. "You're not our standard brand of cleaner," she said.

"I needed the job. Later on I might get something better, they said."

"Be nice having you around," she said, looking with more interest at Hake himself than at his badge. "The rest of the crew'll be here by boat any minute. They'll show you what to do."

Between the dugout and the tower was a long, underwater tunnel. The night crew leader, an Egyptian engineer named Boutros, took his gang through it at a brisk walk. They had seen the tunnel a hundred times, and it was of no more interest to them than his driveway is to a suburbanite. But for Hake it was something to see. Half a mile of nothing but distance. It was like being in a long birth canal, a ten-minute half-trot with spaced red lights before and after, always seeming to stretch out to the same indefinite, maybe infinite, length.

The sunflowers had long since folded themselves into buds for the night. No more energy was coming to the receptor. It was safe for the maintenance crew to come in and start their work. But the generators were still turning, the pumps were thudding, the compressed air was screaming through the criss-cross of thin pipes. Boutros had a spare set of earplugs for Hake. Without them, he was deafened.

The tower was tightly sealed most of the time, but sealed or not, fine sand from the dunes and salt spray from the water found its way inside. That was Hake's job. While the skilled mechanics split off to check and repair the brains and entrails of the system, Hake and a couple of others were set to sweeping and polishing. The first job was the brass railings that surrounded the open central shaft at

every level. Hake, following the finger of the woman working with him, could see where to start. The rails on the
three lowest levels, looking up from the base of the heat
exchanger column, were bright and clean. What looked
like a sudden change to green-black iron in the railings of
the fourth was only the change to the dirt they had to
clean. Far, far up—near the hundred-meter level at the top
of the tower—he could see that the rails brightened and
gleamed again. Cleaning corrosion inside the tower was
another of those jobs without an end.

That part of the job was only make-work and fussiness.
Hake and his co-workers scraped and polished to complete
the fourth level, until Hake was actually sent to push a
broom for a while until it was time to do the more important jobs. The solar collector retained enough heat to generate power for several hours after sunset. Then, with a
suddenness like a crash, everything shut down—the pumps,
the valve motors, the yell and whistle of fluids forced
through tubes—and everyone took earplugs out. There was
total silence for a minute before the pumps started again,
this time at low pressure, and Boutros appeared to wave his
crews toward the stairs.

It was a long climb. A hundred meters of climbing.

When the generator was going and sunpower was pouring in, the pumped air swallowed energy to turn into electricity in the generators. At the same time the flowing air
kept the pipes from burning through. The critical time was
only a matter of seconds at full power. The cavity was
hot—could, in theory, be as hot as the surface of the Sun,
some 9000° Fahrenheit; was, in practice, only about half
that. But hotter than anything Hake had ever encountered.
If the pumps failed, the reflected heat from the sunplants
would convert that delicate grid into slag unless the plants
were deflected away at once. Now that was not the problem, because the sunplants slept. But the pumps were cool-
ing the pipes for Hake's crew, so that they could chip them
free of the thin, tough corrosion of sea-scale that reduced
the heat conductivity of the pipes and wasted energy.

To do that, they had to go up where the heat receptor
was.

A hundred meters is not a great distance, when it is stretched out flat. An Olympic runner can cover it in a matter of seconds. But a hundred meters straight up from the nearest flat surface is something quite different. The physical exertion was the least of it, although Hake reached the top deck panting and shaking. Worse. The wind blew. Clinging to the safety rails, Hake thought his hair would fly off. The tower shook—not entirely in his imagination; there was a bass organ-pipe thrumming that he could feel through the hand-holds. And, although the pumps had swept most of the 4000° heat out of the piping, it blistered his fingers at a touch.

The Arab next to him laughed, spreading his own fingers and pointing to the gloves Hake carried on his belt. Hake set his jaw. They could have reminded him! But he conceded to himself that no reminder would have worked as well to impress the need on him as that one sizzling touch.

But out over the dunes Orion cartwheeled down toward the end of the night. Cool, dry air from the desert smelled of salt, camels and old petroleum. Once he learned to forget the great depth beneath him and get on with the job, it was far from unpleasant to be a hundred meters up in the Arabian night sky.

The job was not difficult. As it was done every night, the salt had little chance to build up. It took only a firm slow rub along each wire-thin pipe, front and back, with the chemically treated cleaning wads. The crew broke for mint tea and peppery coffee, hoisted up from the surface level in buckets, and by the time the sky began to turn cobalt in the east they were done.

Hake went down with the others, excused himself to go to the men's room, and waited there until there were no more sounds from inside the tower. Then he peeped out.

Most of the crew had returned through the tunnel. Some had left by boats tied to the tower's base. He did not think anyone would care much about not seeing him in one place or the other. He had marked the TV monitors that scanned the interior space of the tower and was careful to avoid their fields of view. And he sat down and waited, three levels up from the gentle waves, with a clear view of the shore through one spray-splashed window, and a panorama of the sea's horizons through the others.

The fact that he could see nothing but water in that direction did not mean there was nothing there; the Team would be on its way by now. And on land as well. Peering cautiously over the squat dugout at water's edge, he saw the pink roof of the guard shack. Tigrito and his goons would be there by now, checking their watches. It all looked peaceful, even the tangle of bright plumbing that projected above the eastern headland, the gas-cooling plant and the radar mast of an LH_2 tanker waiting to be loaded.

It would be *sinful* to destroy this. So thought Hake, minister of a church that never used the word "sin," veteran of a quarter century of New Jersey's brownouts and freezeouts and sooty grime. Clean hydrogen was a good. What madness were Curmudgeon and the others engaged in? What madness the world?

The sky beyond the headlands was orange, ready for the sun's entrance on the stage, the color picked up by the plumbing of the LH_2 plant. So many megawatt-hours from this array; and this only one tiny cove, invisible on a map, that could be duplicated a hundred times along this coast alone. No wonder the fight was so intense. The stakes were fantastic.

The pumps throbbed suddenly, and the TV cameras began to swing back and forth in their scan.

Hake jumped. It was time. The sunflowers were beginning to open. The sun was not yet high enough to produce much energy, but he could see the violet ghost image spring into being, halfway up the sky. It laid a trail of oily glitter along the surface of the sea—

And in the middle of that shining trail was a sprinkle of pockmarks.

Bubbles. The invaders were approaching.

The first one up the ladder was Mario, wet suit gleaming in the long slants of sunrise, waterproof tote lashed to his back. He did not speak to Hake, just stripped off his suit and opened the bag to lay out the tools of his trade. Speaking would not have been easy. The pumps were roaring at full force now, and the whole tower thrummed with their noise and the scream of gas through piping. The underwater tug bobbed up to the lowest rung of the ladder, and one, two, three more persons pulled themselves up.

"Stay in this corner!" Hake shouted in Mario's ear. "I rolled a screen over the doorway. You can get to the tunnel without the camera picking you up."

Mario looked at him scornfully, then repeated the orders to the others. That wasn't necessary, except to reinforce the fact that it was he, not Hake, who was running things. He spoke into a radio, listened and nodded. "The others are on their way," he said. "Let's move it!"

Yosper's bully-boy quartet were reassembled here in Al Halwani, rapidly getting out of their wet suits, spreading their treasures on the steel deck. Mario's gear was nose-masks, sleep-gas canisters, slabs of gray-pink plastic explosive. Sven (or Carlos) had his own tools: the camera to photograph the machinery, the kit to take apart any equipment interesting enough to carry away, the detonators to explode Mario's plastic and bring the tower down, when it had been looted of everything worth taking. Dieter (or Sven, or Carlos) carried the biocans of fungus spores. They were to go into the trickle-irrigation system, infecting the sunplants with the wilt. Carlos (or whoever) carried the guns. Bulgarian Brollies and Peruvian Pens, with green-tipped darts like hypodermic needles; one touch, and the victim was anesthetized, in case the sleep gas failed. And a clutch of machine-pistols. They were not nonlethal. Any person who took their thousand-round-a-minute blast would sleep forever, in blood.

The second crew arrived, three persons. Two turned out to be the sheik's men and the third, a-hop with excitement, was Yosper himself. "Goin' like shit through a tin funnel!" he cackled, skinning out of his suit. "We ready, Mario? Get on with it, Hake, lead the way!"

Hake climbed down the ladder and crouched at the door to the tunnel as the others came behind him. Yosper raised himself on tiptoes to peer through the little window, then turned, scowling. "You didn't cover the TV cameras," he accused.

"How could I? They just would have come out and fixed them." It was a true reason, if not a real one, but it didn't solve the problem for Hake. Dieter (or Sven) said cheerfully:

"Not to worry. Give me a minute with the wires." He located and opened a junction-box, and in a moment all the dim red lights beyond the door winked out. "We better move it, Yosper," he said. "They'll be checking that in a minute."

"Then let's go!" Yosper grabbed machine-pistol and sleep-dart projector from the pile and started off at a trot, the others following. Hake lagged, slipped on a nose-mask, and tossed two of the sleep-gas canisters into the darkness behind the Team.

They did not have time to turn around. He heard the clatter of the canisters, the puff of their explosion, a few grunts and gasps, and then the sound of bodies falling.

When he was sure they were all out cold for at least an hour, Hake reclimbed the ladder, picked up the rubbery wads of plastic and the fitted box of detonators and pushed them into the sea, along with as many machine-pistols as he could collect. Then he descended the ladder again, stepping on a thigh here, a spine there, and stumbled through the black tunnel to the control dugout. What he would do when he got to the dugout he was not sure, but at least he could dump the problem on whoever was there. He tripped over a body just before the end—how had anyone managed to get that far?—and reached for the door.

Just as Yosper's voice said softly behind him, muffled through a mask, "You know, Hake, I thought you might try something. Now open the door real easy. What you feel in your back isn't sleepy gas."

Hake stopped still. "You can't blame me for trying," he said.

"Wrong, boy," sighed Yosper. "I can kill you for trying."

Even as Hake started to move, one part of his mind was assessing what Yosper had said: how true it was, but also how irrelevant. If he had a choice, he could not find it.

Three weeks Under the Wire are not much to change the pacific habits of a lifetime, but they had been hard weeks.

The lessons stuck. Fall forward, kick back; twist around, grab for a leg. Hake executed the maneuver flawlessly. His heel caught Yosper just where it was supposed to, lifting the old man off the ground. Yosper brayed sharply, and something rattled away down the corridor as Hake jerked at the leg nearest his flailing arms. The training paid off. The gun was gone, they were hand to hand and Hake had every advantage of youth and size and strength.

But Yosper had been through the same course, more than once, over years. Yosper's skinny knee caught Hake on the side of the jaw, wrenching his head around on his neck and knocking the nose-mask free.

There was a maneuver for that, too. Stop breathing. Find the enemy's nearest vital point, any of the dozen quick and dirty vital points, put him out, get the mask—it was all very clear in Hake's mind, and his body did its best to carry it out. Yosper was before him. The frail old man was incredibly resilient. He could not win against Hake in a one-on-one, but he didn't have to. He only had to delay a decision until Hake was forced to breathe. Hake was straining with every muscle to claw at Yosper's throat, and then, without transition, he was dazedly aware that he was being dragged by the collar into the control room. I did my best, he thought clearly. But what was the good of that, when his best had failed?

Yosper dropped him, and there was silence.

Why silence?

Hake tried to slow the spinning of his head to see what was going on, but nothing was going on. No one was in the room. The monitors were untended, the seats empty. He heard the distant whir of ventilators and the dusty faint crackle of electronics and nothing else, and over him Yosper was standing in a gunfighter crouch.

But there seemed to be no target for his gun; and then a voice, a familiar voice, the voice of one of the Reddis, said, "Put your gun down, Medina," and all around the room men and women were standing up from behind the monitors and desks, and each one held a gun and every gun was pointed precisely at Yosper's head.

* * *

It seemed to Hake that he had been hurting, one way or another, for half his life—had in fact been, most of the time, all the days and weeks since March. The tussle with Yosper had reawakened all of the left-over aches and bruises from Rome and Capri, and his nose was bleeding again. But someone gentle and sweet-smelling was cradling his head and soothing away his pains.

He made the effort to get his head together. "Hello, Leota," he managed.

"Oh, Horny," she crooned, rocking him. It was a pleasant place to be and gave him little incentive to want to move, but he struggled up anyway, breathing deeply to try to get the last of the sleep gas out of his blood. The room was full of people, not only Leota and both the Reddis, but the man from the employment office, Robling, and eight or ten others. Not counting Yosper, who was sullenly spread-eagled against a wall while one of the women pulled articles of armament out of every pocket and crevice.

"You mean we made it?" he demanded fuzzily.

"Well, so far," said Leota, dabbing at the blood on his lip. "Somebody's collecting all the casualties in the corridor; if we can take care of the yacht . . . and then clear up some of the other loose ends. . . ." But all the ends were loose in Hake's gassy brain. He concentrated on trying to follow what she was telling him. The Reddis had set most of it up, somehow assisted by the personnel man, Robling; they had faked a fire at the hotel and got everyone evacuated, and in the confusion Leota and Alys had been liberated. They were all very pleased with Hake, who had apparently done his part superbly, even if he hadn't quite known what it was.

But Subirama Reddi snarled shrilly, "We waste time! The yacht is still out there. It must be decoyed in just now."

Across the room the mask of fury on Yosper's face cleared. He nodded agreeably to the woman guarding him and stepped forward to the radio. Hake managed to get there before him. "Not you, Yosper," he said. "You're a staunch old spook and I don't trust what you'd say. I'll do it."

"Then do it!" snapped Rama Reddi. "Let us complete this and get to the matter of payment!"

Leota cut in. "Absolutely. Go ahead, Horny. Tell them the control room's secure." She squeezed his shoulder warningly.

Someone handed him a microphone. He cleared his throat, looked around and then shrugged. "Curmudgeon?" he called. "Sheik Hassabou? Somebody! Come on in, Curmudgeon. We're all buttoned up and waiting for you."

The radio op clicked off the microphone. "Don't answer anything they say," she warned. "Tell them your receiver's bad. Tell them—"

She was interrupted by Curmudgeon's voice from the speaker overhead. "Is that you, Hake?" he demanded. "What's going on? Where's Jasper Medina?"

"Don't answer," snapped the radio op, but Hake had no intention of answering. They waited, while Curmudgeon vainly tried to raise them and Yosper snarled and fumed from the wall. With Leota's hand clutching his, Hake could believe that all this was real. Reasonable, no. What strange charades they were playing! But all his life had become such a series of charades since the Team had drafted him into their world of outrageous fantasy. It was no more incredible that this patchwork operation should succeed than that spooks and spies should be playing such wretched pranks to begin with.

"Now do it again," Leota ordered. "Talk him in!"

The operator thumbed the switch and Hake took a deep breath. "This is Hake," he said steadily, over the shrill complaints from the radio. "I can't get an answer out of you, but Yosper ordered me to tell you we're all ready. The control dugout is secure, so is the thermal tower. We're waiting."

For a minute or more there was no sound at all. Then Leota sighed, her breath tickling Hake's ear as they both bent over the radar tube. "I think the silly fool is going to do it," she whispered.

On the display they could see the green shadow of the tower, the headlands, the barges waiting with their globular tanks for their cargoes of LH_2 . . . and, yes, cautiously nosing around the headland, the sharp, slim shape of Hassabou's yacht.

"He's coming in!" Robling exulted. "Okay now, you tower operators, do your stuff!"

The dark woman at the hologram monitor reached for her controls. Out of the heavily screened slit at the front of the dugout Hake could see the violet target hologram skid across the sky. Behind, through the clear-glass clerestory panes on the dune side, the sunplants began to nod toward a new focus. Their response time was slow. It would take several minutes, at least, for perfect collimation. But they were moving.

It all happened very slowly. The sunplants could throw ninety-nine percent of the solar flux onto a target—but not all at once. For the next little while they would be tracking in. First they would create a wide patch of warmth, then a swath hundreds of yards wide of discomfort, then a spot smaller than the side of the yacht in which no unprotected thing could survive.

The brilliant star of white at the top of the tower began to blur and darken.

The one-legged man and the controller whispered anxiously to each other. This was a critical time. The cavity receptor was designed to handle intense heat. The structure around it was not. As the spot defocused, thousands, then millions, of watts of heat struck at the polished Fresnel shapes of reflecting steel. The energy of ten thousand horses assaulted each metal vane. But the defocusing was fast enough, barely. By the time the temperature monitor began to redline, the spot had spread. The warning trace wobbled, held steady, then began to decline.

And the yacht stopped and dropped its anchors. The woman at the hologram nodded to Hake.

"Go ahead, Horny," said Leota. "You can be the one to tell them what's happening."

"My pleasure," Hake grinned as he began to understand. Then, into the transmitter, "Curmudgeon! Put your sun glasses on!"

A startled grunt from the radio. Then silence. Then

Curmudgeon's voice, thick and nasty, "Hake, your last chance. What the hell's going on?"

"We're zeroing in on you, Curmudgeon. You have one minute to abandon ship." The yacht was growing brighter every second, as if stagehands were switching kliegs on it from some invisible rafters. "Jump off on the far side," Hake added. "Our aim might not be too good."

The one-legged man scowled and motioned fiercely for Hake to turn off the transmitter. "Watch what you say to them!" he snapped. "They might still get away from the beam—" He stared anxiously out the darkened slit, then began to smile. "I think they missed their chance," he said. "That ship's as good as sunk."

The receiver was rattling with Curmudgeon's voice. "Hake, I don't know what you think you're doing, but if you think you're going to—"

"Not going to, Curmudgeon. It's already done. You have maybe thirty seconds, then I think your hydrogen tank may blow." The sunbeam was contracting and brightening now. Individual shafts of merged beams dipped and wobbled across the surface of the sea, and a palest plume of steam shimmered off some wave-tops. "Fifteen seconds!"

From the corner where he was roped to a chair came Yosper's voice, turgid with rage, "Hake, you little bastard, you're going to wish you were never born."

There was a confused babble of voices from the radio, and then it clicked off again. Even through the grayed glass it was becoming painful to look at the ship. Smoke rose from its side. The paint scorched away. Glass was shattering in the portholes, and the gay line of flags at its masts blew away as ash. The ninety-percent concentration disk shrank to a thousand milliradians, five hundred, three hundred—

The globe of liquid hydrogen on the afterdeck never did blow. It did not have time. Before the heat of its shell boiled off enough of the LH_2 within to shatter the valves, the ninety-percent disk had shrunk away from it, narrowing in on the center of the hull, just above the waterline. Hake could not see that the metal was glowing. The reflectance from the dot of light far overpowered the mere incandescence of steel. But suddenly a dollop of softened metal slid away and splashed into the sea, with an immense production of steam. The vessel rocked wildly and began to settle in the water.

Standing at the darkened window, Hake had a sudden stab of concern. "When it sinks, what'll happen to the people in the water?"

Robling grinned and pointed to the hologram monitor. Already the purple crosshairs were climbing the sky, up and away from the ship itself, and the spot was defocusing again. "Anyway, they're in the shadow. It won't go down for half an hour," he said.

The woman at the control board snapped, "And about time! Do you know what this little game is costing? We do fifteen million dollars a day, and we've already lost an hour's production—"

"Cheap at the price," said the one-legged man. "Let's call the cavalry in."

"I already have," she said. The long-range screen picked them up first, but as soon as Hake's eyes recovered from staring at the bright spot on the side of the dying ship he could see them. A destroyer and two gunboats of the Al Halwani "navy"—probably they *were* the Al Halwani navy —coming in over the horizon, with white bow-waves to show their racing speed.

Hake put his arm around Leota, beside him at the window, and said wonderingly, "We've done it."

"Not quite," said Rama Reddi, cradling a machine-pistol in his arm; and from the other side of the control room, his brother said: "That is so, Hake. You have still to settle with us."

There was more happening than Hake understood. It was not a new situation; he had been living under those conditions for months, but familiarity did not make it easier. Leota rescued him. "Of course," she said, pressing against his arm. "Horny knows. We promised to give you the codes and the keys, and we will."

Yosper yelped venomously, "Slut! You're fooling around with the most muscle in the world!"

"We'll just have to take that chance," said Leota, "although your friends don't really look that dangerous right now." And they were not. They were doing the best they could, and even in rubber boats or struggling in the water itself they were far from toothless. There were half a dozen separate struggles going on in the tiny view of the CRT display. Al Halwani's naval might was up to the challenge. They lobbed vomit-gas grenades at the Team members in the water, and power launches fished them out, one by one, some still struggling, some without fight, scooped out of the water like guppies in a breeding tank.

"We are still waiting," hissed Rama Reddi, meaning that they did not want to wait at all.

"As soon as we get this nailed down," Leota promised. One of the launches was coming in to beach itself before them, and a group of sloppy-looking, but quite efficient, Al Halwani sailors dragged two bound figures into the dugout.

"Now we're getting somewhere," said Leota with satisfaction. "This one I know—" she touched the contemptuously angry Sheik Hassabou with the toe of her shoe—"but who's this other creep?"

"Why, that is one of our leading American sabotage specialists," Hake said. "Good to see you again, Curmudgeon."

The spy was in no position to act, lying on his belly, hands cuffed behind him, one side of his bristly beard slicked down with his own blood. But he could talk. "Every one of you," he said, "is dead. You won't see another sun rise."

Estimating the odds, Hake was not very sure Curmudgeon was wrong. Tied and helpless as he was, there was behind him the immense mastodon strength of the Team, and if Curmudgeon thought it capable of squashing all these impromptu opponents Hake could see no good reason to disagree.

Robling and the hologram operator were trying to get everyone out of the way while they got to the serious business of getting the thermal tower back into production. The Reddis did not want to be out of the way. They had not relinquished their machine-pistols, and they were whispering to each other in their own language, eyes taking in everything that was going on. It would not be possible to stall them very long. But then what?

Hake's head was beginning to clear. It didn't help. He was playing in a game whose rules had never been explained; worse, he couldn't tell which team the players were on. Once upon a time he had thought his life as a clergyman was unbearably complex. Here in this strange-looking room on the Persian Gulf complexity was cubed, muddle was confounded, a simple soul like himself could not tell friend from foe. Ranting Yosper, blustering Curmudgeon, silent and deadly Hassabou were easy to diagnose as enemies. But were the Reddis friends? Unthinkable! Robling, the hologram operator Omaya, the other strangers? Apparently they were. And Leota, encouraging him to fulfill his bargain with the Reddis, surely she was a friend? Of course she was, Hake assured himself firmly, at least a friend; but that was the only "of course" he could find.

Leota, at least, seemed to know exactly what to do. "Let's get on with it," she said, smiling cheerfully at the Hydro Fuels crew.

"About time," grunted Robling, his eyes on the screen where the purple hologram was sliding back to where it belonged. "I think we're okay now. As far as I'm concerned, you people can get on with your private business."

"Here? At this place, with all these witnesses?" Subirama Reddi demanded. "Are you trying to cheat us?"

Leota said firmly, "The deal was that Hake would give you the information, that's all. Said nothing about when or where."

"But—these men are from the Team! In one minute they can change all the codes, and it will be worthless!"

Leota shook her head. "Tell you what. As soon as you've got what you want you can take off. Nobody else will leave here for an hour. Anyway, the prisoners aren't going to be talking to anyone for a while—they'll be in jail in Al Halwani, and I don't think they'll have any visitors."

"Not for twenty-four hours," the one-legged man said, grinning. "I can promise that."

The brothers looked at each other, then shrugged. "Twenty-four hours. No less. In that case he may proceed," Rama Reddi said grudgingly.

"How come nobody asks me if I *want* to proceed?" Hake demanded, anger spilling out.

Leota put her hand on his arm. "Because we made a deal," she said. "Go ahead, Horny. The whole thing. Even tell them about your thumbprint, I promise that part's going to be all right."

Hake took a deep breath. Everybody was looking at him. For the center of attention, he seemed to have very little free will about what he did, and very little time to decide what he wanted. Trading with the Reddis was not the kind of thing he could take pride in. Thwarting one little plan of the Team's was too tiny a victory to last, and the future beyond this moment looked unpromising— "Do it, Hake!" snarled Leota, and her eyes were urgent.

"Oh, all right," he said. "Well. We finance our operations by tapping into other people's bank accounts—mostly cloak-and-dagger fronts for the other sides. To open a line, the first thing I do is present my thumbprint for ID. Then there are some code words." He went on in detail, naming all the bank accounts they were looting, reciting the codes, omitting nothing, while Subirama Reddi took notes and his brother asked questions. Finally Subirama looked up.

"I think we have the procedure, yes. Remains the question of your thumb."

"I'll help out there," Leota said quickly, producing a flat metal box. It contained plastic. "Press your thumb in this, will you, Horny?"

He shrugged and did as he was told. Leota offered the box to the Reddis. "You can make your own thumbprint from that," she said.

Subirama Reddi took it, studied it carefully, and then nodded at his brother. "The payment is complete," he said, "apart from our one-hour lead before anyone else leaves this place, and twenty-four hours incommunicado for the Team."

"Then you better get moving," grumbled Robling. "I want to get all these people out of our plant. Take the gags off those three while we figure out what to do with them."

As the Reddis disappeared, Yosper began to rage. "Traitor!" he yelled. "Boy, you've betrayed the Team, the U. S. of A. and the Lord God, and I pity you when we get through with you! Spreading a few disease germs in Europe, that was all you were good for."

Leota put in, "You mean last spring, when he was a germ carrier for you?"

Yosper glared at her. "Shut up, slut. The sheik'll take care of you, don't worry about that."

"Not unless he wants to kidnap me again. That's a crime, and the Italian government won't put up with it."

The sheik, disdainfully allowing one of the Al Halwani sailors to remove his gag, said in accented English, "My friend the Minister of Justice will not listen to your ravings." He was almost a comic figure, the kohl around his eyes smeared from immersion in the water; but there was nothing comic in his expression.

"What about you, Curmudgeon?" Hake asked. "Have you got anything to contribute to this?"

The Team chief said with dignity, "It doesn't matter, Hake. You're finished. So is Al Halwani."

Robling cut in, "You don't seem to realize that you're facing a jail term, Curmudgeon. We're on to you now."

"And what good will that do you? We don't need to blow up your tower to put you out of business. We've got the stuff to kill off your plants—*and* a new breed of sun-plants of our own, resistant to the disease. You think you can stop one of our choppers from spraying your whole setup, some dark night? Forget it!"

Hake flared, "You can't get away with it. I'll—I'll talk to the President!"

Curmudgeon laughed. "That pipsqueak! He doesn't know about this, and he won't believe you anyway. The Attorney General runs this show."

Hake stared at them, helpless captives, still belligerent. "You know," he said wonderingly, "you people are crazy." And so they were, there could be no doubt, crazy people running a crazy game of sabotage and destruction. They were so *secure*! Curmudgeon and Yosper even seemed to be enjoying it! He detached himself from the surroundings, trying to reason things all out. Was there any way, ever, to put a stop to this endless cycle of mad violence?

Vaguely he heard Leota say to the one-legged man, "I think we've got it all," and saw the one-legged man nod and pick up a telephone. He waited, watching Yosper and Curmudgeon as though they were specimens in a cage, and then spoke into the phone.

Then—"Everybody shut up," he called. "Hake, you might want to take this call." He switched on a loud-speaker extension.

The voice on the other end, cackling with delight, was The Incredible Art.

"Horny? Oh, Horny!" he cried. "It came in just fine! Somebody started jamming about two minutes ago, but it was too late—What?"

The half-second delay made him miss Hake's words. Hake repeated them, staring around at the others. "Art! What are you talking about?"

Half a second. Then—"You mean you don't know? Why, Horny, that's *funny*! You've been on the air! All of you! For the last half hour, by satellite, all over the world!"

XVI

For the first time Hake could remember, it felt safe to relax. He lay bare in the healing sun. His eyes were closed and the pebbly beach stabbed not unpleasantly at his back. Cold drops on his body made him look up. Leota was kneeling beside him as she squeezed water out of her hair. "I wasn't asleep," he said.

She shook her hair onto his face, laughing. "You sure looked like you were having one sweet, self-satisfied dream." He could not look at her directly; the bright sun in the chrome-blue sky was dazzling. He propped himself on one elbow to see her better. Were the intricate tracings on her body really beginning to fade, or was he just getting used to them? He was certainly getting quite chronically used to Leota, to having her nearby, to thinking about her when she was not, To sharing the important parts of a life with her. "Actually," he said, completing a half-dozing thought, "what I was doing was playing chess."

She pulled a shirt around her shoulders and regarded him critically. "You're a weird one, Hornswell Hake," she said, "and you're about to have the damnedest sunburn a human being ever had."

Obediently he turned over to toast his other side. The sensible thing to do, of course, was to get dressed and go on in to Al Halwani, and take up their lives. He wasn't ready to do that. Neither was Leota; it was her suggestion that made them stop the borrowed hydrogen buggy and run down to the beach for a swim. The notion was ludicrously inappropriate to the high-stakes international gangster games they had just been playing; that was what had made it seem just right. "What did you mean, you were playing chess?" she demanded.

"Maybe it was more like doing a jigsaw puzzle," he said thoughtfully. "I was fitting pieces together."

"What kind of pieces?"

"Well—" He craned his neck, to squint up at the burning sky. "Like up there there's the satellite."

"So? There are satellites everywhere."

"But this one was the one we needed." Twenty-two thousand miles straight up; it had taken the pictures from the monitoring cameras and sprayed them all over the world, along with the incriminating words of Yosper and Curmudgeon and the sheik. A chunk of metal no bigger than a piano, but it was there and it had worked.

"I don't *quite* see how that's part of a jigsaw puzzle—"

"And there's the 'thinking with'," he said, rolling over again to face her in spite of the sun. "I was thinking, it's part of a sort of series: Thinking with. Hypnotism. The ecstatic mystical state. Schizophrenia. The hallucinogenic-drug high—they're all so much like each other."

Leota sighed. "Horny," she said earnestly, "if we're ever going to get married, or anything, you're going to have to learn to get the marbles out of your mouth. What are you talking about?"

"I'm sorry. I guess I don't exactly know, except that what they all have in common is a sort of detachment from reality, and when I get back to Long Branch I want to talk about that. To the church, for starters. Then to anybody who'll listen. Now that we're all big TV stars, maybe I can get on the air to talk about it."

She nodded seriously. After a moment, she pointed out, "You said 'I'."

"We. Us—if you'll come along?"

"I might give it a try," she said cautiously. "Are you sure it's, well, healthy?"

He sat up and rubbed his chin. "I could be surer," he

admitted. Then he said, "That was the chess-playing part, trying to figure out what moves come next. For instance. What's the Reddis' move when they find out we gave the whole world the information we sold them? What's the Team's next move in Al Halwani—do they come back some night and defoliate all the sun plants just to get even? What's their next move with me—do they frame me on a drug bust or get me dumped in the Hackensack River?"

"A bunch of real good questions, Horny," she applauded.

"I even have some answers. As for the Reddis, our only move is to keep our eyes open. We've given everything away, so there's no profit for them in us any more; I think we call that game a draw and forget it. I hope," he said. "For the Team, that's harder. I think I know the right move if they just kill off the sun plants, out of meanness, with those spray-cans of bacteria and fungus. There's a resistant strain at IPF, and I think I have a flower from it tucked away. If not, at least I know where to find them. And the move to counter any personal trouble is just what we're going to do anyway. Go public. Raise so much noise they won't dare touch us."

Leota touched his shoulder and frowned. "You're hot. You're going to be really burned if we stay here any longer."

"So let's go," he said, standing up and beginning to put his clothes on. The sun was well up in the sky—it was not even afternoon yet, he realized with astonishment—and it was, when you considered everything, he thought, a really beautiful day. They picked their way barefoot over the sharp pebbles toward the road, Hake relaxed, Leota thoughtful. As they were getting into the hydrogen buggy she said:

"Those sound like pretty good moves. Especially since we don't have much choice. But did you figure out how the game comes out?"

"That's easy," he said, climbing in after her as she slid behind the wheel. "We win." He leaned back and closed his eyes. "Or else we don't," he added. "But either way we play it out, the best we can."

About the Author

Frederik Pohl has been about everything one man can be in the world of science fiction: fan (a founder of the fabled Futurians), book and magazine editor, agent, and, above all, writer. As editor of *Galaxy* in the 1950s, he helped set the tone for a decade of SF—including his own memorable stories such as *The Space Merchants* (in collaboration with Cyril Kornbluth). His latest novel is *Beyond the Blue Event Horizon*, a sequel to the Hugo and Nebula Award-winning novel, *Gateway*. He has also written *The Way the Future Was*, a memoir of his forty-five years in science fiction. Frederik Pohl was born in Brooklyn, New York, in 1919, and now divides his time between Red Bank, New Jersey, and New York City.

DEL REY BOOKS

Try some of Frederik Pohl's tomorrows. Today.

Available at your bookstore or use this coupon.

____**THE COOL WAR, Frederik Pohl**   30137 2.75
A fast moving, thought-provoking look at where we *could* be, some forty years from now, as seen through the eyes of Rev. Hornswell Hake, an unlikely stand-in for James Bond. A Science Fiction Bookclub Main Selection.

____**GATEWAY**   29300 2.50
The HUGO and NEBULA award winner! Rich man or dead man—those were the choices Gateway offered, and Robinette Broadhead happily took his chances.

____**BEYOND THE BLUE EVENT HORIZON**   27535 2.50
The spellbinding sequel to GATEWAY. Winner of THE HUGO, THE NEBULA, and THE JOHN W. CAMPBELL MEMORIAL AWARD.

____**THE WAY THE FUTURE WAS**   26059 1.95
The fascinating look at the world of science fiction by one of it's living legends.

BALLANTINE MAIL SALES
Dept. TA, 201 E. 50th St., New York, N.Y. 10022

Please send me the BALLANTINE or DEL REY BOOKS I have checked above. I am enclosing $.......... (add 50¢ per copy to cover postage and handling). Send check or money order — no cash or C.O.D.'s please. Prices and numbers are subject to change without notice.

Name_____

Address_____

City_____ State_____ Zip Code_____

Allow at least 4 weeks for delivery.

08   G-6